Market Time Conspiracy

Other books by James Duermeyer

Flint Bluff
Heroes in Obscurity
Market Time Conspiracy
Trail of the Outlaw
Singing Creek

The Capture of the USS Pueblo: The Incident,
the Aftermath, and the Motives of the North Korea.

Market Time Conspiracy

James Duermeyer

SPEAKING VOLUMES, LLC
NAPLES, FLORIDA
2020

Market Time Conspiracy

ISBN 978-1-64540-258-9

Chapter One

December 1967
U.S.S. Kawishiwi (AO-146)
Off the Coast of Vietnam

The afternoon sun brutally pounded the gray steel of the large U.S. Navy ship as it cruised in a southerly direction fifteen nautical miles east of Da Nang, Vietnam. Buddy glanced again at the thermometer attached to the bulkhead in the small arms armory where he was working. It read ninety-two sweltering degrees. With the accompanying humidity, he thought it felt more like a hundred and two degrees. His light blue chambray working uniform shirt was nearly dark blue from the sweat on his upper body. He had propped open the watertight metal door to the weather deck, but without another opening into the armory, there was little air moving. How strange, he thought; here it was, nearly Christmas, and he was drenched in sweat.

Buddy had swabbed the barrel of the old rifle at least three times with cleaning solvent, and it still did not meet his standards. As he moved his arm to take another swipe through the barrel, he could see the new crow on his left sleeve. He was especially proud that he had passed his qualifi-cations and advancement test on the first try. He had been wearing the third class petty officer's insignia, "the crow," for only a couple of weeks. He was now Gunner's Mate Third Class Buddy Miller. It made him smile as he repeated the title to himself. He had written his dad to tell him the news. He knew exactly what his dad would say if they were together. "Good job, Buddy!" That's what his dad always said when things went well for his son.

After several more passes of the swab, the barrel of the old M-1 final-ly glistened as he peered into it and, at last, it looked as if it would pass his own standards and those of the chief. Buddy did not understand how the Navy could still have M-1 rifles in their ships' armories. After all, they were an old World War II staple weapon, not a modern one. He had been disappointed when he came aboard the *Kawishiwi* (AO-146) after completing Gunner's Mate "A" school. The sight of the 5"/38 mounts and the six twin 3"/50 mounts were old standard Navy cannonry and did little to excite him after he had learned about the newer, more sophisticated weaponry in use in the destroyer/cruiser fleet. Little of the latest weaponry on which he had been schooled was in evidence on the old oiler. The ship was an auxiliary, a service ship, and not a combatant. Therefore, the Navy did not devote modern weapons money to the ship. Buddy carefully reassembled the rifle, placed it back in the rifle rack, and relocked the security cross bar on the rack.

The chief had told Buddy to clean the pistols in the .45 rack within the next day or two, but it was just hot enough that Buddy decided to take a break. He set his chair next to the open water-tight door so that he could see out to the horizon. The ship was churning through a bright, bluish-green, calm sea; a relative treat for the crew versus other days when the South China Sea rocked the oiler and made life on board considerably less comfortable.

As he gazed out the door, from the corner of his eye he caught a glimpse of a ship moving forward on the port side of *Kawishiwi*. The approaching ship's huge bow sent up white foamed spray to each side of the pointed bow. Just to the side of the bow, the giant ship created its own monster wave which pushed out to each side of the ship, a wave of sufficient size to capsize a small boat. The bright sun suddenly was shadowed by the monstrous visage of the USS *Kitty Hawk* (CV 63). The sights and activities involved in the refueling of an aircraft carrier were not new; he had seen it many times. But it was still exhilarating to see such a mammoth ship come to the *Kawishiwi* for a "drink."

The wartime mission of the old oiler was very simple. The ship was to carry its cargo of mission-essential fuel to the ships operating off the coast of Vietnam. Those ships were the forward deployed units, the ships that were carrying the thunderous weaponry assault to the land-based enemy on shore. The mine sweepers, the destroyers, the cruisers, and even the mighty aircraft carriers with their assortment of airplanes, all required fuel to carry out their missions of fighting the Viet Cong. It was the job of the *Kawishiwi* and her sister oilers to bring the fuel to the war theater.

Buddy put his feet up on the lip of the armory doorway and leaned back in his gray metal chair, watching the carrier approach. He tried to imagine what it must be like to live on a behemoth of battle with over five thousand other sailors. The crew of the *Kawishiwi* consisted of only three hundred twenty-five officers and enlisted men.

He watched as two sailors on the aircraft carrier shot their line-throwing guns toward the *Kawishiwi*. The shots carried two light lines across the abyss between the two ships. The light lines were attached to and followed by heavier rope, which was then followed by cable. Subsequently, two sets of fuel hoses dangled on their harnesses attached to two sets of cables and were slowly fed on pulleys across the cables to the thirsty carrier. One fuel hose would feed JP5 fuel to the carrier to be used in the various aircraft carried in the ship's far-reaching arsenal. The other would carry DFM, the fuel needed for the carrier's boilers.

While the fueling was taking place, another lighter line was rigged between the two ships to allow for the transfer of food stores, mail, and all-important movies. Buddy smiled as he saw the cartons moving to and fro between the ships. He thought to himself that they would have new movies to watch tonight.

The carrier would take on enough fuel for several days of operations before it would need to once again seek out the services of the oiler.

Buddy's eyes moved upward to the carrier's hangar deck opening, where he could see a "skivvy waver" (slang for a Navy Signalman) using hand semaphore to talk with one of the *Kawishiwi* signalmen on the deck above the armory. Buddy had learned only a bit of semaphore in boot camp, but could understand that the men were asking each other where they were from back home, and how much longer they each had until their "wake-up time" (when they would get out of the Navy).

He tilted in his chair slightly so that he could see up to the bridge area of the huge carrier. Officers in their khaki-colored uniforms peered through the glass windowed island of the carrier, intently watching to ensure that the two ships remained at the proper distance apart for refueling.

Suddenly, Buddy's feet were kicked off the lip of the water-tight door, and he took a tumble backwards on the chair as it clattered to the deck.

"What's the matter with you Miller? Don't you have enough to do?" barked Gunner's Mate Chief John Proctor. "I'll bet my next kid's allowance that you haven't even touched those 45's. Well, have you?"

"Geez Chief, you didn't have to knock me on my ass. It already has a crack in it. I might have been hurt even more," said Buddy. He knew Chief Proctor was a great "sea daddy," a mentor to young sailors, and he respected him greatly. He also knew the chief's bark was far worse than his bite, and that the chief had a good sense of humor.

"Kinda hard to bet your next kid's allowance when you aren't even married, Chief," said Buddy.

"That's beside the point, smart ass. And don't be too certain there aren't any little Proctors running around in all of the ports I've been in. Have you even touched the .45's?" asked Proctor.

*****

Gunner's Mate Chief John Proctor was "old school" Navy. He led by example and cared for his sailors from his heart. He expected his men to do their very best without complaining or cutting corners. He was only ten years older than Buddy, but his bold grit, his performance in the service, and his innate intellect had pushed him through the enlisted ranks at an astonishing rate. He had four full rows of well-deserved ribbons attached to his uniform shirt, and proudly displayed above the ribbons was a silver, enlisted surface warfare pin. In addition, he had earned good conduct performance ratings during all of his years in the Navy. He was a "lifer," a career military man who loved the Navy. The fouled anchor tattoo on his upper arm was his personal tribute to the Navy.

The Navy had been John Proctor's opportunity to leave the oppressing poverty of his Omaha, Nebraska, family; a family led by an alcoholic father, and a family that had existed on social welfare programs. Through all of his years of growing up and attending public schools, John's family had been poor. He wore hand-me-down clothing, always needed a haircut and a good scrubbing, and he was forever teased by other schoolmates because of his poverty. The harassment by other children usually ended up in a fistfight, which John almost always won, even though he was generally smaller than his opponents.

High school sports were an outlet and a physical and mental turning point in John Proctor's life. He excelled in contact sports, possessing a speed to match his toughness. With his football performance, he was destined to receive a fine scholarship for college, and he had finally received a well-earned recognition from his fellow students, who now held him in high regard. But that dream ended in his senior year of high school when he was involved in yet another fight with a wise-cracking, smart-ass kid who made a remark about John's mother being a whore. While that remark may have been proven true, it precipitated a fight causing a badly battered opponent whose parents filed a criminal charge against John. But John was lucky and drew an understanding judge in the case. All charges against John would be dropped if he would immediately join the military and leave town. At seventeen years of age, John Proctor found himself in a Navy uniform and never looked back. Therefore, he was eminently qualified to understand the benefits of a Navy career, and he kept his eyes open for smart young men whom he believed could help the Navy and who might also benefit from a secure career.

*****

Chief Proctor stifled a grin. He liked Buddy Miller and knew that the small arms work would get done correctly. The chief just felt that he had to keep "the boys" on their toes and give them the appearance of gruffness now and then. "You've got an hour until chow, so get cracking on a couple of the .45's."

"Aye, aye, Chief," said Buddy and watched the chief walk down the weather deck to check on some of the other GM's at their work stations.

He unlocked the .45 rack and took out one of the pistols. He returned to his chair so he could continue to watch the carrier refueling, and as he watched he began breaking down the gun. He had nearly completed the cleaning of two of the .45's when the underway replenishment lines began to be disassembled and retrieved by the *Kawishiwi* deck crew. In short order, all of the lines and gear that had been strung between the two ships was back on board the oiler. Buddy watched as the Commanding Officer of the *Kitty Hawk* gave an informal "thank you salute" to the bridge of the *Kawishiwi*. In a moment, the distance between the two ships began to grow, and the carrier increased its speed. Soon, Buddy was watching the stern of the giant carrier as its four powerful screws churned up an undulating, white, frothy wake and moved the ship further to port, rapidly putting distance between the two ships. He said to himself, "What a magnificent ship!"

This same scenario took place many times during each day with many different types of ships while *Kawishiwi* was on station off the coast of Vietnam. The ship repeatedly travelled a pre-planned circuit that allowed the oiler to be at specific points at specific times to meet other Navy ships in need of fuel. Each Navy ship operating in the area kept a classified copy of the times and locations of the oilers and the other auxiliary replenishment ships so that they could schedule their activities to meet the auxiliary ships for underway replenishment.

As he replaced the pistol in its rack, Buddy's attention was quickly drawn to the ship's 1MC as it loudly announced that chow for his watch section of the crew was now being served on the mess decks. Listening to the announcement reminded him that he was hungry. Lunch that day had been "shit on a shingle" (creamed chipped beef on toast), not one of his favorites, and he had eaten only some fruit cocktail and dessert. He double checked that he had locked all of the gun racks, went out on the weather deck, dogged down the water tight door, and locked it behind him.

As he made his way through the interior passages of the ship to reach the enlisted mess decks, he passed other junior sailors that he knew. They exchanged greetings or playfully jabbed each other with a punch to the shoulder. Senior petty officers that he met and who knew him smacked him harder on top of his crow. It was their form of offering congratulations on his recent promotion. Periodically, he would stop and place his back to the bulkhead, stand at attention, and render a salute and greeting to any commissioned officer he met walking in the opposite direction in the passageways.

He eventually took a place in line with other members of his duty section, and as the line moved forward he picked up his metal compartmentalized food tray, cup, and silverware. As he looked at the steam table ahead of him and at his metal food tray, he couldn't help but smile inwardly as he thought of movies he had seen where criminal prisoners were depicted in a similar atmosphere: in prescribed uniforms, holding metal trays, and standing in line for their food. The first time he had heard that analogy was from a disgruntled enlistee in boot camp.

Dinner consisted of sliders (hamburgers), green beans, French fries, and apple pie with ice cream. Buddy and his friends were convinced that one of the oiler's bunkers did not contain fuel oil at all. Instead, it contained thousands of pounds of green beans. It seemed like the vegetable was served with every hot meal. After filling his tray, he took a seat at a table with some of his friends. He was hungry, and soon, he had devoured everything on the tray.

He stayed at the table with the other sailors after eating, and the topics of conversation were the same as always among the young men when they were together: girls, the inequities in their treatment by senior personnel, the shitty jobs they were being subjected to, how much longer they had in the Navy, sports, jokes, and girls again. They laughed, told more jokes and outrageous stories, and made fun of one another. This camaraderie marked the high point of the day for Buddy and his young friends. Any free time when they could just be themselves, laugh, and momentarily compartmentalize their Navy life for a few moments made living in their confined shipboard environment much more tolerable.

The group broke up to make room for the next shift of hungry sailors, and Buddy headed for the enlisted berthing area. He opened his small assigned locker and retrieved a notepad and pen. He hopped up into the second bunk in the three bunk tier and sat hunched over with his legs dangling over the side of the bunk. He began writing.

December 10, 1967
Dear Mom and Dad,

I just got back from chow so will write a note before clean-up and movie time. Chow is really not very good. When we have fresh eggs, breakfast isn't too bad. Usually it is powdered eggs. We had hamburgers for dinner tonight. If you load them up with enough ketchup and mustard they taste OK. It seems like we have the same thing all the time. I guess I won't get a good meal at home for quite a while. I sure miss seeing all of you guys. All in all though, I guess the Navy isn't so bad. It sure beats getting shot at. We refueled eight ships today, but since I'm a gunner's mate, I really don't have much to do with the refueling operations. I have made a couple new friends. One of them is even from Des Moines. My chief was kidding me yesterday and told me that since I have made third class petty officer, I will probably get orders to go to another ship. I hope not, because I sort of like being on this oiler.

Well, I guess I'd better go put this in the mail slot on my way to clean-up detail. Say hello to Janeen and Sarah.

Love, Buddy

The 1MC interrupted Buddy's thoughts again, announcing that the cleanup detail was to begin sweeping down the entire ship, *"Now, sweepers, sweepers, man your brooms. Commence a thorough cleaning of the ship from fore to aft. Sweepers man your brooms."*

He hopped out of his bunk and began making his way back to the small arms armory where he had been working earlier. Because he worked in that space, he was also responsible for keeping the armory clean. He dropped his letter home in the ship's mail slot and made his way to the armory. Mail service for ships on station at sea was very infrequent, so there was no telling when the letter he had just written would reach home, or when he would receive mail from home.

Thirty minutes of sweeping and wiping down the horizontal surfaces in the armory followed by emptying the "shit can" (actually called a "chit can" in the Navy, a wastebasket, but sailors preferred calling them "shit cans") made the armory presentable again. He had just finished up when Chief Proctor stepped through the doorway. The chief took a look around and noticed that one of the arms manuals was lying on top of a file cabinet. He walked over and placed it back into a special bookcase designed to keep books from falling out during rough seas.

"What's the movie tonight, Chief?" asked Buddy.

"Hoot Gibson in *Who Pooped in the Saddle Bag*," said the Chief. Buddy already knew that would be the Chief's answer. Even though both men were too young to have ever seen a Hoot Gibson western movie, it was still one of the Chief's favorite lines, and his answer to any question about titles of movies. Proctor had heard his inebriated father use that line sometimes when he was a child, and it just stuck with him.

They both chuckled as the Chief moved around the armory making sure that Buddy had cleaned the space properly.

"What are you going to do with the rest of your life, Shit for Brains?" asked the Chief. Buddy was not offended by the Chief referring to him by a not-so-flattering name. In fact, the chief called everybody "Shit for Brains." The Chief had asked him this question at least a dozen times, and Buddy was somewhat flattered. Underneath the gruff façade, it really meant that the Chief thought enough of him that he was trying to make Buddy consider reenlisting and staying in the Navy as a career. Buddy had actually given the issue some thought, but was not sure that he really wanted to be a "lifer."

"I'm not sure, Chief. But I'm pretty sure that whatever my job in life is, I'll most likely be called Mister, not Gunner's Mate," said Buddy. "I kind of like the sound of 'CINCCIVMIDWEST' (Commander in Chief, Civilian forces in the Midwest)," said Buddy.

"Yeah, yeah, probably Mister Sod Buster or Mr. Chicken Plucker seem more likely. Picking your corn and milking your cows. That's about as close to any female anatomy as you'll ever get."

The Chief paused, and then said, "Seriously Miller, you're the kind of guy the Navy needs, and it's not that bad of a life. With your smarts you could advance and be just as super-duper as me. I'd be honored to swear you in on your next enlistment. From what little I have gained from our talks, it doesn't sound like you have any better prospects on the horizon. Just think about it. I gotta get out of here and go check on the other knuckleheads," and he walked back out onto the weather deck. Buddy's thoughts were again interrupted by the 1MC.

"Now hear this. Tonight's movie will commence in fifteen minutes. I say again, fifteen minutes. Tonight's movie will be 'The Great Escape' *starring Steve McQueen."*

Buddy again locked up the armory and made his way back to the mess decks. The crew of predominately young men loved the action and shoot-'em-up movies. If a sailor really wanted to follow the details of a movie while the ship was underway, he would have to pay close attention to hear all of the dialogue above the ship's machinery noises and the rowdy conversation and hooting of his fellow movie goers. The sailors brought their own "geedunk" (candy or snacks) and soon the tables were littered with candy wrappers and soda cans. The air was thick with cigarette smoke. The villainous Germans in the movie were appropriately booed, and the Allied military men in the movie were cheered as they made their escape. They watched enthralled as Steve McQueen rode his stolen motorcycle in a valiant effort to escape the clutches of the surrounding German military units. The crew all thought it was a terrific movie, and the comments of Buddy and his friends went on for several minutes after the movie concluded.

When the lights in the mess decks were once again switched on, the majority of the men picked up their trash and deposited it in the chit cans. The men who were not on watch drifted off to the berthing area to turn in for the night. Buddy sat up in his bunk for a few minutes reading a Louis L'Amour western novel before lights out, and only casually watched a poker game going on at the corner table in the berthing area. He had always enjoyed reading, and westerns were his favorite. The activities of the poker players were soon stopped as the 1MC advised everyone throughout the ship:

"Now, taps, taps. Lights out in all berthing areas. The smoking lamp is out in all berthing areas. Now, taps, taps."

The men turned into their bunks and all lights except the emergency lighting system were turned off. This was soon followed by the drone of several men's nocturnal droning snores, amid some rather pungent flatulence vapors.

For the officers and crew of a naval vessel at sea, the routine was very nearly the same each day, interrupted only by even more, or varied, work.

*****

Buddy's dream of walking down the hallway of Oskaloosa High School, wearing his letter jacket and holding the hand of busty Shirley Moore in her short-skirted cheer leader's outfit was his favorite dream. In the dream, he kept chatting, laughing, and ogling the petite girl's beautifully endowed chest hidden under her maroon sweater while they passed their friends in the hallway. In the dream, it was his senior year in high school, and he had told Shirley that he loved her, but she had just laughed at him. Her attitude had hurt him greatly. Later in the dream, he and Shirley were kissing while sitting in the cab of his dad's old pick-up, and as it had happened a dozen times before, just as he was moving his hands underneath the maroon sweater, he was disastrously and glaringly awakened by an inopportune-time 1MC announcement:

"Now, reveille, reveille. All hands heave to and trice up. The smoking lamp is lit in all berthing areas. Now, reveille, reveille."

"Damn," thought Buddy. He groaned, yawned, and rolled out of his bunk to shuffle to the head. If he hurried, he would beat the guys who stayed in their bunks to get another five minutes of sleep. He hurriedly washed his face, neck, shoulders and arms, and then shaved. A glance into the shower stalls confirmed the reason for his abbreviated washing. The signs were still hanging on the shower heads stating that the showers were "secured" to conserve fresh water. The old ship's evaporators' output of fresh water simply could not keep up with the demand needed on a working ship in the tropics.

Buddy donned the same smelly work uniform he had worn for the past four days. He hoped that the laundry would soon return some of his laundered uniforms. "This shirt is really ripe," he thought to himself.

He made his way to the chow hall and filled his tray with pancakes and ham, orange juice, and coffee and took his place with his friends. Not surprisingly, breakfasts were rather quiet. It always took an hour or so before the young men truly woke up. They finished chow, lingered another minute over their stout black coffee, and headed back to clean up the berthing area. When they were finished, all the bunks were made up, and the trash was picked up.

"Now, quarters, quarters. All hands fall in for quarters for muster, inspection, and instruction. Quarters, quarters."

This 1MC announcement was almost always immediately followed by several of Buddy's bunk mates shouting that the boatswain's mate of the watch, who usually made the routine 1MC announcements, should "stick his microphone up his ass." This usually drew a chuckle from other sailors, but they all began moving to their assigned stations for quarters.

Buddy moved up several ladders to reach the weather deck and walked to the forward five inch thirty-eight. All of the other gunner's mates were also gathering at the gun mount, and they quickly formed two ranks to the side of the gun mount. Buddy shot an elbow into the ribs of Gunner's Mate Striker Seaman Bob Dawes, his friend from Des Moines, who stood next to him at quarters. It was followed by a retaliatory elbow jab from Dawes. Buddy thought, he's getting better at that. It's starting to hurt.

Bob Dawes was the youngest son of a wealthy family from Des Moines. He had never been a serious student, preferring instead to have a good time in school, date as many female classmates as possible, and stay one step ahead of the local police who seemed to keep an eye on the happy-go-lucky country club prankster.

But the outward appearance exuded by Bob Dawes mostly hid the true young man. The hidden Bob Dawes was an extremely bright, caring person. But growing up in a formal and rather stilted family environment did not allow for displays of feelings. Therefore, Bob substituted a more frivolous, devil-may-care façade. It was this persona that prevailed as he approached graduation from high school. Dawes had not bothered to apply for admission to any colleges. It was just not a priority in his care-free teenage life. Naturally, this drove his over-achieving parents absolutely crazy. But Bob's failure to adequately focus finally caught up with him when his local draft board office sent him a letter. Bob quickly enlisted in the Navy to prevent his induction as an Army infantry soldier. Naturally, the senior Dawes's were not at all happy with this turn of events.

"All right girls, knock off the grab-ass. Atten' hut," barked Chief Proctor as he faced the group. "Stand at, ease," he said, and then did an about-face to wait for their division officer.

While the enlisted men formed up for quarters, officer's call took place elsewhere on the ship. All of the ship's commissioned officers who were department heads, and several of the division officers, met near the bridge and received the day's instructions from the ship's executive officer. Upon completion, the officers made their way to the locations where their respective department and division personnel had formed up.

"Atten' hut," said Chief Proctor, as LTJG (Lieutenant Junior Grade) Mark West, the Assistant First Lieutenant and Gunnery Division Officer, approached the group. "Gunnery Division all present or accounted for, sir," said the Chief as he saluted LTJG West.

"Aye, aye, Chief," said West. "Put 'em at parade rest."

"Parade rest," barked the Chief, and the men relaxed in a parade rest stance, each with their feet apart and hands clasped behind their back.

LTJG West then addressed the division. "I've got some good news guys. We are going to refuel three Pinocchio's today; you know, the wooden guys, the minesweepers. We've got an MSO and two MSC's coming along side shortly, and then we're OOG (out of gas). And because we don't have any more gas, we're heading back to Subic this afternoon. PMS (Preventative Maintenance System) work and painting will go on all the while we head back to the PI (Philippine Islands), but the XO did say that he and the CO were planning to have a swim call and barbecue somewhere along our track back to the PI if the seas cooperate. He also said to pass along that the gunnery spaces are looking good and to keep up the good work. One other thing; for those of you who are needing to complete any of your practical factors for advancement (items for which a sailor must demonstrate a working knowledge in order to qualify for taking an advancement examination), I want you to work with

Chief Proctor. You can break away from your normal work and get those factors taken care of. I want people promoted in this division. The exams are next month, and we have to order the test booklets and score sheets. So get your practical factors done so we can order an exam for you. Any questions? None? Good. Chief Proctor, take charge and dismiss the men."

"Aye, aye, sir." The Chief and the LTJG exchanged salutes, and LTJG West walked away from the group.

The Chief turned to face the division and said, "All right, you know where your assigned work locations are, and I don't want to see anybody picking daisies (loafing) today, you got that?"

There was a grumble of acknowledgement from the group.

"Good. Atten' hut. Dismissed," said the Chief, as all men in the division saluted the chief, he returned the salute, and the group broke formation.

In a matter of five hours, the final ship's refueling would be completed. Buddy was once again in his armory, cleaning .45's and watching the refueling of the last of the three minesweepers. The fuel lines were being brought back aboard following the fueling of the USS *Erne*, (MSC-300), a coastal minesweeper. For some strange reason, Buddy could not take his eyes off the little ship. A chill came over him, and he shivered as he watched the minesweeper's crew secure their refueling rig. Buddy shrugged to dispel the strange feeling that had come over him while looking at the minesweeper. Maybe he was just imagining things.

As the small wooden ship turned away to head back to its war-time station, the *Kawishiwi* set course for the Philippine Islands. The crew fell into the monotonous routine of working all day and standing their duty section watches as the ship made its way toward Subic Bay.

Chapter Two

December 15, 1967
South China Sea
360 Nautical miles from the Philippine Islands

Barring any mechanical problems, the *Kawishiwi* was now one easy twenty-four-hour day out from Subic. At 1100, with a sunny, calm day, and a nearly flat sea, the engine order telegraph on the bridge was set at "all stop." After twenty minutes had passed, the ship's forward momentum had ceased, and the only motion was a slow gentle rocking of the ship in the minimal swells. Olive green cargo nets were attached to and strung from the handrails amidships so that they reached the surface of the sea. Two of the senior gunner's mates on shark-watch duty stood at the ship's rail with loaded rifles. In the event of a shark sighting, all swimmers would be ordered out of the water. If it appeared that a shark or sharks were getting too close to the men as they left the water, the shark would be shot for the safety of the men. Twenty-six sailors, each with his designated swimming buddy were swimming near the side of the ship. The young men shouted, dunked, and splashed each other. Some of the swimmers held onto life vests so that they could simply float and relax in the warm water. A few of the men had swim masks so they could watch the sea life beneath them. True to the CO's word, swim call was being held. Every twenty minutes, twenty-six men climbed out of the sea and ascended the cargo nets. As soon as all swimmers were accounted for, another twenty-six men jumped over the side of the ship or descended the cargo net.

One of the gunner's mates holding a rifle at the rail, laughingly called out, "You can always tell when the 'snipes' (a slang Navy term for a sailor who works in the ship's engineering spaces) get in the water. Just look at the size of that oil slick floating on the water."

One of the engineering sailors who was dog-paddling in the water replied, "Yeah, you're a big man with that gun. Just set the gun down and come on down here, and I'll drown your sorry ass in our oil slick." This was followed by the rest of the enginemen laughing, hooting, and shouting. The young men were just having a good time, with no real malice intended in their good-natured taunting.

The tantalizing aroma of grilling burgers and franks filled the air near the fantail of the ship. The mess cooks had two large barbecue grills loaded with meat waiting for the word to be passed to start chow. A phone talker with a headset on his ears, and who was in communication with the ship's bridge, lazily sat on a nearby bollard watching the activities.

As the last of the swimmers left the water and all hands had been accounted for, the cargo nets were pulled up on deck. The nearby phone talker passed the word to the Officer of the Deck on the bridge that all hands were safely accounted for on deck, and the nets had been taken aboard and were being stowed.

In a moment, the two eighteen-foot diameter screws of the ship began turning once more, and the ship recommenced its journey toward Subic Bay, Philippine Islands. The 1MC soon announced that chow was being served for all hands on the fantail of the ship. A hungry and happy crew, many still in their swim suits, grabbed their paper plates and loaded them with food and found places to sit around on the deck and deck machinery.

Chief Proctor had placed Buddy and two other more senior gunner's mates in charge of the activities following chow. With several hours of daylight remaining, they had set up a skeet shooting area on the fantail of the ship. Shotguns, ammunition, and a box of clay pigeons had been brought from one of the armories. With instructions from Buddy and the other gunner's mates, the shooting match soon began. Each competitor, representing his respective division on the ship, was given ten shots, and the man who broke the most disks would be the winner. The winner would receive a chit that could be used for $100 in merchandise from the ship's onboard store; the same as receiving cash for the lucky participant.

The men who were to compete formed a line, and with the help of one of the gunner's mates instructing the shooter on safety and operation of the shotguns, each took a turn firing at ten clay pigeons. This was the preliminary round that would eliminate the poorer shooters. A second preliminary round reduced the number of final shooters even further. When the competition finally had eliminated all but five shooters, the final rounds would begin. In the final rounds, the shooters each had to try hitting twenty disks.

As the competition progressed, there were very few high scores, until finally, there were two leaders tied at seventeen hits each. Buddy had been nominated by the gunnery division, and he was the final shooter. On land, he could have easily hit all twenty birds. But with the ship slightly rolling, he surprisingly missed number ten, nineteen, and twenty. The score was all tied at seventeen for the three finalists. The three finalists were a second class engineman whom Buddy did not know, Buddy, and Buddy's pal, Bob Dawes.

The final round with the three men began. Sailors and officers gathered around and cheered for their favorites. First up was the engineman. It appeared that every engineman and electrician's mate on the ship was on the fantail rooting for their fellow snipe. The disks were thrown, and the sailor's shotgun answered. The engineman racked up a very healthy score of 18.

Bob Dawes was next up. He loaded and readied the twelve gauge in his hands, put it up to his shoulder, and cried, "Pull." The bird flew and split in dozens of pieces as the shot interrupted its flight. Over and over,

Dawes blasted the flying targets. But on the seventeenth shot, he missed the mark. He would now have to hit all three of the last shots to beat the engineman.

Dawes paused and let the shotgun rest across his arms as he drew a couple of deep breaths. He checked to ensure that the gun was loaded and slowly raised it to his shoulder. Three shots in rapid succession followed, with three accompanied shattered clay pigeons. Dawes had finished with nineteen hits. He was now in the lead.

Buddy Miller took the shotgun from Dawes, loaded it, and raised it to his shoulder. In a remarkable display of rapid shooting, only interrupted by reloading the gun, Buddy had shattered eighteen pigeons. Chief Proctor had unobtrusively moved to stand only three feet behind Buddy. After a final loading of the gun, two more shots were fired, resulting in two more shattered disks. Buddy had hit all twenty targets and won the contest. The gunnery division was cheering and the snipes were all booing and good-naturedly shouting that the contest had been rigged. However, many of the men came by and clapped Buddy on the back, expressing their congratulations.

As the men disbursed and the gunners picked up the guns and ammo to be re-stowed in the armory, LTJG West handed a chit for $100 to Buddy which he could use at the ship's store. Chief Proctor stood to one side and watched.

"Congratulations, Miller. I'm glad you showed the rest of those guys that the gunners are the guys who know best how to shoot. Here's your prize. Don't buy too much geedunk," said LTJG West.

"Thanks, Mr. West," said Buddy. "Sir, can I talk to you for just a minute?"

"Sure," said West. "What's on your mind?"

Buddy stumbled a bit, but then started to talk. "Sir, I was wondering if it would be all right if I gave this $100 prize to someone who really needs it more than I do. You see, he has a problem that he needs to take care of and could use the chit to help him get squared away. Could I please do that, sir?"

LTJG West just stared blankly at Buddy. He could not figure out how $100 worth of merchandise from the ship's store would solve any kind of problem, unless it was an extraordinary case of a sweet tooth. But he thought better of prying into a seemingly innocuous situation. "Miller, you are a strange guy. Is this other sailor in our division?"

"Yes sir," said Buddy.

"Well, tell him to come see me if he needs more help. But I guess it would be OK to give it to him."

Chief Proctor had overheard the conversation and joined Buddy as LTJG West walked away.

The Chief followed Buddy back to the armory and watched as Buddy began breaking down the shotguns for cleaning. "All right, Miller, what's going on? How dumb can you get, turning down a hundred bucks. And who's the lucky s.o.b. that you are going to give this to?" said Proctor.

"I don't think I want to talk about it," said Buddy.

"OK, be that way, but I'll take that chit and tear it up," said Chief Proctor, and he reached forward to grab it. But Buddy held it back, keeping it.

"All right, all right. I guess you'll find out in the end," said Buddy. "Dawes has gotten himself in a bind. The dipshit went and got himself in a poker game with the Weasel."

The Weasel was actually Boatswain's Mate First Class Mike Brady. Brady ran an unauthorized, underground, but almost constant game of poker. He specialized in fleecing the younger, gullible sailors, and he had a couple of henchmen confidants who were his muscle for sailors who could not pay off their debts incurred from the shady poker game.

Although Brady had gone to Captain's Mast at least once and had been fined for his shenanigans, it did not stop him from restarting a new game every chance he could.

"Oh, Jesus," groaned the Chief. "How much does he owe him?"

"A hundred and fifty dollars," replied Buddy, "and he doesn't have the money."

"And what do you think you are going to do about it?" asked Proctor.

"Well, I thought I might give Dawes the chit, and he could go and talk to the Weasel and get him to take the prize chit as payment for Dawes' debt," said Buddy.

Chief Proctor began laughing. "You numb nuts. Do you really think that Weasel will listen to Dawes? If some green little sailor comes into Brady's domain down there in the bosun's locker, he's liable to get the chit taken away and all of his other cash and jewelry will also turn up missing." There was no longer a smile on Proctor's face. "No, no, Miller, this is not a job for you or Dawes," said the Chief. "I'll take care of this problem, but I'm also going to have a man-to-man talk with that dumb shit Dawes. Gimme' the chit."

Buddy handed the chit to the chief and watched as Proctor ambled away.

Chief Proctor had a distinct dislike for the first class boatswain's mate. This was not the first time that BM1 Brady had fleeced one of the junior sailors under Proctor's supervision. Proctor would not have been nearly as irritated if the deck division, which Brady belonged to, had a chief with the guts to take care of Brady. Unfortunately, old Boatswain's Mate Chief Weaver was afraid of Brady and stayed clear of any discipline for his leading petty officer. Weaver was biding his time as he neared retirement and didn't want to take on any tough problems. At this stage in his career, he was a poor excuse for a leader.

*****

The boatswain's locker was located at the forward part of the ship. It was meant for storage of the supplies needed for the deck gang. All sorts of ship's hardware, rope, and paint were stored in that space. But BM1 Brady had also cleared out a section of the space to hold his poker games. A large canvas cloth was attached to the overhead between the water tight door of the compartment and the poker table, so that passersby could not see the table if they looked in the door. But at 2200, under cover of darkness, Proctor knew this was where he would find Brady, and he moved to the door of the bosun's locker.

Proctor glanced around, then quickly pulled the dogging lever and opened the door. He stepped through the door and was met by a second class boatswain's mate. Another stood beside the canvas drape.

"Stand aside, monkeys," said Proctor, as he moved to the canvas drape. He pulled it aside to see BM1 Brady dealing cards to five junior sailors. Proctor looked at the junior sailors and told them in no uncertain terms to make tracks and "get the hell out of there."

"Aw, c'mon, Chief. I'm ten bucks ahead," said one of the sailors.

Chief Proctor reached down and lifted one side of the poker table and flipped it over. "I said, get the hell out of here and never come back." With eyes as wide as silver dollars, the sailors grabbed their white hats and scrambled out the water tight door.

"Brady, call off Humpty and Dumpty there. I want to talk business with you," said Proctor.

Brady fiercely looked at the chief and then over to his two goons. "Hang on boys; let's see what our favorite gunner's mate has to say. What's on your mind Proctor?" said Brady.

23

"That's Chief Proctor to you, Weasel. I want to make you a proposition. You're holding a chit on one of my guys, GMSN Dawes."

"Yeah, so what. The little shit bird decided that he wanted to play cards with me, and now he owes me a hundred and fifty bucks. So why is that your problem?" said Brady.

"Because everyone knows you run a poker game about as straight as a lightning bolt. And unlike you, I care if my boys get into trouble, and you're the worst trouble on this ship."

The two men glared at each other for a few seconds. Then Chief Proctor continued. "But I want to solve this little problem. What do you say?"

"Keep talking, Gunner," said Brady.

"I've got a chit in my pocket worth a hundred bucks at the ship's store. I'm willing to give you the chit if you will take Dawes off your books. It's as simple as that," said Proctor.

"Let's see if I've got this straight. You're going to give me a chit worth a hundred dollars to clear out a debt worth a hundred and fifty." Brady looked at his cohorts. "What do you think, boys? I think we're getting screwed," said Brady.

The two burly petty officers grinned at Brady and dumbly nodded.

"I don't think we like that deal, Proctor. So why don't you get your slimy khaki covered ass out of my bosun's locker. My boys will show you to the door."

From the corner of his eye, Chief Proctor noticed movement as the two cohorts began to make a move to grab him. But Proctor knew that action would be coming, and he leaped to the side of BM1 Brady. As he passed a rack of marlinspikes and fids, lined up in a rack on the bulkhead, he grabbed a fourteen inch steel marlinspike. While holding Brady with one arm, with his other arm he held the marlinspike's sharp point against BM1 Brady's neck, just above his collar bone.

"Tell the two monkeys to back off, or this marlinspike slips right into your yellow neck," said Chief Proctor.

Brady's face turned red with fury, but he soon nodded and the two sailors backed away.

"One more time, Brady. I'm going to throw this chit on the deck, and Dawes' debt is wiped out. Isn't that right?" said Proctor. "A simple head nod will suffice."

Brady slowly nodded his head, and Chief Proctor threw the chit on the deck with his free hand.

Looking at the two petty officers, Chief Proctor said, "Why don't you two boys move on over to the other side of the room there." The sailors looked at Brady, who slowly nodded his head, and they complied, giving Proctor an unobstructed pathway to the door.

"Brady, I don't want to hear about any of my boys being sucked into your crooked card games. If any of them show up here, tell them to get lost. Is that understood? If not, we can take this whole sordid business up with the XO," said Proctor.

Again, Brady nodded.

Chief Proctor had opened the water tight door and shot through it before Brady or his cohorts even knew that he had moved. The heavy metal marlinspike made a sharp clanging sound as it hit and bounced on the steel deck when Proctor threw it back over his shoulder as he passed through the door. The situation was satisfactorily resolved. Well, almost. Two days later, GMSN Dawes showed up at morning quarters sporting a black eye and some other assorted bruises. After dismissal from quarters, Chief Proctor asked Dawes what had happened to him.

"I'm not sure, Chief. But a couple deck apes knocked me around a little bit, and then told me my debt was paid with BM1 Brady. And they said something about giving their regards to you," said Dawes.

Chief Proctor surveyed the physical damage to Dawes and decided that it could have been much worse.

"Serves you right, dipshit. I think you've learned never to get in another card game with the Weasel," said Chief Proctor, and Dawes grinned slightly, nodded his head, and wandered away.

Buddy had overheard the conversation. "Gee Chief, do you think that's fair that they beat up on Dawes, even though his debt was paid?"

"You just don't understand, Miller. Those goons always start adding interest to debts, and then you end up having one of them go through the pay line with you each pay day, and that can go on for months. So there's no such thing as a debt being paid off easily. Dawes got off cheap, and I hope he learned his lesson. A few bruises are just Brady's way of giving him a parting shot. But they won't bother him anymore," said the chief. "Now, don't you have work to do?"

"Yeah, Chief. And thanks for getting Dawes off the hook," said Buddy. He shook hands with Chief Proctor and hustled off to the armory.

Chief Proctor watched Buddy walk away, and thought to himself, "Pretty damn naïve, but a good kid!"

Chapter Three

The three young men walked across "Shit River." Henry threw a nickel toward one of the Filipino kids standing in a canoe on the water below them. The boy jumped out of the canoe and dove into the river, which carried all the raw sewage of the Philippine city of Olongapo, to retrieve the coin. In a moment the boy returned to his canoe, waving the coin in the air.

"Throw me more coins, sailor," yelled the boy, but the three American sailors walked on.

After leaving the *Kawishiwi* and passing through the main gate of the U.S. Navy base at Subic Bay, they had crossed the foul-smelling river to begin walking on Magsaysay Drive in Olongapo City. Buddy, GM2 Henry Lucas from Brownwood, Texas, and Bob Dawes were headed toward their favorite watering hole on the main street of Olongapo. A group of *Kawishiwi* sailors frequented one bar more than others. The bar was called the *At Ease Bar.* But the sailors had all dubbed it the "Mad Disease Bar," for its notoricty of having prostitutes who produced a few minutes pleasure and months or more of social disease discomfort. Through hard lessons learned from their friends, the three young men did not spend their hard earned money on any of the "pleasure girls."

They stopped at one of the many money exchanging booths at the corner of Gordon Avenue and Magsaysay, and each of the young men changed a few of their American dollars into Philippine pesos. As they continued down the dirt street, the noise was nearly deafening. Rock and roll music poured out of the doors of the bars they passed. Bar employees with battery-powered megaphones each beckoned passersby to enter their bar. Gaudy, but gaily colored Jeepneys with their radios blaring, honked and raced along the street carrying passengers to their destinations. Many of the Navy's Seventh Fleet ships were in port, and the city was full of sailors and marines out to have a good time. The bar girls and prostitutes would be busy that evening.

As they walked, they passed the *Rosanna Club, Oceans 11 Club, California Club,* the *Fortuna Hotel,* the *Cat Walk Club,* the *New Life Club,* and dozens of other bars before reaching their destination. Buddy, Henry, and Bob pulled chairs up to a table in the At Ease Bar where some of their shipmates were sitting. Another round of ice-cold San Miguel beers arrived in their wet, brown bottles, and the stories and good-natured teasing bounced around the table. A loud, enthusiastic Philipino band was playing its rendition of American popular rock and roll tunes, but it was almost comical to hear the singers murder the lyrics.

A couple of the younger sailors were teasing Henry Lucas. Henry had recently been promoted to gunner's mate second class and had reenlisted after his promotion.

"Henry, you goon; you've turned into a lifer," said one of the sailors, and this was followed by jeers and laughter by his friends.

Henry did not mind the ribbing. He was smart enough to have figured out that without having the means to obtain a college education, and coming from a poor family in Brownwood, Texas, he would be facing a dead-end manual labor job if he got out of the Navy. He just grinned and said, "Say what you will boys, but I'm making more 'moolah' than any of you."

"Hey Henry, let's go and spend some of your big E-5 cash. Let's go pull some slots," said one of the sailors, and soon they were all leaving the bar and heading for another bar that doubled as a casino.

"You're staying by me, Bob," said Buddy. "We both know what a great poker player you are," he said as he jabbed Dawes in the ribs.

The bar/casino was a walk-up. It was on the second floor of the street-side building. As a result, there was a constant stream of military patrons and local female hustlers going up and down the stairs. Periodically, the upward and downward flow of people would stop while an amorous couple groped each other in a spur of the moment embrace. This was followed by the jeers and shouting of others on the stairs to get the traffic moving once more.

As they entered the bar/casino, the furnishings were a stark contrast to the scene on the street below and the dark, lurid stairway leading up to the casino. The decor of the bar was mostly an ivory-white in color, with dark burgundy carpet. Several small gold and glass chandeliers hung from the decorated ceiling. Dealers and waitress staff were all dressed in black and white uniforms with black bow ties. It was a relatively nice, fun place for the military patrons to hang out; but it was also clear that the establishment was successful in parting those patrons from their hard-earned money.

Buddy and Bob Dawes played the craps table and only bet on red or black. They lost a few bucks and then quit to watch as the other gamblers around them slowly, but surely, lost their cash. When Henry Lucas had had enough, he told the group he was heading back to the ship. Buddy and Bob went with him.

As they walked back to the base, passing the gaudy, loud businesses, Henry said, "This has got to be the strangest place on earth. If you get back home and try to tell somebody about Olongapo, they will laugh at you. But mark my words, boys. You'll never forget this place, and that's for sure."

*****

It was a Saturday afternoon, and there were fifteen sailors jammed into the cab and in the back bed of a haze gray pick-up truck. Two large trash cans filled with beer and soda were also in the back of the truck. They were headed for a fast pitch softball game at one of several ball fields on the base. The Navy Special Services office on the base maintained the baseball fields, swimming pools, and other recreational venues for the sailors to use. The ship also had its own funds for recreational needs. Any profit generated by the ship's store could be used for such purposes. As a result, all members of the *Kawishiwi*'s baseball team had uniforms, and they were a sharp looking bunch of players when they took the field for warm-ups.

Their opponents soon arrived in their own ship's pick-up truck. The *Kawishiwi* team had to stifle a laugh as a rag-tag bunch of players from the USS *Ute*, an ocean-going fleet salvage tug climbed down from their truck. They wore no uniforms per se, but all their players wore an assortment of faded red t-shirts and caps and jeans or cut-off jeans.

The beer and soda-filled trash cans were dragged to the respective dug-outs, and after a bit more warm-up time, the game got underway. The *Ute* team was up first, and though they were able to get a couple hits, they were unable to score.

The *Kawishiwi* team now faced the *Ute*'s pitcher. And that was about all they did; faced the pitcher. *Ute*'s pitcher was extremely fast, and the *Kawishiwi* batters were three up, three down.

The innings went on, and the Ute team was able to amass enough hits to put runs on the board, while *Kawishiwi*'s batters never honed in on the opponent's pitcher. The game ended with *Kawishiwi* team being beaten 3-0 by the Ute team.

After the game, the two teams stood around talking and drinking. The young men swapped stories and jokes and good natured ribbing. *Kawishiwi*'s team captain said, "When you guys are pulling a target sled for us next time, don't be surprised if there is an errant shot from a 5 inch." That remark drew laughter and jeers. Everyone knew it was only a joke. The crews of the two ships knew each other well, as they were both in the same auxiliary ship squadron. When the beer ran out, and the stories began to be retold, the teams parted as friends and would certainly meet each other on the baseball diamond again in the future.

*****

It was Christmas Eve. Buddy had the quarterdeck watch. On a large ship in port, there was also a commissioned officer standing watch on the quarterdeck. These officers on the quarterdeck watch were usually the most junior officers on the ship. An ensign was on watch with Buddy, but Buddy did not know him very well.

Buddy was in his tropical whites with a holstered .45 pistol covering his hip as the holster hung from his web belt. Also attached to the web belt was a small pouch containing two loaded clips for the pistol. Buddy stood to the side of a podium facing the end of the ship's gangway which rose up to the ship from the pier. There was a green, cloth-covered log book lying open on the podium. This was the official ship's log. Period-ically, Buddy made notations in the log when the messenger of the watch reported to the quarterdeck after making his rounds on the ship. As the quarterdeck watch, it was the officer and enlisted man on duty who would ensure that only authorized personnel came aboard the ship.

The base and the ship were quiet. A number of the base activities were closed down for Christmas, and many of the ship's crewmembers had taken leave to either go home to Hawaii, the home port of the *Kaw-ishiwi*, or to make other travels during the quiet time. Buddy and the ensign were standing the second "dog watch," from 1800 to 2000. With only twenty-five minutes until "colors," he had just sent the messenger to find and ensure that the sailors who would lower the forward jack and the stern ensign were properly standing by. The messenger would also go to the wardroom to alert the Officer of the Deck that colors would soon be observed.

A few minutes later, the 1MC announced, *"First call, first call to colors."* From his vantage point on the quarterdeck, Buddy could see that the Officer of the Deck (OOD) had taken a position on the deck in front of the stern ensign. A sailor stood at the ready, each holding the flags' halyards at the bow and stern of the ship. Five minutes after the call to colors, a whistle sounded over the 1MC, followed by a recording of the bugle call, "Retreat." As the bugle call was played over the 1MC, the OOD saluted the ensign being lowered at the stern while the union jack on the bow was simultaneously lowered. Buddy and the officer on the quarterdeck faced the stern of the ship and saluted as the U.S. flag was lowered. After the ensign was fully lowered and the musical notes of 'retreat' were completed, the 1MC sounded the command, *"Carry on."* With evening colors completed, Buddy had only a few more minutes in his watch standing until he would be relieved.

The gray dusk settled in. Weather deck lights were turned on, and the ship was once again relatively quiet. The gentle, rhythmic, slapping against the hull by small wind-driven waves lulled Buddy. Even standing at the podium, he could not help getting drowsy. His mind wandered, and he began to think about other Christmases; Christmases when he was younger, when he was happily with his family, and when he was home.

Chapter Four

December 24, 1960
Miller Farm
Mahaska County, Iowa

1960 had been a good year. All aspects of the American economy had now fully shifted from producing equipment for use in the now fading-from-memory Second World War and Korean War, to goods and services that the American consumer really wanted. Jobs were plentiful in the teeming cities, and American farmers were producing unheard of crop yields to feed a hungry nation, as well as providing exports to feed a hungry world. The Miller farm was no exception. The recent harvest had given the Millers the necessary income to purchase and repair equipment, maintain their home, and keep money aside for next spring's planting.

Mr. and Mrs. James Miller and their three children lived on the same Iowa farm where James's father and grandfather had fought the elements to make an honest, yet difficult agricultural living. They did not know how to live any other lifestyle, and they had no interest in any other career. Their family roots were deep in the fertile, black, Iowa soil.

The powerful machines used in the age-old process of harvesting a corn crop were not flawless. Invariably, a considerable amount of corn kernels were cast outside the yawning chute opening that sent the yellow gold into a collection bin on the corn picker after having been machine stripped from the corn cob. It was these tasty morsels which drew the game birds to the fields following harvest time. It was through one such field that Jim Miller and his son walked slowly on this very cold, frosty morning, carrying their shotguns.

Jericho William Miller loved the funny, crunchy noise made by his boots in the new, dry snow. As he walked, the snow made a scrunch sound that vibrated through the soles of his boots, tingling his feet. The temperature had hovered at the zero mark all through the night before, and his hands were cold as he and his dad walked in parallel rows between the foot-high corn stubble. The sun was bright and had just cleared the eastern horizon on this new, late December day. The sun on the fresh snow produced a million tiny sparkles of light that made him squint from the brightness. They had been walking for nearly two hours on this Christmas Eve morning.

He looked down at his feet as he walked. He watched for a moment as the toes of his boots continued to trade the lead, putting one foot out in front of the other. He had gotten the new insulated, winter, pac-type boots at the start of hunting season. With their insulation and felt insoles, his feet were warm; not like some of their earlier outings. He liked that. It made hunting much more comfortable. Yet his fingers certainly knew Jack Frost's bite. They were cold and a bit stiff inside his fur-lined leather gloves.

His dad walked about fifteen feet to his left, and said very quietly, "How 'ya doing Buddy? Let me know if you get too cold."

His dad did not call him Jericho, or William; nobody did, except his mom when she got really mad at something he had done. Most of the time, everybody just called him Buddy. He was not sure how he came to be named Jericho William Miller. His mom always said something about a highly regarded ancestor who had fought with the Iowa infantry in the Civil War. Although the story had been told to him several times, it still meant little to him. He was simply too young to understand or appreciate the significance. When friends in school asked him what his real name was, he always told them William. It took too much time and some embarrassment to explain Jericho.

Ranger, the Miller's "psychotic" Brittany spaniel was seventy-five feet in front of them, bounding back and forth across the future path of the boy and his dad. His dad called the dog psychotic, and said it was the dumbest dog they had ever had. Instead of methodically working the corn field ahead of the men, the dog tended to just play and run and would not hold a point more than five seconds before jumping at any bird he stumbled onto.

Hunting had been good this fall and winter, and their freezer at home was well stocked with quail and pheasant. Venison roast, sausage, and venison back strap also occupied the freezer. In the fall and winter, Buddy and his dad spent at least a couple of hours nearly every Saturday tramping the harvested corn fields on their farm. It was a special time for the boy. Whenever he went hunting with his dad, he felt like an adult, carrying the heavy 20 gauge pump across the fields. Twelve year old Buddy shifted the Remington 870 in his arms as he watched the dog coursing in front of them. Buddy made sure the muzzle of the gun pointed to the right, away from his dad.

The glimpse of the breaking rooster pheasant was instantaneously followed by the dull brown of two hens as they broke from cover and ran ahead of Buddy toward the roaming dog. Buddy swung the gun into firing position. The birds spotted the dog, panicked, and cackled an even louder alarm, as they lifted to flight. Buddy led the rooster as it gained speed and height, fired the shotgun, and immediately pumped a new round into the chamber. But it was not needed. The rooster had become motionless in flight, crumpled, and plummeted to the snow. The hens continued to cackle and flew for cover in the adjoining woods.

"Great shot Buddy!" said his dad. "I was looking out to the left and didn't even see those birds. Let's go pick him up and head for home. I'm pretty darn cold, and a good hot cup of coffee or cocoa would taste awful good right now."

They both switched on their guns' safeties, walked to the fallen roost-er, and Buddy picked him up. He stuffed the bird into his game pouch, and Jim and Buddy began walking perpendicular to their previous path. They walked a considerable distance across the furrows to get to the edge of the corn field. This would bring them to the gravel road where they could more easily walk to the parked pickup truck a quarter mile down the road. When they reached the truck, Buddy threw the bird in the truck bed, and both he and his dad unloaded, then broke their guns for the ride back to the house.

The old, dirty, rusty, faded red International pick-up truck objected to the turning of the key in the ignition. If it were possible for a machine to have arthritis, the old truck demonstrated an acute case. Zero tempera-tures thickened the old truck's motor oil and made the aging engine cantankerous. Jim Miller stomped on the accelerator several times before the engine reluctantly turned over. The starter growled over and over, and just when it looked like the old truck wouldn't start, the engine coughed and wheezed to life. Many times his dad had said that it was about time to get a new truck, but then, each time the old truck sputtered to life, his dad just grinned and patted the truck's dashboard.

"Guess she's got a few more miles left in her," he said as he adjusted the manual choke and the stubborn heater control to get the maximum heat in the truck's cab.

Ten minutes later they had parked the truck at the back of the house, and Buddy grabbed the two shotguns. He walked over and opened the door to the back porch where he removed his gloves, coat, and boots, then opened the door to the kitchen and entered the house as his dad went toward the barn to clean the pheasant. His mom had bread baking for lunch, and she poured Buddy a cup of cocoa and put it on the kitchen table. Buddy went to the basement, retrieved the gun cleaning kit, and returned to sit at the kitchen table while he began cleaning the two guns. He sipped his warm cocoa while he worked.

"Buddy, I've told you before, you need to put down some newspaper on the table before you start cleaning those guns. Don't be getting that smelly old gun cleaning oil on my kitchen table," said his mom. Buddy got the previous day's morning *Des Moines Register* and spread it on the table. He glanced at the sports story about the six-girl basketball tournaments that were presently taking place around the state, and then began cleaning the guns.

His dad returned from the barn, washed his hands, and rinsed the bird at the kitchen sink. He carefully wrapped the dressed-out bird in aluminum foil and walked out to the back porch where the family kept a freezer. He opened the freezer door and added the bird to the meat supply.

As he came back into the kitchen, he said, "Irene, you should have seen the shot Buddy made today. I think he's gotten so he can outshoot me," said Jim.

Irene and Buddy Miller just smiled. In truth, there was not a person in Mahaska County that could outshoot Jim Miller. His prowess with a rifle or a shotgun was proven every year at the Southern Iowa Fair. He had won the shooting contests for several years and had a shelf full of trophies and ribbons won in those contests. In addition, he usually won the skeet tournament held each year at the local Izaac Walton League annual picnic and pig roast.

Jim grabbed a mug and filled it with the hot coffee from the stove, which he had brewed before going hunting. He sat down at the table, blew on the steaming mug, and watched as Buddy ran gun solvent-saturated swabs through the gun barrels. Cleaning the guns was a job that Buddy didn't even need to be asked to do, and after two years of hunting with him, Jim knew the job would be done correctly. Jim smiled to himself when he remembered how much smaller Buddy had been when he started hunting with him two years ago.

"Where are the girls?" asked Jim.

"I took them over to the Nelsons so all the girls could play together. I'll go get them in a few minutes."

Irene had taken the fresh bread from the oven, and while it cooled, she put sandwich fixings on the counter. Jim and Buddy would have roast beef sandwiches for lunch before they did their chores. "Now don't forget, you two, that you will need to get cleaned up for supper so we can go to church tonight," she said as she sliced the bread and made the sandwiches. "I have to go get the girls, and I will eat with them when I get back." She stripped off her apron and hung it on the oven door handle. She pushed up the sides of her hair and went to get her coat. In a couple of minutes, Buddy and his dad heard the grinding of the old pick-up starter followed by the chugging of the old truck as it headed out to the road.

"Better finish up, Buddy. I'm worried about the sows, and their pens need cleaning. It won't be long now 'til farrowing time," said his dad.

Jim Miller kept a maximum of only twelve sows on the farm. While keeping livestock was work intensive, they were almost always a guaranteed money maker as the market for hogs seemed to hold steady every year. Pigs were like an insurance policy. Even in times of bad weather for producing a good corn crop, and poor corn prices, the hog market was almost always stable and profitable. Each year, Jim would pay for the services of a neighbor's boar to impregnate the sows. In the winter or early spring all the sows had their piglets. At four months old, most of the weaned gilts, the castrated shoats, and the oldest of the mother sows would be sold. But Jim would keep the younger sows and a few of the gilts for the next year's crop of piglets. This process took place every year and helped augment the farm family's annual income.

Buddy and his dad trudged through the light snow to the farrowing shed, located a considerable distance from the house to minimize the drifting smell. They opened the big double door. The strong smell of confined hog manure and its associated ammonia and methane gas would certainly be overpowering to someone unused to it. But Buddy and his dad accepted the odor as just another part of their farm operation. They each grabbed a large grain shovel and entered a sow's pen. The filthy, saturated straw was shoveled out of the pens and taken outdoors to be picked up later and loaded into a manure spreader. After the pens had been cleaned out, they spread clean straw in each enclosure. Fresh water and swine meal were put in each pen's feeder. Buddy lingered in the pen of one of the sows.

"Beulah girl, how are you?" said Buddy. Beulah was to be Buddy's 4-H project for next summer's fair. Buddy had spent a great deal of time with the pig as a gilt so she would become used to having him near her, washing her, and making her less fearful of other humans. After the sow had her piglets, Buddy would need to begin working almost daily with the sow so that she would walk with him and cooperate in the show ring at next summer's county fair.

"Are you feeling all right, girl? It won't be long now," said Buddy. He gave her a swine biscuit treat and moved to the next pen.

"I figure another week to ten days," said Buddy's dad, referring to the upcoming time when the sows would begin having their piglets. They worked through the afternoon, and by the time they had finished with their chores, it was nearing supper time. They put away their shovels and moved to the outdoor water pump. At the pump, they rinsed their boots and hands in the frigidly cold water and passed the parked pick-up as they made their way to the house. Obviously Irene was back with the girls. They continued to the back porch where they took off the boots and hung their coats and hats on pegs on the wall of the back porch.

The unmistakable, delicious smell of oysters being simmered in butter prior to being added to the soup stock filled the kitchen. When supper was finally ready, the family sat down to a traditional Christmas Eve dinner consisting of rich, buttery oyster stew, relishes, fresh-baked bread, and oven-fresh Christmas cookies. After saying grace, the family quietly enjoyed this once-per-year delicacy.

Later, the Millers scrubbed up, dressed for church, and backed the old, black, four-door Plymouth out of its shed for the ride into town. Irene never liked riding in the old car. She sniffed her nose every time she got in it. By virtue of the car's unique smell, she was certain there were mice living somewhere in the bowels of that Plymouth. She was probably right. Mice loved to crawl into more snug surroundings for the winter.

The family attended the candle-light Christmas Eve service in town. The children enjoyed going to church because they could see all of their school friends. That was one drawback to living on the farm. They did not have many friends close by. Another attraction of the candlelight service was that the children were allowed to hold their own lighted candles during the service while the beautiful carols were sung by the small church choir and the congregation.

The old Plymouth lurched on the ruts in the country road and groaned in the icy temperature, but chugged faithfully homeward after the service. The yawning youngsters quickly changed into their pajamas, brushed their teeth, and were soon tucked into bed. Tired as they were, the final conversations of the children centered on the arrival of Santa Claus, which they were assured by their parents would happen sometime during the night.

But even after midnight, Irene's work was not yet over. She still had to prepare for tomorrow's festivities and the large meal that would be enjoyed by the family. Exhausted, she finally toppled into bed at two a.m. Christmas morning.

The two sets of grandparents were still living and had homes in town. Early Christmas morning, Irene's parents' dark green Pontiac sedan nosed into the farm lane, jounced sluggishly, approached the house, and the four grandparents stepped out of the car. Their arms were soon loaded with brightly wrapped presents and food dishes which they were unloading from the car. Sarah and Janeen, Buddy's younger sisters, spilled out of the front door of the farm house to run giggling toward their grandparents.

"Hurry, Grandma. We've been waiting for you to open presents!" said Sarah. Soon, everyone had a place to sit in the large living room of the house. A warm crackling fire in the fireplace took the edge off the cold in the old farm house. Extra kindling and logs were piled neatly to one side of the hearth. Buddy was charged with reading the tags on the presents and distributing them. The conversation among the adults and the laughter of the children banished all worries and concerns of everyone in the room.

When, at last, everyone had a small pile of gifts waiting to be opened, Jim Miller opened the worn family Bible and began reading the Christmas story aloud. *"There were shepherds in the field nearby tending their flock. An angel of the Lord appeared to them, and the glory of the Lord shone around them, and they were terrified. But the angel said to them, do not be afraid. I bring you good news of great joy that will be for all the people. Today in the town of David a Savior has been born to you; he is Christ the Lord. This will be a sign to you: you will find a baby wrapped in cloth and lying in a . . ."*

Chapter Five

"What's up, Miller? What's going on?" Buddy was irreverently jerked from his reverie by the voice of his buddy Henry Lucas. "You've only got another five minutes on watch. Let's go into town."

Buddy's thoughts had only reluctantly pulled back from his fond memories of Christmas at home when he was younger, and he began to focus on his friend gently punching him in the shoulder. He was still feeling melancholy over the fact that he was not home for the holidays.

"For crying out loud, Lucas, it's Christmas Eve. I'm not going into that stinking town tonight. I'll make you a deal, though. You buy me a beer, and I'll go to the EM club with you," said Buddy.

"OK, you're on," said Lucas.

Just then the men were joined by a second class Electronics Technician (ET) who was Buddy's relief on the quarter deck watch, and a LTJG who was the officer's relief. After briefing the ET on the ship's status and alerting him to anything out of the ordinary, the ET took over the watch and strapped on the web belt and pistol. Buddy signed his name and closed out his watch in the green-covered log book. He and Lucas then headed below to change into civilian clothes.

Forty-five minutes later, Buddy and Henry were sitting in the bar at the EM club, each nursing a beer. The juke box was loudly playing a variety of popular rock and roll tunes and was being fed an endless string of quarters so there was never a break in the music. But even with the noise of the music, the club seemed a bit somber. The patrons were young men who were far from home in time of war, and most of them were fondly remembering their Christmas Eves when they had been home. The talk among the young men was quiet and sometimes melancholy as they talked.

"What did you like best about Christmas, Henry?" asked Buddy.

"Oh, that's easy; being out of school, with no homework and no teachers. I always liked those two weeks," Henry replied. "How about you?"

"I guess it would be the food," said Buddy. "We would have the grandparents over for Christmas dinner, and my mom would fry up a mess of quail along with turkey or ham. Man, that quail was so good, fried up in butter and bread crumbs. And pie for dessert. Cherry pie was my favorite. And you know what? I honestly miss the snow."

"Not much snow in Brownwood," said Henry. "We'd just get a little bit once in a while. I really miss my mom's Tex-Mex chili that we would have on Christmas Eve. Then we would have a huge barbecued brisket on Christmas, with home-made butter rolls. Geez, my mouth is watering." But after a few more seconds of silence, Henry then broke their mood by saying, "Let's go play some pool."

The young men ordered a beer refill and headed to an adjoining room where there were several pool tables. But as they went through the door, they heard shouting.

"Oh, Jesus, when did Dawes sneak in here?" said Henry as he looked across the room at one of the far pool tables. What he saw was a sailor he knew from the ship, one of the Weasel's buddies, known simply as Sam, holding a pool cue in the air. In front of him was the cowering figure of Bob Dawes. "I thought Dawes said he was staying on the ship tonight," said Buddy.

As Buddy and Henry walked up, they diplomatically asked Sam what was going on. Sam said, "This slime ball owes me five bucks, and he says he doesn't have the money to pay me. So, I figure a pool cue busted over his head is what he needs to wake up."

Henry turned to Dawes. "You got any money, Bob?"

Dawes shook his head no.

"Put the pool cue down, Sam. Here's your five bucks," said Henry as he handed the money to Sam.

"Let's go Bob," said Buddy, and the three men went back to the bar, where they found a table and sat down.

"Dawes, you don't have the sense to pour piss out of a boot if the instructions were written on the heel!" said Henry. "Didn't you learn anything from getting beat on by those shit heads?"

"Hey, I'm pretty good at pool. I thought I could beat Sam," said Dawes as he gave them one of his boyish, million-dollar smiles.

"Oh sure, and pigs will be flying at sunset," said Buddy, as he walked to the table from the bar. He put three fresh beers on the table and sat down.

They clinked their Budweiser bottles together as Henry said, "Well boys, here's to Christmas Eve in Subic!"

*****

Turkey, dressing, mashed potatoes, and all the ice cream a man could eat was served on Christmas day, along with the obligatory green beans. The men on the *Kawishiwi* spent the day relaxing and thinking of their families back home. Buddy wrote his family and dropped the letter in the ship's mail box. In all likelihood it would not reach Iowa for at least two weeks.

Christmas Day
Dear Mom and Dad,

The ship is in port at Subic, and I don't have duty today. It's a strange way to spend Christmas. I'll catch up on some reading and just goof off with some friends. I went to the Navy Exchange on base a couple weeks ago and did my shopping. So I sent you guys some presents. I hope you get them in time for Christmas. Chow was good today. We had turkey and dressing and all the ice cream we could eat. Wish I had a nice warm slice of Mom's cherry pie to pile the ice cream on. It sure was not as good as being home and eating with you. We will head out again next week and get back to fueling ships again. Wish I was there with you guys. Merry Christmas and Happy New Year.

Love, Buddy

*****

In a few short days the *Kawishiwi*, topped off with over seven and a half million gallons of fuel in her bunkers, would again return to the waters off Vietnam; it was a hard-working auxiliary ship supporting the front line warriors. Through much of the month of January, the *Kawishiwi* made repeated runs to Romeo station off the coast of Vietnam, fueling the forward deployed ships until she would return to Subic Bay to replenish her dry fuel bunkers.

Chapter Six

In the Combat Information Center (CIC) of the *Kawishiwi*, radarmen, electronics technicians, and radiomen gathered around their equipment, keeping alert to the ship's progress, contacts on radar, and to message traffic. They relayed the information they gathered to the Officer of the Deck who was located on the ship's bridge.

When refueling was taking place, the men were always busy at their jobs. Periodically, however, when the ship was not refueling other ships, the activity in CIC slowed to the point where fewer men could carry out CIC's work. Some of the men would then take time to play cards, read, get a snack, or catch a quick nap. In addition, when no other ships were nearby for fueling, and radio traffic was light, the radiomen would switch the radio frequencies, which they monitored in order to pick up the activities of other military units. They especially enjoyed hearing the voices of the tactical aircraft pilots, both Navy and Air Force as they carried out their bombing and strafing missions over both North and South Vietnam.

*****

Cobra one, Aardvark one, over.
Aardvark one, this is Cobra one.
Cobra one, target in site, maintaining two angels, over.
Roger Aardvark one, Cobra and Willie Fudd have eyes on, out.

Seven minutes later.

Cobra one, Aardvark one, over.

Go ahead Aardvark one, over.

Roger, Cobra, half payload away. Triple A too great for second run. Aardvark two with a near miss and damage. Request permission to cruise Point Delta prior to Bingo and RTB.

Roger Aardvark, permission granted. See you at home. Out.

The *Kawishiwi*'s CIC gang knew this to be a Navy flight of three F-4 Phantoms who were from the Kitty Hawk which was code named Cobra, led by Aardvark One, who was conversing with the carrier regarding the mission of the three planes which had been sent to destroy pre-determined targets in the north. The *Kawishiwi* was close enough to the carrier's present operating area at Yankee Station to have watched the three planes on radar as they left the carrier.

Navy Lieutenant Commander Steve Andrews, the flight leader, also known by his call sign of "Goose Neck" waggled his wings at his two companion planes and the three planes turned eastward toward Point Delta. As they left the coast line behind them, they approached Point Delta, several miles east of land, and several miles south of the latitude of the DMZ. At the instant that each of the three planes crossed Point Delta, they each released their unused bombs.

Goose Neck, Billy Club.

What's up?

Take a look at my belly, would you, I've got a strange noise down there.

Lieutenant Commander Andrews maneuvered his plane to go beneath LTJG Bryan's plane and then looked up at the bottom of Bryan's plane.

Whoa, Billy Club, you've got some fine ventilation, with a little patch of loose skin. That's probably making your noise. There must be ten or more holes in that fuselage. Got anything showing on the board?

No, no warnings and everything seems to be working OK.

They continued their return flight and were vectored back to the steaming Navy carrier, USS *Kitty Hawk.*

Point Delta was used by the Navy and the Air Force to rid U.S. tactical planes of their unused ordinance before returning to land at their respective home bases. This unexploded ordinance, primarily bombs, was too dangerous to have hanging on an airplane as it made its sometimes rough landing at Air Force Bases or Navy Aircraft Carriers.

The waters at Point Delta contained an enormous number of unexploded bombs of all types. This unexploded stockpile grew with every day of the war. Although the waters at Point Delta were generally charted to be of sufficient depth, the danger of exploding underwater bombs always existed for watercraft that were traversing the location and had not heeded the warnings on nautical charts of the area.

This procedure of the fighter planes and bombers expending their unused ordinance at Point Delta was not clearly known to the CIC gang on the *Kawishiwi.* They did not know for sure what Point Delta was used for. They just knew it was a great pastime to eavesdrop on the Navy and Air Force pilots.

The Navy planes approached the carrier and began preparing for landing.

Just to be on the safe side, boys, Aardvark three will follow me in. Billy Club, you come in after us.

His two wingmen rogered up and watched as Andrews lined up to the carrier. He landed without incident, and his plane was quickly moved to the side. Aardvark Three followed, also caught the wire, and was quickly moved off the landing portion of the pitching deck.

Cobra, Aardvark Two.

Go ahead Two.

Could you get a spotter to look at my flaps and gear? When I popped them down, I heard a strange noise, over.

Roger, do a dirty pass, and we'll take a look. Out

LTJG Bryan lined up his Phantom and passed slowly over the deck of the ship. At least six sets of binoculars were trained on the undercarriage of the plane as it passed above the ship with its flaps and gear down.

"Uh, oh," said Commander Fred Banks, as he stared through binoculars at the passing plane. "Tell Two that his right gear looks damaged, and his tire is shredded. Alert the deck crew to prepare for a crasher."

The radioman went back on the line.

Aardvark Two. Be advised that your right gear appears damaged and your tire is shredded, over.

An audible, but quiet, "damn it" from the mouth of Aardvark Two came from the overhead speakers on the bridge of the *Kitty Hawk*.

Two, you are cleared to land. Deck is clear, net is up, and crew is standing by. Over

Roger.

LTJG Eddie Bryan was a good pilot, but not a great pilot. He took his Phantom on a very large race track while he tried to calm his nerves. Every landing of an airplane on a carrier is a controlled crash. The plane drops to the deck of the rolling ship with a thunderous crash to be caught on a cable by the arresting hook hanging from the underside of the plane. If the controlled crash is successful, as it is in almost all cases, the plane and the pilot will fly another day. But if something is amiss in the carefully orchestrated landing, the odds of a catastrophe skyrocket. LTJG Bryan was fully aware of the problem as his stomach churned. What he did not know was how the plane would react as it hit the deck, minus a fully functional landing gear and tire.

The "dirty" condition of the plane with its gear and flaps down necessitated that Bryan give the plane more throttle as he dropped to six hundred feet. As he watched his angle of attack (AOA) indicator, he could see that his speed was correct, with the center yellow light lit. He dropped to four hundred and seventy-five feet and was now ninety degrees from the upwind approach leg. He kept his speed and turned into the wind. He could now see the "meatball." It was dead center in the light display. He eased the throttle ahead slightly to hold his speed. The orange light rose slightly, and he eased the stick forward to put the meatball in dead center. He was doing fine. But suddenly a large gust of wind hit the starboard side of the plane causing it to lift the starboard wing. Bryan brought the stick over, but it was too late. The plane had moved to the left, and he had lost altitude. The meatball became red, and the carrier's landing signal officer triggered a button on his hand-held "pickle," which lit up the meatball light display, signifying that Bryan was getting a wave-off. LTJG Bryan's stomach flopped, and he jammed the throttle forward while pulling slowly back on the stick. Even in a dirty condition, the F-4 jumped forward and began climbing rapidly.

LTJG Bryan's flight suit was wet with perspiration as he leveled off at six hundred feet on the downwind leg. Once again he watched his AOA, turned to the ninety degree point and continued the slow turn while dropping to the proper altitude. As he caught sight of the meatball, he brought the nose of the plane up slightly and tapped in a bit more throttle. All on-deck eyes were on the Phantom as it began the approach to the ship. The meatball was locked in the center. In ten more seconds the plane properly crashed onto the deck. As it hit, the right landing gear buckled, dropping the starboard wing to the deck. But the arresting hook had already caught one of the five cables. As it hooked, the plane took a violent jerk forward and to the right because of the crumpled landing gear, harshly pitching LTJG Bryan's body to the left and forward against his shoulder straps. His helmet banged against the seat support. The plane had decelerated from 150 miles per hour to a dead stop in only a second. Bryan closed the throttles. His helmet crackled with sound.

How you doing in there, Billy Club? It was LCDR Andrews asking.

LTJG Bryan responded. *Well, Goose Neck. It's another one I walk away from. Guess it's a good day.*

LTJG Bryan would indeed fly again another day.

*****

Forty minutes later in the *Kawishiwi* CIC.

Homerun, this is Rattler Four, over.

The *Kawishiwi* CIC gang listened to another pilot. This time it was a flight of four Air Force Phantoms, a 'four ship', which had lifted off in Thailand and were closing in on their target.

Go ahead Rattler Four, over.

Homerun, we're on final approach. Small convoy on trail. Will engage. Out.

Seven minutes later.

Homerun, Rattler Four, over.

Homerun, over.

Homerun, Rattler Four. Cargo delivered. Two bandits on us and we are engaging, out.

Ten minutes later.

Homerun, Rattler Four.

Go ahead Rattler Four.

Yaaahoooo. Rattler Six got a kill and the other Fresco Charlie hightailed it. Five's got some wing aeration, but he's OK. We're strolling to Point Delta to let seven unload and then will be RTB.

Roger, Rattler four. Homerun out.

Rattler Four out.

The *Kawishiwi* radiomen were in awe of the pilots, whether they were Navy or Air Force.

"How about those guys. They did a bombing run and took out a Charlie plane. Boy, I sure would have liked to be in the back seat of one of those planes," said one of the radiomen.

"They wouldn't let you," said another sailor. "You'd puke all over the back of the pilot." The CIC guys laughed. They knew this particular sailor's reputation for frequent seasickness.

Chapter Seven

It was not always monotonous hard work for the oiler's crew. February found the *Kawishiwi* in Hong Kong for some much needed rest and recuperation for the deserving crew of the oiler. The ship was anchored in the harbor, and two liberty boats carried crew members to and from the ship to explore the exotic port.

Enjoying their brief work respite, Buddy Miller, Henry Lucas, and Bob Dawes were seated in *Custer's Last Stand*, a favorite Hong Kong bar for the crew of the oiler. They were drinking green bottles of Tsing Tao beer with a couple of other crew members and listening to a Hong Kong rock band butcher the latest American music.

Henry loved to jab Bob Dawes. "What do you think, Dawes? Should we find you a nice friendly poker game to get into?"

"Aw, lay off, Henry. I think I've learned my lesson," said Bob. "Besides, I promised my mom that I would get her something nice while we were here in Hong Kong so I've got to save my moolah."

Buddy happened to be looking at the bar's entrance. "Uh, oh. Heads up," said Buddy. "There's Proctor coming in the door. What do you suppose he wants?"

The Chief rarely associated with his subordinates on the beach. That's just the way it was. Chiefs usually went on liberty together, not with the junior petty officers.

Chief Proctor pulled up a chair and sat down at the table. A very scantily, provocatively clad Chinese waitress brought a fresh round of beer to the table with another bottle for the chief. The three gunner's mates were surprised when the chief paid for the round. The conversation was light and interspersed with the latest jokes they had each heard.

In a few minutes, the Chief leaned over to Buddy and said, "Miller, I need to talk to you. Grab your beer and let's go over to another table where it's quieter." The young men looked at each other, and Buddy shrugged his shoulders to signify he had no idea what the Chief wanted, but he rose with Chief Proctor to move to another table. After they were seated, the Chief leaned close to Buddy.

"Here's the deal, Miller. Before I left the ship tonight, I got stopped by Radioman Chief Binns. He had a couple messages he wanted to show me. It turned out to be two sets of orders that had just been received in the radio traffic. The XO hadn't even seen them yet."

"OK, so what?" said Buddy.

"The orders are for you, knucklehead," said the Chief. "And the other set of orders is for Lucas. I told you when you made rate that you would probably be picked up for independent duty. Well, this is it. You're going to the USS *Erne*, (MSC-300) out of Sasebo. But she is doing Market Time over here right now. This is really a hot shit assignment. What do you think about that?"

Buddy just stared at the Chief and did not say anything. As far as he was concerned, it was not all that exciting. He would much rather remain on the *Kawishiwi*, where he was accustomed to the routine and had made several good friends. But he also knew that independent duty, where a petty officer was the only one on board a small ship who had a particular rating or job, really was a career enhancing opportunity for a sailor. Apparently, these orders would place Buddy on the *Erne*, where he would be the only gunner's mate on the ship.

Buddy thought he probably should say something. "Where's Henry going?" he said.

"Henry? Are you listening to me at all? What the hell do you care? I'm telling you about your orders, and you are asking about Lucas. Geez Miller, focus here will you? You're getting a plumb assignment that is a huge career enhancer. And that's why I wanted to talk to you alone," said the Chief.

Buddy knew what was coming. It would be another of Proctor's pep talks about making the Navy a career.

"Buddy, you really need to give serious thought to making the Navy a career. Without a doubt, you will make second class on that minesweeper, and at that point you need to re-up. This is the type of assignment that will either make your career or break it. I'm just telling you that you are getting a hell of an opportunity. Just think about it," said the Chief.

Buddy took a swallow of his Tsing Tao and carefully set the bottle back on the table. "You're right, Chief. I'll think about it. Now, where's Henry going?"

"Oh, Lucas has been riding my ass for weeks about getting a transfer to brown water duty on a PBR (river patrol boat, a small, well-armed boat used in river operations). Well, he got what he wanted. He'll be headed for a PBR. Probably get his ass shot up, but that's what he wanted. But he's already a lifer, and knows PBR duty is also a career enhancer. It's a good career move, but it's dangerous, that's for sure," said Proctor. "I'll tell him about his orders as I leave. Remember, I wouldn't have made my way to this sleazy bar you guys call home unless I seriously thought you had what it takes to help the Navy." The Chief rose from his chair and started to turn around to go.

"Thanks, Chief. I appreciate it," said Buddy.

"Don't get too shit faced. I'll see you at quarters in the morning." And with those words, the chief turned and headed for the door of the bar. But he stopped at the table where Henry and Bob were sitting, said a few words to Henry, slapped Henry on the shoulder a couple times, and walked out the door.

As Buddy walked back to the table he heard Henry, "Whoo Hoo, I'm gonna be a brown water sailor. Hot damn, Vietnam! PBR's, just what I wanted!"

As Buddy sat down, he said, "Be careful what you ask for, Henry. You might just get your ass shot off."

"Yeah, ain't it great?" said Henry, showing a toothy grin.

The two petty officers compared their next duty stations in speculative story after story, interspersed with stupid jokes, while Bob Dawes listened intently to the two senior men. In the loud, smoky bar the beer flowed freely. Against his better judgment, Buddy kept up with Henry and was soon feeling no pain, and his concerns about his upcoming duty station were forgotten. The three young men were quite inebriated when they decided it was time to head back to the ship.

As the three sailors ambled in a somewhat reeling manner down the sidewalk, crossed several streets to make it to the boat pier, and slumped against the wooden benches of the liberty boat as it made its way back to the *Kawishiwi*, thoughts swirled in Buddy's addled mind. GM2 Henry Lucas was excited. He was getting exactly what he had wished for. On the other hand, GM3 Buddy Miller was very unsure of his next assignment.

*****

Buddy left the *Kawishiwi* temporarily in April 1968 to spend two weeks in a Gunner's Mate refresher course at Subic. The course was designed to prepare the class members to assume the responsibilities and accountabilities as the leading gunner's mate in a small Navy command. As usual, Buddy had no problems with the course work. In fact, the course had piqued his interest to the point that he was beginning to look forward to his new job on the small minesweeper. However, he was not happy that the *Erne* was another command that had no significant, modern armament. He had been hoping to work with more sophisticated weaponry. He had also learned that as the lead gunner's mate, there was a possibility that he could have a seaman or striker also assigned to the weapons division, working under his supervision.

The USS *Erne*, (MSC-300), a coastal minesweeper, was home ported in Sasebo, Japan. But the small ship was involved with the Navy's Market Time Operation, wherein, U.S. Navy ships and a squadron of U.S. Coast Guard ships patrolled and made a barrier line along the coast of South Vietnam, intercepting Vietnamese water craft to inspect for contraband and goods that could be used by the North Vietnamese military.

Operation Market Time had begun almost immediately after U.S. forces spotted a camouflaged ship just north of Nha Trang in February 1965. The ship was carrying weapons, ammunition, and medical supplies to North Vietnam. Operation Market Time had continued in effect for U.S. forces since March 1965.

Market Time ships at sea had airborne help from U.S. patrol planes based in South Vietnam and Thailand that kept watch farther out at sea and warned the Market Time ships when unknown foreign ships were headed their way. While carrying out Market Time duties, the *Erne* was attached to U.S. Military Assistance Command, Vietnam, Task Force 115, which included radar picket ships, ocean-going minesweepers, and the coastal minesweepers. The *Erne*, along with these other Navy ships, was on Market Time duty as the *Kawishiwi* left Subic in late April to resume its fueling station off the coast of Vietnam. GM3 Buddy Miller would transfer to the *Erne* while it was at sea.

Chapter Eight

May 5, 1968
USS **Kawishiwi**
Romeo Station, Vietnam

The first week in May 1968 found the *Kawishiwi* at Romeo Station, its fueling area. The ship moved slowly from north to south in a race-track pattern nearly fifty nautical miles in length. Like frantic, desperately paddling ducklings, a multitude of different Navy and Coast Guard ships would hurriedly make their way to the unmarked racetrack in the ocean to meet the oiler for fuel, parts, and mail.

Shortly before breakfast, Henry Lucas and Bob Dawes watched as Buddy Miller shoved the last of his clothing and belongings into his already stuffed green canvas sea bag. Buddy would not have a chance to eat breakfast. He pulled the flap tight on the top of the bag and latched the shoulder strap hook into the black metal eye. He was finished packing. Chief Proctor strode into the enlisted berthing area and found the three men.

"Let's go, Miller," said the Chief. "CIC has the *Erne* on radar and comms. She'll be here in about fifteen minutes."

"OK, Chief," answered Buddy.

The four men climbed several ladders and made their way to the underway replenishment rigging points on the main deck. A destroyer was seen distancing itself from the oiler after having completed its refueling in the early morning light. It churned a white, frothy wake as it gained speed and crossed the bow of the oiler to return to its patrol area. In silhouette, a small ship could be seen closing the distance to the oiler's port bow. The oiler slowed slightly, but kept its steady course. Soon the small wooden minesweeper turned slowly to port and took its place on the oiler's port side, running parallel to the larger ship. Refueling lines were passed between the two ships and made secure to padeyes on the bulkheads of the ships above their fueling stations. The top speed of the little minesweeper was only thirteen knots. The two ships cruised side by side at between ten and twelve knots. It would be up to the minesweeper to adjust its speed to stay with the oiler. *Kawishiwi* would not change its course or speed while another ship was alongside.

There was a knot in Buddy Miller's stomach as he watched the fuel lines being rigged and a bosun's chair being attached to another line between the two ships. When the deck crew was ready, Buddy was told to strap on a life jacket, climb into the chair, and put his sea bag on his lap. He stuffed his white hat into the waistband at the back of his pants and climbed into the chair. A small safety line was placed across his lap, and he was instructed on how to release it quickly in the event the rigging broke, and he was swept into the sea. As he was absorbing these instructions, the proper signals were given by the minesweeper's deck crew, and the bosun's chair lurched away from the oiler and began swinging to and fro in the wind. Buddy was now suspended from a pulley which rode on a cable strung between the two ships. The pulley assembly had a rope attached to both sides of it, the ends of which were held in the hands of sailors on both of the ships. As he sat in the chair, the rope and pulley continued moving, and the chair, with Buddy strapped in, slowly moved between the ships. Buddy only snatched a quick glance at the ocean below him and quickly looked back to see Henry and Bob, with big grins on their faces, flipping him the bird, and then waving. He waved back. He would miss those two friends.

"Gunther, you horse's ass, how the hell are you?" shouted Chief Proctor. He was shouting at a chief who was standing on the deck of the *Erne*.

"That's Senior Chief horse's ass to you, Proctor," said the senior chief on the *Erne*. "What number wife did you leave pregnant at home this time?" obviously referring to the fact that Chief Proctor had taken the plunge into holy matrimony more than the norm. In fact, Chief Proctor had been married to four different women. Once, he was even married to more than one woman at one time, a situation which nearly drove him to the "nut farm" and almost cost him his career before he finally got it all straightened out. He had vowed to remain single following that incident.

"None of your damn business, Senior Chief. You're just jealous," said Proctor.

"Oh yeah, like I want six kids running around, too!" laughed Senior Chief Gunther.

In truth, although there were several marriages in his background, Proctor had no children that he was aware of.

"Good to see you, shipmate," said Proctor. "Stay out of trouble."

"You too, my friend," said Gunther, as the two men waved at each other.

Buddy looked over at the smaller ship and watched as its deck gang hauled the bosun's chair to the *Erne*. He also noticed that the deck crew on the *Erne* was laughing and pointing. He looked down and saw that somebody on the *Kawishiwi* had pasted a length of toilet paper to the heel of his boondocker work boot. He tried to lean over and pull it off, but the chair and his sea bag made that impossible. He looked back and saw Henry and Bob laughing. He would have liked to flip them the bird, but with everyone on both ships watching him, he just waved again as the chair came to the deck of the minesweeper. Buddy got out of the chair, leaned over and tossed the flapping toilet paper over the side. A second class boatswain's mate told Buddy that the XO was on the bridge and wanted to see him as soon as he was aboard.

He hoisted his sea bag onto his shoulder and climbed two ladders to the bridge.

Chapter Nine

May 5, 1968
USS **Erne**
Off the Coast of Vietnam

With a lump in his throat, GM3 Buddy Miller set his sea bag on the deck and stepped onto the awning-covered bridge. He quickly scanned the small area. The bridge was a bit crowded with three officers in khaki, a quartermaster, and a phone talker. An ensign seemed to be giving orders, leading Buddy to surmise that the ensign would be the current OOD. A LTJG (lieutenant junior grade) stood to the side of the bridge, and a LT (lieutenant) sat in a large chair that had been turned to watch the replenishment activities between the two ships. Generally only one man on the bridge sat in a big chair, and Buddy knew that would be the Captain of the *Erne*. That left the LTJG to be the XO. Buddy approached him and saluted.

"Gunner's Mate Third Class Miller reporting aboard, sir," said Buddy.

LTJG Gus Bamino, the ship's executive officer, returned the salute. "Glad to have you aboard, Miller. You come highly recommended."

This remark took Buddy aback, and the surprised look on his face revealed his thoughts.

"Relax, Miller. It's sometimes a real small Navy," said the XO. "Word of the good guys, and of the shit birds, gets around. We were told you were a good guy. We'll soon find out if that's true."

Pointing to the officer sitting in the chair, he said, "That's our CO, LT Sam Yates."

Buddy quickly saluted the commanding officer, and the salute was returned.

"The OOD is Ensign Steve Meyer. He's also the ship's engineering officer."

Buddy quickly looked at the ensign, but the ensign paid no attention to Buddy, as he was intently making sure that the *Erne* held her position properly next to the *Kawishiwi*, which towered over the small mine-sweeper. A mistake by the OOD could have disastrous results if the small ship were to veer into the side of the oiler.

Replenishment of the minesweeper was soon completed, and the high-line gear was being dismantled and brought aboard the respective ships. Soon there were no lines between the two ships, and the CO walked out to the bridge wing and saluted the CO of the *Kawishiwi*.

"The ship is clear, Mr. Meyer. Let's take a very slow turn to port and get away from the oiler," said the LT Yates.

"Aye, aye, Captain. Five degrees left rudder," said Meyer, speaking into the voice tube that was connected to the pilot house one deck below. The helmsman, located in the pilot house below, shouted back up the voice tube, answering, "The rudder is five degrees left, sir."

The ship began turning very slowly to port, increasing the distance between it and the oiler. When the distance was greater, the XO again turned his attention to Buddy. "Miller, you will report to the First Lieutenant, Ensign Jack Kramer. But you need to go down to the ship's office and let the yeoman and personnelman get your orders and paper-work up to speed. Then you can look for Ensign Kramer. Ship's office is down on the port side on the main deck. When you are in the office, tell the yeoman that I said he should show you around the ship and find you a bunk. Understood?"

"Yes sir," said Buddy, and he saluted, turned, and walked to the back of the bridge. He picked up his sea bag and climbed down the ladders to the main deck. As he began walking to the ship's office, he quickly noticed that the small ship did not ride anything like the big oiler. The small ship was rocking from side to side with regularity, and Buddy was not used to the motion. He was concerned that he might become seasick as he began to feel a bit nauseous. But he proceeded on and walked through the water-tight door into the interior port passageway, where he soon discovered that the ship was not air conditioned. It was unbelievably hot in the interior of the ship. He found the ship's office, knocked lightly on the door, which had been propped open, and stepped into the office. There were two sailors sitting at desks in the tiny office space, and a third desk and chair sat next to their two desks. The back of the vacant chair at the third desk was plainly stencil-painted with the letters 'XO'. A gray electric fan fastened to the bulkhead droned and vibrated wearily as it attempted to move the thick, sticky air around the office.

The two sailors in the office turned in their chairs. "Ah, you must be FNUGY," said the second class petty officer. Buddy had been in the Navy long enough to know that FNUGY was the acronym for 'fuckin' new guy.' "My name is Wayne Briggs, ship's yeoman. I guess you must be Miller. We got a copy of your advance orders last week."

"Yep, I'm Buddy Miller," said Buddy.

"This piss-poor excuse for a sailor is PN3 Donny Sorenson," said Briggs pointing at the third class petty officer sitting at the next desk. This crude remark resulted in a sound punch to the shoulder of Briggs by Sorenson.

"Lemme have your files," said Briggs. Buddy opened the top of his sea bag and pulled out three worn manila folders; his personnel file, his pay record, and his medical file and handed them to Briggs, who in turn, handed them to Sorenson.

"So how was that ride in the bosun's chair?" asked Briggs. "Since we are so far from home port, a lot of our guys have arrived that way. Kinda scary, huh?"

Buddy chuckled. "Yeah, I didn't look down very much. When I came aboard I had to report to the XO. That scared me more than the ride over in the bosun's chair. The XO said you might be able to show me around and find me a bunk."

"OK, Jericho William Miller," said Briggs as he quickly perused Buddy's orders. He set the papers aside and said, "Glad to have you aboard. Let's go and I'll show you around."

"Nice meeting you, Sorenson," said Buddy as he hoisted his sea bag. He and Briggs left the office and moved forward in the ship. They reached the enlisted mess deck, and Briggs pointed out the posted "Watch, Quarter, and Station Bill," the document that listed the duty section to which each sailor on the ship was assigned, and the location where each sailor was assigned for different activities of the ship, such as general quarters, fire parties, and sea detail.

"I'm sure Mr. Kramer will get you on the watch bill a.s.a.p. We can always use another watch stander," said Briggs.

They moved through another water-tight door into the crew's berthing area. Briggs pointed out an empty bunk and told Buddy that would be his. "Your locker is over on the bulkhead. Pick one that doesn't have a lock on it, and it's yours. There are supposed to be clean sheets in each empty locker; that is, if no one has filched them. The head is right next to us through that door," said Briggs. "When you dump your sea bag, come back to the office, and I'll take you to meet Mr. Kramer."

"OK, thanks," said Buddy.

Twenty minutes later, after stowing his gear and making up his assigned bunk, he was back at the ship's office. He and Briggs then went to the officer's wardroom. They knocked on the door and entered. Two officers sat at the wardroom table doing paperwork. Briggs first introduced him to LTJG Jerry Clark, the Operations Officer. He then introduced him to Ensign Jack Kramer, the First Lieutenant and

Minesweeping Officer. Kramer had been poring over paperwork on the table. The documents appeared to be part of the Navy's Preventative Maintenance System.

Each Navy ship and shore command had specific periodic maintenance duties assigned to each piece of equipment at that command, or ship, in order to ensure that the equipment would continue to operate properly and to prolong the life of that item. This system was known as the 3M system (maintenance and material management). Maintaining the proper records attesting that the required maintenance had been completed was a tedious and never-ending chore.

Buddy could plainly see that Ensign Kramer was elbow-deep in the 3M records. After standing and shaking hands with Buddy, Kramer said, "Boy, am I glad to see you, Miller. You're just in time to help me make sense of these gunnery PMS sheets. They are way behind, and I don't have time to be working on this. Sounds like a good job for you. Did Briggs find you a place to bunk?" asked Kramer.

"Yes sir, I'm squared away," answered Buddy.

"Thanks, Briggs, I'll take him from you now," said Kramer.

"Aye, aye, sir. See you later, Miller," said Briggs and left to return to his office.

"Sit down here with me, Miller, and lend me a hand with this mess."

Buddy sat down next to Ensign Kramer, and for the next hour and a half, the two men straightened out the weapons records and brought all of them up to date. There were six PMS procedures that needed to be performed on some of the small arms, and they were all in the ship's armory.

"Here are the six cards you need to do the work procedures on the small arms. The guns are in the armory, of course, and here's my extra key for you to the armory," he said as he slipped a key from the key ring he wore clipped to his belt and handed it to Buddy. "The armory is out on the weather deck up forward on the starboard side. You can't miss it. It's the only water-tight door up there."

"Glad to have you aboard, Miller," said Kramer. "We've been without a gunner's mate for a month now. I understand we might be getting a striker too, but I haven't seen any orders in the radio traffic. Go ahead and take off, and I'll catch up to you later. Chow should go down in about an hour."

"Yes sir," said Buddy, and he got up from the table, took the six maintenance cards, and found his way out to the starboard weather deck. He had not formed any opinion of Ensign Kramer in his short time with him, but thought he seemed like a reasonable guy to work for.

Buddy worked the worn, brass key into the brass padlock on the armory door. The lock opened reluctantly. He noted to himself that he would need to oil the padlock to keep it from further corroding and becoming inoperable in the corrosive salt air. It was obvious that this had not been done properly in the past. As he pulled the water-tight door, it screeched on its hinges and required extra effort to get it to swing open. Like the lock, its hinges needed lubrication. As the daylight entered the armory, and Buddy could see the interior, he drew in a quick breath of surprise. The tiny armory was a shambles. Trash, paper, and filthy, oil-covered rags covered the deck. Of the two overhead lights, only one lit as he flipped on the light switch. He groaned. The previous gunner's mate must have been a real slob, he thought. That would also explain why the weapons PMS records were so fouled up. Buddy wondered if a thorough inspection had ever been held in the armory. He looked over at the racks of M-1's and .45's and groaned again. Not only would he be in charge of these old small arms, but their condition also reflected the gross negligence of the previous gunner's mate. The entire small arms inventory would need to be cleaned and oiled, and the armory itself would need a thorough straightening, cleaning, and painting. Well, he knew what he would be doing for the next few weeks. Then his eye caught a strange sight. Lying on the deck, next to the rifle rack, were four Russian Kalashnikov AK-47's, with several clips and loose ammunition. Buddy had never seen one of these rifles up close, and he picked up one of them to examine it. It, too, was dirty and not well maintained. Buddy wondered where these rifles had come from since they were not U.S. Navy weapons. He placed the rifle back with the others.

For the next hour, Buddy picked up the trash and straightened up the armory as best he could, and then started in on the PMS cards. He completed two of them and was about to start the third, when Ensign Kramer stuck his head in the door.

"C'mon Miller, we've got a contact to take care of. Lock up and come with me," said Kramer.

Buddy had no idea what Ensign Kramer was talking about, but he locked the armory and followed Kramer. They passed the open watertight door to the mess deck, and he noticed that most of the crew was eating lunch. He guessed that he would miss lunch as he proceeded on with Mr. Kramer.

He then noticed that the ensign was wearing a .45 in a holster attached to a web belt around his waist. This seemed odd. Where had Mr. Kramer gotten the pistol? They proceeded to the fantail, and Buddy was shocked again to see two sailors and a senior chief standing near the rail holding three rifles. Again he wondered where these guns had come from. As he glanced up forward on the weather deck, he also saw another sailor manning a .30 caliber machine gun which was fastened by a pin mount to a stanchion. There was a phone talker standing by the group on the fantail, wearing a headset plugged into a jack on the bulkhead below the gunwale. He also noticed another man standing with the sailors. He was wearing a gray uniform and was obviously Asian.

"See that little boat over there?" said Ensign Kramer to Buddy as they walked to the fantail of the ship.

Buddy focused on a small fishing boat rocking in the swells off the *Erne*'s starboard bow. "Yes sir," said Buddy.

"That's our target vessel. We're going to stop him and search him. Since this is your first look at how 'Market Time' works, you're going to sit this one out and just watch," said Ensign Kramer. "Pay attention, though, because I want you involved in the future. Understood?"

"Yes sir," said Buddy.

"We will first find out if the occupants speak English. If they don't, Ensign Binh will interpret for us. He's the South Vietnamese officer we haul around with us for that purpose," said Kramer.

Buddy now understood why the Asian officer was standing on the deck of the *Erne* watching the procedures.

The *Erne* approached the small fishing vessel that looked like a miniature junk. It was brown in color with a small orange-tinted sail, which had weathered to a very dirty orange-gray. The boat had a small raised poop deck on the stern of the boat, and several ropes hung over the sides. A small red pennant flew from the mast above the odd-shaped sail. Ornamental eyes were painted on the two sides of the bow of the small boat. As the ship came alongside of the fishing boat, two shirtless men could be seen on the boat. Ensign Kramer spoke to the two men, asking their permission to come on board their boat and examine their papers. One of the men apparently understood English and nodded his head.

"Let's go," said Ensign Kramer, and one of the sailors with a rifle followed Kramer as they climbed over the rail of the *Erne*, descended a rope ladder, and jumped gingerly onto the deck of the junk. They were followed by Ensign Binh. The senior chief and the other armed sailor remained at the rail of the *Erne* and loosely held their weapons ready, while keeping a sharp eye on the small fishing boat below them.

"You too, Miller. I want you to watch this first hand," said Kramer. Buddy did as he was instructed and, although he was unarmed, he climbed over the rail to join the men on the deck of the junk.

Ensign Kramer did not need to ask for the papers from the fishermen. The individual who had indicated that he understood English handed Kramer a clear plastic envelope containing a sheaf of papers.

"Come here, Miller, and look at this. This top sheet is the one we really have to see. It shows the names of the people assigned to be on this boat and who the owner of the boat is. It also tells their occupation. Almost all of the papers on these boats we examine are going to say that the boat is owned by a fisherman and his family. Look here," he said pointing to the document. "This fellow's family name is Nguyen, and he is a fisherman. Over half of the people in Vietnam have that same family name. The next name is the middle name and the third name is the given name. It's not the same as the order of naming in our culture. See, his middle name is Hai and the given name is Sang. Hai usually means he is the oldest son in his family. In most cases, you address Vietnamese people by their given name. You will learn more about this as you gain experience." Buddy was thoroughly confused.

Ensign Kramer continued, "Then, we want to see the paper that contains this particular seal. It is given to owners of watercraft who are loyal to the South Vietnamese Government. And the last paper we look for is a current license, also issued annually by the government. If all these things check out, we consider them to be OK. But hell, the whole works could be counterfeit; we wouldn't know," said Ensign Kramer, as he handed the documents to Ensign Binh who immediately began studying all the papers. Because it was he who knew the laws and the language, it was Binh who would give the final OK to Ensign Kramer that all the papers were in order. While Binh continued to riff through the papers, Kramer turned his attention to the fisherman.

Testing once again to see if the fisherman understood English, Kramer asked, "Have you had good luck fishing today, Mr. Sang?"

The fisherman nodded his head and replied, "Fishing has been good." Kramer thought to himself, great, the old guy understands and speaks a little English.

"We need to look at your boat, sir. Would that be all right?" asked Kramer. The fisherman had been through this routine before, so he knew his boat was going to be inspected no matter how he answered. He nodded his head in assent.

For the next thirty minutes, Ensign Kramer, the armed sailor, and Buddy pulled open all hatch covers, built-in cabinets, and drawers. They examined all spaces and the living quarters in the small boat. Buddy stayed with Kramer to learn what and where to look on the boat for contraband.

"We are especially looking for guns or munitions; anything that could help the cause of the North. If we have any doubt, we confiscate the items or throw them over the side. Weapons, we keep so they won't go diving for them later," said Kramer.

Next, they examined the small hold of the boat and saw that it indeed contained a large quantity of fish. The ensign stepped down onto the ladder going into the hold and removed a small oil lamp that was hanging next to the ladder and lit it using a wooden match he found in an old tin can tacked to the bulkhead near where the lamp had hung. He and Buddy climbed down into the hold and carefully kicked aside fish until they could stand firmly on the deck. "Shuffle your feet from side to side and look down. You are looking for trap doors," said Kramer. After a few minutes Kramer was satisfied that there were no hidden compartments under the fish. "Let's go," he said. They climbed back out of the hold. Binh handed the documents to Kramer and quietly told him the documents checked out OK. Kramer handed the envelope of documents back to the fisherman.

"Thank you, Mr. Sang. Good luck with your fishing." The fisherman smiled and bowed slightly at the waist.

Kramer, Buddy, the armed sailor, and Ensign Binh climbed up the rope ladder and over the rail of the *Erne*.

"Tell the bridge we are finished with the inspection, and the boat checked out OK," said Kramer to the phone talker. The phone talker relayed the message to the bridge. As the small fishing boat moved clear of the ship, the minesweeper's diesels revved audibly, and the *Erne* moved further away from the fishing boat.

Kramer turned to Buddy. "Come with me, I need to talk to you about our procedures and rules of engagement."

Buddy noticed that the senior chief and the other two armed sailors were walking off with their rifles. "What about the guns, sir. Shouldn't I go lock them up?" he asked.

"Nah, we'll just need them again later," said Kramer.

This remark bothered Buddy. He was going to be held accountable for the small arms on the ship, and at present, he did not know how many were assigned to the ship, nor did he know where all of them were at any moment. He also knew that this loose arrangement with the small arms was not in accordance with Navy directives regarding the accountability and safe-guarding of weapons.

He followed Ensign Kramer into the officer's wardroom. He watched as Kramer poured two mugs of coffee from an electric urn secured to a bulkhead of the wardroom. He handed one to Buddy and sat at the wardroom table. "Have a seat, Miller," said Kramer. Ensign Kramer disappeared into the tiny officers' stateroom and returned with a couple sheets of paper.

"You need to read these, Miller, and give them back to me after you have read them. Basically they will spell out our mission while doing Market Time, and also tell you under what circumstances we are to confiscate property. And finally, those papers will pretty well spell out what to do in an emergency, such as when one of the boat people becomes aggressive or threatens us with deadly force. In other words, it's our rules of engagement. Just initial them after you read them and give them back to me. If you have any questions, be sure to ask me," said Kramer.

For the next thirty minutes, Buddy and Ensign Kramer got better acquainted as they talked about their home towns and some of the details of their personal lives.

"So you played football in high school, eh Miller. You'll have to talk to the XO some time about his football days. He was a hot shot running back at the academy and got some kind of big deal award for it. I don't remember all the details about it," said Kramer. "I ran cross country and track in high school instead of football."

Ensign Kramer continued to go over other details regarding the ship and Buddy's duties. "I've got you on the watch, quarter, and station bill," he said. "You need to check it out on the mess decks. Since you are the new guy on board, you've got the bridge mid-watch tonight. I'll be up there with you since I've got the mid-watch OOD duty."

The two men talked a bit longer, until Ensign Kramer told Buddy he could go. "You probably need to get back to the armory. I know our previous GM left the place looking bad. Let's just say he didn't leave the ship under the best circumstances and left in a hurry. Stop by the mess deck and see if the cook can fix you up with some lunch. I know you didn't eat. I'll see you later, Miller."

"Yes sir," said Buddy, and he turned and left the wardroom.

After leaving the wardroom, Buddy made his way to the mess deck. The cook handed him two slices of bread and several slices of bologna. Buddy slathered on some catsup and mayonnaise and continued aft to the fantail before turning to go to the armory. As he was about to go forward on the weather deck toward the armory, he heard his name being called.

"Miller, come here." It was the senior chief overseeing a couple of the deck crew who were making equipment repairs to some of the mine-sweeping gear.

Buddy walked over to the senior chief. "We haven't been introduced, so I'll do it myself. I'm Senior Chief Boatswain's Mate Ray Gunther. I guess you're Miller," said Gunther.

"Yes, Senior Chief. I'm Buddy Miller," said Buddy as the two men shook hands.

"Well, glad to have you aboard," said Gunther. "Do you know the first thing about guns? 'Cause it's a damn sure thing your predecessor didn't know his ass from the barrel of a cannon. Every damn gun on this ship is a mess. Do you think you're up to the job?" asked the chief.

"I hope so, Senior Chief," said Buddy.

"Yeah, well I hope so too," said Gunther. "Let me know if there is anything you need, and I'll try to help you to get the armory squared away."

Just as the Senior Chief was about to turn away, Buddy said, "Senior Chief, there are a couple things I could use. I really need a bunch of cleaning supplies for the armory. I also need an electrician to fix a light in the armory. It's darker than the bottom of a well in there."

"OK," said the Senior Chief. "Go back down that starboard passage-way and you will see the supply office. The storekeeper is in there. Tell him what you need, and he will get his striker to bring the stuff to the armory. I'll round up an electrician and send him to the armory in 30 minutes. That should give you time to complete your business with the SK."

"Thanks, Senior Chief. I appreciate your help," said Buddy. Just as he was about to leave, Buddy turned back to Gunther. "Say, Senior Chief; Mr. Kramer made a remark to me that I wonder if you know anything about. He said that my predecessor left the ship 'in a hurry' and not under the best of circumstances. What did Mr. Kramer mean by that?"

The Senior Chief looked at Buddy for a few seconds, and finally said, "I guess you will have to ask Mr. Kramer what he meant." He then waved Buddy off and turned his attention to the two boatswain mates sitting on the deck, who were greasing wire sheaves used in the mine-sweeping equipment. "C'mon girls, we haven't got all day. We've got to get this gear put back together and stowed away before chow," growled the Senior Chief.

Buddy made his way to the ship's supply office, a space so small that only a small desk and several file cabinets fit compactly into the space. He found the storekeeper pounding away on a typewriter, completing supply records. The second class storekeeper looked up and said, "Who are you, and what do you want."

"I'm Buddy Miller, and I'm the new gunner's mate," said Buddy.

"Well great, now we know who you are. I'm SK2 Sam Cosgrove. Now what do you want?"

Buddy wasn't sure why he was not getting a very friendly reception, but by the look of the stacks of papers piled on the desk, file cabinets, and the deck, the storekeeper was swamped in work. "I need some supplies for the armory," said Buddy.

"Well, Miller, right now you are a low priority. The CO and XO want to see their quarterly supply reports, and I've got to get this to them yet today. Tell you what; see that stack of blank 1250 requisition forms over there? Take a few of them with you, fill them out, and bring them back, and we'll see about getting your supplies. Now get the hell out of my office, I've got work to do," said Cosgrove.

Buddy was taken aback, but managed to respond. "Cosgrove, I've never done a 1250. I don't know how to order supplies."

SK2 Cosgrove exploded. His face became red, and he rose from his desk. "Listen, Miller. You're a petty officer, and you don't know how to fill out a 1250? How did you make third class? Anyway, I just told you I can't help you right now, so get lost!"

But just then, a skinny, dark-haired sailor wearing black-framed Navy issue glasses stuck his head in the door of the office and said, "I got the break-outs done for the galley, Cosgrove. What should I do now?"

Cosgrove diverted his attention to the sailor and said, "Newton, get the hell out of here, that's what I want you to do. Wait a minute, hang on. Newton, this is the new gunner's mate, Miller, and he needs supplies. Take him with you and pick up some blank 1250's and help him fill them out. That should get both of you out of here for a while. Now scram!"

Newton grabbed a short stack of forms and led Buddy to the mess decks where they could sit at a table. The aroma of cooking food filled the space and reminded Buddy that he was now very hungry. He had thrown half the bologna sandwich over the side when Senior Chief Gunther began talking with him. Newton stuck out his hand. "I'm SKSN Robert Newton, but everybody just calls me Fig," he said.

Buddy shook his hand. "GM3 Buddy Miller, glad to meet you," said Buddy. Then Buddy told Newton what materials and supplies he needed for the cleanup of the armory.

"Oh, that's easy. Everybody uses that stuff all the time, so I know the stock numbers by heart. Here," said Newton, "I'll show you how to fill out these requisitions."

For the next twenty minutes, Buddy and the storekeeper striker, New-ton, completed the forms for Buddy's supplies.

"Don't let Cosgrove bug you," said Newton. "He's really a great guy and really smart. The problem is that on a small ship, the storekeeper's job is almost a twenty-four hour job. And he's got reports that are due to the old man."

When the two men broke up their meeting, Newton took the forms with him. "I'll have the supplies for you in the morning."

"Thanks, Newton, I appreciate it," said Buddy.

"Fig, just call me Fig," said Newton, and he smiled and walked away.

Neither man had any idea that their individual destinies would inter-twine in the future.

Just then two mess cooks entered the mess deck and began wiping down tables and filling salt and pepper shakers in preparation for the evening meal. Buddy could surmise that he would not have time to return to work in the armory, so he made his way to the berthing area where he washed his face and hands. He then wandered aft to the fan tail to wait for the call to eat.

By the time the 1MC announced supper for the crew, Buddy had met most of the men on the ship who were not on duty as they also waited on the fantail for chow. The men formed a line to pass the galley window where they picked up a tray and silverware and told the two galley cooks what they would like. The metal trays flew through the two cooks' hands as they were filled and handed to each sailor. The men then found vacant seats on the benches at the mess tables and devoured their food. Soon there was no evidence of the grilled Spam slices, mashed potatoes, canned corn, apple sauce, and a cookie that had minutes before been in the partitioned slots on Buddy's tray. He drained the last of the milk in his glass and set it back on the tray. A loud belch erupted from a sailor several seats away from Buddy. This was followed by laughter and jokes from his tablemates.

As he looked around the mess deck, most of the men had finished their dinner, and the majority of them had an after-dinner cigarette in their mouth. The conversation picked up, and a few new jokes were told. Buddy could see this was a tight-knit crew. A pang of loneliness hit him, as he realized that he was now an outsider. It would be several days before he felt comfortable as a member of the *Erne* crew. In a few minutes, he made his way back to the berthing area and broke out his writing paper and a pen.

> *May 5, 1968*
> *Dear Mom and Dad,*
>
> *It's been a heck of a day. I am now onboard the* Erne, *a coastal minesweeper off the coast of Vietnam. It's a strange little ship. It's all made of wood. They claim a wooden ship will not set off a certain kind of mine. I hope that's true. They transferred me to the* Erne *from the* Kawishiwi *in a chair hanging from some cables set up between the two ships. A little scary. I've met my new Department Head and the XO and CO. There are only about fifty guys on this ship. I've met quite a few of them. I haven't found anybody from Iowa yet, though. The gun armory is quite a mess. I guess the guy before me was not well liked and was a slob. Have you started the planting yet, Dad? Wish I was there to help. Say hello to Janeen and Sarah.*
>
> *Love, Buddy*

The 1MC interrupted Buddy's thoughts, announcing that the evening's movie would be shown on the mess decks. The movie was going to be '*Grand Prix*' with James Garner and Eva Marie Saint. It sounded like a good one to him, so Buddy made his way back to the mess decks. However, he only watched the first hour and then made his way back to his bunk. He was tired and wanted a nap before going to stand the midwatch. He didn't bother to take his clothes off. He crawled into the bunk and was soon asleep.

At 2315, he was shaken awake in his bunk by the messenger of the watch.

"Wake up Miller, you've got the next watch," said the sailor.

"Yeah, yeah, OK," mumbled Buddy. He rolled out of his bunk, opened his locker, got his toothbrush, tooth paste, a bar of soap and a towel, and went to the head. He stood in front of the urinal for a moment, then quickly washed his face, brushed his teeth, pushed his hair back, and put on his white hat. He restowed his gear locker and then stopped on the mess deck where a large tray of peanut butter and jelly sandwiches was available for the watch standers. This midnight rations snack, known as "mid-rats," is common throughout the Navy. After grabbing a sandwich and a small juice container, Buddy made his way to the bridge and relieved the bridge phone talker. He put the headphones on, made a quick phone check with other phone talkers stationed at posts within the ship, slipped the strap of a set of binoculars over his head, and munched on his sandwich while he let his eyes adjust to the dark. With the exception of the green glow of the radar repeater, the only lights on the bridge were red because the red lights would not interfere with the men's night vision. Buddy watched as Mr. Kramer went through the ritual of relieving LTJG Clark, who was the Officer of the Deck.

At the end of their briefing each other, Mr. Kramer said, "I relieve you, sir."

He was answered by Mr. Clark saying, "I stand relieved."

Rather loudly, Kramer then said, "This is Mr. Kramer, and I have the deck and the conn." The two sailors on the bridge (the quartermaster of the watch and Buddy, the phone talker) and the two sailors in the pilot house (the helmsman and the engine order telegraph operator) all loudly answered, "Aye, aye, sir." Now with only three people on the bridge and two in the pilot house, the watch settled in for their four hours.

During the night, the ship would stay on a specific course and speed, moving slowly back and forth along a ten nautical mile line. Their speed was only five knots to conserve fuel. Each length of their track, before they reversed their course, took nearly two hours. Their navigational fix was taken by the quartermaster of the watch using radar and navigational lights on the shore of Vietnam. It would be a boring watch, but the sailors preferred a mundane watch during the nighttime hours. It was all Buddy could do to keep his eyes open. Periodically, he would put the binoculars up to his eyes to watch the passing of small fishing boats. The boats had either colored electric lights or oil lanterns fastened to the boat for navigational lights. But this was not always the case, and he was told to keep a sharp eye out for any fishing boats not displaying navigational lights. On those boats, it was common that only a small white work light would be seen. When this occurred, Buddy would let the OOD know what he had seen. If necessary, the ship would take evasive action, but if the fishermen were able, they would normally move slightly to be out of the way of the larger passing ship.

"XO on the bridge," shouted the quartermaster, announcing that the Executive Officer had just come onto the bridge. This announcement is a common practice to let the OOD know when either the CO or XO come onto the bridge. Buddy thought this seemed rather odd that the XO had come to the bridge so late at night. It was now 0130 in the morning, and the XO was wandering around the ship.

"Everything OK, Jack?" asked LTJG Bamino, as he walked over and looked down at the radar repeater.

"Yes sir. Everything seems to be pretty quiet," said Kramer.

"Couldn't sleep. Too damn hot in the stateroom," said the XO. "Nice breeze up here on the bridge, though."

"Yes sir," said Kramer.

The XO turned his attention to Buddy. "Hey Miller. Mr. Kramer tells me you used to play football. Is that right?"

Buddy lifted one of the earpieces on his headphones off of his ear and parked it behind his ear. "Yes sir, I played high school ball."

"What position did you play?" asked Bamino.

"Quarterback, sir."

"Were you any good?" asked Bamino.

"Well sir, we were a pretty small school, but we won our conference," said Buddy.

The two men talked for a few more minutes. It turned out that Bamino had been a halfback at the Naval Academy and loved to talk about football. He told Buddy that his two favorite teams were the Dallas Cowboys and the Washington Redskins. He could never make up his mind which team he should root for when the teams played each other. He also told Buddy that the only other football player on the ship was Ensign Meyer who had played for a small college in the Midwest before joining the Navy. Buddy was a bit ill at ease. After all, he was only a third class petty officer discussing football with the XO of the ship. He was a bit relieved when the XO turned his attention to Mr. Kramer.

"Guess I'll wander around a bit more, Jack, and go back and try to get some sleep. Carry on," said Bamino, as he turned and left the bridge.

"Aye aye, sir," said Kramer.

After he was gone, Ensign Kramer said, "I should have warned you, Miller. The XO has a habit of wandering around the ship late at night and is liable to just show up on the bridge during the late watches. I guess he doesn't need much sleep. Say, did you get a chance to read those Market Time procedures and rules of engagement?"

"Not yet, sir. I'll take care of that in the morning and give them back to you," said Buddy.

The rest of the watch went smoothly, and at 0345 the new watch section came on duty. As soon as Buddy was relieved, he went straight to his bunk, stripped off his clothes, went to the head and took a quick shower, and fell into his bunk, immediately falling asleep.

Chapter Ten

November 1965
Community Stadium
Mahaska County, Iowa

It was the homecoming game of his senior year, and it was the best homecoming ever! It was also the final conference game of the season. The outcome of the game would determine the Central Iowa Conference football championship. At five o'clock in the afternoon of a beautiful, cool, late fall Saturday, the crowd was still cheering. Buddy was numb. Twenty seconds before, he had initiated a triple reverse, a play that the team had practiced, but never before used in a game. The third and final hand-off recipient of the football was the quarterback, Buddy, and he had taken the ball, sped around a cleanly blocked end, and sprinted into the end zone for a touchdown. The Grinnell defenders had been completely juked and all ended up on the wrong side of the field to defend the non-ensuing run. Buddy had had the field to himself and easily scored the winning points in the final minute of the game. With the remaining two games of the season against non-conference teams, Oskaloosa High School was now the Central Iowa Conference football champion. The buzzer ending the game was followed by the bleachers being emptied of fans as they crossed the old cinder track and streamed onto the field. The players and coaches were mobbed. Jim and Irene Miller found Buddy, and Jim clapped their son on the shoulders while his mom gave him a kiss on the cheek. Suddenly, Shirley Moore was also there in her cheerleader's uniform and also kissed Buddy on the cheek, but quickly returned to the rest of the cheerleading squad.

The Oskaloosa players scooped up their coach and carried him off the field, up the embankment to the track level of the stadium, across the cinder track, and into the nearby home team locker room; a pathetically sad, wooden clapboard building which clearly showed signs of its age, its wooden floor pocked by hundreds of football cleats over the years. The exuberance of the young men was at a joyous peak. Even though they quieted briefly to listen to the congratulatory remarks by the coach, few of the team paid much attention. The team erupted in cheers again when the coach was finished and began a dog pile on top of Buddy. Finally, the celebrating frenzy came down to a lower level, and the players stripped off their muddy, sweaty uniforms and headed for the showers. Their spirits were sky high, and they still had a homecoming dance to attend that evening.

Later, the rock and roll band, made up of students from nearby Central College, not only looked like, but sounded very much like the Beatles. The band was well known in central Iowa, partially because of their mode of transportation. They drove to gigs in a bright red, chopped, 1950 Ford two-door sedan. It was remarkable that all of the band members and their musical equipment would fit into the small Ford. The band occupied a temporary stage in the high school gymnasium. The lights had been dimmed in the large room, and even the teacher chaperones were dancing to the slow tunes. As Buddy and Shirley slowly dance-stepped around the polished floor, they were probably unaware that they were experiencing the best, carefree, happy moments of their lives.

Two hours later, it growled, moaned, and protested, but the old International pickup burst to life in the chilly, fall, night air. Following the light cast by its rusty, dim headlights, Buddy drove the truck to Five Points, a popular parking place in the country where five dusty, seldom-used, gravel roads converged. Nearly twenty cars were parked along the road, all containing at least one amorous couple. White swirling steam and smoke poured from the tailpipes of the idling cars. Radio station KIOA broadcasting from Des Moines played from the car radios and could be heard through the steamy glass windows of the cars. Buddy let the old pickup idle so the heater would keep it reasonably warm in the cab of the truck. He and Shirley had removed their coats and were soon locked tightly in each other's arms. While the kissing continued, Shirley had allowed Buddy to rest his roving hand on the bodice of her gown, and the couple's kisses were ever more passionate. Shirley's hand had moved to Buddy's inside thigh . . .

Now reveille, reveille! All hands heave to and trice up. The smoking lamp is lit in all berthing areas. Breakfast is being served for all watch standers. Now, Reveille, Reveille!

Buddy groaned. He had half awakened earlier and was enjoying memories of his senior year of high school when he was brought to full wakefulness by morning reveille. He rolled over in his bunk. He hated that 1MC more every day. He slowly spilled out of the bunk and while rubbing his eyes, groggily walked to the head to begin another day at sea.

Chapter Eleven

July 1968
USS **Erne**
Off the coast of Vietnam

   Buddy stayed extremely busy during the first few weeks that he served on the *Erne*. A great deal of time was spent talking with Ensign Kramer and the XO, and finally resorting to showing them the Navy's written directives on the safeguarding and accountability for small arms on a Navy vessel. Apparently, the previous gunner's mate had not bothered to show these regulations to the officers and probably didn't care to follow the rules anyway. Finally, the two officers relented, and from then on, no small arms were in the hands of ship's personnel, except the .45's issued to the CO, XO, and Mr. Kramer. All other weapons were locked in the armory and brought out and issued to boarding party members when they were needed. Buddy was assured by Ensign Kramer that only Buddy, Mr. Kramer, and the XO had keys to the armory. Every rifle and hand gun on the ship had been inventoried, broken down, and thoroughly cleaned and oiled. The inside of the armory had been scrubbed and repainted. Buddy had even built a new wooden rifle rack to be used for storage of confiscated arms. The small armory had never looked better. When a subsequent inspection of the armory and the arms records was conducted by the XO, it revealed that the weapons section was in tip-top shape. As a result, Buddy was verbally commended by the XO for his excellent work.

   Among the papers and books kept in the armory was the small arms inventory book. Every time he opened that book, Buddy was reminded that the ship's small arms inventory reflected a glaring gap in one of the previous inventories versus the present inventory. Buddy had learned that his predecessor had actually stolen and sold two Navy issue Colt .45's on the black market in Subic Bay. His theft had been discovered, and the sailor had been placed in confinement by the Naval Investigative Service until a court martial could be held. The outcome of the court martial had been a dishonorable discharge and a prison sentence. Buddy's predecessor was serving time at the Federal prison at Fort Leavenworth, Kansas. His actions had reflected badly on the command, which explained a lot as to why the CO and XO of the *Erne* took a special interest in their new gunner's mate.

Buddy also took great pains to overhaul the ship's larger weapons. The ship had two stanchion-mounted .30 caliber machine guns that were brought from the armory and manned during Market Time inspections, and a twin .50 caliber machine gun mount affixed to the deck on the bow of the ship. The mounts for all of these guns had been cleaned, primed, and repainted. All of the weapons were now cleaned, oiled, and ready for use. The .50 caliber twin mount had been an especially challenging problem. Aside from the paint flaking off all the metal surfaces and the rust on the mounting hardware, Buddy's predecessor had neglected the preventative maintenance on the guns themselves and had not always kept them covered. As a result, salt residue had built up on the guns, and corrosion of the guns' mechanisms required a great deal of work to bring them back to pristine condition. But Buddy had taken his time, with pains-taking attention to detail. Following this long refurbishing process, all guns were test fired at sea. All of the ship's arms were now in excellent working order, with the exception of one of the M-1 rifles and one .45 handgun.

While cleaning and testing the weapons, Buddy discovered that the firing mechanism on one of the M-1's was overly worn. This resulted in the rifle having a super-sensitive trigger; so sensitive, in fact, that the rifle could discharge even when handled roughly without a finger on the trigger. It could unexpectedly fire by just being bumped. In short, the rifle was unsafe. Buddy isolated it at one end of the rifle rack so that he would not issue it to anyone during general quarters drills or vessel inspections. He also discovered that one of the .45s was missing part of the firing assembly, and on further inspection, he discovered that the breach of the pistol was out of round. The opening was distorted and would not accept an ammunition round. The gun had been somehow mishandled and could never be fired, but he also discovered that it had been robbed of firing mechanism parts for use in repairing other weapons. The pistol was, therefore, useless and would have to go through the normal Navy procedure for disposal in the near future. He set that firearm to the side with the unsafe rifle, and later told Ensign Kramer of the situation with these two firearms. Kramer responded to Buddy, telling him that he would inform the XO.

Some days later, while the *Erne* was still at sea, Ensign Kramer came to Buddy and told him that the CO wanted to have a day of target practice. Old paint cans and empty oil drums were to be used for targets. All hands who would be involved with the ship inspections were familiarized with the weapons they would be using and allowed to fire all of those guns. But for some odd reason, Mr. Kramer told Buddy to save every bit of spent ammunition casing brass. When the day of target practice was completed, Buddy had several large garbage bags full of spent brass, which he stored in a corner of the armory.

Chapter Twelve

Marty was tired of his friend's harassment. For the last week he had received a daily message from Dex. His OCS classmate was drifting around WestPac as the XO on a big old auxiliary oiler, the *Kawishiwi*, idly firing off these messages to him, while he had problems of his own. Being a friend was one thing. Being a pest was another.

CDR Martin Shear read over the message one more time. Yeah, same old crap. And then he had to grin. CDR Abraham Dexter was one of his best friends. How they had ever managed to get through and graduate from OCS was still a mystery to the two of them. Too many hangovers and late hours spent at the *Black Pearl* in Newport almost washed them both out of OCS. Dex needed a favor from his old friend and sent Shear a daily message asking for his help. Apparently, Dexter was gung ho to get some sailor off of his ship. Shear mumbled to himself. "OK, Dex, you are going to owe me one. Poor kid. I don't know what you did to piss off your XO, but it must have been something."

Shear walked over to the desk of his senior chief and handed him the latest message from CDR Dexter. The senior chief, who oversaw the placement of scores of sailors every day, read the message and looked up at CDR Shear.

"Is he serious? All this trouble for a lowly seaman?" said the senior chief.

"'Fraid' so," said Shear. "The kid must have done something really stupid. I don't want to know how you do it, just make it happen, please."

Even before Shear had walked back to his office, the senior chief had pulled up the personnel file from the data base on his computer and had begun the process of constructing the transfer orders on GMSN Robert Dawes.

Chapter Thirteen

July 25, 1968
*USS **Erne***
Off the coast of Vietnam

The tropics were always an ungodly, torrid bitch. Even this early in the morning it was so hot that following quarters, the crew laid on the deck in any modicum of shade provided by any piece of deck machinery that they could find. They would have to "turn to" soon enough, but until then, they relaxed as best they could. The *Erne* was running as fast as its top speed of thirteen knots would allow. They were chasing a course to intercept an oiler for refueling of the small wooden minesweeper.

Forty minutes later the 1MC announced: *All hands report to replenishment stations. All hands report to their replenishment stations. Refueling will take place on the port side.*

The minesweeper had caught up with the oiler and took its place on the starboard side of the ship, dropping its speed slightly to maintain nearly eleven knots, thereby matching the speed of the oiler. Buddy had walked to the fantail to watch with mild curiosity, since it was his old ship, the *Kawishiwi*, which would be supplying their fuel. The entire procedure was no longer a novelty since he had seen it many times over the course of the last few months. He watched as lines were strung between the ships, followed by the fueling lines being rigged. The fueling process then began, with the unseen diesel fuel pouring into the *Erne*'s fuel tanks. A mail pouch was sent across to the *Erne* on a light line. Buddy was munching on a far-overripe, not very tasty apple, when suddenly his eyes caught sight of Chief John Proctor waving at him from the *Kawishiwi*. He was happy to see the Chief and waved back. Oddly, the Chief kept shaking his head from side to side and throwing up his hands. Buddy did not know what to think of the Chief's pantomime. But then he watched as a bosun's chair was being rigged. That could only mean one thing. Someone was coming across from the *Kawishiwi* to the minesweeper. In a moment, a sailor dressed in tropical whites and carrying a sea bag which covered the side of his face approached the bosun's chair, climbed into the rig, and placed his sea bag upright on his lap. The chair swung to face the minesweeper, and Buddy dropped the apple on the deck, his mouth hanging open. The promised and much anticipated gunner's mate striker being transferred to bolster the weapons department on the *Erne* was none other than GMSN Bob Dawes. Buddy groaned audibly as Dawes spotted Buddy and waved. Buddy feebly returned a half-hearted acknowledgement wave. "What have I done to deserve this," said Buddy under his breath.

Thirty minutes later, as Buddy was applying thick, dark colored grease to the twin .50 swivel mount, Ensign Kramer brought Dawes to meet Buddy. "Hey Miller, here's your new GM striker. His name is Robert Dawes."

Dawes set his sea bag on the deck and stuck out his hand. Buddy slowly wiped remnants of grease from his hands with a rag and shook hands with the wide-grinning Dawes and said, "Yes, sir, I know Dawes from the *Kawishiwi*."

"Well, great," said Kramer. "How about you take Dawes then to find a bunk and make sure he gets checked in at the ship's office. I'm glad we finally got you some help, Miller."

"Yes, sir, so am I," replied Buddy, and Kramer walked away.

"Man, isn't this great," said Dawes, still grinning. "It'll be just like old times, eh Buddy."

"Yeah, sure," said Buddy, as he looked away from Dawes. "C'mon, I'll get you to the ship's office."

Later, after Dawes had checked in at the ship's office, stowed his gear in the enlisted berthing area, and changed into his dungarees, he found Buddy sitting in the small armory with the weather deck door fastened open. Buddy was idly looking out at the gently rolling sea.

"Hey, this is a pretty neat little armory," said Dawes as he poked his head through the open door. "Mr. Kramer gave me a key to this place as he passed me on the mess decks." He then caught sight of the wooden rifle rack that Buddy had built for the confiscated weapons. "Wow, look at that. AK-47's. Where'd you get those?"

Buddy was still trying to digest the fact that Kramer had given an armory key to Dawes. How many damn keys are there to this armory, he thought. Buddy just looked at Dawes. Finally he said, "We got them in ship searches," but did not explain to Dawes what that meant.

Bob Dawes was now beginning to feel the cold attitude of his friend. "Hey, Buddy. Are you mad or something? You don't seem to be in a very good mood," said Dawes.

Buddy turned in his chair and stared for a long moment at Bob Dawes. "Bob, you've got to be one of the last persons I expected to be transferred to the *Erne*."

"Chief Proctor said you would probably say that. But I passed my practical factors for third class, and I have not been in any trouble since you left the *Kawishiwi*," said Dawes. "Well, other than that little fracas with the XO one night when I was standing bridge watch." Dawes did not elaborate, and Buddy thought to himself, why even ask? Dawes continued, "Chief Proctor also said to tell you that he doesn't know how I ended up with orders, since I was not due for a new assignment for probably another year. Proctor thinks it was probably some kind of SNAFU at BuPers. Even so, I think we will make a good team. I think it's great!"

Bob Dawes's blind, but bubbling, enthusiasm was still readily apparent and was mildly infectious to Buddy. He began to rethink the situation. Maybe it wouldn't be so bad to have Bob on board. After all, he knew Bob's weak points, and he generally did what he was told. If he could just keep Dawes from goofing around and getting them both in trouble – it was a big "if."

"Bob, here's the deal," said Buddy. His face was cold, and his stare bored into Dawes's eyes. "This ship had a lousy gunner's mate prior to us, and because of that, I seem to get a lot of attention from the old man and the XO. But so far, I have made a few small changes and everything is good. I don't want you screwing it up. I think you know you didn't have the greatest reputation on the *Kawishiwi*, and that might even be the reason you got sent off of there early. And even if we are friends, I expect you to pull your weight and do a good job. If you don't, I'll have Mr. Kramer make you a permanent mess deck helper. Is that plain enough for you?"

Dawes was visibly hurt. The exuberance drained from his face. A non-smiling Bob Dawes swallowed. He had never seen his friend this serious. He knew Buddy meant what he said. But in seconds, the smile returned. "Don't worry, Buddy. I won't let you down."

*****

The tropical heat was relentless and stressed the small ship and its crew. The non-stop pace of remaining at sea wore on equipment and men alike. Machinery on the ship was not designed to withstand the continuous pounding the small ship took in rolling seas while carrying out its Market Time activities. The fresh water on the ship was nearly gone, and the overworked evaporators had finally ceased functioning. The ship would soon be out of fresh water. The Chief Engineer, Ensign Meyer, had predicted the impending break down due to the worn parts of the evaporator and had reported the situation to the CO two weeks prior. The necessary parts needed for repair of the evaporator had been ordered by radio message and had arrived for pick up at Cam Rahn Bay. The *Erne* turned its bow westward toward land and was headed into the base to retrieve the parts and make the needed repairs. Captain Yates guided the small ship and docked it at the Sea Bee pier, where the ship would pick up its parts and supplies. The plan was that the ship would remain in port at the pier while the ship's crew made the repairs. Without the ability to make fresh water, the ship could not get underway.

As the *Erne* was made secure at the pier, Buddy happened to look at a nearby pier where six dark green small boats were tied. The boats were substantially armed, aluminum hulled, river craft. Such watercraft were part of what the Navy called the "brown water Navy." It was their job to patrol the tributary rivers in Vietnam which flowed to the sea and into the huge Mekong Delta, intercepting all watercraft and occasionally looking in on villages along the rivers. When necessary, they would engage small enemy forces along the river. It was dangerous work, and it was exactly to this type of boat that Buddy's friend Henry Lucas had been ordered. Buddy wondered if Henry was anywhere around. But he had no time to think more about that, as he was kept busy while the ship was in Cam Rahn Bay.

Almost immediately after tying up, work parties made up of the storekeepers and deck crew, including Buddy and Dawes, began stowing previously ordered food provisions which had been brought to the pier for transfer to the ship. Mail bags were brought aboard, and the critical engineering parts were lowered to the engine room to begin repairs. While the flurry of activity surrounded them, Ensign Kramer called aside Buddy and Dawes.

"Look over at the pier, you two. See those two chiefs walking toward the pier with clipboards in their hands? They are from Mine Squadron Nine. The XO told me they are here to see you gunner's mates. As soon as the brow is clear, they are coming aboard to give you an unannounced inspection." Dawes looked quickly at Buddy, and Buddy groaned.

"What's the matter with you two? You've got the weapons department squared away, don't you?" said Kramer.

"Yes, sir," said Buddy. "But I'm not positive it will meet with their expectations."

"Well, heads up. Here they come," said Kramer.

They were two senior chiefs. Ensign Kramer walked over and returned their salute as the two senior enlisted men crossed the brow. They introduced themselves to Ensign Kramer and then to Buddy and Dawes. Kramer led the way to the armory, followed by the two senior chiefs and the two gunner's mates. Dawes and Buddy looked at each other again as they walked, and then stared straight ahead.

"They don't have a very friendly look, do they Buddy," Dawes quietly remarked. Buddy ignored him.

When they had all reached the armory, Ensign Kramer opened the door.

One of the senior chiefs had his clipboard up and was writing. He then looked at Kramer and asked, "How many people have keys to the armory, Mr. Kramer?"

Ensign Kramer replied, "The XO, me, and the two GM's."

"Hmm," said the senior chief. "You might want to rethink whether a non-rated sailor has a need for a key to this space," he said, looking directly at Dawes and then Ensign Kramer.

For the next thirty minutes the two senior chiefs looked at every written record and every piece of weaponry in the armory. They picked up and inspected every firearm in the armory. Buddy showed them the malfunctioning rifle and the pistol that needed to be discarded. The senior chiefs continued to take notes. Buddy thought that since the inspectors were there, he would ask them how to get rid of the confiscated AK-47's. He was told that the MINERON staff would pick them up in the morning for proper disposal. The chiefs then inspected the two .30 caliber machine guns and moved to the bow of the ship to inspect the twin .50's. They worked the mechanisms of the guns and continued making notes. Their only comment to Ensign Kramer and Buddy was that they should try to obtain a tighter fitting cover for the twin .50's to better protect the guns from the salt spray at sea.

"Mr. Kramer, we are through with our inspection. Could you please take us to the CO's cabin?" The officer and two chiefs walked away from the two gunner's mates.

"How come we don't get to go along?" asked Dawes. "Doesn't seem fair since we do all the work."

"Don't worry, we will certainly hear about it in a little while," said Buddy. Later, as Buddy and Dawes were doing some touch-up paint work on the .30 caliber stanchions, they paused to watch the two senior chief inspectors walk across the brow, leaving the ship.

Buddy and Dawes looked at each other, shrugged their shoulders, and continued with their work. "Well, I guess we will know soon enough what they had to say," said Buddy.

By mid-afternoon, all the stores had been taken aboard the ship, and the repairs had been made to the cantankerous evaporator. The minesweeper was again ready to sail. The 1MC had announced that all hands should make preparations for getting underway. It seemed strange then, that Ensign Kramer had sought out Buddy and asked him to accompany him. They climbed the ladder to the bridge, where the OOD and CO were getting the ship ready for departure. The XO was standing to the side of the bridge.

"Excuse me Captain. You wanted to see us?" said Kramer.

Captain Yates turned in his chair and stepped onto the deck. "Yeah, Jack, I've got something I wanted to give to Miller." He turned and faced Buddy. "Miller, Mr. Kramer has already been briefed on this. Those two inspectors that pulled that surprise inspection on you gave me their report. Basically, they said that our weapons department is in the best shape they have ever seen on any of the MSC's. They gave the ship a Bravo Zulu, and I wanted to give you the same. This is a Letter of Commendation that I wrote for you, and it will go into your personnel file. Congratulations on your progress for the ship, Miller. Keep up the good work." The CO then shook Buddy's hand and gave him a copy of the letter.

Buddy was speechless for a moment, but then saluted the CO and thanked him. The CO returned the salute, and continued preparations for getting the ship underway. "Make sure that letter gets into Miller's file, Jack."

"Aye, aye, skipper," said Kramer, and he and Buddy left the bridge.

Before they parted, Kramer echoed the CO's sentiment. "Great job, Miller. I'm glad I've got you in my department."

Buddy went below and put his copy of the letter in his locker in the berthing area. He then proceeded topside to stow the painting gear he and Dawes had been using in preparation for getting underway. He told Dawes what had happened. "Wow, a letter from the old man! Way to go Buddy," said Dawes.

*****

The next two weeks went by quickly for the *Erne* and her crew as the ship remained on station conducting its inspections of native fishing craft. Prior to each inspection, Buddy would open the armory and issue the small arms to the participants in the inspection. Then, he and Dawes would tote one of the .30 calibers, along with ammunition, to the main deck and place it in its stanchion. The inspections during those two weeks had gone smoothly, and the only contraband seized had been an old rusty sword which was in such poor condition that it probably should not even have warranted the seizure. It had been thrown overboard as soon as they were out of sight of the small fishing boat from which it had been taken.

Chapter Fourteen

The day dawned bright and hot. August weather was showing promise to be an exact copy of what had been a stiflingly hot July. Breakfast for the crew had been completed, and the ship prepared to begin its interception of small native fishing craft for inspections. As they approached their first inspection of the day, the weapons had been broken out and distributed, and Buddy was manning the .30 caliber on the main deck. It was a routine stop, and Mr. Kramer, a deck crew sailor, and the interpreter were onboard the Vietnamese fishing boat questioning its crew and searching the small boat. All eyes of those on the bridge and the deck of the minesweeper were focused on the boarding crew and the persons on board the small fishing boat. Buddy was also watching the inspection party. But from the corner of his eye, Buddy caught a motion. He glanced toward the bow of the *Erne* and locked his eyes onto Bob Dawes, who was standing near the front port quarter of the ship, a position from where he was not readily visible to the personnel on the bridge. Dawes was wearing a web belt with a holster. In his hand was a .45 pistol. Dawes was repeatedly placing the pistol in the holster, and then quick-drawing the gun from the holster. Each time he drew the gun, he made a firing motion of the gun, spun the gun two times on his finger, which was placed in the trigger guard, and returned the gun to the holster. Dawes was oblivious to what he was supposed to be doing.

Buddy's mouth dropped open. What the hell was Dawes up to now, he thought. That damn idiot is going to get us both in hot water. Just as Buddy was about to turn his attention back to the inspection party, time seemed to slow down, and he watched as the .45 pistol, which had been spinning on Dawes's finger, suddenly made a slow motion arc up into the air, turning over and over until gravity pulled it to the surface of the ocean where it hit with a quiet "thunk," sinking into the murky sea, never to be seen again. Dawes suddenly turned his head and looked directly at Buddy. For what seemed much longer, but was only seconds, the two men's eyes were locked on each other. Buddy then quickly turned his attention back to the boat inspection team. He then made a furtive glance to each side and up to the ship's bridge. It appeared that no one seemed to have seen Dawes's stupid action. Buddy's heart was racing, and his head was pounding. What am I going to do now, he thought.

There was nothing Buddy could do for the immediate time being. The ship took on three more boat inspections in rapid succession, which took them well past lunch time. In the early afternoon, with no more inspections scheduled, all small arms were once again stowed away, and the inspection team finally had time for lunch. Buddy sat at the lunch table, along with other members of the inspection team. Bob Dawes sat across the table from him, but no words were passed between the two young men. Buddy had no real appetite. As the sailors left the mess decks, Bob Dawes finally leaned across the table and said, "Geez, Buddy, I'm sorry. What are we going to do?"

Buddy just stared at Dawes. "Let's go to the armory," he said. It had been nearly four hours since Dawes had flipped the pistol in the drink. They entered the armory, and Buddy closed the weather deck door behind him. As he turned back around, his emotions took over, and he slapped Bob Dawes across the face and backed him into a corner. He put both hands on Dawes's chest and kept him pinned against the bulkhead. Buddy was irate.

"You stupid son of a bitch; you ask me what we are going to do. I know exactly what we are going to do. We're going to march in to see

Mr. Kramer, and you are going to tell him everything. I told you I was not happy to see you come on board the *Erne*, and sure enough, you've got us in a jam. And not just a little jam. You have to go and lose a Navy weapon. Damn it Dawes, you have pushed our friendship to the limit. I can't cover for you this time. I don't know what will happen to you, but I'm not going to look through iron bars at Leavenworth like my predecessor is doing! You promised me when you came aboard that you wouldn't let me down. And now look at what you've done." Buddy's face was bright red, and spittle was popping from the corners of his lips as he shouted at Dawes. It took all of Buddy's will power to keep him from throwing Dawes across the room.

Dawes was terrified. Buddy was a half a head taller than Dawes and at least twenty pounds heavier. Dawes was afraid that Buddy was going to beat him up. And then he made the stupid mistake of opening his mouth. "I don't want to go to jail for this, Buddy. I didn't mean to drop the .45 over the side, you know that. I was only having fun, and besides, it was only the .45 that has to be surveyed for disposal anyway. It wasn't one of our better guns."

The next sound in the small armory was a simultaneous "thud" and sharp "crack" of Buddy's fist hitting and breaking Dawes's nose. The blood began streaming from Dawes's nose, and he began sobbing. The sound of Dawes blubbering and the oozing blood from Dawes's nostrils took away some of Buddy's anger. He looked over at the pistol rack and confirmed Dawes's story. The inoperable .45 was indeed missing. Buddy reached down and grabbed a couple of clean rags and threw them in Dawes's face. Dawes began gingerly wiping the blood and mucus from his face.

"C'mon," said Buddy.

They made their way to office of the ship's corpsman. The corpsman took a look at Dawes and immediately asked, "What the hell happened to him," as he began pushing cotton swabs up Dawes's nose.

"He was putting a rifle into one of the racks and it fell and hit him in the nose," said Buddy. Dawes glared at Buddy but said nothing. The corpsman soon stopped the bleeding, and then taped up Dawes's nose to hold it in place to heal. He gave Dawes some pain medication and told him to come back in forty-eight hours, and he would re-pack the dressing. The corpsman didn't believe for a minute that a falling rifle had broken Dawes's nose. He had patched up his share of sailors who had been injured in fist fights.

Buddy and Dawes then went to the ship's wardroom and knocked gently on the door. As soon as they heard the word "enter" they opened the door. The CO and XO were sitting at the table with LTJG Clark and Ensign Kramer. The officers were looking over some radio traffic and placing plotting marks on a navigational chart that was opened on the table.

"Jesus, Dawes, what the hell happened to you?" asked the XO.

Dawes drew in a quick breath and hesitated, then slowly said, "A rifle hit me in the nose and busted it." But when he said rifle, it sounded like "rible," and when he said nose, it sounded like "node."

The four officers burst out laughing, and it was several seconds before the XO finally said, "What can we do for you gentlemen?"

Buddy looked at Ensign Kramer and said, "Mr. Kramer, could we speak to you in private, please?"

The CO and XO looked at Jack Kramer, but said nothing.

"Sure, I guess so," said Kramer. "Let's go out on deck." Buddy and Dawes followed him to the fantail.

"What's up guys?" asked Kramer. For the next fifteen minutes Buddy related how Dawes had flipped the inoperable .45 over the side of the ship. He also told Kramer that the gun that was lost was to be surveyed, due to it being inoperable. (During the 1960's and early 1970's, the Navy disposed of worn out equipment by a process called "surveying." Written records were kept when the procedure was utilized to ensure proper disposition). While Buddy told the story, Ensign Kramer shifted his eyes from Buddy over to Dawes and back again. Several times, a barely audible "shit" was uttered by Kramer.

As Buddy finished relating the event, Kramer continued looking at the two gunner's mates. "I thought that would have been one of the first things that you guys would have been taught in 'A' school. Guns are not toys. Geez, Dawes. Did you graduate from junior high school?"

"Yes, sir," said Dawes, as he looked down at his shoes.

"That was a rhetorical question, Seaman Dawes," said Kramer as he glared at the sailor. "Well, you know what happens from here. I've got to tell the XO and CO. My guess is that the old man will hold a mast. Jesus Christ," said Kramer as he shook his head from side to side and walked away.

After evening chow, Buddy was leaning on the rail at the fantail talking to a couple other sailors, including Donny Sorenson.

"Hey, Miller. I just filed that letter from the CO in your personnel file today. Good job, man," said the personnelman.

"Oh, yeah, thanks Donny," said Buddy, but he was still in no mood to receive accolades, knowing that his fellow gunner's mate had just screwed up. And his actions would reflect poorly on the reputation of the weapons department. As he was thinking, he remembered an old Navy saying that he had heard in boot camp years ago. It said, "One 'aw shit' wipes out ten 'atta boys' every time."

Senior Chief Gunther approached the group of sailors on the fantail. "Make yourselves scarce, boys. I want to talk to Miller alone for a minute." As the sailors moved away, Buddy had no idea why the senior chief had singled him out.

"Ever been to a Captain's Mast, Miller?" asked Gunther.

"No, Senior Chief," answered Buddy.

"Well, it just so happens that in addition to being every enlisted man's 'sea daddy' on this boat, I'm also the Chief Master at Arms. Because of that, I also attend every Captain's Mast and act as an advocate for the enlisted man at mast," said Gunther. "So I want you to give me your honest opinion about your striker. Is he worth saving?"

The direct question caught Buddy off guard. He was not sure how to answer the question and didn't answer right away. For the next few minutes, he told the chief everything he could about Bob Dawes. In the end, he told the chief that he thought Dawes was worth saving, but that he was horribly immature.

Senior Chief Gunther nodded his head. "OK, that's the read I got of him too," said Gunther. "Now tell me about the .45 that took a dive. I heard that it may have been scheduled for survey. Is that right?"

Buddy told the Senior Chief that it was indeed correct. The pistol was missing several operating parts and could not be fired even if the parts were obtained due to the misshapen cartridge receiver.

"Have you got any survey forms in the armory?" asked Gunther.

"Yes, Senior Chief," said Buddy.

"Let's go get one," said Gunther.

The two men went to the armory, and Buddy handed a survey form to the Senior Chief.

"I don't want your stinking blank form. Fill the damn thing out," said Gunther.

Sheepishly, Buddy began filling in the multitude of blank boxes on the form, completing the paper work to properly dispose of the inoperable pistol. While Gunther impatiently paced to and fro within the confines of the armory, five minutes later, Buddy handed the completed form to Senior Chief Gunther. As he handed him the form, he said, "Isn't this a little weird? I mean, usually the form is filled out to get the CO's approval to dispose of a piece of gear. Our gun is already gone," said Buddy.

The Senior Chief just looked at Buddy. "Miller, you're such a rookie. My first piece of advice to you is just keep your trap shut and watch the old Senior Chief in action. I'll take it from here. Oh, and Dawes's mast is at 0900 tomorrow morning," said Gunther, and he turned and left the armory, taking the completed survey form with him. Buddy stood for a moment, shrugged his shoulders, and locked the armory door as he left. He was not real sure what the Senior Chief was up to, but he knew that when Gunther was on a scent, it was better to just stand back and watch the more experienced man operate.

> *August 15*
> *Dear Mom and Dad;*
>
> *I am OK. We have a lot to do on the ship, and I manage to keep up. I have told you about Bob Dawes from Des Moines coming onboard the ship to work for me. He has only been here a few weeks and has already gotten himself in trouble. He has to go to Captain's Mast in the morning. He is still my friend, but boy, he needs to grow up and he makes me so mad some-times. Weather is still the same, horribly hot and muggy. Say hello to the girls.*
> *Love, Buddy*

GMSN Bob Dawes was dressed in tropical whites and stood outside the CO's stateroom door along with Senior Chief Gunther. A thick bandage ran across the bridge of his nose, and cotton plugs were in his nostrils. Both of his eyes were blackened, and he was a sorry sight. At exactly 0900 on August 16, Senior Chief Gunther knocked gently on the CO's door and opened it after hearing the CO say "enter." The XO and CO were both in the cabin, both standing with their hats on, facing the door to the cabin. Dawes had been prepared by the Senior Chief.

"Gunner's Mate Seaman Robert Dawes reporting as ordered, sir," said Dawes as he saluted the CO. The CO returned the salute.

"Uncover," said Senior Chief. Dawes complied, removing his white hat.

The CO began to speak. "Seaman Dawes, you have been charged . . ." but before the CO could go farther, he was interrupted by Senior Chief Gunther.

"Captain, if I may interrupt just one moment."

"What is it, Senior Chief?" said Captain Yates, looking at Gunther with an annoyed expression.

"Um, well, sir, I know this is not the most opportune time to do this." As he spoke, he pulled some papers from his hip pocket. "But last night, Mr. Kramer asked me to have you sign this, and I completely forgot. Could I get you to sign this form please?"

"What the hell's wrong with you, Senior Chief? We're trying to conduct a Captain's Mast here." But as he said it, he pulled a pen from his breast pocket and signed the form. "What is this, anyway; a survey form?"

"Mmm, yes sir. I'll just take that, and we can get on with our mast," said Gunther. He put the signed form back in his pocket.

The CO was still a bit taken aback by the seemingly trivial and unnecessary interruption. He stared at the chief for a moment, but then resumed the procedure.

"Seaman Dawes, you have been charged by your Department Head, Ensign Jack Kramer with two violations of the Uniform Code of Military Justice. These charges are, 'Careless operation of government equipment; specifically a Navy issued .45 caliber pistol,' and 'Failure to safeguard valuable government property while it was in your possession, specifically a Navy issued .45 caliber pistol.' This is now your opportunity to speak. Do you have anything to say in your defense?"

Dawes was absolutely frozen. His mouth opened, but he did not say anything. He was scared to death, and it was obvious. He could not speak on his own behalf. Both the CO and XO watched him, but Dawes remained silent.

"If I may speak on behalf of Dawes, sir," said Senior Chief Gunther.

"Isn't that a bit unusual, Senior Chief? After all, you are the Master at Arms in this proceeding," said the CO.

"Yes, sir, but I think Seaman Dawes might need some words in his defense," said Gunther.

"Very well, proceed."

Senior Chief Gunther unconsciously hitched up his trousers while collecting his thoughts, then gave it his best shot. He relinquished the facts that Seaman Dawes struggled with bad judgment and was still an immature young sailor. He also told the CO that Dawes was not a bad young man – just immature. He said that he believed that Dawes would someday make a good sailor and be an asset to the Navy. And finally, he told the CO that the pistol in question was a worthless frame, incapable of firing, and that it was to have been surveyed anyway. "With all due respect, Captain; because of these facts, I believe that Seaman Dawes should be shown leniency."

"Leniency!" said the CO with a raised voice. "The sailor carelessly tossed a Navy .45 over the side, or have you forgotten? I'm not sure he deserves leniency."

But the CO curiously watched as the Senior Chief slowly removed the same papers from his pocket that he had only moments before given to the CO to sign. Gunther slowly opened the papers, seemed to be reading them, and ever so slowly refolded them and put them back in his pocket.

A light suddenly came to the face of Lieutenant Sam Yates. "God-dammit, Gunther. Is that the survey form for this .45 we are talking about?"

Senior Chief Gunther dropped his face, and then looked back up at the CO. "Why, yes sir. I believe it is." A small sly grin came to Gunther's face.

The CO glared at the Senior Chief. But then he lowered his head, made no sound, but his belly could be seen shaking a couple times. He knew he had been had by the crusty old chief.

The skipper raised his head, looked at Dawes, and said, "After hearing the testimony, I believe that a charge of unsafe operation of government equipment is not warranted since the equipment in question was inoperable. I'm throwing that charge out. As far as the second charge goes, it certainly was not valuable government property. However, it was still government property, and Seaman Dawes did not safeguard it properly. Therefore, I am sustaining that charge, even though the word valuable probably should not have been in the charge. Therefore, Seaman Dawes, I am reducing you by one pay grade to Seaman Apprentice, and I am fining you one hundred dollars, to be taken out of your next two pay checks. I am also suspending your reduction in grade on the condition that your conduct does not require further discipline in the next three months. That is my judgment. This Captain's Mast is concluded. Oh, one more thing. Give the Senior Chief your key to the armory." Dawes unfastened the key from his key ring and handed it to Senior Chief Gunther.

"Cover," said Senior Chief Gunther. Dawes placed his white hat back on his head. "Hand salute," said Gunther, and Dawes saluted the CO. The CO returned the salute. Dawes dropped the salute, did an about-face, and he and Senior Chief Gunther left the CO's cabin.

Senior Chief Gunther turned to Dawes after the CO's cabin door was closed. "Dumb ass. Now go get your work uniform on and report to Mr. Kramer." Gunther walked away, while Dawes was still trying to figure out what had happened. But as near as he could figure, he would not be going to Leavenworth prison, a fact for which he was very grateful.

Later in the morning, Buddy and Dawes were using chipping hammers to remove some paint and rust on the forward, twin fifty mount when they were approached by Ensign Kramer.

"You are one lucky son of a bitch, Dawes. I hear the Senior Chief went to bat for you," said Kramer.

Dawes had told Buddy the outcome of the mast, but not the whole story.

"What do you mean, Mr. Kramer?" asked Buddy.

"Well, do you remember giving the Senior Chief a survey form?" asked Kramer.

Buddy answered that he did.

"Well, it seems that Senior Chief Gunther had the old man sign the survey form for the .45 just as the mast started. He caught the CO off guard, and pretty much knocked out half the charges against Dawes. I guess only a senior chief could be that crafty and still get away with it." Ensign Kramer was laughing as he walked away.

After Kramer was gone, Buddy scowled at Dawes and said, "Since it's obvious that you are not going to Federal prison, don't you think it might be a good idea to go and thank the Senior Chief for what he did for you?" Dawes nodded his head in agreement. Buddy continued, "I would suggest you go find him and take care of that, and tell Gunther you will buy him a steak dinner when we get back to port." Dawes jumped up and took off to find Senior Chief Gunther.

*****

The afternoon sun was brutal as it hit the small ship heading to its assigned inspection area.

Attention all hands. It was the XO on the 1MC. *The ship serviceman will be giving haircuts on the fo'csle for the next three hours. Without exception, ALL hands will get a haircut before we reach our assigned patrol area. Mr. Clark, you will be first in line.*

That last remark by the XO brought a chuckle to the sailors. It was recognized by the crew that LTJG Clark sometimes let his hair get pretty shaggy.

For the next couple of hours, the crew formed a line and had their heads buzzed by the clippers of the ship's barber, who was in reality, one of the wardroom stewards. The barber only knew how to do one haircut; every man's head was soon shaved down to a nub. Even a none-too-happy LTJG Clark rubbed his white-skinned pate after being subjected to the clippers. At least everyone now had a regulation haircut, no matter how funny some of the men appeared. Bob Dawes started laughing after Buddy had gotten his head shaved down and returned to the armory where Dawes was working.

"What are you laughing at, Bob. You need to go look in a mirror," said Buddy, as he walked away from a still laughing Dawes.

Dawes ran his hand over his head, front to back, repeating it several times. His smile soon faded. "Good thing it grows back," he said.

*****

A few days later, the ship received orders from the squadron commander detaching *Erne* from Market Time duties. The ship was to return to its home port in Sasebo, Japan, for upkeep, repairs, and much needed rest for the crew. Another coastal minesweeper, the USS *Albatross*, would be relieving the *Erne*. In addition, the ship was granted a rest and recreation stop in Hong Kong while enroute to Japan. This stop would also serve as a refueling and replenishment stop. All of this was good news for the crew. They had grown quite weary of the at-sea routine and looked forward to liberty on dry land. The transit time for the little ship to return to home port was from eight to ten days, depending upon the weather, the sea state, and barring any breakdowns in the ship's operating equipment. Therefore, the interim stop in Hong Kong was greatly appreciated by the crew, but would also allow the ship to take on fuel and fresh food. Fresh meat and produce were scarce while the ship was at sea and would be a welcome addition to the crew's diet.

Chapter Fifteen

The news of the Hong Kong liberty port stop was exciting to Buddy Miller and Bob Dawes. It would be the second time they had been to Hong Kong, so they knew it to be an exciting liberty port and were looking forward to experiencing it again. The ship set a generally northeast course heading into the South China Sea. The weather was cooperative, and they made good time. Their careful course avoided the many islands dotting their navigation charts as they made their way to Victoria Harbor and Hong Kong Island. At an outer harbor buoy, the ship embarked a Hong Kong harbor pilot, who was helped aboard the ship as he crossed from the pilot boat to the *Erne*. With the harbor pilot on board and Lieutenant Yates at the conn, the *Erne* picked its way through scores of ships and junks to move to its assigned berth. The *Erne* would join other American Navy ships in the harbor, as well as naval ships from various other countries. The minesweeper approached and finally tied up at a pier reserved for provisioning ships. U.S. Navy ships often times anchored in the harbor, but because the *Erne* was small, and would be taking on provisions, a vacant berth at the pier had been assigned to the ship.

Buddy and Bob Dawes stood near the rail on the ship's port bow as the city of Hong Kong drew near. Smaller boats crisscrossed the *Erne*'s bow and stern, narrowly missing the ship as it moved forward. The young men were in awe of the huge city with its multi-structured skyline, which literally marched up the side of a mountain. The huge San Miguel beer sign loomed over the China Fleet Club, a recreation and shopping complex that catered to visiting mariners. Later in the evening, this sign and thousands of others across the city would be lighted in wondrous blinking neon rainbows of color; a visual overload. As the ship neared its berth, vehicles and people could be seen as a colorfully undulating, noisy mass, swarming on the city's streets. Small red and crème colored Mercedes diesel taxi cabs blew their horns as they zipped along the avenue close by the piers. Buddy and Bob looked at each other and grinned. They were like two small boys, looking forward to the circus; the Hong Kong circus of life.

No sooner had the ship shifted its electrical load to shore power and connected to the fresh water and telephone lines on the pier, than small vendor boats began circling on the water side of the ship. These boats were manned by one or two trinket hawkers, or in some cases, families were in a boat. They were all trying to sell something to the curious sailors standing and gaping at the rail of the *Erne*. But soon, one slightly larger boat nudged its way through the throng of smaller craft and actually tied up to the side of the *Erne*. The CO, XO, and Ensign McCoy, the supply officer, had seen the boat and had come to meet it. From the boat, two young Chinese women climbed over the rail of the *Erne*. They were dressed in no-nonsense dark navy blue slacks and traditional embroidered white cotton shirts. One of the women had a colorful red, white, and blue scarf around her neck and carried a small notebook, which she soon opened. By her demeanor, she was clearly the leader of the two women. Both women bowed as they were introduced to the three ship's officers. After pleasantries were exchanged in English, the two women and the three officers made their way forward to the wardroom.

Meanwhile, the sailors were having a good time shouting and haggling with the boat vendors, resulting in money being passed to vendors and hastily purchased merchandise of low value was handed back aboard the ship to the individual sailor purchaser.

The 1MC broke in on the good time the sailors were having bartering with the vendor boats.

Now sweepers, sweepers, man your brooms. Commence ship sweep down, cleaning and stowing from fore to aft. Liberty call will be in one hour for those persons not in the duty section, after an inspection of the ship's cleanliness by the Executive Officer. Sweepers man your brooms.

Department Heads sought out their leading petty officers and chiefs to make sure that a thorough cleaning of the ship was completed before liberty, warning them that a less than satisfactory cleaning job would mean that the slackers would be forced to forego their much-anticipated liberty.

While most of the sailors began tidying up the ship, thirty minutes later, the CO, XO, and Supply Officer emerged from the wardroom with the two Chinese women. They all wore smiles, except Ensign McCoy. McCoy conferred for a moment with Jack Kramer who was standing to the side watching a couple of the senior sailors still having their bartering fun. Kramer was smiling as he glanced over at Ensign McCoy. McCoy definitely was not smiling and wore a serious expression.

At the appearance of the CO and XO, the remaining senior sailors drifted away from the ship's rail and went to look after their junior men who were assigned to the cleaning details. The small vendor boats could see that they would be making no more sales and moved away from the ship, while the boat belonging to the two Chinese women waited at the aft quarter. Ensign Kramer soon tracked down Buddy and Bob Dawes and told them to go to the armory and bring all the bags of spent brass which the ship had been keeping after each ship's gunnery practice. Several large bags of spent cartridge brass were soon brought to Kramer who was waiting on the fantail. As Buddy and Dawes brought the brass to the fantail, simultaneously SK2 Cosgrove and SKSN Newton, along with Ensign McCoy, all struggled to the fantail each carrying a case of frozen food. There were two cases of beef steaks and one case of pork roast. They were soon followed by one of the mess cooks carrying a case of three pound coffee tins. These were all stacked on the fantail near the rope ladder that was hanging over the side of the ship. After all of the materials had been inspected by the two women, the leader gave a signal to crewmen waiting on the boat, and two Chinese deck hands scrambled up the rope ladder, jumped onto the deck of the minesweeper, and began handing the merchandise back to the waiting boat. When all the material was on the Chinese boat, the two ladies turned and bowed to the CO and XO, then turned and climbed over the rail and descended to their waiting boat, which quickly untied and departed in a cloud of foul diesel smoke.

Buddy was standing next to Senior Chief Gunther as the Chinese boat left.

"Hey, Senior Chief, what was that all about and who were those women?" he asked.

Senior Chief Gunther chuckled. "I keep forgetting what a rookie you are," he said, and clapped Buddy on the shoulder. "The boss of those ladies was the famous Mary Soo. She runs a business here in Hong Kong of painting U.S. Navy ships. She almost always uses women in her painting crew. The reason for that is that Mary Soo also runs an orphanage, specializing in rescuing young orphan girls whom she puts to work for her when they are old enough. She's a pretty enterprising woman and is well regarded in the Hong Kong waterfront community." The chief continued, "In the great and wonderful rules of Uncle Sam, we are not allowed to pay them in U.S. currency to paint the ship, so Mary Soo takes payment in food items and metal scrap. They especially like the ammunition brass. They can melt that down and make other products from it. And that, my rookie gunner's mate friend, is how Navy ships get painted in Hong Kong. And when you go on liberty in Hong Kong and you happen to buy some brass trinket to take home, you're probably buying back some of your old ammo brass. How's that for free enterprise?" Gunther laughed at his own joke.

The small wooden ship remained in Hong Kong for five days. During that time, Mary Soo's crew constructed scaffolding and walkways on floating platforms that were attached to the ship. Compressors and electric lights were rigged, and the exterior of the ship was completely repainted by Mary Soo's crew in only three days, working nearly around the clock with flood lights in use for night-time painting. The painting crew wasted no time. Time, indeed, was money to the hard-working women of Mary Soo's painting company.

*****

For two of the five days in Hong Kong, Buddy and Bob Dawes had coinciding days during which they did not have the duty. During those two days, the young men went on liberty together and wandered the stalls of the China Fleet Club, eyeing the various goods sold in the orient. At a money changing stall in the Fleet Club, they exchanged most of their U.S. dollars for Hong Kong dollars. Then they bought electronic items for themselves and gifts for their families back in Iowa. They also took a tram ride to the top of Victoria peak, visited Tiger Balm gardens, and rode a tour boat to Hong Kong's famous floating city. The young men reveled in being tourists in a strange, but wonderful city. At the end of the day, when fatigue overtook them, they returned to the ship and stowed away their purchases. Since there was no spare room in the berthing compartments, the merchandise was safely stowed in the ship's armory. They were so worn out that they simply went back to the China Fleet Club for a couple beers and returned to the ship to get some sleep.

Their final evening of liberty, as dusk's purple hues settled over the mountains majestically perched next to the harbor, and after they had grabbed a quick snack on the mess deck, the two gunners headed back into Hong Kong to explore the night life of the fabulous city.

But on this final evening of liberty, as they made their way to the fantail to cross the brow and leave the ship, they were stopped by Senior Chief Gunther. "Where are you two tadpoles going?"

"We thought we would find a place to get a decent meal and then head for somewhere that has ice cold beer and maybe some China dolls," said Dawes, as the grin spread across his boyish face.

"Whoa, slow down you two. You need to listen to me for a minute. I want you to stick around the *Erne* crew. We're going to have a ship's party. All of your shipmates are going to be at one place tonight, and I'm giving everybody a map so they can find their way there. We're all going to a bar called *Custer's Last Stand*. There is a great restaurant right next door called *Jimmy Lee's*. You eat there and tell them you are part of the *Erne* crew. They'll give you a good deal. The bar is going to have an American band, and the beers are a quarter." Turning his head slightly, Gunther said, "Are you listening, Dawes?"

Bob Dawes had been watching the last of the cute, female painters who were cleaning up their working gear near the stern of the ship, but he started when the chief mentioned his name. "Oh, yeah, Senior Chief, the Custard Pie Bar. We'll be there."

"That's what I figured," said Gunther. "You didn't hear a word I said. Now look, Miller, you've got to take this foul ball under your wing. Wandering around at night by yourself in Hong Kong is not a good idea. You might end up with some rather unsavory characters who would just as soon rob you as look at you. So I want all the crew to stay together. Heck, even the officers will be there."

A groan escaped from the two young men at the thought that they would be watched by the officers.

The Senior Chief continued. "What I forgot to mention is that there will also be a whole lot of lovely ladies at Custer's, just waiting to help us spend our money. Miller, am I getting through to you?"

"Yep. Thanks, Senior Chief. Looks like we're headed to Jimmy Lee's," said Buddy as he took the copy of the map from Gunther's hand. "Let's go, Bob."

As the young men walked down the pier leaving the ship behind, Dawes started his carping. "You've got to be kidding, Buddy. You're not really going to listen to the old chief, are you? We've got places to go and things to see. We don't have to stick around the rest of the guys. We can make our own fun."

Buddy pulled up short and turned to look at Bob Dawes. "Listen here, lame brain. You're darn right I'm going to listen to the chief. He's twice our age and has been around the world a couple times. He knows what he's talking about and always tries to help us when he can. I guess you don't remember that he pulled your bacon out of the fire at Captain's Mast. You better start listening to that old man, Dawes. I'm headed for Jimmy Lee's." He started to walk off, studying the map as he walked, and said over his shoulder, "Are you coming or not?"

Dawes quickly caught up. "Geez, you don't have to get all pissy about it. I'm coming." With the help of Gunther's hand-drawn map, they were able to walk through the narrow streets of the sprawling city to the restaurant. It was not more than a mile from the ship's location, but without the map it would have been much more difficult to find, hidden among the myriad of look-alike business fronts and alleys.

If one counted the small market stalls selling ready-to-eat food, there were probably a million restaurants in Hong Kong. *Jimmy Lee's* was the same as any number of other similar restaurants. It was not fancy, and yet, was not seedy. It was clean, friendly, catered to clientele who were not wealthy, and it served large portions of good Asian food. It was a favorite of tourists and visiting military personnel. As Buddy and Dawes stood on the sidewalk outside the restaurant, they observed the usual pictures of various prepared food dishes displayed in the window of the restaurant. Since the descriptions and prices below the pictures were written in Chinese, the men had no idea what any of the delicacies might be. And since they had not quite figured out the conversion rate of Hong Kong dollars to U.S. currency, they were also unsure of the real cost of the entrees. They entered the restaurant, and a young attractive hostess seated them at a table. A frenetic waiter took their drink order, and soon, two near-quart-sized Tiger beers were on the table. It was readily apparent that over half of the patrons in the crowded restaurant were American military personnel; they just had that look, even in their civilian clothes. As Buddy and Bob sipped their beers, they looked around at all of the other patrons. In addition to the Americans, interspersed in the noisy conversation of the diners, they could overhear the distinct English dialects of both British and Australian individuals.

Suddenly, Bob Dawes jumped up and shouted to Buddy. "Look, Buddy, over at that table. It's Chief Proctor." Buddy followed Dawes's pointing finger and finally saw the Chief. He was seated with two other men. Buddy and Dawes also knew them to be from the *Kawishiwi*, although they did not know them personally. They were first class petty officers from the *Kawishiwi* weapons department. "Let's go say hello to him," said Dawes as he grabbed his beer and moved toward Proctor's table.

The *Kawishiwi* had pulled into Hong Kong the previous afternoon, and the bar was full of sailors from the oiler. Chief John Proctor had also spied his two former gunner's mates and rose from the table. Since he and his companions had not yet eaten, he asked Buddy and Bob to join them. Introductions were made and the sea stories began. The constant conversation was interrupted only by their waiter. Proctor gave the meal orders for everyone at the table and the waiter disappeared, only to quickly reappear with another round of the large Tiger beers. At a lull in the story and joke telling, Chief Proctor turned to Buddy.

"My sources tell me you are doing a great job on the *Erne*, Miller. They tell me you took over a completely FUBAR'd division and put it in good order."

Geez thought Buddy. How does Proctor hear about everything going on in the *Erne*? He obviously has spies.

The Chief continued and turned and looked at Bob Dawes. "They also tell me that you continue to be one of the biggest screw-ups in the Navy, Dawes." Bob Dawes just looked at the chief and grinned. But Buddy could see the hurt in Bob's eyes. Chief Proctor looked back at Buddy and said, "And I want you to know, Miller, that I had nothing to do with getting Dawes transferred to the *Erne*. Scuttlebutt is that our XO might have had a hand in talking to the Bureau." Bob Dawes stared at the label on his beer bottle and said nothing in response.

Their food arrived, delivered by four small women carrying trays nearly as wide as the women were tall. Steaming platters of sea food, vegetables, and noodles were placed in the center of the table on a large turning lazy susan. The centerpiece platter around which all the other platters were placed contained a large bed of green cabbage with a huge purple onion in the center. The onion was decorated to look like an octopus, with black olives for eyes and a bright red pimento for a mouth. Radiating from the purple onion head were twelve octopi tentacles. Buddy thought it was odd that the octopus had twelve legs instead of eight. The whole platter was then sprinkled with pink, steaming shrimp and small whole-roasted fish. The platter was reasonably attractive, even with the strange, onion-headed octopus. The platform holding the various dishes could be turned to allow access to all platters by everyone at the table, and the ravenous sailors soon made short work of many of the dishes. Another round of Tigers arrived while the men ate. But it took Chief Proctor to lead the way on the octopus.

"Fried calamari, gentlemen. Octopus arms. Just spear one and cut it up. It's good." He demonstrated by chomping on the chewy tentacle. The others followed his lead, and it was not long before the octopus had lost its legs. Only the creepy looking purple onion was left on the platter.

After most of the food platters were empty, Chief Proctor told the men they were in for a treat. The dishes were cleared from their table, and more waiters appeared with bowls containing what looked like a mound of brown rice for each man. But to the sailors' surprise, liquor was quickly poured on each mound and lit. A flaming bowl was placed in front of each man.

One of the petty officers at the table said, "OK, Chief. I give up. What is this stuff?"

Chief Proctor laughed. "When the flame goes out, take a spoonful and eat it." Almost simultaneously, the men took a spoonful in their mouths and all of them grinned. Proctor laughed again. "It's deep fried ice cream," he said. "This place is famous for it." The table then became quiet, with no one talking. They were all too busy eating the delicacy. Buddy thought to himself; I've seen a million dairy cows in Iowa, but this is the first time I ever saw fried ice cream.

*****

After finishing and paying for their meal, they all followed Chief Proctor through the adjoining door to the bar next door. It was loud and dimly lit. The natives were restless at *Custer's Last Stand*, and the joint was jumping. An Anglo band was playing some of the latest American and British rock and roll tunes, and the place was packed with American, British, and Australian military men and petite young Chinese women gyrating around the dance floor. At the back of the main room were four pool tables with patrons standing around the tables giving encouragement to their favorite players who were playing matches for five dollars a game. Along one wall was a bank of slot machines, certainly rigged so that there were seldom winners. Prostitution was legal and licensed in Hong Kong. "Pleasure girls" freely roamed the floor. It was the kind of place sought out by sailors on liberty.

"Proctor, you old bastard!" someone shouted. The group turned to see Senior Chief Gunther moving toward Proctor.

"Gunther, you horse's ass!" said Proctor. The two old friends shook hands, grinned, and clapped each other on the shoulder. They were about to walk off together, when Gunther turned around and grabbed Buddy and Dawes.

"Listen you two. Remember what I said. You stay with the group and don't wander off by yourselves. When it gets to be time to go back to the ship, you grab a cab or walk back as a group. You got that?" said Gunther, and he walked away to join Proctor.

Buddy and Dawes spotted some of the other *Erne* sailors and joined them at a large table. Each of the sailors had a Chinese girl on his lap. Bespectacled Robert "Fig" Newton, wearing a big grin on his face and a girl on his lap motioned for Buddy and Dawes to sit next to him at the table. In another moment, two more women appeared and soon occupied the laps of Buddy and Dawes. The beer flowed, and the band kept playing. The dance floor remained crowded as the sailors struggled to appear that they knew how to dance to the latest rock and roll tunes. But alcoholic inebriation and dancing are not necessarily compatible, making for some rather comical physical moves on the dance floor. Although they may have been a dance choreographer's nightmare, they were all having a good time. The women, who were employed by the bar, en-couraged the sailors to buy them drinks, which were actually watered down tea. The bar owner made a healthy profit from the girls' work of enticing the men to buy drinks.

One of the other *Erne* sailors at the table called their attention to a table some distance from them. "Hey, get a load of that. It's most of our officers all at one table." Only Ensign McCoy was missing as he had the duty on the ship. "What's the deal with that? Why are they all together?" One of the engineering senior petty officers spoke up and told them that Ensign Meyer, the engineering officer, had just been promoted to LTJG. And because of his promotion, he had to host a "wetting down" party, where he had to buy drinks for the rest of the wardroom.

"Poor slob," said Dawes. "He has to buy all the other brass drinks. I think Meyer has 'lifer' written all over him."

"Aw go easy on him," said the engineman. "He's a hard ass, but he runs a good department. He's a whole lot better than some of the other ones I've worked for. And besides, I'm a lifer too." This comment raised a round of jeers and teasing of the career man at the table.

As afternoon turned to evening, the women began encouraging the men to leave the table and follow them for some "special time." The prostitution laws allowed the women to take a man to the individual prostitute's small bedroom, which she rented from the bar owner. Rows of these bedrooms lined a hallway on the second floor of the bar.

With the prostitute on his lap, Dawes leaned over toward Buddy and said quietly, "Loan me ten Hong Kong dollars."

Buddy gave Dawes a blank look, but then said, "Payday is Monday. I want it back then."

"Yeah, yeah. I'll pay you Monday," said Dawes, and Buddy handed him a ten Hong Kong dollar bill. As Dawes pocketed the bill, Buddy locked eyes with Chief Proctor who had seen the money change hands from his seat at a nearby table, and almost simultaneously they both scowled and shrugged. A moment later, Buddy glanced back around and noticed that Bob Dawes had left the table.

The band played on, and the beer continued to flow freely. From time to time, before they had spent all of their money, sailors could be seen drifting up the back stair case of the bar, each with a girl hanging on his arm. They would return a short time later to rejoin their friends. It was, indeed, a profitable night for the owner of *Custer's Last Stand.*

*****

At two minutes before one a.m., the band played "Anchors Aweigh." At the conclusion of the song, the bar lights were turned up, and the band began packing up their gear. The night was coming to a close.

"Gentlemen, if I could please have your attention." It was CDR Dixon, the XO of the *Kawishiwi* trying to quiet the boisterous, inebriated sailors. "Guys, we need to head back to the ship. We need to start walking to the small boat pier and hop the liberty boat back to the *Kawishiwi*. Stick together with your buddies and make sure everybody gets back on the liberty boats. The XO of the *Erne* has asked that the *Erne* crew start walking back to their ship too. Be careful guys."

Fig Newton sidled up to Buddy and asked him, "Have you seen Dawes? He disappeared a long time ago, and I haven't seen him. I wanted to get the five bucks back that he owes me so I could take a cab."

Buddy chuckled as he looked back at his friend. "Good luck, Fig. Dawes never seems to have any money and almost never pays anybody back when they loan him money. Looks like you'll be walking back with me."

Slowly the crowd began to thin as the sailors and officers trickled out the door of the bar to the street to begin walking back to the liberty boat pier. The sailors laughed and stumbled their way along the sidewalks shouting barbs at each other, always laced with good-natured profanity. More than once, a knot of sailors would halt to allow one of their group to grace the curb with a sample of his stomach contents while the poor swabbie was jeered and laughed at. Was it any wonder that the senior petty officers and chiefs almost demanded that the young men stay together as a group to look after each other? Many of the sailors were just kids, doing a man's job in a military uniform.

The bar was almost empty. Chief Proctor and a couple of his gunner's mates from the *Kawishiwi*, along with Senior Chief Gunther, Buddy, Fig Newton, and a couple boatswains' mates from the *Erne* were the only remaining patrons. They were exchanging departing remarks and preparing to leave the *Last Stand*. Instead, the door to the bar burst open and three burly sailors in whites, with a shore patrol brassard circling their upper arms entered the door. Billy clubs hung from their web belts, and white helmets sat atop their heads. A barefoot white man wearing only white, Navy-issue boxer shorts hung his head between the shore patrol sailors. Buddy quickly looked at Chief Proctor and Senior Chief Gunther.

One of the shore patrol group, a big, burly, first class machinist mate spoke up. "This guy claims he belongs to a party going on here. Says his name is Dawes, and he is off the *Erne*. Does he belong to you guys?"

"Aw, shit," said Senior Chief Gunther. "Yeah, he's ours. What's he done now?"

"Well, it isn't what he has done. It is what was done to him," said the shore patrol spokesman. "It appears that he wandered off with one of the hookers from this bar. He says her name is 'Maria.' Hell, I think half the hookers in this town use that name. Anyway, she took him to a couple of her male accomplices down one of the back alleys. They didn't beat him up, but threatened to cut his nuts off, and then they took everything he had on him except his skivvies. So, we don't have any charges on him, and you can have him. I'll tell the bar owner about this. He won't be real happy it was one of his girls, and she will probably find herself without a job. This guy's all yours," and the shore patrol men walked over to the bar to talk to the owner.

The sailors were left standing, looking at each other. Suddenly they all burst out laughing when one of the boatswain's mates went behind Dawes and pulled his skivvies down around his ankles. Dawes was left naked as his birthday.

"Hey Dawes, nice to see you still have the family jewels," said one of the sailors.

"You're damn lucky you're still in one piece," said Senior Chief Gunther, as he watched Dawes slowly pull up his shorts. "You have got to be the stupidest sailor I have ever met. And believe me, there's a shit load of them. But you're number one!"

Almost on the verge of tears, Dawes spoke up. "Aw, leave me alone, you guys. I already feel pretty damn stupid. How would you guys like to wander around Hong Kong in your underwear?" His remark only brought on another round of hysterical laughter.

Chief Proctor rejoined the group. He had been talking to the bar owner and held some used clothing in his arms.

"These clothes cost me ten Hong Kong. Senior Chief will collect from you on Monday and send me the money. Now put these on, and let's get out of here."

In a moment, another round of laughter arose and was not about to die down. Dawes had put on the pants, which came up at least four inches above his ankles, and then put on a pair of pathetic looking flip flops. Then he put on the t-shirt. It was pink in color, and written in bold letters on the front of the shirt were the words, "I Love My Sailor."

The shore patrol group was leaving the bar and stopped to see what the laughter was about. They soon joined in the hilarity. One of them said, "Maybe we should throw him in the brig for being, you know, one of those 'funny boys'. They're not allowed in the Navy." The shore patrol detail walked out of the bar still laughing. It had been a great ship's party, and even Bob Dawes was smiling again as the minesweeper group returned in the wee hours of the morning and walked across the brow of the *Erne*.

Later in the morning, after breakfast, as the ship held quarters before getting underway again, a pink t-shirt with "I love My Sailor" written on the front was seen flapping in the breeze high up on one of the ship's flag halyards. It had been spirited away very early in the morning by one of the signalmen and hauled up for the ship's company to see. The Dawes story from the night before had made its rounds on the ship. Bob Dawes was a reluctant celebrity of sorts, but even he saw the humor intended. But this incident, along with previous occasions when he had received the scorn of the men whom he most admired, was making a heartfelt impression on the young man and was beginning to form Bob's future personality in a more positive manner. He was starting to mature, to grow into manhood, and leave behind his lack of responsibility. But there was still a great deal of progress to be made.

After another eastward transit of several days from Hong Kong, the ship and crew rounded the headlands of the island of Kyushu, Japan, and made their way to their home port of Sasebo, located on the western side of the island. The ship slowly made its way through the harbor traffic and edged closer to its designated berth. In the cooler climate of Japan, the crew was in dress blues while manning the rail. As *Erne* got closer, the crew could see wives, children, and girlfriends, whom they had not seen for several weeks, waiting and waving on the pier. Buddy and the other sailors were standing on the starboard side of the ship as it neared the pier. From his location, Buddy could hear the OOD, who was standing above him on the bridge wing, shouting orders to the helm. LTJG

Meyer was conning the ship. His helm orders would soon bring the ship to a stop next to the pier.

"Rudder amidships," was followed shortly by "All back one-third." The ship shuddered as the screws chewed the water under the stern of the ship, stopping the ship's forward motion. LTJG Meyer soon gave the final orders. "All stop. Throw over lines one, two, three, and four." The ship was back in its home port.

*****

For the next six weeks the slower pace of in-port duties allowed the crew to be at home with their families and rest from their long days at sea. But a great deal of work would be done while the ship was idle. Needed repairs were completed on all systems in the ship including mechanical, electrical, and weaponry. The store rooms were soon restocked with all materials needed for the ship to make its next deployment. Spare parts, ammunition, food stuffs, fuel, and other items were stowed in their proper places. Preventative maintenance in all departments was brought up to date. Even the living quarters and berthing spaces were thoroughly cleaned and given a fresh coat of paint. There was no idle time for the crew during the day; however, they had liberty every night if they were not in the duty section. But like all ships in the Navy, the *Erne* belonged at sea. Their time in Sasebo would soon end.

October 1
Dear Mom and Dad,

The ship is back home in Sasebo. It sure is nice not to be bouncing around at sea. We are catching up on our work on the ship. We had a nice time in Hong Kong on our way back to

Japan. I'll tell you all about it when I get home. Sasebo seems like a real nice place, and we are eating lots of different Japanese food. The weather is a little cooler here in Sasebo. I like that. Say hello to the girls.

Love, Buddy

Chapter Sixteen

October 9, 1968
USS **Erne**
Home Port, Sasebo, Japan

One morning following quarters, all hands met on the fantail of the ship. Captain Yates took this opportunity to hand out awards to the crew. Vietnam Service medals were presented to the members who had earned them by virtue of their service in the war zone. In addition, he presented certificates to four of the enlisted men who were receiving promotions. Two men were promoted to first class petty officer, another to second class, and Robert "Fig" Newton was promoted to storekeeper third class.

Captain Yates concluded the awards ceremony by saying, "To all of you I just want to say that our crew is performing in a manner that brings credit to the *Erne*. I'm proud of all of you. You're doing a great job." He then hesitated a moment and continued. "These past weeks have been wonderful for all of us. Six weeks in port with our families, and a chance to do some sightseeing here at our home away from home have been great. But we all knew that soon the *Erne* would be called on again to take up Market Time duties. That time has come. We have been ordered by Commander Naval Forces Japan to put to sea tomorrow. But because of this short notice for you, liberty will go down at 1400 this afternoon and will cease at 1200 noon tomorrow. Department Heads, we will not have a formal muster at noon, but will take roll call on station just prior to shoving off. XO, take charge and dismiss the men." Captain Yates left the group and walked forward to his cabin.

Immediately after the sailors were dismissed from the awards session, Fig Newton came up to Buddy and Dawes.

"OK guys. Now that I've got my crow, we're going to celebrate to-night, especially since we have to head out again tomorrow. I'm buying the first round at *Mama Kito's* tonight," said Fig.

Mama Kito's was a favorite hangout of the crew when the ship was in its home port. It was a combination bar/restaurant and bath/massage establishment. Since they were newer to the crew and had only been in Japan for six weeks, Buddy and Dawes had only frequented *Mama Kito's* one time, but had not gotten a bath or massage. Drinks were more expensive at the bath house, and since there were much cheaper places to get a beer, they had not been back since.

"You're on," said Dawes, while Buddy silently nodded his head.

*****

The first inkling that Bob Dawes was beginning to reason through a situation for his advantage came that afternoon prior to liberty call. He was approached by one of the operations department's senior petty officers, Pete Wyans. Wyans was married, and he and his wife were parents of a toddler daughter.

"Hey Dawes, you want to make some money?" said Wyans. Strange-ly enough, Wyans was already dressed in civilian clothes.

Bob had a sneaky feeling of what was coming, but he said, "Sure."

"How 'bout taking my duty tonight? My wife will kill me if I don't get off the ship before we head out again," said Wyans. "I'll make it worth your while. How about if I give you twenty-five bucks to take my slot on the roster?"

Bob Dawes owed money to several people on the ship and needed to pay off those debts. But he had promised Buddy and Fig that he would go with them to Mama Kito's. He didn't answer Wyans, just looked at him, and gave the appearance that he was thinking it over.

"C'mon, Dawes, help me out here. I've got to get out of here and give some lovin' to mama. How about thirty-five?"

"Aw, I don't know. I promised a couple other guys I would go with them tonight," said Dawes. But as he said it, he was already hatching a plan. There was a gamble involved, but he thought he could work it out.

"Dawes, I've got to get off the ship. What is it going to take to get you to take my duty?"

"Well, here's the deal, Wyans. I'm just a poor little stinking seaman. I don't make much money. You need to sweeten the pot for me," said Dawes.

"All right, all right, how much?"

Dawes looked at Wyans and smiled. "It'll cost you seventy-five bucks." Dawes even started to turn away to start walking.

The 1MC interrupted this game of high finance. *Attention. Liberty call, liberty call for all hands not in the duty section. Liberty will expire at 1200 tomorrow.*

"You shit bird, Dawes. See if I ever do anything for you." But even as he said it, Wyans was reaching in his pocket and fishing out the money. He barely had the seventy-five dollars, but soon slapped it in Dawes' hand. "I hope you choke on it," said Wyans as he fairly ran to the ship's brow and sprang onto the pier. He raised and waved his middle finger at Dawes as he trotted toward the end of the pier.

Dawes just chuckled, and shouted, "Say hello to wifey for me!" as he pocketed the cash.

Dawes had to work fast. He went to the vending machine on the mess decks and bought two cold Cokes. Then he made his way to the supply office where he knew he would find SK2 Sam Cosgrove. The door to the supply office was open, and he walked in. Ensign Ted McCoy was just leaving to head out on liberty. Cosgrove was sitting at his desk, as usual, working.

"Hey Dawes, what's cooking," said McCoy as he moved to the door to leave.

"Not much, sir. Have a good time on liberty," said Dawes.

McCoy gave Dawes a thumbs-up sign and a conspiratorial wink and was gone.

Cosgrove looked up at Dawes. "OK dipshit. What do you want?" said Cosgrove. Cosgrove was dressed in a dirty tee-shirt and dungarees. An overflowing ash tray sat on the desk, which was covered with papers and books.

"Oh, c'mon, Cosgrove. I come in peace. I even brought you a Coke," said Dawes. Along with the other clutter, Cosgrove's desk was littered with empty Coke cans. The man was addicted to the sweet soda. "So how's it going, anyway?"

Cosgrove knew a game was afoot. He dropped his black government-issue ballpoint, the one with a chain and tape around it so no one could filch it – as if that would stop a sailor who wanted it. He turned in his chair and scowled at Dawes while lighting up another Winston. "What do you want?"

"Well, you're not going on liberty, are you Cosgrove?" Dawes already had overheard Cosgrove bitching at lunch that he had too much work to do to leave the ship.

"I might, and then again, I might not," said the storekeeper, as he blew cigarette smoke from his mouth.

"Well, I thought that maybe if you were staying on the ship, I could slip you ten bucks to take my duty." Cosgrove never paid any attention to the watch bill. He only knew when he had duty, and today was not one of those days.

"You slimy little bastard. Do you think I would take your duty for a measly ten bucks?" Cosgrove laughed.

Dawes thought to himself, keep laughing you jerk. We'll see who laughs last here. "All right, all right, I could go as high as fifteen bucks."

"Dawes, you don't have fifteen bucks to your name. And just because I know you don't have the money," said Cosgrove, "I'll make you a deal. I'll take your duty, but it will cost you twenty-five greenbacks. Now get the hell out of my office, you slime ball."

Dawes turned his back to Cosgrove and counted out the twenty-five dollars. He then spun around and slapped the twenty-five dollars on the desk in front of Cosgrove. A look of complete disbelief came over Cosgrove's face as the cigarette butt between his fingers burned him, and he brusquely mashed it out in the ash tray.

"You're actually taking Pete Wyans place on the watch bill. Make sure you tell Mr. Clark. He's the OOD tonight. Thanks, Cosgrove," and Dawes quickly turned and hurried out of the supply office, but not before seeing the red flooding the face of the storekeeper. He also couldn't help but hear Cosgrove yelling, "You're an asshole, Dawes!"

Buddy and Fig Newton were waiting for Dawes on the mess decks. They had already changed into civvies. Dawes hurriedly changed clothes, and the three sailors walked to the fantail to cross the brow and head for town. On their way, they passed the still-open door of the supply office. "You're an asshole, Dawes!" once again boomed out of the open door as they passed by. Dawes chuckled and began to enlighten his companions while they were walking down the pier.

"Here's the ten bucks I owe you, Buddy, and here's the five I owe you, Fig." He did the quick calculations in his head. He had also paid five bucks to two other guys in the berthing compartment as he got dressed.

"Not a bad day boys. I've got twenty-five bucks in my pocket and didn't even have to work for it. And just because old Wyans wanted to be home so bad with his wife. Geez, I hope I never get that pussy whipped," said Dawes.

*****

As they made their way across the Navy base, they avoided the Enlisted Men's Club, where they could have had a cheap beer and something to eat. But they all agreed that the food tasted too much like that served on the ship. Because it was a Navy-run facility, the odds were good that the cooks in the club used the same recipes as those on the ship.

Buddy, Dawes, and Fig stopped at a street-front noodle shop to eat an early dinner. They had all eaten here in the past. They stopped on the sidewalk at the front of the shop and looked at the various menu choices displayed in pictures in the shop window. A bowl of noodles with vegetables and a bit of meat, along with a Kirin beer was a very inexpensive, yet nourishing, dinner, not to mention that it was a great improvement over the bland tasting ship's food. A reed-thin, smiling Japanese man came out of the restaurant with a pad and pencil. He bowed and smiled at the young men. He had done this hundreds of times with visiting military men. The three sailors pointed to the picture in the window of the menu item they each wanted. The proprietor bowed again and motioned for them to come inside the restaurant.

The steaming bowls of noodles and the chilled beer soon arrived at their table. In Japan, it was not considered bad form to suck up and slurp your noodles from your noodle bowl. It was a good thing too, as the three sailors noisily slurped from their noodle bowls and periodically downed a swallow of their beers. Their game attempts to use their chop sticks were humorous to the few other Japanese diners who were idly smoking and furtively watching the three Americans. The expressionless faces of the other patrons belied the fact that they thought these three sailors were entertaining, indeed. The young men paid their tab, bowed to the shop owner, and left the restaurant. They wandered a few streets, looking in shop windows and watching the people of this country that was so foreign to them. Periodically, they would enter a shop to browse and perhaps purchase a snack or souvenir trinket. As the afternoon wore on, with the sun casting longer shadows from behind the city's buildings, they decided it was time to head for *Mama Kito's*.

*****

Mama Kito's establishment had been in its present location near the waterfront for decades. Before the Americans became more or less permanent at their Sasebo naval base after the Second World War, local fishermen and sailors patronized the iconic combination bar/restaurant/bath house/massage parlor, and house of prostitution. The atmosphere was smoky, and the background music was pure string-plucked tinkling Japanese. Food and drinks were not necessarily cheap. But it was a quiet, relatively safe place to have a couple of beers to relax, followed up by a soapy bath and a remarkable deep muscle massage. If one was so inclined after his bath, there were several separate rooms for activities of a more intimate sexual nature. Aside from two very burly male bartenders and a door man, all of whom doubled as bouncers, the staff was comprised of women.

No one really knew if there was a real Mama Kito. But everyone who entered the well-known establishment was sure to see the small, frail-appearing Asian woman of advanced years, dressed in one of her several brightly-hued silk kimonos, tied with an equally colorful obi, who sat at a small corner booth in the bar, watching through small tortoise-shell framed spectacles. Her hair was impeccably coiffed, albeit almost white, and she wore gold-trimmed lacquered chop sticks in her hair.

Small pearl stud earrings adorned her ear lobes. Although old, she still glowed with a natural beauty. She was always there and seldom moved except to drink from either an elegant hand-painted tea cup or a large water tumbler, or to light and smoke aromatic brown-wrapped cigarettes affixed to a black lacquer cigarette holder. But her darting black eyes never stopped moving and missed nothing. The staff of women would occasionally cast furtive glances her way. Visitors to the establishment assumed that this was Mama Kito, but no one ever asked, nor did the staff volunteer the information. To all gaijin, she was simply "Mama San." But to locals and employees, she was a revered force, not to be crossed.

As the three sailors entered the front door of *Mama Kito's*, they met the steely eyes of the stoic doorman, dressed in a brass-buttoned crimson tunic. A brass-handled, ornately engraved dirk hung at his side in an open, ringed, partial holster, which revealed the formidable, gleaming blade. The young men carefully and quietly walked past the doorman, casting quick glances at each other. All agreed that it would be unwise to ever get in a physical confrontation with that fellow.

They sat at a table with two other sailors whom they did not know. But in a few moments, with introductions made, the sea stories and jokes soon bounced merrily around the table. Listening to the stories, Buddy absently flattened a mosquito on his arm that had been buzzing his head for a few minutes. A spot of blood and a dead mosquito were the result. After two rounds of beer, Fig left the table and was seen speaking with one of the hostesses. He returned to the table with a grin on his face.

Speaking to Dawes and Buddy, he said, "Drink up boys. See that little dolly over there? We're going to follow her and get a scrub down and massage."

As they finished their beers and rose to leave the table, the other two sailors who remained at the table spoke up. "Have fun boys," as they raised their beer bottles and gave the departing trio a knowing, ribald laugh.

Buddy, Dawes, and Fig followed the lithe young woman in her white kimono through the crimson beaded doorway at the back and to one side of the bar. They walked down a short hallway and came to a surprisingly brightly lit perpendicular hallway, where everything was either painted or tiled in white. Small, well-lit, white rooms led off both sides of this hallway. The young woman motioned for each of the sailors to enter an individual room.

As Buddy entered his assigned room, he soon saw that the floor was tiled in white, with white walls, and a large white deep-sink. Small fluorescent overhead fixtures brightly lit the room. In the tile floor, there was a water drain opening in the center of the room. A worn, wooden, four-legged stool perched over the drain opening. To one side of the room was a small tubular rack of shelving which contained clean, folded, white towels, and room to place clothing. Next to it was a massage table, covered with a waterproof, brown vinyl top. The only other color in the room was provided by two large, framed, landscape pictures, both depicting a ruggedly beautiful, coastal scene. The room was stark, yet calming. A young woman entered the room behind Buddy and gently closed the door. She was wearing white, short shorts and a white, short-sleeved blouse. As Buddy turned, she bowed and spoke to him in English.

"Welcome to Kito bath," she said. As the woman was bent over, Buddy could not help but notice that she did not have undergarments beneath her white shirt. As she straightened at the waist, Buddy could see that she appeared to be a few years older than he. She was not especially pretty, but was not homely either. Her hair was tied on top of her head with a white ribbon. "Please, what is your name?" she said.

Buddy answered, and simply said, "Buddy." He was beginning to feel nervous and a bit apprehensive. He was wondering how this was going to play out.

"Oh, Mr. Buddy. Very nice to meet you. I am Tomika. Please call me Tommy."

"OK," said Buddy.

"Please Mr. Buddy, come over here and place your clothes here." Tommy had moved to the small clothing rack and motioned for Buddy to place his clothing on the rack.

At this point, Buddy thought seriously about leaving the room. The woman, a complete stranger, wanted him to disrobe in front of her. But he did as he was asked and took off all his clothes except his skivvies. As he turned back to the woman, she lowered her head, and said, "Mr. Buddy, please remove your underwear."

Buddy could feel his face getting red. Reluctantly, he turned away from the woman and pulled off his undershorts. While he was doing that, he could hear water running. He turned, with his hands strategically placed, but trying to appear natural. Tommy did not turn away from her task of running water into the large sink.

Tommy then said, "Please sit here," as she motioned toward the wooden stool.

Buddy took his place on the stool while Tommy adjusted the water temperature at the sink. She had also taken a rubber hose and a large white plastic bucket from the sink and was using the hose to fill the bucket, which was soon full of sudsy water. The woman pulled the bucket next to Buddy's stool and held the end of the hose in her hand. She then used the hose and her hand to completely soak Buddy down. The water was hot, and the small room began to get steamy with the heat. Buddy was soon all wet, and his skin was turning pink from the hot water. Tommy then retrieved a sponge from the bucket and squeezed soapy water onto Buddy's head and washed his hair and head. She continued sloshing the hot soapy water onto Buddy and worked her way down his body, washing as she got lower.

While she worked, she asked Buddy where he was from. She asked about his family, what his father did for a job, and about his sisters. Buddy enjoyed the conversation, and she reciprocated by telling him about her family, and where she lived. She alleged that she enjoyed her job and liked meeting the visitors to the bath.

By now, Tommy was also very wet, and it was very apparent she was wearing no upper undergarments. Her shorts were either lined, or she had on underpants. Her shirt stuck to her small frame, and her small breasts were covered only in the opaque, wet, whiteness of her shirt. Buddy watched her nipples and began to be uncomfortable. As Tommy worked, he watched her as discreetly as possible. But he felt his penis stirring into an erection. This embarrassed him, and he mentally fought the urge. He was barely able to remain calm.

"Please stand up, Mr. Buddy," said Tommy.

Buddy did as he was told, and Tommy began scrubbing his penis and groin, and moved around back to scrub between his buttocks. Buddy was losing the mental battle over his erection. It rose a bit more.

Thankfully, he heard Tommy say, "Please sit, Mr. Buddy," as she moved in front of him on the stool. She continued washing, moving down Buddy's legs, finishing with his feet. She then turned the bucket on its side to run the water down the drain. After rinsing it, she placed it back in the sink. Turning back to Buddy, her shirt continued to cling to her small breasts. She came over to Buddy and began to rinse the soap off of him. She ran the hot water on Buddy and used her free hand to go over the skin to make sure the soap was all rinsed off.

As she worked down to Buddy's abdomen, she asked, "Do you like the bath, Mr. Buddy?"

Buddy nodded his approval.

Holding the water hose in her hand and running the hot water over Buddy's stomach, Tommy leaned into Buddy and quietly spoke into his ear. "Would you like special, Mr. Buddy?"

This caught Buddy completely by surprise. He had to ask. "What is the special?"

Her response was even quieter, whispered in his ear, "Blow job." Buddy couldn't believe what he had heard. The crude words, spoken so easily from the mouth of the woman with whom he had just made pleasant conversation, and who had given him the best bath he had ever had, left him surprised. It had been so pleasant, and now it seemed so incongruous. Whenever he had previously heard the crude two word term for oral sex, it had always been from other men; never in the company of a woman.

He replied very quietly, "No thank you, Tommy." Tommy smiled, bowed, and continued to rinse the remaining soap from Buddy. When she had finished with the rinse, Buddy watched through the steamy air as Tommy turned off the water. She turned back to Buddy and then went over to the towel rack and brought two large white towels over to Buddy. She then went completely over his body, roughly toweling him off until his skin tingled and he was dry. She handed the towels to Buddy. She then went over to the towel rack and retrieved more towels which she laid over the massage table.

"Please come over to the table," said Tommy. Buddy followed, while wrapping the towels around him. Tommy motioned that Buddy should get on the table, lying face down. As he got on the table, Tommy took the two wet towels from Buddy. He was soon lying naked on the table. Tommy began working on Buddy, kneading the muscles, and grinding the palms of her hands into the muscle. The hard pressure on the muscles was, at times, uncomfortable, but soon, as she continued to work, Buddy's mind began to wander. Surprisingly, he was getting very sleepy, even though his muscles were being pummeled by this small woman. He dozed intermittently.

In time, she finished Buddy's back side. "Please roll over, Mr. Buddy," she said. Buddy was only slightly away from being asleep and did not think about it. He just rolled over on his back. Tommy placed a towel across Buddy's groin. Somehow the sensation of the towel being placed on his privates brought Buddy out of his sleepy state. He opened his eyes, turned his head, and stared right at two, small, beautiful breasts. Tommy had taken off her wet shirt and was beginning to massage Buddy's arm. She took no notice of Buddy staring at her chest. Tommy worked down his body and soon climbed up on the table. She was straddling Buddy's legs as she kneaded his thigh muscles. Buddy watched the small breasts bouncing as she worked, and the towel across his groin began to rise. There was no stopping it.

Tommy jumped down from the table. "Stand up, Mr. Buddy." Buddy held the towel to his body. Tommy also wrapped a towel around her upper body. "Come with me, Mr. Buddy." She took him by the hand, and they left the white room. They walked a short ways down the hall, and she led him into another room. This room was decorated in red, gold, and black and was sparsely furnished. There was a bed on one side of the room. Tommy closed the door to the room and gently faced Buddy. She dropped her towel and slowly bent and removed her damp shorts and undershorts. She then turned a switch on the wall, and the lights became very dim. Facing Buddy, she gently removed the towel from his hands and stroked his stomach, groin, and alert penis. Buddy audibly groaned and leaned and kissed the small woman. She then pulled him down onto the bed with her. Her expert hands guided Buddy in his first real love making. After the first explosion, it did not take the young gunner's mate any time to reload for a second climax. Buddy Miller's days of being a virgin came to a wonderful and glorious end at the hands of a Japanese, professional, "woman of pleasure."

*****

The two sailors sitting in the bar were still there; considerably more inebriated, but still there as Buddy slowly made his way from the rooms behind the bar to the barroom. He had never felt better in his life. Every muscle in his body was relaxed. He felt like walking gelatin and seriously just wanted to lay down somewhere and go to sleep.

"Have a good time?" asked one of the inebriated sailors.

Buddy leaned down and put his head on his crossed arms on the table and closed his eyes.

The two sailors both laughed. "Yeah, I guess he did."

In a few minutes, Bob Dawes walked from behind the bar and joined the group. He too put his head down on the table and closed his eyes, drawing a roar of laughter from the two sailors.

At least thirty minutes passed before Buddy opened his eyes and raised his head. He looked across the table at the snoring Bob Dawes. The two sailors who had co-occupied the table were gone, but other tables in the bar area now had occupants who were drinking and talking. Bob Dawes snorted, smacked his lips, and peered through slit eyelids. Slowly he raised his head. "God, I'm thirsty, and hungry too," said Dawes.

A hostess in her short black skirt and white blouse came to their table and took their order for beer and noodle dumplings. The ice cold beer trickling down the throats of the two young men revived them, making them more alert. Their food soon came, and they said nothing as they ravenously ate. Buddy finally was alert enough to ask, "Have you seen

Fig?" Dawes didn't reply. He simply looked around and shook his head negatively while he continued chewing.

They had finished eating when two more of the *Erne* crew came through the front door and joined them at the table. For the next couple hours the beer flowed and more food came to the table while the four crew members laughed and told stories. Finally, at nearly ten-thirty p.m., Buddy was wiped out. He felt so tired that he could barely stand up. But he slowly rose, briefly fished in his pockets, threw some money on the table, and turned to Dawes. "Dawes, I've got to get back to the ship and get some sleep."

Dawes struggled to his feet. "Hang on, I'll go with you."

Buddy then remembered and looked at the two sailors still seated at the table. "Hey you guys. Fig Newton came in here with us and went in the back, but he hasn't come out. Can you guys keep an eye out for him and make sure he gets back to the ship?"

"No problem, gunner," said one of the sailors.

Buddy and Dawes then turned and slowly walked out the door, flexing their leg muscles, willing them to cooperate. With a somewhat rolling gait, they made their way toward the ship, crossed the brow, and ambled to the berthing area. As they parted for their own bunks, Dawes mumbled, "What a day!" The same thought was in Buddy's head as he fell into his bunk. Reveille would come very early the next morning.

*****

No one had seen him at breakfast. Nor did he show up at quarters. Ensign McCoy sought out Buddy and Bob Dawes as they were cleaning small arms in the armory. "OK, you two. I understand that you were with Newton last night. He didn't show up at quarters this morning. Where the hell is he?"

Buddy and Dawes looked at each other and then looked back at Ensign McCoy. Buddy answered, "Sorry sir, we don't know. We were with him at Mama Kito's last night, and we left early and came back to the ship. We alerted a couple of the Ops guys that were there to keep an eye out for him, but we don't know what happened to him after that."

"Great. You guys are a big help." McCoy turned and walked off mumbling under his breath.

"Holy shit, Batman," said Dawes. "What do you suppose happened to Fig? Ooh, I'm glad I'm not in his shoes right now." The same thought crossed Buddy's mind, but he still worried about his friend.

As it so happened, Dawes could have been in Fig Newton's shoes. They were empty. One was lying upside down in the middle of the room, and the other one was under the bed in which Fig and a comely, well-endowed Japanese prostitute were entwined. Both Fig and the prostitute were naked and dead to the world asleep. Sexual acrobatics and athletic endeavors artfully taught to the eager near-sighted little storekeeper by the skillful prostitute had lasted far too long into the night, leaving both young people in the arms of Morpheus.

The dreaming lovers were rudely awakened by a senior staff member at *Mama Kito's*. She slapped the exposed buttocks of the prostitute and shook the young sailor. "Sailor, wake up. You miss ship. It eleven-fifteen," she shrieked.

The words that he had heard only yesterday, "shoving off at noon," buzzed into Fig's brain. Realization of the time electrified Fig into action. He was now fully awake and in a panic. He dropped to his hands and knees while searching for underwear, socks, shoes, and the rest of his clothing on the floor of the bedroom. He pulled on his pants, slid into his shoes, and put his arms in his shirt sleeves as he ran out the door.

No doubt this same scenario had been played out numerous times in the past, and nearby Japanese citizens doing their daily sidewalk sweeping paid little attention to the comical sight of a westerner with colorful clothing all askew, slap-slapping in untied shoes down the middle of the street heading for the U.S. Navy base.

As he ran, Fig Newton became aware that he must not be fully awake. The world appeared fuzzy, yet bright. Unconsciously he reached up to touch his face, only to discover that he was without his black-framed Navy issue eyeglasses. A loud moan gurgled from his mouth as he kept on running. He gripped his military ID card in his hand and held it at eye level as he passed the gate guard at the base. The guard called out, "You'll never make it, buddy!" Fig's breath was now mixed with a rasping sound as he kept running. He could see the superstructure of the minesweeper. But then he heard it. Three long blasts on the ship's whistle signified that the ship was beginning to back away from the pier. Line handlers on the pier had now thrown over three of the four hawsers that had held the ship to the pier and one line handler was now lifting the last rope over the pier bollard. He intended to throw it into the water for the ship to pull aboard. But suddenly, as he was just about to let go of the rope, a dark shape flashed in front of the line handler, and the rope was snatched out of his hand. Fig was now flying through the air hanging on the rope that would soon bang against the side of the ship. There was a loud 'thump' as Fig and his snared rope hit the ship.

The deck crew on the main deck of the *Erne*, who had been pulling the hawser on board, suddenly lost their grip as the rope became heavier with the weight of Fig grasping onto it. Fig and the end of the roped submerged in the water. But the deck crew quickly grabbed the elusive rope again, and four men strained to pull the rope up the side of the ship, with a wet and very bruised Fig Newton hanging on for dear life. As the ship backed away from the pier, he was hauled under the lowest cable life line of the ship and laid out on the forecastle. Poor Fig lay there gasping for air, thinking that he might die of oxygen deprivation at any moment.

Senior Chief Gunther had watched this whole scenario unfold, and it brought forth memories that he would certainly not share with anyone. An inward smile on his face remained hidden. He walked forward and glanced up to see the XO peering out one of the bridge windows. LTJG Bamino was shaking his head back and forth, but he too wore a grin. Everyone who was topside on the ship as it backed away from the pier that day had seen the comedy. It would be the talk of the crew for several days.

"What the hell are you doing lying around on my deck!" bellowed Gunther. "And you are out of uniform, sailor. Get the hell out of my sight and get your uniform on!"

Fig attempted to sit up, then stood up, and groaned as he stood.

"What the hell's the matter with you?" snarled Gunther.

"It's my side, Senior Chief. It's killing me," moaned Fig.

"Get your damn uniform on and see the corpsman," said Gunther. "Now get going." Fig, obviously in pain, hobbled away.

Buddy and Bob Dawes, standing by the forward gun mount, watched Fig gingerly walking aft.

"Living on this ship is more fun than going to the county fair," said Buddy, which brought a laugh from Dawes. But Dawes also knew that the cloud that had followed him around due to his mischief had suddenly moved away and was hovering over Fig Newton. Dawes could not help but feel better, but he also felt bad for his buddy Fig.

Chow that evening kept the mess decks full. Everyone wanted their slice of Fig. The poor young man was roasted as the barbs flew thick and fast. At Fig's expense, the hilarity and ridicule rolled from table to table, and probably would have gone on longer, but Senior Chief Gunther departed chief's quarters and wandered into the mess decks. He had heard enough.

"All right you guys. If you are through eating, get to your assigned cleaning stations. The XO wants the ship to have a good sweep down before movie call. Now scram!" said Gunther.

In a few minutes, the mess decks were empty, and the mess cooks began wiping down the tables. Senior Chief Gunther and Fig Newton stayed behind, and as Buddy and Dawes were about to leave, the chief grabbed them. "You guys sit down here too."

"What did the corpsman say, Newton?" asked the Senior Chief.

"He says I probably have a couple cracked ribs from when I hit the side of the ship. And he said I have a lot of contortions."

"Contortions! Don't you mean contusions?" said Gunther.

"Oh, yeah, contusions, whatever that is," said Fig.

"It means you've got a bunch of bruises. You're gonna live. Miller and Dawes, I wanted you to stay here because I'm going to give you a piece of my mind, right along with Newton. For the future let this be a lesson to you. If you go on liberty with a buddy, you stay with him and make sure he gets back to the ship. You should never have left him in that whorehouse. If you can't get your buddy to come back to the ship, you grab some other guys and physically haul him back. Leaving Newton there was wrong. Geez, all you have to do is look at the guy and know he is gonna need somebody to look after him. Have you got that?"

Buddy and Dawes both mumbled their acknowledgement.

Turning his attention to Fig Newton, Gunther said, "What the hell were you thinking, Newton. You could have killed yourself swinging on that mooring line."

"Well, I didn't want to miss ship's movement. I know that's a real bad thing to do," said Fig.

"Yeah, that can be brig time," said the Senior Chief. "But the Captain still wants to hold mast tomorrow, so you're at his mercy. Now tell me why in the hell you could not leave Kito's. No whore is worth going to mast over. You're a sailor first. I mean, it's probably your first time having sex, but geez, she's just a hooker, for God's sake."

"Aw, she's not really a hooker, Senior Chief. She's just trying to make some money to send to her poor family."

Gunther could not begin to count the number of times he had heard that old story.

"Bullshit. She's a whore, dumb ass," said Gunther

Fig's eyes glared. "It, it, it's not like that Senior Chief. Polly's really a nice girl, and we love each other. We're going to get married. She told me so . . ."

Before Fig could go further, all three of the other men began laughing.

Senior Chief started in on him. "Polly. Polly is it? Listen, shit for brains. She probably said something like; 'I love you, no shit,' didn't she? And then she told you that you were the only sailor she ever wanted to stay with, didn't she? And then she told you she wanted to get married, didn't she? Did she also tell you that if you paid her a little more, then she wouldn't have to make love to other sailor boys? So I'll bet you gave her all your money, didn't you?"

Fig's silence answered that question.

"And did she also tell you that she would have another 'appointment' right after you left the joint?"

Tears were welling up in Newton's eyes, but the Senior Chief went on. "Newton, she's a whore. She came from the streets, and that's where she's at home. She's making good money for easy work, and I mean easy. Her job is to make you happy and take you for all the money she can get from you. Probably by now, four other guys have screwed her since you left that joint. You don't mean shit to her unless you give her money. And you sure as hell wouldn't want to take her home to the states to meet your momma, now would you? What are you going to say around the dinner table when your family wants to know what kind of work she does? Oh, man, would that ever be a pretty sight. Am I getting through to you, numbskull?"

The tears rolled from Fig's eyes. But he was getting the message.

"You're a good kid, Newton. And you're a good sailor. You've got to be to put up with that dumb ass Cosgrove for a boss. But you've got a lot to learn," said Gunther. "At least a half dozen guys on this ship have gone through the same thing you have." He almost said that he was one of them, but that little secret would never cross his lips. "Have fun on liberty. Spend some time with the girls if you want to. But never, ever think that a whore would make a good wife. It will never happen. She only wants your money and will get you in big trouble. Learn from this mistake." He paused for effect. "Anything you want to say to me?"

Fig looked up at Gunther. "Thanks, Senior Chief."

Gunther stood up to leave and gave Newton a squeeze on the shoulder. "You guys need to get to your cleaning stations." He walked back toward chief's quarters.

October 10
Dear Mom and Dad,

We are now leaving Sasebo and going back to Vietnam. I had a great time in Japan. Visited a lot of interesting places and had fun. I think I told you that my friend from Des Moines who was with me on the Kawishiwi has transferred to the Erne. *He seems to be growing up, and we get along well. And I have a couple other friends who are pretty good guys. But one of them got himself in some trouble, and will have to go see the Captain tomorrow. You just would not believe how hot and hu-*

mid it is over here. It makes me wish for a winter in Iowa. Got-ta go.

Love, Buddy

By 1100 the next morning, Captain's Mast was concluded. For being AWOL at quarters the previous day, Fig was barred from receiving his promotion to third class, and fined $100, which would come out of his next three paychecks. Fig did not understand it at the time, but his promotion had only been delayed. He would be able to put on his crow in sixty days. In addition, although it didn't mean much to him when the Captain said it, to Fig's credit, the Captain had told him if he had missed ship's movement, the punishment would have been much more severe. For the next twenty-four hours, a crest-fallen SKSN Newton's chin never raised up from his chest. But the young sailor's irrepressible spirit would soon help him get past this learning experience.

Chapter Seventeen

October 17, 1968
USS **Erne**
Off the coast of Vietnam

Once again the ship had made the long, rough-water passage from Japan to take its place off the coast of South Vietnam. They had been at their assigned station for a few days when they raced to meet the always-in-motion *Kawishiwi* to be refueled. Two bags of stale, lost-in-transit mail finally caught up with them and dangled from the high line as they were pulled across to the minesweeper. In addition, a young, second class boatswain's mate, BM2 Mark Schmitt, holding his duffle bag on his lap, swung from a bosun's chair and was brought aboard the *Erne* to report aboard as an addition to the crew.

Senior Chief Gunther was standing on the rocking fantail of the *Erne*. He held an old-style megaphone to his mouth and was shouting across to the *Kawishiwi*. The recipient of his conversation was GMC John Proctor, who was leaning on the rail of the oiler, shouting back at Gunther.

"What's this I read in the message traffic about some jackass named Proctor being promoted?" shouted Gunther.

A rightfully proud Chief Proctor was laughing as he said, "It's true, you old fart. I put the star on next month." John Proctor was being promoted to senior chief, with his name appearing on the list of advancements distributed by radio to the fleet. Although relatively young, Proctor's exemplary record played an influential role in his early promotion.

Gunther continued. "I didn't think they promoted kids with milk on their breath. Be that as it may, congratulations, John. You deserve it."

"Thanks, Ray, I appreciate it. You keeping Miller and Dawes under control?"

"Yep, they're doing OK." The refueling rig had been disconnected between the ships, and the two chief petty officers waved at each other as the ships began moving apart. The large silhouette of the big oiler became steadily smaller as it continued on its assigned course to replenish other Navy ships in the region.

The sunny, hot, sticky days rolled on. The monotonous routine at sea was broken by the intermittent inspections of Vietnamese water craft. But the ship had found no contraband for the past several days, and all inspections had been rather routine.

Chapter Eighteen

October 20, 1968
USS **Erne**
Off the coast of Vietnam

October 20 started out just like all other days; hot and muggy. The ship was slowly churning through the swells approximately four miles off the coast from Cam Ranh Bay. The non-duty personnel were roused from sleep by the 1MC announcing reveille. The last of the heat-subjected sour milk was poured on dry cereal, or rehydrated powdered scrambled eggs were ladled onto metal trays as the crew sat down for breakfast. Sweat-soaked chambray work shirts clung to the frames of the young sailors gathered around the mess deck tables. Those assuming the 0800 watch ate quickly, followed by a quick smoke, in order to relieve the watch. Quarters was soon held for the rest of the crew.

Buddy was not feeling well that morning. His throat was sore, his nose and sinuses were congested, and he had a splitting headache. He was sure he was coming down with a cold. He thought, how strange; getting a cold in weather conditions from hell. He snuffed his nose and went to quarters, fighting off an occasional spell of dizziness. After quarters, Buddy and Dawes broke out primer, brushes, and chipping hammers and were working on the forward mount when they heard:

Attention. Boarding party report to the armory. Boarding party report to the armory.

Both Buddy and Dawes stood up and laid their chipping hammers at the base of the gun mount. "What the hell's going on?" said Dawes.

"Let's go," said Buddy, and he and Dawes headed for the armory. As they came around the corner, they saw that the door of the armory was open. Weapons had already been issued to personnel, and they were moving to the fantail of the ship. The XO was standing at the armory door handing out rifles.

"Glad you're here," said LTJG Bamino. "We got a flash message that we have a junk out here with a bunch of weapons. I went ahead and gave rifles and ammo to the boarding party, because the junk is right off the starboard quarter. You and Dawes grab another rifle and a machine gun and take your places." Dawes picked up the .30 caliber machine gun and an ammo can while Buddy grabbed a rifle and an ammo sling. As the XO walked aft, Buddy closed the armory door and followed him. As he walked aft, he wished to himself that this would not take long. His headache was worse, and he was still fighting waves of dizziness.

As he reached the fantail, he could see that their intended junk was now close by. In only a few moments it would be in a position to board.

Buddy had just helped Dawes place the .30 caliber on its stanchion when he heard, "Miller, come here a minute." It was Senior Chief Gunther who was standing by Schmitt, the new boatswain's mate. Dawes took over at the machine gun, and Buddy grabbed his rifle and walked over to Gunther and Schmitt. Schmitt held a rifle in his hands and was attempting to draw back the slide on the rifle. It would not move. "Miller, trade rifles with Schmitt here. He can't seem to get this one to operate."

"Senior Chief, do you think this is a good idea. Schmitt has never been on a boarding party, and also has not been checked out on the weapons," said Buddy.

"Look. I'm just doing what Kramer ordered me to do. It'll be OK. He told me he has fired M-1's before, and I'll keep an eye on him," said Gunther.

The sailors exchanged rifles, and Gunther and Schmitt followed Ensigns Kramer and Binh who were crawling over the ship's rail to the junk below. As they left, Buddy quickly worked on the rifle, but to his disgust, he discovered it was the old M-1 that was mechanically unsafe for use. Someone had picked up this rifle from the armory and issued it to Schmitt. If Buddy had been at the armory to issue the weapons, it would never have left the armory. Standing at the fantail rail, Buddy carefully made the rifle ready to fire, being careful not to touch the unpredictable trigger. Switching the safety to the off position, he kept the muzzle up as he watched the boarding party on the junk. BM2 Schmitt, with a rifle across his arms, was standing next to Senior Chief Gunther observing. Ensign Kramer was examining the documents of the vessel, with Ensign Binh interpreting. All pertinent data was being recorded in the log book carried by Kramer.

As the boarding party began their search through the junk, Buddy studied the Vietnamese family. There was an older, white-bearded man sitting on the deck with a woman of similar age sitting next to him. A younger man was seated on the deck next to the legs of a standing woman. A black canvas bag was next to this seated man, and a fold of fishing net lay across his lap. This couple appeared to be the parents of four children; two teenaged boys, old enough to help with the tasks involved in a family fishing boat, a teenaged girl, and a younger girl. Buddy thought to himself; so much for the intelligence message the ship had gotten. This was just another family making their living by fishing.

The sun was shining directly in Buddy's vision. He turned slightly to avoid the sun in his eyes, but now could not see all the family members on the boat. For only a second, he glanced up and saw Bob Dawes attentively manning the .30 caliber. Turning his attention back to the boat, he could only partially see the family as he watched Ensign Kramer and the petty officer searching the boat. It seemed to be another routine stop, and Buddy's mind relaxed slightly, followed by the muscles in his hands, arms and shoulders.

"He's got a gun!" shouted BM2 Schmitt.

The synapses in Buddy's brain crackled to life sending millisecond flashes the length and breadth of his body. The resultant scenario was also carried out in milliseconds. Buddy's head turned with all focus on the occupants of the fishing junk. The rifle barrel followed as if he were tracking a pheasant in flight. A micro-glimpse of the seated fisherman signaled Buddy's brain. The man was removing a black handled instrument from the black canvas bag. The man's hand was wrapped around the black handle, which was now fully visible. Buddy's rapidly firing neural network sent the message to prepare to apply pressure to Buddy's trigger finger to fire the rifle. Other impulses sent doubt signals in the brain, overriding any command to pull the trigger. As a result, Buddy's index trigger finger only exerted enough pressure to keep the finger in place on the trigger. But even so, the infinitely light pressure on the trigger of the malfunctioning rifle caused its own chain of events, from which there would be no pause. Metal acted against other metal in the inner workings of the firing block of the rifle. The spring-loaded bolt was released and slammed its pin into the center of the primer at the rear of the cartridge case, causing an explosion, and sending a lead projectile from the muzzle of the rifle. The entire incident had taken place in a time span of less than two and a half seconds.

A curl of smoke wafted away on the breeze as it escaped the muzzle of the old M-1 rifle. All eyes on the ship and the junk turned to the man who had been sitting on the deck. He was now lying on the deck in a curious pose. His body was slightly twisted from the direction his head faced. Shining crimson liquid covered the entire left side of his head and face. His hand still gripped the black-handled gun. Only it was not a gun. Ensign Kramer had knelt beside the man and lifted his hand. The instrument that had been declared a gun, clattered to the deck of the junk. It was a black-handled fisherman's tool. The handle was indeed, pistol-grip shaped, but it was attached to a curved shaft with a blunt hook on the end of the shaft. The tool was used for repairing fishing nets.

Kramer continued to hold the man's hand. He clumsily felt for a pulse. None was discernible. Kramer looked up at the bridge of the *Erne* and shook his head from side to side, triggering a screeching, high-pitched keening by female members of the family. The ship's corpsman was hurriedly sent over to the junk. He too felt for the man's pulse and subsequently shook his head. He could find no pulse and was, therefore, sure the man was dead.

The booming voice of Captain Yates called out. "Mr. Kramer, bring your boarding party back aboard immediately."

Kramer was still looking at the face of the man, and then at his wife. "Aye, aye, Captain." His eyes then turned to the four children. The stare returned by one of the teenage boys made his blood run cold. The boy's eyes seemed to enlarge, and a deadly, hot, seething anger could be seen in the light of his eyes. Kramer shuddered. "Boarding party back to the ship!" he said. Buddy had also seen the deadly look in the teen-ager's eyes.

Buddy had not moved since the shooting. He was only partially aware when Senior Chief Gunther and Ensign Kramer removed the rifle from his hands. But as they removed the rifle and attempted to eject the clip from the weapon, it inexplicably fired another round. This bullet hurtled into the air harmlessly.

"The damn gun is haunted!" said Gunther.

At the sound of the second shot, Buddy appeared to faint. He slumped onto the deck of the ship. Buddy's exhausted brain slowed down. He was only dimly aware of the angry radio conversation erupting from the speakers on the bridge of the ship, where it was heard by all topside personnel. Captain Yates had wasted no time in reporting the incident to his superiors and was being directed to take the ship into port at Da Nang. He was ordered to report to the field office of the Military Assistance Command Vietnam (MACV). Following the order, the ship made a slow turn to starboard.

The corpsman quickly looked at Buddy. He looked up at Senior Chief Gunther and Ensign Kramer and said that he thought Buddy must be suffering from shock. At the chief's direction, Buddy was carried to the berthing compartment and placed in his bunk.

Senior Chief Gunther turned to Ensign Kramer. "Sir, I'll take the log book into CIC while you go talk to the Captain." Ensign Kramer handed over the log book and headed for the bridge for what he believed would probably be the ass chewing of his life. He was correct.

All armament was returned to the armory, where Bob Dawes again stowed all articles in their proper place. Except for one item, which he hid where only he could find it later.

Senior Chief Gunther did not go directly to CIC with the log book. Instead, he went to the ship's office. YN2 Briggs was sitting in the office typing on his IBM Selectric typewriter. The print ball whizzed and spun around as the yeoman typed. He looked up when the Senior Chief came in. "What's up Senior Chief?"

"I just need to make a couple copies," replied Gunther. He then placed the green log book on the Xerox machine, and made several copies of pages in the book. "OK, Briggs. We needed a copy of a couple pages out of the boarding party's log book. Thanks for the use of your copier."

"Anytime, Senior Chief," said Briggs, and he returned to his typing.

Gunther folded the copies he had made and stuffed them in his pocket. Then he took the log book to CIC.

*****

Through the remainder of the day and that evening, the *Erne* steamed north and northwest toward Da Nang. As they approached the port in darkness, the *Erne* would hold short of entering Da Nang and wait for sunrise. The ship would anchor well off the coast and enter the harbor in the morning. Later that night, as the ship rocked slowly while held firmly by its anchor, no moonlight was visible as the sky was overcast with a low ceiling of clouds. Complete darkness at 0100 hid the two figures who stealthily opened the door to the armory and entered. They were overheard as they spoke quietly.

"Damn it, Schmitt, are you sure this is the one?"

BM2 Schmitt was not positive, and he was scared. He was sure he was somehow going to get in trouble over this whole incident, and even more so if he did not say what the officer wanted to hear. "Y, y, yes sir," he stammered. "I'm pretty positive."

"Good. You keep your damned mouth shut about this. You got that?" said the officer.

"Yes sir."

The officer locked the armory, and under cover of darkness, carried the rifle aft and climbed the ladder to the upper deck, while the stunned boatswain's mate followed closely behind the commanding officer.

GMSN Bob Dawes had the roving mid-watch. In the pitch-black dark, he was crouched on hands and knees behind the deck bollards. He had heard the entire conversation between the two conspirators. He whispered to himself, "Holy shit!"

On the opposite side of the ship, also in hiding, another figure had heard most of the conversation and subsequently melted into the darkness.

*****

Buddy was not showing any signs of improvement throughout the night. In the morning, when the corpsman checked on him again, the corpsman found that Buddy had a temperature of one hundred and one. Therefore, he made his recommendation to the XO. Later in the morning, when the ship docked in Da Nang, a call was made by the corpsman. In less than thirty minutes, a military ambulance arrived on the pier. Buddy Miller was taken from the ship and placed in the Da Nang military hospital. He was quickly diagnosed as having a raging case of malaria.

The ship would not be leaving Da Nang for several days. A full investigation was being conducted into the shooting of a Vietnamese civilian by a member of the crew of the *Erne*. Each morning after quarters, Lieutenant Sam Yates, the Commanding Officer of the *Erne*, and Ensign Jack Kramer, the ship's First Lieutenant reported to the Navy Judge Advocate's Office on the Da Nang base. Also in attendance at these meetings were special agents of the Naval Investigative Service; the Chief of Staff of the Mine Squadron, who had flown to Da Nang from Sasebo as soon as word of the incident had been received in Japan; and Navy JAG attorneys from MACV and Naval Forces Japan. Captain Yates was being grilled by all of these people. Each day, Yates would return to the ship in a foul mood. At dinner time, the CO would leave the ship to frequent the Officer's Club on base for dinner and drinks. He would return to the ship at midnight, demonstrating an uncertainty in his walk caused by a more than adequate intake of spirits. The cycle repeated itself for three days. On the fourth day, only the CO attended the meeting, and he returned to the ship in the afternoon in much better spirits. He and the XO went to dinner that evening. Later, they both returned to the ship with neither exhibiting signs of over indulging.

For two full days after the incident, Bob Dawes carried out his duties but remained deep in thought. He was at a loss as to what he should do. After quarters on the third day, he knocked on the door to the chief's quarters and asked to speak to Senior Chief Gunther. The old chief and the young sailor walked to the supply office. The chief opened the door to the office.

"Cosgrove, here's four bits. Go get yourself a Coke and make your-self scarce. I'm going to use your office for an hour."

Cosgrove protested. "This is my office, Senior Chief. You can't make me get out."

Gunther took one step toward Cosgrove, threw the two quarters on his desk, and stood looking down menacingly at the storekeeper.

"All right, all right. I'm leaving, but I'll be back in an hour," mumbled Cosgrove.

"You can come back in your office when I'm gone. I'll leave the door open when I'm finished," replied the Senior Chief.

For the next hour and a half, the supply office door remained closed. Bob Dawes left no detail out of his discussion with the old Senior Chief.

Nothing that Dawes told Senior Chief Gunther surprised him. Senior Chief Boatswain's Mate Raymond (Ray) Gunther had nearly thirty years of naval service under his belt. He had been around the world on a number of Navy ships and had served under some of the finest skippers in the Navy, as well as some of the worst. He had seen the best in men and the worst in men. Men working under his supervision in the deck gangs were not generally known as the brain trust of a ship. Ray Gunther was an anomaly. He possessed the intelligence and reasoning ability to have been successful at any college. But coming from a poor family, college had not been an option. Instead, he chose to make the Navy his career. He was a natural leader and teacher who gained a tremendous amount of satisfaction in seeing young men excel and reap the rewards of his teaching. He also had an innate ability to quickly determine the character, work ethic, and moral compass of a young man by observing the individual for just a few hours. He was seldom wrong in his assessments. But it was not just the young enlisted men that he carefully observed. He had the uncanny ability to size up, in the same manner, the young commissioned officers with whom he served, and at the present time he was feeling very uncomfortable serving under Lieutenant Sam Yates.

Chapter Nineteen

On the fifth day in port, the behemoth shape of the *Kawishiwi* was unceremoniously pushed into place by yard tugs and took up the berth on the opposite side of the pier to which the *Erne* was moored. The oiler had minor mechanical problems which could be fixed more easily while the ship was attached to shore power and water. If all went according to plan, they would put back to sea in two or three days. That afternoon, there was a visitor in the chief's quarters on the *Kawishiwi*. The old Senior Chief and the new Senior Chief huddled over Cokes and quietly conferred. Late that evening, under cover of darkness, Senior Chief Gunther crossed the brow of the *Erne* with a package, carefully wrapped in a canvas tarp. He walked down the pier and once again climbed the gangway ladder of the *Kawishiwi*. He returned to the minesweeper three hours later.

*****

It had been six days. Buddy Miller was responding to the medical treatment. The headaches were diminishing, and his fever was under control. It would be a few days before he could be released back to his command. His doctor was a young, very able, Army captain. After thoroughly questioning Buddy, he had theorized that Buddy had been bitten by a malaria-infected mosquito somewhere in the ship's travels in the recent weeks. The exact location was immaterial. The outcome had been certain.

Even though the immediate medical problem experienced by Buddy Miller was under control, a larger, more difficult problem was beginning. The nightmares had begun. Each dream began with the deafening sound of gunfire. This was followed by a thick haze of impenetrable gun smoke. In his dream, Buddy tried mightily, but was unable to see through the roiling, deep, gray haze. Ever so slowly, the twisting and turning haze began changing color. It became faint yellow, followed by a more vivid orange. Finally it turned blood red, still writhing angrily. Slowly, the haze began emitting droplets of blood. The droplets enlarged and ran to the bottom of the vision. Then, the upper part of the haze also dropped slowly until the vision was clear, revealing a new horrific sound and scene. Two screaming women and two younger girls were standing in a circle. Within the circle was a man lying prone on a wooden platform. The women parted slightly to reveal more of the man. The upper part of the man's torso held his head. But it was not a full head. It was only half of a head. The left half was missing. In its place was a flat red sheen of blood. The half face, with its one eye, looked directly at Buddy. The eye shone like a dull, pulsating orange light. The half mouth curved in a downward slanting sneer. Then the man's right arm rose. In the grip of the man's hand was a fishing net repair hook with a black handle. While the four wailing women shrieked even more loudly, the male apparition then lunged the hook of the tool forward at Buddy. At this point, Buddy always woke, drenched in sweat, gasping for breath.

During his daily rounds, Buddy's attending physician asked Buddy many of the same questions each day. He was aware from nurses' reports that Buddy was not sleeping well. He questioned Buddy about this, and, with a furrowed brow, made hasty notes in Buddy's medical file. Eventually, the doctor had no further reason to keep him in the medical ward, and Buddy was released from the hospital and returned to full duty on the *Erne*.

*****

When he returned to the ship, Buddy found himself to be a pariah. He was avoided by the majority of the crew and all of the officers. To the enlisted men, he was acknowledged to be someone in trouble. Staying away from Buddy was done in order that some of the guilt didn't "rub off" on any of them. It was not as if they disliked GM3 Miller. They just preferred to keep their distance. The officers were even colder in their treatment of Buddy. They knew their skipper was under fire in the midst of an investigation. No officer on the ship wanted to appear to take sides other than being on the side of the CO. It would be very detrimental to their treatment and their future careers to cause any perception otherwise. The exceptions to this cold treatment were Dawes, Fig Newton, and Senior Chief Gunther. For reasons unbeknownst to Buddy, the old senior chief had no qualms about conversing with Buddy; even to the point of asking him more questions about the incident. Many of his questions centered on the mechanical condition of the rifle which Buddy had been holding at the time of the shooting. Buddy was grateful to his friends, but was still sensing a severe loneliness brought on by his treatment by the rest of the crew.

Buddy's ostracism did not last long. Early one morning, an attractive woman crossed the brow carrying a briefcase. She was dressed in officer's khakis, wearing a skirt and low black heels. She had a gold maple leaf on her right collar point, and a Judge Advocate General (JAG) Corps insignia on the left collar point. She saluted the ensign and was escorted to the Captain's cabin. Five minutes later, the CO left the ship. He did not seem to be in a pleasant mood as he hurried across the ship's brow. A few moments later, the messenger of the watch came to Buddy and told him that he was to report to the Captain's cabin. Buddy had no idea what this was about.

He climbed the interior ladder to the upper deck and knocked on the CO's door. He was taken aback when a female lieutenant commander opened the door.

"Are you GM3 Buddy Miller," she asked.

"Yes, ma'am."

"Miller, I am Lieutenant Commander Joan Anderson. I have been appointed by the Judge Advocate General to be your defense attorney in the special court martial proceedings."

Court Martial! Court Martial! The words clanged in Buddy's brain. His stomach rolled. "What court martial, ma'am?" It was all Buddy could think of to say.

LCDR Anderson then elaborated. "From your reaction, I guess no one had the decency to even tell you that you have been charged under the Uniform Code of Military Justice and that a court martial will soon be convened. Is that right?"

Buddy nodded. Numbness washed over him. How could this be happening, he thought.

For the next few minutes, Buddy and LCDR Anderson talked informally and got to know each other. All the while they were talking, Joan Anderson made methodical notes on a yellow legal pad. She explained that she was from Texas and had come into the Navy under a program in which the Navy assisted her in paying for law school at Southern Methodist University. Under contract, at the completion of law school, she entered the Navy JAG Corps.

After informalities, LCDR Anderson's demeanor became strictly businesslike while she explained that an informal investigation had been completed; the result of which was that the commanding officer of the *Erne* believed that the violation of the UCMJ was so severe, and that there was sufficient evidence surrounding the shooting incident to warrant the convening of a special court martial. She went on to explain that by virtue of Captain Yates junior rank, he did not have the authority to convene a court martial. Therefore, the Commanding Officer of the Mine Squadron would be the convening authority. In addition, she attempted to bolster Buddy's feelings by explaining that a special court martial is the intermediate level of court martial, and that they were fortunate that the upcoming proceedings would not be a more serious general court martial. She then carefully went through the intricacies of the military's form of trying a case in court. She explained that Buddy had been charged under the Uniform Code of Military Justice. The charges against him were under Article 892, Failure to obey an order or regulation; and Article 134, the "catch-all" article that can be phrased to include "bringing discredit upon the armed forces."

With a lump in his throat, Buddy asked, "Am I going to jail, Commander?"

"Not if I can help it," said Anderson. At the end of thirty minutes, LCDR Anderson asked Buddy if he wanted a Coke. Buddy said yes. She cranked the handle on the ship's internal squawk box phone, rang the ship's quarterdeck, and asked the quarterdeck watch to send the messenger of the watch to the captain's cabin. After a moment, there was a rap on the door. She opened it, handed the shocked sailor two dollars and told him to get her two Cokes. While they waited, LCDR Anderson asked a multitude of questions. She asked him all about his family, the family farm, his hobbies, his interests, and his participation in sports. The answers to those questions gave the attorney a candid picture regarding the character of GM3 Buddy Miller. Even in that short discussion, she had formed the opinion that she was defending a young man of good character and morals. This assessment served to make her task somewhat less daunting. They paused when the messenger brought them their soft drinks.

Another half hour of questioning passed, and LCDR Anderson had nearly filled a yellow legal pad with notes. She left no rock unturned. Buddy was exhausted and had a pounding headache. Her final questions were about Buddy's friends in the Navy. Who were they, and where were they located? They talked about friends he had on the *Kawishiwi* as well as those on the *Erne*. LCDR Anderson finally set her pen down on her legal pad and flexed her tired writing fingers. Buddy thought they were finished.

"Now it's your turn, Miller," said Anderson. "I want you to ask me any question that comes into your mind. Give me all your thoughts about the incident and tell me anything that you think I should know." Time once again passed quickly as Buddy, through the pain of his pounding headache, narrated everything he could about life on the *Erne* and the incident in specificity. LCDR Anderson at last dropped her pen for the final time.

"I want to thank you for your time, Miller. You have been very help-ful." LCDR Anderson reached into her briefcase and gave two business cards to Buddy. "I want you to give one of these cards to Senior Chief Gunther and tell him to call me. Will you do that?"

"Yes, ma'am," said Buddy.

"I have a set of temporary orders here for you." She retrieved some papers from her briefcase. "These orders will get you off the *Erne* while the court proceedings are going on. You probably don't want to stay here right now, do you?"

Buddy acknowledged that he would be more comfortable somewhere else.

"I have a Bachelor Enlisted Quarters (BEQ) reservation for you. You will have to report to our office each morning after chow just so we know you haven't run off somewhere; not that you've got anywhere to go in Vietnam. Then you will carry out the remainder of the day under temporary duty with the base armory. As a good gunner's mate, I'm sure you can help those guys out at the armory. So, the bottom line is that you will not be confined, but you are only to be at one of five places on the base. If you are not at my office, and I need to call you, I will call your BEQ room, the chow hall, the armory, or the base gym. If I can't reach you, you could end up in bigger trouble. Do you understand?"

"Yes, ma'am," said Buddy.

"Our next meeting will be at the MACV JAG office after I have had a chance to talk to some other witnesses; probably in two or three days. I will call you to set up the meeting. In the meantime, if you think you need to talk to me, my number is on the card. The trial is set for one week from today. But most of these trials get pushed back a day or two. It'll be tight, but we will be ready. It would probably be a good idea if you packed up your gear and went on over to the BEQ while the CO is gone. Make sure you give a copy of those orders to the ship's office so the XO sees them." She looked him in the eye. "I think it's going to be OK, Miller."

"Yes, ma'am," said Buddy, but he felt no confidence.

*****

Bob Dawes sat on his bunk and watched as his friend stuffed his belongings into his sea bag. Buddy was almost done packing and was anxious to leave the ship. Buddy walked with Dawes through the berthing compartment, then the mess decks and aft to the fantail. Fig Newton and Senior Chief Gunther were waiting near the brow to say farewell. Buddy put his sea bag on the deck and straightened his white hat. He looked down at his shoes as he said, "I'll miss you guys."

Senior Chief Gunther put his hand on Buddy's shoulder. "Keep your chin up, Miller. I have a feeling that we haven't seen the last of you yet." The Chief glanced at Bob Dawes, but quickly returned his eyes to those of Buddy. "If you get really hard up for company, give one of us a call and we'll come over to the 'Q' and play cards or something."

"Yeah, we'll even bring the beer," said Fig.

The three men watched as Buddy hoisted the sea bag to his shoulder and made his way down the pier. As Buddy walked away, Gunther and Dawes left the fantail and went their separate ways. No one heard as Senior Chief Gunther mumbled under his breath as he walked back to chief's quarters, "I'm gonna get that little son of a bitch."

His friends had predicted it. He was already lonely for company after he had shown his orders to the desk clerk at the BEQ, gotten his key, and checked into his room.

*****

Buddy settled into a routine. In the evening, he either watched a movie that was broadcast on the base television station, or he read. Then he went to sleep. Every night at approximately one a.m. the same frightening nightmare unfolded, awakening him. He would try to read for a while and finally get back to sleep. He figured he was only getting a maximum of four hours of sleep at night. He got out of bed at six a.m., showered, shaved, and dressed. Then he walked to the base chow hall, ate breakfast, and came back to his room. He brushed his teeth, made up his bunk, and walked to the JAG office at seven thirty, where he said good morning to the civilian receptionist who wrote his name in her desk calendar. Buddy then walked nearly a mile to the base armory to go to work. He had had one more meeting with LCDR Anderson, but his confidence level did not rise following that meeting. The attorney had told him that they would meet one more time before the trial.

November 5, 1968
Dear Mom and Dad,

I am sorry to tell you that I have gotten myself into some trouble. While we were searching a Vietnamese junk for contraband, I accidently shot a fisherman who was on the boat. It was a bad mistake. I don't know what will happen to me. The Navy is going to take me to a court martial and I am really scared. The Navy gave me an attorney and she seems to be very good. But I sure wish I knew how this was going to come out. Please don't worry about me. Maybe say a prayer for me. I miss all of you.

Love, Buddy

Chapter Twenty

Military Advisory Command, Vietnam (MACV)
Munitions Storage Facility
Da Nang, South Vietnam

The work Buddy was temporarily assigned to was interesting. He became friends with a couple of the permanently assigned army guys who worked in the armory. Buddy had never seen a large cache of munitions such as that contained in the warehouse armory. The armory held the entire gamut of military ammunition. The partially in-ground warehouse covered two acres and was a depository for small arms rounds, medium caliber ammunition, mortar rounds, artillery rounds, and rows and rows of bombs to be used primarily by the Air Force. The main responsibilities of the men working at the facility were to receive new shipments, properly store the munitions, and issue ammunition to commands as they arrived in trucks to pick up their supplies. Buddy had quickly caught on to the procedures and soon learned to drive a fork lift for moving and lifting the cases of ammunition and pallets of bombs.

One day, he was working with his Army friend, Sergeant Ben Carson, in the aircraft ordinance area, moving pallets of bombs to storage. As they worked, they noticed three Air Force Officers and a civilian walking toward the pallets of bombs. The civilian had a lanyard around his neck which held an ID card with his picture, his name, and the company name, Honeywell, on it. He was obviously a military contractor. He was carrying a stack of papers on a clipboard. The officers were particularly interested in one pallet and were poring over the data sheets attached to the pallet. They compared this data to the sheets held by the civilian. They carefully examined the bombs' fins, the cable assemblies attached to the fuse heads, and the pointed fuses on each bomb. Their conversation became rather loud and heated. They motioned to Sergeant Carson to come and talk with them. Ben joined the three officers while Buddy continued to work. After talking with Ben, the three senior officers and civilian soon left, and Ben returned to his fork lift.

When they had a moment to talk, Buddy asked Ben, "What was that all about?"

Ben replied. "Well, I don't have all of the details since I never get out of this place to hear the latest gouge. But there is talk that some of the Air Force fly boys are getting killed by those bombs; something to do with defective fuses. The rumor is that several pilots have been killed by the bombs detonating as they are released from the plane, rather than when they reach the ground target. Supposedly, several pilots who were carrying that bomb on their planes have been killed. Heck, there has been a bunch of brass coming in to this place looking at that particular bomb. They all just stand around scratching their heads and taking notes, but it doesn't seem to make any difference. The same model bomb keeps getting shipped here, and we just keep sending it out to the Air Force guys. Way above my pay grade, but it sort of seems to me that if there is a problem, then something should be done about it. Rumor is that somebody is covering it up. At least that's what I hear. But I don't know anything. I'm just a lowly sergeant."

Buddy's curiosity was piqued. He hopped off his fork lift, walked over to the pallet that had been examined earlier, and studied the bombs. Ben watched him, but continued carrying out his work. Soon he joined Buddy.

"So what do you suppose makes these things go off prematurely?" asked Buddy.

"Your guess is as good as mine," said Ben. "But I also hear they are working on some kind of new smart bomb. It's going to be guided by some kind of special light, called a laser. Beats the crap out of me what that could be. But it will probably make these old mechanical fused bombs obsolete. C'mon, let's get back to work."

Chapter Twenty-One

November 15, 1968
Office of the Judge Advocate General
Da Nang, South Vietnam

It was all he could do to keep the piece of toast and glass of milk down as he walked to the JAG office that morning. His stomach was tied in a knot. At 0800 the sun had cleared the surrounding hills and the heat was already bearing down on the military base. Buddy's tropical white uniform shirt was beginning to stick to his back. The trial was to begin at 0900, and he was to meet LCDR Anderson at her office. The court room was in the same building.

LCDR Joan Anderson was ready. She yawned. She had not left her office until nearly midnight the night before. During the past few days, her witnesses had been prepped and told what time to arrive in the court room. Evidence was secured and would be brought to the courtroom. She finished her third mug of steaming black coffee just as Buddy Miller was shown to her office.

"Good morning, Miller. How are you feeling this morning?" said Anderson. She was dressed in her khaki uniform.

"Not very good, ma'am," said Buddy. He looked as bad as he felt. He had tossed and turned most of the night before, getting little, if any, sleep.

"Well, I gotta tell you, Miller, I feel pretty darn good. I think you are going to be surprised at what happens today. You want some coffee?" said Anderson.

"Mmm, no ma'am. My stomach doesn't feel very good right now."

"OK, just sit tight there. I've got a few things I need to write down here and then we can head out," said the attorney. But first, she rose from her desk and walked to the side where she opened a locker. She retrieved a set of tropical whites on hangers and carried the uniform out the door of the office. She returned in a few minutes dressed in the whites and carrying the khakis. She laid the khakis on a chair and returned to her desk, where she began writing once again.

At ten minutes until nine, on an overcast morning on November 15, 1968, less than a month since the unfortunate shooting of the civilian, LCDR Joan Anderson and GM3 Buddy Miller walked into the court room. All eyes turned to watch them take their places at a table. Their table was one of two that faced another longer table. At the table next to them were seated two Navy JAG officers, a lieutenant and a lieutenant commander. They would be the prosecuting attorneys representing the mine squadron commander.

In a few minutes, six men entered the court room and took their seats at that long table. A JAG Corps Navy captain sat in the center. He would be the presiding official, equivalent to the judge in the case. The other members of the court martial panel were two Navy Commanders, an Army Lieutenant Colonel, a Marine Corps Lieutenant Colonel, and a Navy gunner's mate master chief. They would serve as the deciding panel, equivalent to a jury. A court reporter sat to the side of the panel. A Navy first class petty officer, wearing a legal aide insignia on his sleeve, stood by the closed door of the hearing room.

The make-up of the panel was a bit unusual, as it included members from branches of the military other than the Navy. It reflected the fact that with individual mission priorities, and the backlog of JAG cases, it was sometimes difficult to secure a panel comprised of members from a single branch of the service.

The captain at the center of the long table spoke. "Good morning, counselors. My name is Captain William Marshall, and I will be the presiding official at these proceedings today."

For the next few minutes Captain Marshall read through a presentation of the procedures that the court martial would follow. He also stated that he had already sequestered the witnesses in the case. They were being held in various offices in the building. After completing his reading, he turned and faced Buddy. "Petty Officer Third Class Jericho W. Miller, you are charged with two infractions of the Uniform Code of Military Justice. They are Section 892, Article 92; 'Failure to obey an order or regulation, resulting in the shooting of a Vietnamese civilian;' and Section 934, Article 134, 'Bringing discredit to the Armed Forces, specifically the Navy.' Has your attorney advised you of the charges against you?"

Buddy was a bit surprised when he heard his formal name and that the Captain had addressed him. He quickly recovered. "Yes, sir."

Captain Marshall then turned and asked the prosecution table if they were ready to try the case. His question was answered affirmatively by LCDR Todd Boyd, the lead prosecuting attorney.

LCDR Boyd had just told another of his characteristic stretches of the truth. LCDR Todd Boyd was a product of a moneyed Eastern family. He had never truly worked a full day in his life including a considerable portion of the nine years he had been in the Navy. When faced with naval law cases, he relied very heavily on his legal staff and junior officers to carry the load.

Well over a decade ago, when Todd Boyd approached high school graduation, he only half-heartedly applied to several colleges. This was at the frenetic urging of his father who was wise enough to know that the military draft was imminently facing his son, unless he pulled some strings with family friends to get his son into an acceptable college. Boyd had subsequently attended a fine Ivy League school, to which his father had contributed large sums of money. Todd Boyd was not a stupid young man. On the contrary, he was very intelligent. But applying himself to work tasks and to academic rigors was not his forte. Hence, his father's contributions to the university had certainly helped Todd Boyd gain admittance to the school, and he completed his undergraduate work with little difficulty, while achieving an enviable grade point average. Acceptance and completion of law school was accomplished under similar circumstances, but the strength of his academic record along with his lack of personal life challenges meant that Todd Boyd was admitted to and attended a third tier law school, wherein his competition from fellow classmates was not overly challenging. To his credit, Todd Boyd had finally managed to focus his intellect in order to complete law school, which he did handily. And somewhat surprisingly, at the conclusion of law school, Boyd, by a very slim margin, passed the bar exam.

Having ensured that his son graduated from law school, albeit a less prestigious institution, Boyd's father also knew that there was value to having a military officer's experience on a resume. He knew the experience could perhaps help his son later gain employment in a better law firm and/or enter politics at some point in his career. So, once again, his family's influence with their elected representatives in Washington helped to guide Todd Boyd to a Navy direct commission in the JAG corps, which would then allow Boyd to practice military law.

Due to the mercurial nature of the military during time of war, Boyd had now been around long enough to have served under several different commanding officers. Yet, his military experience was not stellar. He had served as second chair on a multitude of cases, but his solo performances had never been taxing cases. He was assigned to cases such as extended AWOLs and failure to pay debts and could successfully process those cases in his sleep. In the Miller case, he had miscalculated. He thought this case was also simple. After all, Miller had shot an innocent civilian, and that seemed pretty cut and dried. As a result, he had not properly researched and prepared for the case. His lack of attention would soon come back to bite him.

Contrary to what should have been a conscientious, comprehensive study of the case, LCDR Boyd had not investigated this case in detail, nor had he conducted thorough, in-depth interviews and preparation of his witness, and those of the defense. He left that to the legal aides in his office and the junior officer who had accompanied him and who would sit in the second chair. In this case, his subordinates had failed him. He just didn't know it yet. He was also relying on the testimony of one prosecution witness. This was also a mistake. Yet, he believed this case was locked up. The kid had shot a civilian, case closed.

Oh yes, another item of interest was that LCDR Boyd was certified at the bar, sometimes the wrong one. The previous evening at the officer's club on the Da Nang base, LCDR Boyd and his junior attorney had imbibed in far too many bar spirits. Boyd was not even remotely mentally or physically prepared for trial. Sadly, he was unaware of the complexity of this case.

Captain Marshall then turned to LCDR Anderson and said, "Commander Anderson, are you prepared to try this case." She also answered affirmatively.

"Very well, then. Prosecution may present its first witness," said Captain Marshall.

"Prosecution calls Lieutenant Samuel Yates," said LCDR Boyd, as he rose and smiled at Captain Marshall.

Once again, Buddy was sure his stomach was going to embarrass him. Nausea gripped him as the court room door opened, and Sam Yates entered. The stoic expression on the face of Lieutenant Yates belied the fact that he was just as nervous as Buddy Miller. But he was confident that his status as a commissioned officer in the world's greatest Navy would put this matter to rest at the expense of a mere third class petty officer. Captain Marshall swore him in and listened as Lieutenant Yates held his hand aloft and swore that he would tell the truth. He then took the chair that was located to the side of the panel.

For nearly an hour, LCDR Boyd asked questions of the Commanding Officer of the *Erne*. He established the fine military record of the Lieutenant, and what a fine fellow Sam Yates was. These were all "soft ball" questions meant to paint a picture that the Lieutenant was a superlative junior Navy officer, above reproach in this most unfortunate affair that happened to occur on Lieutenant Yates' impeccable ship. At the end of an hour, Captain Marshall declared a ten minute recess. When the court reconvened, LCDR Boyd resumed his questioning of Lieutenant Yates, asking more specific questions.

"Lieutenant Yates, did you observe Petty Officer Miller shoot a Vietnamese fisherman on October 20, 1968?"

"Yes, sir, I did," answered Yates.

"Was Petty Officer Miller under orders to shoot the fisherman?"

"No, sir, he was not."

"Were the fisherman and his family a threat to your ship, Lieutenant Yates?" said Boyd.

"No sir, I don't believe they were."

"Do you base that opinion on the fact that their documents were all in order?" asked Boyd. LCDR Boyd had just committed a rookie error. He had asked a question for which he did not know the answer.

Unsure of how to answer the question, Yates simply answered, "No."

Himself now confused, Boyd pressed on. "Do you mean that you did not base your opinion on the documents, or that their documents were not in order?"

It took ten full seconds for Lieutenant Yates to answer, but he finally said, "I don't know if their documents were in order."

Stepping further into the mire, Boyd asked, "Lieutenant Yates, doesn't the ship keep a record of the names of the owners of water craft that you inspect?"

"Yes sir, but when I looked at the log book, there was no entry for that inspection. It appears that Ensign Kramer, who kept the log book had not completed an entry yet when the incident occurred," said Yates.

Unknown by every individual in the court room, save one, the Commanding Officer of the USS *Erne* had just crossed the unseen, but always felt, line of ethical behavior and had perjured himself.

Boyd then moved on to another topic.

"Lieutenant Yates, did you know Gunner's Mate Third Class Miller well?" asked Boyd.

"Yes. I believe so," answered Yates.

"Would you say that he was a 'squared away sailor,' an impressive sailor?"

"Oh, I wouldn't say that he was impressive. He was just an ordinary sailor, I think," answered Yates.

"Is Petty Officer Miller the only gunner's mate on the *Erne*?"

"No, there is also a gunner's mate striker. He was even less squared away than Miller," said Yates.

"Umm, would that be Gunner's Mate Seaman Robert Dawes?"

"Yes, sir," answered Yates.

"Lieutenant Yates, as I understand it, the *Erne* has recently been involved in Operation Market Time. Is that correct?"

"Yes, sir."

LCDR Boyd was trying his best to phrase his questions so that Lieutenant Yates would need to speak as little as possible.

"I understand that under the procedures of Market Time, your ship was authorized to stop, board, and search Vietnamese vessels for contraband. Is that correct?"

Again Yates answered affirmatively.

"Lieutenant Yates, in order to carry out your duties, were you given directives and procedures for dealing with a non-cooperative and/or combative crew of a vessel you were searching? In other words, did you have written rules of engagement in these circumstances?"

Yates answered, "Yes, sir, we certainly did. They were promulgated by MACV to all units assigned to Operation Market Time."

LCDR Boyd pulled a paper from the stack in front of him on his table and showed the paper to Lieutenant Yates.

"Lieutenant Yates, is this a copy of those rules of engagement?"

Yates answered that it was.

"Do those rules of engagement allow a sailor on your ship to indiscriminately shoot at a Vietnamese civilian?" asked Boyd.

"No. There must be specific cause to open fire," said Yates.

"In your opinion, Lieutenant Yates, was there sufficient cause for Petty Officer Miller to open fire on the civilian?"

"No, I do not believe there was," answered Yates.

"And, was everyone involved in the boarding party, including those sailors holding guns while the boarding was in process, required to have read and signed a copy of these rules of engagement?" asked Boyd.

"Yes, sir."

"Lieutenant Yates, it is my understanding that Petty Officer Miller was in those boarding parties. Did Petty Officer Miller sign those rules of engagement?"

"Yes, sir, he did."

"Lieutenant Yates, have you ever seen Miller's signed copy of the rules?"

"No, sir. But I have been assured by my First Lieutenant, Ensign Kramer, that they were signed by Miller," answered Yates.

LCDR Anderson quickly raised her hand and verbally objected to the hearsay evidence. Her objection was sustained by Captain Marshall.

Lieutenant Samuel Yates was a Naval Academy graduate. He was typical of many of the Navy's career officers at that time. Their careers were guided by both written principles, as well as several unwritten principles. One unwritten principle was that Officer Fitness Reports, written by the officer's superior, could make or break an officer's career. Therefore, an officer must always strive to do exemplary, unblemished work, thereby gaining favor with his superior who would write the report. Another principle was that in order for an officer to be promoted more readily, the officer must strive for and achieve command of a Navy ship at sea. By virtue of his unblemished, and seemingly stellar career so far, Lieutenant Sam Yates had achieved both of these goals early in his career. But there was another unwritten principle that was generally never discussed. It was the "CYA" principle.

The "cover your ass" principle is not unique to the Navy. Indeed, it appears in the hallowed halls of government, academia, and private industry. In all likelihood, it rears its ugly head in all endeavors occupied by men of flawed character. In its Navy form, it meant that if anything detrimental was about to occur, or had occurred, an officer possessing said flawed character needed to be prepared to defend his actions, even if it meant sacrificing a person junior in rank to do so; or tailoring a story which might contain somewhat stretched half-truths, or outright untruths, in order to again deflect the blame for an incident to someone other than that officer. Lieutenant Samuel Yates was determined that his career would not be besmirched by this whole ugly incident. The "cover your ass" principle had just been skillfully demonstrated by a struggling and very apprehensive Lieutenant Sam Yates.

Lieutenant Yates had been interviewed and prepped for this court martial by the demonstrably short-sighted LCDR Boyd. In his preparatory meetings with Boyd, Sam Yates felt that many of the details of the case had been blithely passed over and/or ignored by LCDR Boyd. Yates was not sure if Boyd had demonstrated the proper skill in moving the blame for the incident away from him. As a result, he was very uneasy sitting on the witness stand. But his ingrained arrogance allowed him to believe that ultimate due process would throw the blame for this incident squarely in the lap of the junior petty officer, GM3 Buddy Miller. In fact, he had taken certain precautions to ensure that outcome would occur.

Lieutenant Yates was not the only person in the room paying close attention to the questions of LCDR Todd Boyd. Captain William Marshall was closely watching the performance of Boyd. As a nearly thirty-year practicing attorney who had seldom lost his assigned cases, he was highly respected. His record was impeccable. It was not chance luck that placed him in the position of presiding official/judge in this case. Instead, it was demonstrated, skillful expertise which placed him in the role as the judge. As an expert in his craft, he could spot a phony a mile away. As he watched Boyd in action his opinion was rapidly forming. Not only that, but he was also intently studying Lieutenant Sam Yates.

LCDR Boyd continued his questioning. "Lieutenant Yates, during discovery, defense shared with me that there may have been a malfunctioning rifle on the ship, and that this rifle was the one that was in Petty Officer Miller's hands when the shooting incident occurred. Were you aware that there was a faulty rifle on board your ship?"

There was an ever so slight pause before Yates answered. He knew in his heart that he was going to once again dodge what should have been his moral obligation. "I do not believe there was a faulty firearm on the ship." A slight pink hue crossed the Lieutenant's face, but other than that he showed no emotion.

Boyd then asked a final question. "Lieutenant Yates, based on your firsthand knowledge of the case, is it your belief that GM3 Miller violated the Uniform Code of Military Justice; specifically, those two articles for which he has been charged?"

Yates answered, "Yes, I believe he did."

When he heard that response, Buddy lowered his head, looked down, and closed his eyes at the table where he was sitting. He felt that he was certain as to the outcome of the case and that his fate was sealed.

LCDR Boyd smiled at Captain Marshall and said, "I have no further questions for this witness, Captain."

Captain Marshall had seen enough. He now opined to himself that Boyd was a phony. "Very well," he said and turned to LCDR Anderson. "Commander Anderson, you may proceed."

LCDR Anderson rose from her chair. "Captain, I would like to defer my questioning of this witness for later and request that I be allowed to retain my right to cross examine."

"Your request is granted. We will take another ten minute break." As the participants rose to leave the room, LCDR Anderson turned to Buddy and patted his arm. "You may not know it, Miller, but this is going even better than I imagined. It's all going to be OK. Go out in the passageway and get yourself a drink of water." She rose then to leave the room.

After everyone had returned to their seats, Captain Marshall asked LCDR Boyd to call his next witness. "I would like to call Petty Officer Miller to the stand."

Buddy continued to fight the nausea as he stood and walked slowly to the witness chair. He was sworn in by Captain Marshall and sat down. His face was ashen. He was visibly nervous, with shining, small beads of perspiration on his temples. A growing headache pounded unceasingly, thereby distracting Buddy with the pain. LCDR Boyd rose from his chair, looked at Buddy and began his questioning.

"Petty Officer Miller, while you and the others in your boarding party stopped and searched a Vietnamese junk on October 20, 1968, you shot one of the junk's crew, didn't you?"

Buddy swallowed and said, "Yes, sir."

"In fact, Petty Officer Miller, you shot and murdered that Vietnamese fisherman in cold blood that day, didn't you?"

LCDR Anderson quickly rose to her feet. "Objection. The prosecutor is injecting non-fact. If the prosecutor will examine this case, it has never been established in the record that the fisherman, in fact, died. I surmise that prosecution framed their charges with this fact in mind and is the reason that prosecution did not charge Petty Officer Miller with murder under the code."

Captain Marshall was momentarily taken aback. The wheels spun in his head as he reached a conclusion. His regard for Joan Anderson just took a huge leap upward. She had managed to introduce a key element into the proceedings with just a simple objection. With a sideways glance to the members of the court martial panel, he turned and faced LCDR Anderson.

"Objection sustained. The panel is instructed to ignore any reference to killing or murder. Commander Boyd, you will not make any such reference in the future. You will structure your questions accordingly," said Captain Marshall.

The court room was silent for a full minute. Boyd stared straight down at the papers in front of him. The panel glanced at each other and appeared slightly confused.

LCDR Boyd was stunned and continued to nervously shuffle the stack of papers on the table in front of him. His mind was racing. He thought this case was going to be over by noon. He thought that all he had to do was get a confirmation of Miller killing the fisherman and sit back and let the panel decide the damn kid's fate. Now he was going to have to deal with the charges.

He continued. "All right, Petty Officer Miller, isn't it true that you shot and wounded that Vietnamese fisherman on October 20, 1968?"

"Yes, sir," answered Buddy.

"Were you aware at the time of the shooting that your ship, the USS *Erne*, was under a set of rules of engagement?"

"Yes, sir."

"Prior to today, have you ever read those rules of engagement?" asked Boyd.

"Yes, sir."

"In fact, weren't you required to read those rules, sign them, and return the copy to Ensign Kramer, the First Lieutenant?" asked Boyd.

"Yes, sir."

"So, Petty Officer Miller, why did you blatantly choose to defy those rules of engagement and shoot the fisherman?"

"I, I don't believe that I defied those orders," said Buddy.

"Petty Officer Miller, why would you believe that you did not defy the orders?" asked Boyd. Boyd could not help himself. He just kept asking questions that were not in his own best interest.

"Umm, because the rules of engagement say that deadly force can be used when a military unit is under attack by an opposing force," answered Buddy.

Boyd momentarily read the rules of engagement in silence. He then looked up and asked, "And did you believe that the ship or members of the crew were in danger from attack?"

"Yes, sir."

"Oh come now, Petty Officer Miller. How could you possibly think that a man sitting on the deck of his boat while mending his fishing nets could pose a deadly threat to members of the crew of the *Erne*?" Boyd asked gloatingly.

"Well, sir, I was always taught that a gun in someone's hand is a deadly danger, even when there is no harmful intent," said Buddy.

LCDR Anderson was amazed. Miller was doing great on the stand, and Boyd just kept digging himself into deeper quicksand.

Damn it, thought Boyd. I never should have asked that question.

"You said gun, Petty Officer Miller. Wasn't it, in fact, a fishing net tool that the fisherman had?" asked Boyd, who was grinning broadly. "And if it was a fishing tool and did not present a danger, then it is obvious that you defied the rules of engagement, didn't you?"

"Well, yes, sir; um, I mean no, sir. You see, as the man drew the tool from his bag, the handle looked like a pistol handle and gun barrel, and a crew member yelled that the man had a gun."

LCDR Boyd decided that he had made his point on the violation of the engagement rules; or at least as well as he could. It was time to attack the other charge. "Petty Officer Miller, would you agree that shooting a Vietnamese civilian, who is not a member of the enemy's military force, is not in the best interest of the Navy and the United States Government?"

The question confused Buddy. "I, I guess so," he said.

"In fact, shooting an unarmed civilian brings discredit to the Navy and the United States Government, doesn't it?" said Boyd.

LCDR Anderson was instantly out of her chair. "Objection. Calls for an opinion. The witness is being asked for an opinion for which he is not qualified to answer, and for which he could unknowingly incriminate himself."

"I am going to allow it. I would like to hear what Petty Officer Miller has to say," said Captain Marshall. Captain Marshall was also trying to get a read on Buddy's character.

"Yes, sir, I guess so," answered Buddy. It was all he could do to keep tears from forming. There was no one in the room that felt worse about the shooting than Buddy Miller.

Gotcha, thought LCDR Boyd. So much for that charge. He once again shuffled the papers in front of him. He then came to the narcissistic conclusion that he had proven both the charges as best he could. "I have no further questions, Captain," said LCDR Boyd.

Captain Marshall was shocked. In all the years of working as an attorney, this was probably one of the shoddiest displays of attorney work he had ever witnessed. He knew LCDR Boyd's boss at the JAG Corps at seventh fleet. He intended to have a talk with him after this circus was over. "Very well. Commander Anderson, the witness is yours," said the Captain.

LCDR Joan Anderson rose from her chair and began her questioning of Buddy. "Petty Officer Miller, we will not need to talk about the shooting incident again. You have admitted to shooting the civilian, and if the prosecutor had read all of his discovery documents, the shooting was stipulated in my submission."

LCDR Boyd was not even paying attention when his skill as an attorney was impugned, and the barb went over his head. Captain Marshall, however, heard it and thought to himself that the proceedings might now, indeed, get interesting.

"Petty Officer Miller, you stated that you had read the rules of engagement. Is that correct?"

"Yes, ma'am."

"Petty Officer Miller, did you sign those rules of engagement as having read them; and did you give the signed copy to Ensign Kramer?" she asked.

"No, ma'am."

LCDR Boyd's head jerked up, and he looked back and forth from Buddy to LCDR Anderson. It was just another detail that Boyd had not personally verified in his trial preparation.

LCDR Anderson paused for a moment and then asked, "Why didn't you sign the rules of engagement."

"I meant to, but we were so busy that I just forgot and put them in my locker on the ship. I guess Ensign Kramer forgot about them too, because he never asked me for them again."

Now, Captain Marshall was immediately alert, as well as the other panel members. Even LCDR Boyd was now listening.

"Petty Officer Miller, going back to the scene of the incident, you remarked that there was a sailor who shouted out that the fisherman had a gun. Who was that sailor who shouted that phrase?"

"It was BM2 Schmitt. Mark Schmitt," said Buddy.

"Was Petty Officer Schmitt normally in the ship's boarding party?"

"Umm, no ma'am. He was new to the ship and had not yet been trained to be in the boarding team. He should not have been on the team."

"Did you inform anyone that Schmitt should not be on the team," asked Anderson.

"Yes, ma'am, I told Senior Chief Gunther, but he told me that Mr. Kramer had ordered him to put Petty Officer Schmitt on the team. Mr. Kramer had told him that Schmitt knew how to handle M-1s."

"Petty Officer Miller, was Petty Officer Schmitt issued a weapon at the time of the boarding of the junk?"

"Yes, ma'am."

"Who gave him the weapon?" asked Anderson.

"I don't know for sure because I wasn't there when he received the weapon," said Buddy. "Usually I issued the weapons to the participants, but on that day the XO had already opened the armory and was passing out weapons. And I didn't know it, but the XO issued a faulty rifle to BM2 Schmitt," said Buddy.

"How do you know that?"

"Senior Chief Gunther had me take the faulty rifle that Schmitt had and I gave my rifle to Schmitt," said Buddy. "I ended up with the faulty rifle."

"Objection," said LCDR Boyd. "We have not established that there was any faulty weapon."

"Sustained," said Captain Marshall, who was still listening intently.

Undaunted, LCDR Anderson continued. "Since we apparently haven't yet established that the gun was faulty, I'll ask this question. Petty Officer Miller, as a trained gunner's mate, would you have ever issued the gun you were using for use by boarding party members?"

"No. I was sure that it was unsafe," answered Buddy.

"Why didn't you go and get another rifle to use?"

"There wasn't time. The junk was already being secured to the side of the ship when I got the rifle from Senior Chief Gunther," said Buddy.

"OK," said Anderson. "When you heard Schmitt yell that the fisherman had a gun, what did you see?"

"I looked at the people in the junk and saw the man pulling what looked just like a pistol from a bag that was next to him," said Buddy.

"So what did you think?"

"When I saw the gun, I thought the man was going to shoot somebody in the boarding crew."

"So you feared for the safety of the crew. And what did you do then?" asked Anderson.

"I swung my rifle around to bear on the man. But as I stopped the swing, the gun sort of went off by itself." Buddy was tearing up. "And the man slumped down on the deck." A tear crept down his cheek, and he quickly wiped it away.

"So you didn't really pull the trigger of the rifle," she asked.

It took him a few seconds to compose himself. Then Buddy replied, "Well, I had my finger in the trigger guard, and I was just thinking about pulling the trigger when the gun went off. But I am sure I did not pull the trigger."

Again LCDR Anderson paused, and this time she consulted the papers in front of her on the table. She found what she was looking for and asked, "Petty Officer Miller, what type of guns are on the USS *Erne* and how many are there of each.

Captain Marshall was not sure why LCDR Anderson had asked the question, and he was wondering why Boyd was not objecting to the relevancy of the question.

"The ship is allowed to have sixteen M-1 rifles, two twelve gauge shotguns, two .30 caliber machine guns, twelve .45 caliber pistols, and a twin mount .50 caliber machine gun."

"Petty Officer Miller, the weapons department on the *Erne* was in pretty bad shape when you arrived, wasn't it?" asked Anderson.

"Yes, ma'am."

"I would like for you to tell the court all about that, and what you did when you got to the *Erne*."

LCDR Boyd rose quickly from his chair. "Objection. I fail to see the relevance here," he said.

Captain Marshall nodded, but remained quiet for a few seconds. "I will give this a bit of leeway. Objection overruled. Commander Anderson, please proceed."

For the next twenty minutes, Buddy told the court about how his predecessor had gone to prison for theft of a weapon, and how the records and the maintenance for the department both needed a great deal of attention. He described how there had been no accountability for weapons being checked out of the armory and how he had set up an accountability system with the blessing of the executive officer, and how he had collected all keys to the armory except those of Ensign Kramer, the XO, and he and the gunner's mate striker. He also told the court that the system made him the sole issuer of fire arms except in emergency. He described how he had cleaned everything up and had the department in very good shape. So good in fact, that he had received an excellent rating by the mine squadron inspectors, which resulted in the CO giving him a letter of commendation.

Captain Marshall laid the pen, with which he had been writing, down on the yellow tablet in front of him. As he rehashed previous testimony in his head, the words, "The son of a bitch lied" went through his brain.

"Captain, I have no further questions for the witness at this time. I would like to reserve the right to recall this witness if necessary," said LCDR Anderson.

"Very well," said Captain Marshall. "Commander Anderson, I believe we have time for one more witness."

"Thank you, Captain. I would like to call Boatswain's Mate Second Class Mark Schmitt," said LCDR Anderson.

In a moment, a visibly nervous BM2 Mark Schmitt entered the room and Captain Marshall asked him to be seated at the witness chair, where he was quickly sworn in.

LCDR Anderson began. "Petty Officer Schmitt, how long have you been attached to the *Erne*?"

"About three months," said Schmitt.

"Prior to the *Erne*, where were you serving?"

"I was on the *Kitty Hawk*, ma'am," said Schmitt.

"While you were on the *Kitty Hawk*, did you have the opportunity to handle any weapons?"

"No, ma'am. I was on the deck gang. We didn't handle any weapons."

"Other than the incident in October on the *Erne*, when was the last time you had handled an M1 rifle?"

"Umm, I guess that would have been in boot camp nearly ten years ago. But we never fired those rifles. We just marched around with them once in a while."

"So Petty Officer Schmitt, did you tell that to Mr. Kramer when he asked you about being in the boarding party?" asked Anderson.

"Yes, ma'am. I told him the same thing I just told you. But he said it was OK. He wanted me to get the experience of being in the inspection party."

"Petty Officer Schmitt, do you know how to load and fire an M1? And do you know how to clear a jammed M1?" she asked.

Mark Schmitt looked down. He was still wondering how he had gotten mixed up in this whole mess. "No, ma'am."

"Petty Officer Schmitt, did you know prior to putting that rifle in your hand back in October that there were certain rules of engagement for dealing with Vietnamese civilian population?"

"No, ma'am. I've heard about it since that incident," said Schmitt.

"Have you ever read and signed a copy of those rules?" asked Anderson.

"No ma'am."

"Petty Officer Schmitt, is it true that you shouted to the boarding party crew that the fisherman had a gun?"

"Yes, ma'am." Schmitt drew a quick, audible breath and blurted, "But I really did think it was a gun when I saw it."

"When you yelled that the fisherman had a gun, what did you think would happen?" she asked.

"Well, I thought that . . . well, I thought . . . Oh, I didn't know what would happen. But I sure didn't want Miller to get in trouble." Schmitt's composure was gone.

"Thank you, Petty Officer Schmitt. Just a couple more questions. Petty Officer Schmitt, has Captain Yates made any demands on you since the incident on October 20th."

Schmitt's head jerked and his speech stumbled. "I, I don't know what you mean."

"Has the Captain ever ordered you to do something that you didn't think was right?"

Schmitt's face flushed. This was the moment he had dreaded. Both of his feet started moving, in turn moving his knees. He faced the floor and answered, "Yes, ma'am."

"Did Captain Yates order you to go with him to the ship's armory on the night of the shooting and remove a rifle?" asked Anderson.

The sound of Captain Marshall's pen falling to the floor broke the tension for only a few seconds.

"Yes, ma'am," said Schmitt.

Almost in unison, all members of the panel leaned forward in their chairs, intently listening to the testimony of BM2 Schmitt.

"Did he order you to give him the rifle that had been used in the shooting?" asked Anderson.

"Yes, ma'am, he wanted me to give him the rifle that I had traded to Petty Officer Miller on the fantail."

"Did you do that?"

"Yes, ma'am, except that I didn't really know which rifle it was. I just wanted to get out of there, so I gave him the first rifle I could see."

"What did Captain Yates do then?"

"He took the rifle and told me to keep my mouth shut," said Schmitt. Schmitt's white uniform shirt was nearly soaked through with perspiration.

LCDR Anderson continued. "Thank you Petty Officer Schmitt. I know that was hard to talk about. But we must keep going. Did Captain Yates ask you to do anything else that you thought might be improper?"

"I don't remember," Schmitt replied.

LCDR Anderson again consulted her papers. "Let me help your memory. Did you retrieve a green log book from the ship's CIC and take it to the Captain?"

Petty Officer Schmitt visibly slumped, put his elbows on his knees and covered his face for a few seconds with his hands. He then raised his head and said, "Yes, ma'am."

Gently, LCDR Anderson asked the next question. "Were you in his cabin with him when he asked you for your knife?"

"Yes, ma'am."

"And what did the Captain do with your knife?"

"I watched him cut a couple pages out of the log book. He kept the pages and gave me my knife, and told me to put the log book back in CIC."

"Did the Captain say anything else?"

Schmitt's face became very red with embarrassment. "He told me to keep my damn mouth shut or he would use the same knife to cut off my balls."

She paused briefly, and then LCDR Anderson said, "Thank you very much Petty Officer Schmitt. You have been very helpful. And by the way, if anyone asks you what you talked about in here today, you just tell them that the court told you that you were not supposed to answer that. OK?"

"Yes, ma'am."

"Commander Boyd, your witness," said Captain Marshall.

Boyd slowly stood up. He blinked his eyes four times slowly. In his mind, he had put the pieces of Schmitt's testimony together, and finally was coming to a conclusion. "No questions, Captain; but I would like to reserve the opportunity to cross, if necessary."

"Granted," said Captain Marshall. Turning to Schmitt, he said, "Petty Officer Schmitt, you are free to go."

As Petty Officer Schmitt left the court room, there was complete silence. It was as if all the air had suddenly been sucked out of the room. No one spoke. The panel was trying desperately to digest that they had just heard. In fact, to the panel it seemed unbelievable; but not to LCDR Anderson. Captain Marshall stared at the ceiling while the rest of the panel looked down at their notepads. Finally, Captain Marshall straightened up in his chair and said, "We will reconvene at 0800 tomorrow morning."

*****

He was mentally drained. He felt like his brain was stuffed into a pressure cooker. Buddy could not put a rational thought together as he trudged slowly back to the BEQ from the chow hall that evening. He had eaten only a dish of butterscotch pudding and had a glass of milk. If he was asked, he probably would not even remember what he had eaten for dinner. He just wanted to sleep, but an uninterrupted dreamless sleep was out of the question.

As he neared the BEQ, a base taxi, belching diesel smoke and fumes from a rusty, dangling tail pipe shrieked its brakes as it stopped in the street next to where Buddy was walking. He paid it no heed and continued walking. The taxi cab doors opened and then slammed shut.

"Hey Miller. Hey dumb ass!"

Hearing his name, Buddy stopped and turned. A grin crossed his face. Fig Newton and Bob Dawes walked quickly from the cab to Buddy's side. They were carrying two large grocery bags.

"What are you guys doing here?" asked Buddy. But he was very happy to see his two friends.

"C'mon, we've got to get to your room. I'm not supposed to be here," said Dawes.

When they reached Buddy's room, a six pack of beer, a six pack of soda, and various snacks were removed from the grocery bags. The distinctive sound of beer can pop-top openers followed, accompanied by the sounds of cellophane snack chip bags being ripped open.

"OK, Buddy, we're not allowed to talk about the trial, so let's tell sea stories and have a good time," said Dawes. "In fact, I'd probably be in trouble if anyone knew I was here. I will tell you this, though. Tomorrow is going to be a fun day at the old court house; just wait and see. Turn on that miserable TV and see if we can catch any sports," said Dawes as he stuffed his mouth with potato chips.

They passed the time watching a grainy-pictured hockey match between Chicago and Detroit being broadcast from the states, and in which none of them had any interest. They were sure that it had probably been filmed over a week ago anyway.

His friends stayed for over two hours. Buddy laughed with them and felt relaxed. It was wonderful to be able to talk to someone other than attorneys and others associated with the trial. After his friends left, Buddy brushed his teeth, and with a slight alcoholic buzz in his head, he crashed on his bunk.

He got three good hours of sleep. He dreamed of working on the farm with his dad, driving the tractor in a perfectly straight line as the planter dragged behind inserting the seeds that would later become tall green tasseled stalks holding the livelihood of the Miller family. He could smell the black earth as the tractor moved through the field. He saw the old pick-up bouncing over the field as his mother brought his lunch out to him. His little sister, Janeen, waved to him from the cab of the truck. Buddy smiled in his sleep. He awoke to go to the bathroom.

He returned to bed and was asleep when the nightmare started again. This time, his field of vision was a churning red mass that appeared to be glistening wetly. The explosion of gunfire began parting the red screen to once again reveal the shrieking, keening women gathered around the bloody body of the fisherman. The women turned toward him. Their faces were elongated downward, giving them a horrific ghostly appearance. In unison, they all raised their arms and pointed at him while the ghastly shrieking continued. Suddenly the vision of the net repair tool slashed across his vision, and the women were gone. But the bloody-faced man became larger, growing until just his head was visible. Half of the head was missing, with bloody wet pulp where the other half should be. The remaining eye stared directly at him. The half-mouth opened and closed as if trying to speak or scream. Buddy awoke, loudly moaning and covered with sweat. There would be no more sleep that night.

Chapter Twenty-Two

0900, November 16, 1968
Judge Advocate General's Office – Courtroom
Da Nang, South Vietnam

They all rose as Captain Marshall entered the room. "Please be seated," he said. "I believe that when we adjourned yesterday, you were ready to call your next witness. Is that correct, Commander Anderson?"

LCDR Anderson rose and said, "Yes, sir. I would like to call Lieutenant Junior Grade Gustavo Bamino."

The executive officer of the *Erne* soon took his place on the witness chair and was sworn in by Captain Marshall.

LCDR Anderson began her questioning. "Good morning Lieutenant Bamino. I have just a few questions to ask you. Hopefully this won't take too long. Lieutenant Bamino, you serve on the USS *Erne* as the Executive Officer under command of Lieutenant Samuel Yates. Is that correct?"

"Yes, ma'am."

"Lieutenant, in the ship's armory, were you aware that there were any faulty firearms? And if so, could you tell us how you were made aware of the faulty weapons?"

"Yes, ma'am, I was aware of there being two faulty weapons; an M1 rifle and a .45 pistol. I was made aware of them after being told by Ensign Kramer, and by our MINERON weapons inspection team briefing following their inspection some time ago."

"Lieutenant Bamino, after you were made aware of the faulty weapons, did you apprise your commanding officer of the situation?" asked Anderson.

"Well, I didn't have to. I was with Captain Yates when the inspection team told him about it at their briefing, so he was aware of it without me telling him."

"Fine, thank you. Now Lieutenant, I want you to think back to October 20, the day of the shooting. Did you, in fact, issue weapons from the armory to the boarding party on that day?"

"Yes, I did."

"Was it normal procedure that you would issue the weapons to the boarding party? And if it was not normal procedure, please tell the court why you were issuing weapons," said Anderson.

"Normally, Petty Officer Miller, the ship's gunner's mate would issue the weapons. He and I had worked out that procedure to ensure accountability for the issued weapons. But on that day, I did not find Miller immediately, and the CO was kicking my behind to get ready to board the junk. We had been given an urgent message that this particular junk would be carrying contraband, and the CO wanted to make sure we were prepared to quickly board the junk. So I went ahead and opened the armory and started issuing weapons."

"Lieutenant, as you issued those rifles, were you aware of the location of the faulty rifle?"

LTJG Bamino lowered his head. He knew where this line of questioning was leading. He lifted his head and answered, "No, ma'am."

"So, Lieutenant, do you think it is possible that you could have issued that faulty rifle to one of the crew members?"

He looked straight at the attorney and answered, "Yes, ma'am."

"Thank you Lieutenant, I just have a couple more questions. The *Erne* is a rather small ship isn't it?"

"Yes, ma'am."

"And because it is so small, you and the CO bunk in the same cabin, do you not?"

"Yes, ma'am."

"At any time following the shooting on October 20, did the CO, Lieutenant Yates, bring a rifle into your cabin?"

"Yes, ma'am."

"Did Lieutenant Yates say why he was bringing the gun into the cabin?" asked Anderson.

"No, ma'am, not exactly. He said something about wanting to take the rifle to the base armory for some calibration. I didn't know what he meant by that, but I learned a long time ago not to question him when it was none of my business," said Bamino.

"Is that rifle still in your shared cabin?" asked Anderson.

"No, ma'am."

"Do you know where it is?"

"No, ma'am."

"Thank you Lieutenant. I have no further questions, Captain Marshall."

"Commander Boyd, your witness," said Captain Marshall.

LCDR Boyd rose and asked, "Lieutenant Bamino, did you see Petty Officer Miller shoot the civilian in the fishing boat on October 20th?"

"Yes I did," answered Bamino.

"And Lieutenant Bamino, as an officer in the United States Navy, would you agree that shooting a civilian for no apparent reason would not be in the best interest of the Navy?" asked Boyd.

LCDR Anderson rose from her chair. "Objection, calls for an opinion."

"I'll allow it," said Captain Marshall.

"Yes, I suppose it would not be in the Navy's best interest," said Bamino.

That's all I need to hear, thought Boyd. "No further questions, Captain."

Captain Marshall stared at LCDR Boyd for a few seconds, and finally said, "Please call your next witness, Commander Anderson."

"Yes, sir. I would like to call Gunner's Mate First Class Paul Stroud."

Buddy was curious. He had never heard Stroud's name before and wondered who this might be.

Stroud entered the court room, took the witness chair, and was sworn in.

"Petty Officer Stroud, thank you for coming here today. Would you please tell the court where you work," said LCDR Anderson.

"Yes, ma'am. I am attached to MACV in the weapons repair facility."

"And please tell us what you do at that facility."

"Well, just like the name says, we repair small arms mostly. The Market Time small boats and other ships bring us weapons that need repair. Some of the weapons, like the old M1s have been around since the Second World War, and some of them are in pretty bad shape. So we repair and recalibrate them and return them to their command," said Stroud.

"Thank you. Petty Officer Stroud, did you recently receive two M1 rifles from the USS *Erne*?"

"Yes, ma'am."

"Could you please tell the court the circumstances of receiving those rifles, and who brought them to you," asked Anderson.

"Yes, ma'am. The first rifle we got was brought to us by a Lieutenant. His name was Yates. He said he was from the USS *Erne*, and they had this rifle that they wanted checked out. He asked me to check out an M1 that he said was faulty, and he wanted it fixed. But we checked it out, and there was nothing wrong with it."

"Let me stop you there for a second," said Anderson. She shuffled through some papers on her desk and retrieved a document. She handed the document to Petty Officer Stroud. "Petty Officer Stroud, do you recognize this document?"

"Yes, ma'am. It's the work order for the M1 I was talking about. See, the serial number ends in 46, and that is Lieutenant Yates' signature on the bottom of the work order."

"Please tell the court the date on the work order," said Anderson.

"October 23, 1968," answered Stroud.

"So, if I understand correctly, Lieutenant Yates brought that rifle to you on October 23. Is that correct?"

"Yes, ma'am."

"Petty Officer Stroud, can you please tell the court where that rifle is now?"

"Yes, ma'am. We still have it at the armory. It was never picked up by the ship, or Lieutenant Yates."

Captain Marshall dropped his head, and if one looked carefully at the Captain they would have seen his stomach pulsing as he laughed to himself. He then leaned back in his chair and crossed his arms across his chest. He was enjoying the testimony. On the other hand, Buddy Miller was listening also, but he still did not grasp the significance of the testimony.

"Petty Officer Stroud," she said as she retrieved another sheet of paper from her stack. "Can you please tell the court what this document is?" asked Anderson.

Stroud looked at the paper and answered. "Yes, ma'am. This is the work order for the other rifle from the *Erne*. It was brought in on let's see, looks like October 24. See, the weapon's serial number ends in 73, and it was another M1. But boy, that rifle was really screwed up."

"Who brought that rifle to you?" she asked.

"It was a senior chief by the name of Gunther. See, he signed the bottom of the work order. He asked us to thoroughly check out the rifle and write up what we found. But he also asked that we not repair the rifle. I thought that was kind of odd. But we did the report for the senior chief, and he picked up the rifle a couple days later. But when he picked it up, I told him that he better never load that weapon because the firing mechanism was so worn that it could go off at any minute without anyone even pulling the trigger. I don't know why, but he even smiled when I told him that. I thought that was kinda odd."

LCDR Anderson was retrieving another piece of paper. "Is this a copy of the write-up that you did for Senior Chief Gunther?"

"Yes, ma'am. See, I even wrote that this rifle is unsafe."

LCDR Anderson walked over to the court room door and opened it. She then turned and walked back into the room, followed by one of her legal assistants who was carrying a rifle. The assistant handed the rifle to GM1 Stroud. "Petty Officer Stroud, would you first check to make sure the weapon is not loaded. I don't think the court would like to have a loaded weapon in its midst. Captain Marshall and the panel smiled as Stroud struggled with the bolt of the rifle. There was no clip in the gun. After struggling for several seconds, he managed to slide the bolt back, confirming that the gun was not loaded.

"Petty Officer Stroud, is this the faulty, unsafe weapon that we discussed?"

Stroud turned the rifle over in his hands and looked at the serial number of the weapon. "Yes, this is the one. See the serial number that ends in 73 matches the number on the work order. By the way, you saw how much trouble I had in opening the breach of the rifle. It is really messed up and ought to just be junked."

"Thank you, Petty Officer Stroud. I have no further questions, Captain Marshall," said LCDR Anderson.

"Your witness, Commander Boyd," said the Captain.

By this time, LCDR Boyd had surmised that this entire case was marching down a path which was leaving him far behind. He had decided that there was no point in embarrassing himself even further. He did not even straighten up in his chair. He waved his hand and said, "No questions, sir."

Smart boy, thought Captain Marshall. Just sit there in your chair and don't say anything stupid. You finally figured out where this case is headed.

"You are free to go Petty Officer Stroud. I think we have time for one more witness before lunch, Commander Anderson." The legal assistant placed the faulty rifle on the floor behind the members of the panel.

"Thank you, Captain. I would like to call Ensign Jack Kramer."

A rather uneasy appearing Ensign Kramer entered the court room, was sworn in, and took his seat. LCDR Anderson then began her questioning. "Ensign Kramer, you are Petty Officer Miller's Department Head on the USS *Erne*, aren't you?"

"Yes, ma'am."

"Ensign Kramer, there has been previous testimony regarding the rules of engagement for the *Erne*. Are you familiar with them?" she asked.

"Yes, ma'am, I am."

"And isn't it true that you had each crew member who was going to be involved in the boarding parties read and sign those rules?"

"Yes, ma'am," answered Kramer.

"Ensign Kramer, I want you to think carefully about your answer. Do you have a copy of those rules of engagement signed by Petty Officer Miller?"

Jack Kramer seemed to flinch slightly, but answered, "No, ma'am."

"In fact, Petty Officer Miller never did give you his signed copy, did he?"

Kramer again squirmed slightly and answered, "No, ma'am."

"Ensign Kramer, did you ever tell Lieutenant Yates, your CO on the *Erne*, that you had received Petty Officer Miller's signed copy of the rules?"

"No, ma'am, he never asked me about it," said Kramer.

A smile again appeared on Captain Marshall's face. He did not make any effort to hide it.

"Ensign Kramer, did Petty Officer Miller ever speak to you about having any faulty weapons in the *Erne*'s armory; in other words, weapons that could not be used?"

"Yes, ma'am. He told me about an M1 and a .45 that were inoperable, and I passed that on to the XO, LTJG Bamino," said Kramer.

"Ensign Kramer, let's talk a bit about Petty Officer Miller. When Petty Officer Miller came on board the *Erne*, what was the overall condition of the weapons department?"

"Well, it was a bit of a shambles. His predecessor did not do his job properly and even got in some trouble about it. He had to leave the ship. But Petty Officer Miller did an outstanding job in getting the department back in line. Everything was ship-shape when we were inspected after that."

"In fact, Ensign Kramer, Petty Officer Miller did such a good job that you recommended him for a Navy Achievement medal, didn't you?" asked Anderson.

"Yes, ma'am. I gave the recommendation to the XO, but when it got to the CO, the CO made the XO change it to a letter of commendation instead."

"So the CO gave Petty Officer Miller a letter of commendation for his excellent work. Is that correct?" asked Anderson.

"Yes, ma'am."

A quick smile crossed Captain Marshall's face, but disappeared just as quickly.

"Now, Ensign Miller, as Petty Officer Miller's Department Head, you also wrote his performance evaluations, didn't you?"

"Yes, ma'am."

"And how did you rate him, let's say, on the last two evaluations," asked Anderson.

"I rated his last two evaluations as straight 4.0s," said Kramer.

"So you graded him as outstanding in all categories?"

"Yes, ma'am."

"Thank you. Ensign Kramer, as the Weapons Department Head, can you tell me how many small arms the *Erne* carries? Let me be more specific. Do you know the number of M1 rifles in the *Erne*'s armory," she asked.

"Yes, ma'am. I believe there are sixteen M1s."

"Do you by chance know how many are in the ship's armory right this minute?"

Ensign Kramer squirmed in his chair. "No, not right this minute. I would need to take an inventory. Why? Is something missing?" asked Kramer.

Captain Marshall and the panel could not hold it in. They all chuckled. Ensign Kramer's face turned red.

LCDR Anderson smiled and said, "Don't worry Mr. Kramer; I do not believe that anything is unaccounted for. Just a couple more questions. As I understand it, Boatswain's Mate Second Class Mark Schmitt is a member of the *Erne*'s crew, isn't he?"

"Yes, ma'am."

"On the second or third day that Petty Officer Schmitt was on board, did you order Petty Officer Schmitt to be in the boarding party on October 20th?" asked Anderson.

The crimson returned to Kramer's face. He knew where this was going. "Yes, ma'am."

"Ensign Kramer, isn't it true that Petty Officer Schmitt had received no formal training in the boarding party procedures?"

"Yes, that's true." Jack Kramer now could feel the spotlight on himself and he was extremely uncomfortable.

"And Ensign Kramer, isn't it true that Petty Officer Schmitt had never even seen or read the rules of engagement for the boarding party members?"

Kramer visibly swallowed. "Yes that's true."

LCDR Anderson paused for a few seconds and debated with herself. She then asked, "Why did you put Petty Officer Schmitt on the boarding party when you knew it was wrong to do so?"

Kramer looked down for a few seconds. "I just wanted him to get some experience. Ninety-nine per cent of our inspections are just routine. I didn't think anything would go wrong."

She decided to take a shot in the dark. "And yet you had been told by the XO that this particular junk was very likely carrying contraband. Isn't that true?"

"Yes, ma'am."

Bingo, thought LCDR Anderson. He just admitted to poor judgment.

Anderson continued, "Wouldn't you say, then, Mr. Kramer, that your poor judgement contributed to the situation of which we are discussing today?"

Kramer did not answer.

At the table of the judge and panel, Captain Marshall was smiling inwardly. He was enjoying this immensely.

"That's OK, Ensign Kramer, you don't have to answer that last question. But I do have a couple more questions. It is my understanding that each time you searched a junk, you wrote a record of the inspection in a log book. Is that correct?"

"Yes, ma'am."

"And on October 20th, did you make a record of that boarding?"

"Yes, ma'am."

She shuffled in her stack of papers again and retrieved two sheets of paper.

"I want you to take a look at these pages. They are dated October 20, 1968. Can you tell me if this is the record you wrote in the log book that day? Notice that the name of the fisherman, by virtue of his boat's ownership document and citizenship papers is there. Is this your writing and the notes you made in the log, Ensign Kramer?"

Where in the hell did she get those, thought Captain Marshall. This just gets better all the time.

"Yes, ma'am, those are my notes," said Kramer.

"I notice that the log is not signed by you. Why is that?" asked Anderson.

"Well, when the shooting occurred, the Captain told us all to get back on the ship. I guess because I was in a hurry, I did not sign the log. But those are my notes," said Kramer.

LCDR Anderson pulled the green log book from the table in front of her and brought it over to Ensign Kramer.

"Ensign Kramer, is this the log book that you used to write the records of your ship boardings?"

"Yes, ma'am," said Kramer.

"Good. Could you please look in the log book and find your log entry for October 20th."

Ensign Kramer leafed through the book and sat with the open book on his lap. He shuffled pages on both sides of the open book. "I don't see the pages for the 20th. They don't seem to be here."

"Do you know where the pages could have gone?" asked Anderson.

"No, ma'am," replied a bewildered Ensign Kramer.

"Thank you, Ensign Kramer. I have no further questions, Captain Marshall," said LCDR Anderson.

Captain Marshall looked at LCDR Boyd, who simply waved and shook his head no.

"Commander Boyd, you will need to tell me your intentions. The court reporter cannot record silent responses, and we need your answer for the record," said Captain Marshall.

He straightened slightly in his chair. "No questions, sir," said Boyd.

"Great," said Captain Marshall. "This seems like a good time to break for lunch.

LCDR Anderson reached over and patted Buddy on the arm. "It's going great, Miller. Just hang in there; it's going to be fine."

Buddy was only slightly relieved by the attorney's pep talk. He had pieced together some of the testimony and responses to questions and could see that there was more to this court martial than just the issues with him. But he still was not convinced that everything would come out OK for him. He was still confused as to where LCDR Anderson had gotten the log records, the rifle, the armory reports, and everything else that she had presented. He could only conclude that she had some good sources.

*****

As the parties returned from lunch, Buddy and LCDR Anderson were walking together. Just prior to entering the court room, they passed one of the offices where witnesses were being held. In that office, Buddy saw Bob Dawes sitting on a chair reading a copy of *Navy Times*. Dawes saw Buddy and waved and grinned at him. Buddy groaned, but waved back and continued walking. He could not help but wonder how Dawes would screw something up. "What's Dawes doing here?" he asked LCDR Anderson.

"He's going to testify on your behalf," she said.

"I don't know if that is such a good idea," said Buddy.

LCDR Anderson chuckled. "Miller, just wait and see. I keep telling you this is all going to come out OK. C'mon, we don't want to keep Captain Marshall waiting."

After everyone was seated, Captain Marshall said, "Commander Anderson, you may call your next witness."

"Thank you Captain. I would like to call Gunner's Mate Seaman Robert Dawes."

Momentarily, the court room door opened, and a legal aide escorted Bob Dawes to the witness chair where he was sworn in.

"Seaman Dawes, are you presently serving on the USS *Erne*?" asked LCDR Anderson.

"Yes, ma'am," replied Dawes.

"As a gunner's mate, do you serve alongside Petty Officer Miller?"

"Yes, ma'am."

"I would like you to think back to the events on October 20th. Were you serving in the boarding party that day?"

"Yes, ma'am, I was at the .30 caliber stanchion."

"From your position, were you able to see the shooting that occurred that day?"

"Yes, ma'am, I could see it real well," said Dawes.

"In your own words, can you please tell us what happened that day?" asked Anderson.

Dawes hesitated a few seconds and then said, "Well, the boarding party, that is Ensign Kramer and the interpreter and one of the boatswain's mates, were on this junk, and they were checking the papers on the boat and searching around on the boat. All of the sudden, BM2 Schmitt yelled that the guy on the boat has a gun. And as the guy pulls this thing out of his bag, it really did look like a pistol. It had a black pistol grip. I sure thought it was a pistol. Anyway the next thing we know, Buddy, er, I mean Petty Officer Miller shot the guy. And that's about it . . ."

"OK, Seaman Dawes. What happened after that?" asked Anderson.

"Mmm, the CO called all the boarding party back onto the ship, and I went with the boarding crew to our ship's armory and restowed all the weapons and ammo."

"But you didn't restow all of the guns, did you?"

"No ma'am. When Senior Chief Gunther brought me the gun that Buddy, I mean Petty Officer Miller was using, I made sure it was unloaded, and then I hid it."

"Where did you hide it?" she asked.

"Well, back behind our small arms rack, there's a little space that goes behind the rack. I put the rifle in there," said Dawes.

Both Captain Marshall and Buddy were listening with rapt attention as Bob Dawes continued telling his story.

"What ever happened to that rifle, Seaman Dawes?"

"This whole shooting thing was eating me up. I knew that Buddy was going to be in big trouble. I really didn't know what to do to help. So I went to see Senior Chief Gunther and talked with him. While we were talking, I told him that I had the rifle hidden. He was really happy to hear that, and the next night he came and got the rifle. I don't know what ever became of it after that."

"That's fine. Now Seaman Dawes, can you tell me how many small arms were in the inventory of the *Erne*'s armory? In fact, can you just tell me how many M1 rifles the ship has?" asked Anderson.

"Oh, yes ma'am. It's sixteen. I should know. We have to inventory them every two weeks."

"When was the last time you inventoried those rifles, Seaman Dawes?"

"Well, we had a formal inventory just a couple days before the shooting. All sixteen rifles were there." Bob Dawes looked down, then looked back up and squirmed a bit in his chair. "I hate to say this, but I have been in the armory several times since then, and I think there are two rifles missing. I guess one of them would be the one I gave to the Chief. But I don't know anything about that second missing rifle. So I'll probably get in trouble again over that."

LCDR Anderson smiled at Dawes. "I don't think you will get in any trouble Seaman Dawes." She then went back to the documents on her table and removed one and handed it to Dawes. "Please tell the court what this document is."

"Umm, yes, ma'am. It's a copy of the inventory sheet for the M1s in our ship's armory," replied Dawes.

"Now, all the serial numbers of the rifles are there on the sheet. Can you tell me if there was a faulty rifle in that group, and if so, what the serial number of that rifle might be?" asked Anderson.

"Oh, yes ma'am. It's this one right here," said Dawes pointing to the sheet.

"For the court, Seaman Dawes, please read aloud that serial number."

Dawes read the serial number aloud. It was the same serial number as the rifle that had previously been submitted to the court, and ended in 73.

"Are you positive, Seaman Dawes?"

"Oh yes ma'am. And it's the same rifle that I hid after the shooting that day," replied Dawes.

"All right then. Let's go back to October 20th again. Did you have the mid-watch that night?" asked Anderson.

"Yes, midnight to four a.m."

"Did you overhear a conversation that night between your CO and BM2 Mark Schmitt?"

"Yes, ma'am."

"Can you please tell the court where you were and how you heard this conversation?" asked Anderson.

"Well, I had the rover watch. It was about 0100, er, 1 a.m., and I had just come up to the fantail from after-steering, and I leaned against the rail, looking up at the sky. It was so dark, darker than a pimp's heart. Oh, sorry ma'am."

"That's OK, go ahead," said Anderson.

"Anyway, there were no stars. I thought that was odd. Then, I heard voices and looked forward. Two men were at the door to the armory, and they were opening the armory door. I almost challenged them, since it was my armory. But then I recognized the skipper's voice. He was talking to BM2 Schmitt."

"How do you know it was Schmitt?" asked Anderson.

"Because the Captain asked him, 'Are you sure this is the right one, Schmitt?' That's what he said, so I knew he was talking to Schmitt."

"What happened then?"

"I didn't know what they were up to, so I sort of hid behind the deck bollards and watched," said Dawes. "After that, the CO had a rifle in his hand, and put the padlock back on the armory door and said something again to Schmitt. Something about keeping his damn mouth shut. And then the CO went through the mess deck door, and Schmitt was following him. I hung back and followed them, and I think they may have gone to the CO's cabin."

The thought flashed through Captain Marshall's mind. The dumb son of a bitch is getting nailed by a seaman. Serves him right.

Boyd rose and said, "Objection, witness is speculating."

"Sustained," said Captain Marshall.

"That's fine, Seaman Dawes. Thank you for your help," said Anderson. She turned to Captain Marshall. "No further questions, Captain."

Captain Marshall turned to LCDR Boyd. "Questions, Commander Boyd?"

"No questions, Captain," replied Boyd.

"Seaman Dawes, you are free to go," said Marshall. "Commander Anderson, do you have any other witnesses?"

Bob Dawes looked over at Buddy, smiled and winked. Buddy could not help but return the smile. He suddenly realized what his friend had done for him. He would be eternally grateful. His eyes followed Dawes out of the room.

"Yes sir, I would like to call Boatswain's Mate Senior Chief Raymond Gunther."

A legal assistant left the room and momentarily returned with Senior Chief Gunther, who was sworn in and seated.

"Good afternoon, Senior Chief. Thank you for taking the time to be here today," said LCDR Anderson as she started her questioning.

"Happy to be here, ma'am," said Gunther.

"Senior Chief, it is my understanding that you serve aboard the USS *Erne*, and that you are the deck and weapons department's leading petty officer. It is also my understanding that you are the senior enlisted man on that ship. Is all of that correct?" she asked.

"Yes, ma'am, that is correct," replied Gunther.

"And Senior Chief, we have had several meetings prior to this trial haven't we?"

"Yes, ma'am, we have."

"And in our first meeting," she paused and looked at her notes, "on the 25th of October you brought me something. Can you tell the court what you brought to me, and what we talked about at that meeting?"

"Yes, ma'am. I brought you an M1 rifle and a report from the base armory. The rifle was the gun used in the shooting of the Vietnamese fisherman on board the *Erne* on the 20th. The armory report confirmed that the rifle was unsafe and should never be used."

"How did you happen to get that rifle?" asked Anderson.

"GMSN Dawes gave it to me. He had been hiding it. When I got it, I took it off the ship and kept it in safe-keeping with a friend on another ship until we could get it to the armory and have it tested."

While he talked, LCDR Anderson retrieved the rifle and handed it and a document to Gunther.

"Senior Chief, is this the rifle we are talking about?"

"Yes, ma'am. See the serial number matches the armory report."

"Are you certain, Senior Chief?" she asked.

Senior Chief Gunther chuckled. "Yes, ma'am. Look over here on the bottom of the shoulder stock. See that little vee notch cut there that doesn't match the color of the stock?" He showed the stock to LCDR Anderson.

"Yes, I see it," she said.

"Well that notch is there because I put it there with my own knife before I gave the rifle to you as evidence. It's not that I don't trust you. I just wanted to be sure," said Gunther.

LCDR Anderson chuckled, along with Captain Marshall and the rest of the panel members.

"OK, and you subsequently brought me some other things too, didn't you?"

"Yes."

"Please tell the court what those items were," said Anderson.

"I brought you copies of the October 20th pages from our boarding party log book. I had copied those pages right after the shooting incident. And then I put the log book back in our ship's CIC."

"Senior Chief, can you please tell the court why you copied those pages?"

"Yes, ma'am. I got a funny feeling watching the CO after the shooting that this whole incident might get pushed over into Petty Officer Miller's lap. And I didn't think that would be quite right. So I just copied those pages for my own satisfaction to make sure nothing happened to them."

LCDR Anderson showed him a document. Is this a copy of the pages you copied?"

"Yep. I mean, yes, ma'am. See my initials are down there in the bottom corner of the page."

LCDR Anderson looked closely at the document and smiled. "Oh, so that's what that is. I guess you never mentioned that to me before."

"OK, Senior Chief. Let's go back again to October 20th. Late that evening, did you overhear a conversation between your commanding officer and another sailor? And if so, could you please tell the court about that incident?"

"Well, it was about one in the morning of the 21st, the night after the shooting. My stomach was giving me fits and it woke me up; too much coffee before I hit my rack. Anyway, I got out of my bunk and went out on the port weather deck. I had just finished a smoke and was walking forward to go up on the bridge to see if everything was OK when I heard voices. I was curious so I walked around the front of the superstructure to the starboard side and saw that the armory door was open. I heard the voices more clearly and recognized one of them as Captain Yates. Then I heard him say something like, 'Are you sure this is the right one, Schmitt', and realized he was talking to BM2 Schmitt. Schmitt told the CO something about being pretty sure it was the one. Then the CO closed the armory door to lock it. A rifle was in his hands. As he closed the door, I slipped back down the port side of the ship and stayed out of sight. I did not see either of the two men after that, and I went back to chief's quarters to think about what I had seen."

"That's fine, Senior Chief. On the 20th of October, were you ordered to put BM2 Schmitt in the boarding party to search the junk?" asked Anderson.

"Yes, ma'am. I was told by Ensign Kramer to put Schmitt in the boarding party. I argued with him because Schmitt had not been trained yet, but I did as I was told. Petty Officer Miller argued with me about that too, but I told him that Kramer wanted it done."

"OK, Senior Chief. I am going to ask you one more question for the interest of the panel, and I want you to answer truthfully, giving me an honest opinion. If you had been in Petty Officer Miller's shoes on October 20th, would you have fired your weapon at the fisherman?" she asked.

"Objection, speculation," said LCDR Boyd.

"I'm going to allow the answer," said Captain Marshall. "Go ahead, Senior Chief.

Senior Chief Gunther sat for a few seconds with no expression on his face, and then answered. "Ma'am, with all due respect to you and the panel, I do not believe that Petty Officer Miller intentionally fired that rifle. The damn gun was a disaster and could have gone off all by itself. That was verified by the armory report. In answer to your question, no, I would have waited another few seconds before firing to make damn sure it was the right thing to do. And I think that is what Petty Officer Miller would also have done had it not been for that piece of crap of a rifle. Beg your pardon, ma'am. Petty Officer Miller is a fine young man, and I have every confidence that he did not intentionally shoot that civilian. His impeccable character and his training would not allow that to happen."

"Objection, opinion," blurted LCDR Boyd.

"I'm going to allow it, Commander Boyd, since it goes to the heart of the character of the plaintiff, and defense asked for an opinion."

"Thank you Senior Chief. You have been very helpful. No further questions, Captain," said LCDR Anderson.

"Senior Chief, you are free to go," said Marshall.

Gunther looked over at Buddy and smiled, and he, too, uncharacteristically winked at Buddy. Buddy grinned.

"Commander Anderson, do I understand that you might still have one witness remaining?" asked Captain Marshall. He knew very well who that witness was going to be.

"Yes, sir, Captain. At this time I would like to recall Lieutenant Samuel Yates," said Anderson.

Hot damn, thought Captain Marshall. I am going to enjoy this.

As he stepped through the door to the court room, Lieutenant Sam Yates was not happy. He incorrectly thought that his testimony would have put that damn Miller behind bars. In fact, he could not imagine why he was even being brought back except that the stupid defense attorney did not question him the previous day. His thoughts now focused on the present.

"Good afternoon, Lieutenant. I have a few questions for you, and I will remind you that you are still under oath. Let's start at your previous testimony in this court room. You stated that you felt that Petty Officer Miller was not a very impressive sailor. I think your words were something to the effect that he was just an ordinary sailor. Is that pretty much what you said?" asked Anderson.

"Yeah, I guess that's about what I said," replied Yates.

LCDR Anderson handed Sam Yates a document. "I believe what you have in your hands is a letter of commendation written for Petty Officer Miller. Is that correct?" she asked.

Yates continued looking at the document for a few seconds, then looked up and answered, "Yes."

"And did you sign that letter, sir?"

"I guess so," said Yates

LCDR Anderson looked quickly at Sam Yates. "I believe the answer to that question should have been yes. You did sign it, didn't you?"

"Yes, I signed it." Sam Yates twisted in his chair and handed the letter back to LCDR Anderson.

"Would it be correct then, Lieutenant, that Petty Officer Miller was better than just ordinary, or do you give these letters out to your whole crew?" she asked.

"OK, OK, I guess he was an above average sailor. But he still shot somebody," said Yates.

"We'll get to that, Lieutenant. Now, you also stated that you believed that there were no faulty guns in the ship's armory, isn't that correct?"

"Yes, there were no faulty guns on my ship." Lieutenant Yates crossed his legs and clasped his hands across his knee.

"Lieutenant Yates, I will remind you that you are under oath, and I will ask you again if you were aware of any inoperative weapons on the *Erne*?" she asked.

"Not that I was aware of," said Yates.

Hmm, thought Captain Marshall. Not so definitive now are you, Yates?

"Lieutenant Yates, weren't you aware that there was an inoperative .45 pistol on your ship? After all, you signed a survey form to have the pistol turned in to salvage. I have a copy of that survey form right here," said LCDR Anderson as she pulled the document from her stack of papers and handed it to Lieutenant Yates.

"Oh, yeah, now I remember this gun. I thought you meant rifles."

"Oh you did? Well, let's talk about rifles then. Lieutenant Yates, how many faulty rifles are on board the *Erne*?'

"I already said that I don't think there are any," said Yates, but he dropped his crossed knee and squirmed slightly in his chair.

"Lieutenant, I am handing you another document. This document is the report from the MINERON staff that completed an inspection of your armory several weeks ago. That report says that in addition to the inoperative .45, there was also an M1 that was unsafe. Were you aware of that? Didn't you see this report?"

Sam Yates' face had turned a soft pink color. He sat looking at the report. Then Yates said, "I don't remember seeing this report."

Outwardly it was not apparent. But Captain Marshall was laughing on the inside. You sorry, lying bastard, he thought to himself.

"Lieutenant Yates, according to other witnesses, the MINERON inspectors came to your cabin after their inspection, with Ensign Kramer and the Executive Officer. Mr. Kramer and Mr. Bamino both verified that they were there with you when you saw this. They both testified that you all discussed this report. And isn't this the same report for which you felt justified in giving the letter of commendation to Petty Officer Miller?" asked Anderson.

Crap, thought Yates. Now what do I do? "Yes, I believe I do remember that, now that you bring it to my attention."

"Lieutenant Yates, after you saw this report, did you take any action to have those two faulty weapons removed from your ship?" she asked.

"No, I just assumed that the First Lieutenant would take care of it," answered Yates.

"OK. Lieutenant Yates, do you know how many rifles are allotted to the *Erne*? Do you know, sir?"

"No, I don't know for sure. Probably around fifteen or twenty."

"Well, in previous witness statements, the correct number of M1 rifles seems to be sixteen. Do you know how many rifles are on board the *Erne* right now?" she asked.

Lieutenant Yates twisted again in his chair and coughed lightly. He finally took the easy way out to answer. "I would think that there were sixteen, but I don't know for sure," he said.

LCDR Anderson went around behind the panel and retrieved the rifle which had been lying on the floor behind the panel.

"Lieutenant Yates, I am handing you an M1 which is assigned to the armory of the *Erne*. Let me assure you, sir, that this is the same rifle which was held in the hands of Petty Officer Miller when the shooting occurred on October 20th," said LCDR Anderson.

It was out of his mouth before he even knew he said it. "That's impossible!" said Yates. He quickly coughed loudly in a feeble attempt to draw attention away from what he had just said. How the hell could this be, thought Yates. After all, he alone knew where that rifle was.

A smile spread across Captain Marshall's face.

LCDR Anderson caught herself before she laughed. Instead, she just smiled innocently. "No, Lieutenant. This is indeed the rifle. Previous witness testimony has assured the court that this is the rifle. I am also giving you another document," she said as she handed him a piece of paper. "It is a report from the base armory attesting that this rifle is unsafe. See, if you look right here at the serial number on the rifle and that one on the report, they match," she said as she pointed out the numbers to Yates.

"Can you also see who signed that report for the ship?" she asked.

Gunther, thought Yates; I'll have his ass for this. "Yes, it looks like Senior Chief Gunther," said Yates.

"So this leads the court to believe then that there was at least one unsafe M1 rifle on the *Erne*. Would you agree, Lieutenant?"

What the hell can I say, he thought. "Yes, I guess so," he said.

She took the rifle from Yates and placed it back behind the chairs of the panel members. As she returned to face Yates, she said, "So Lieutenant, if the *Erne* has sixteen such rifles assigned to its armory, and we have one rifle here today, I guess there are probably fifteen there now. Would you agree?"

"Yes, I guess so," said Yates.

"But you know what, Lieutenant. We did an inventory of the *Erne* armory, and there are only fourteen there now. It appears that another rifle is missing." LCDR Anderson then walked a few paces away from the witness chair and then walked slowly back to face Yates.

"Lieutenant Yates, why did you take the other rifle from the armory?"

Yates face brightened at least two more, deeper hues of red. "I didn't take any rifle. I don't know what the hell you are talking about."

"Lieutenant Yates, previous testimony in this court room leads us to believe that you ordered BM2 Schmitt to accompany you to the *Erne* armory and get you the rifle that had been used in the shooting on October 20th. Do you deny that?"

Yates knew that only Schmitt knew about that. He did not know that two other witnesses had corroborated the story. "I don't know what you are talking about," said Yates.

LCDR Anderson signaled to her legal aide. He walked out of the court room door. Lieutenant Yates tropical white shirt was now saturated with sweat.

In a few moments, the legal assistant reentered the court room. He was carrying a rifle. A sweat droplet dropped from Lieutenant Yates chin, making a small wet spot on the thigh portion of his white pants.

LCDR Anderson took the rifle and handed it to Lieutenant Yates. "Lieutenant Yates, this rifle is also assigned to the *Erne* armory. But do you know where the court obtained the rifle?" she asked.

Lieutenant Yates, by now was pretty certain where the rifle had come from, but he answered, "I have no idea."

LCDR Anderson then withdrew a document, and handed it to Yates. "Lieutenant, the document is self-explanatory. Your signature is on the bottom. Why did you remove this rifle from the *Erne* armory and take it to the base armory?"

Yates simply stared at LCDR Anderson. He no longer had the will to bluff his way through this quagmire. He did not answer.

"Let me help you Lieutenant. You have maintained that there were no inoperative guns on the *Erne*. That has now been proven false. But to back your assertion, you took the rifle which you thought was defective to the base armory. You instructed the armory to examine the rifle and fix it if it was faulty. But then you figured that the rifle would be safe at the base armory while the investigation and court martial were being conducted, and you would pick it up later."

"Objection, prosecution is speculating and testifying," said LCDR Boyd.

"Duly noted, Commander Boyd," said Captain Marshall.

At her signal, LCDR Anderson's legal assistant took the rifle and placed it by the other rifle behind the panel.

From her table, LCDR Anderson retrieved another document, slowly read it, and brought it around the table and handed it to Lieutenant Yates.

"Lieutenant Yates, what is this document that I have given you? Could you please tell the court?"

Yates answered, "Well it looks like some kind of medical report."

"That's correct, Mr. Yates. Could you also tell the court the date of the report and the name of the patient? See, it's listed right there," said Anderson as she pointed to a location on the document.

"Umm, the date is October 23, 1968, and the patient's name is J.W. Miller," said Yates.

"And Lieutenant Yates, can you please tell the court what is listed as the diagnosis of Petty Officer Miller," said Anderson.

"Malaria, advanced state," said Lieutenant Yates.

"Lieutenant Yates, were you aware that Petty Officer Miller had a high fever associated with malaria on October 20th?" asked Anderson.

"No, I didn't know that," answered Yates.

"Don't you think that the CO of a small ship should know if he has a key member of a boarding party that is not at full performance due to an illness?"

"I suppose so, but neither the corpsman nor the XO told me that Miller was ill," said Yates.

While Yates answered the question, LCDR Anderson retrieved the green log book. She handed it to Lieutenant Yates.

"Lieutenant, as I understand from other witness testimony, the *Erne* kept this log book and recorded the circumstances of every Vietnamese water craft that you stopped and inspected. Is that correct?"

"Yes, ma'am," answered Yates.

"Lieutenant Yates would you please read the log entry for October 20th, the day of the shooting incident?" asked Anderson.

Lieutenant Yates opened the log and leafed through the pages. He already knew what he would find. "I don't seem to find the page for October 20th," he said.

"Oh, let me help," said LCDR Anderson. She then handed him the copy of the log page for October 20th. As he took the document, Sam

Yates dropped the log book on the floor. The bang that the heavy book made as it hit the floor sounded like a gun firing. He slowly bent over and retrieved the book.

"If you look at the notes, you will see the date, and you will see the fisherman's name, Ninh Ba Chau. Those notes have been verified by three other witnesses in this trial to be the log entry made by Ensign Kramer as he examined the fishing boat on October 20th. But for some reason, that original page is not in the book. Lieutenant, if you open the log book and examine the space in the book where that page should be, do you notice anything strange about that page?"

"No, I don't know what you mean," said Yates.

"Look closely at the spine of the book. Don't you see where the page for the 20th was cut out of the book?"

Yates looked closely at the book, but made no comment.

"Lieutenant, do you have any idea who might have cut that page out of the book?" asked Anderson.

"No," he said, and abruptly closed the log book.

"Well, Lieutenant, the court knows who cut those pages out. The court knows that you ordered BM2 Schmitt to help you cut those pages out. That action occurred in your cabin. Don't you remember that?" she asked, and smiled very slightly.

Again, Lieutenant Sam Yates simply stared at LCDR Anderson. His eyes, however, were glazed.

LCDR Anderson gently removed the log book from Yates' hands and walked to her seat. "I have no further questions, Captain Marshall," she said.

"No questions," said LCDR Boyd. He didn't need to be asked by Captain Marshall. This case was dead in the water.

"Very well," said Captain Marshall. "Lieutenant Yates, I would like for you to return to the witness holding room. We will come and get you as soon as we can. The panel will come with me. I need to make some phone calls. Both Counsels and Petty Officer Miller may leave the room, but remain close to the court room. We will return in a few moments."

*****

It was closer to an hour and a half that the judge and panel were away. As they returned to the court room, they carried their notes and file folders. LCDR Anderson, LCDR Boyd, Boyd's second, and Buddy followed them into the court room. "Everyone just take a seat. We're waiting on someone to help us," said Captain Marshall. "They should be here shortly."

In a few moments, the court room doors opened and three Marines, one a captain and two non-commissioned officers entered the room. They wore the arm band of military police, and all wore camouflage uniforms. A military .45 was attached to each of their web belts.

The captain in the group made a brisk salute and said, "Captain Harmon, reporting as ordered, sir."

The two attorneys and Buddy were at a loss as to why three armed Marines had entered the court room. But suddenly, Buddy panicked. He quickly thought that the marines were there to take him away. He looked at LCDR Anderson and he thought, how could she remain calm when they were going to take him away? Although it was just a slight case of paranoia, it seemed to Buddy like the two enlisted marines kept looking at him.

Captain Marshall pointed at the legal assistant and said, "Would you please go tell Lieutenant Yates that we are ready for him?"

A moment later, as he entered the court room and saw the armed Marines, Sam Yates thought to himself, good. They're here to take Miller away. Maybe this thing will finally be over.

"Take a seat, please, Lieutenant, on the witness stand," said Captain Marshall.

Yates took his seat with a look of mild curiosity on his face.

"Lieutenant Yates, I have asked you to return to the court room," said Captain Marshall. "As an officer of the court acting on behalf of the Military Advisory Command Vietnam, I have been authorized to place you under arrest."

Yates head jerked as he heard the words. "Under arrest." This could not be happening. The stupid kid was supposed to go to jail. He turned and glared at LCDR Boyd, who looked back at him without expression. He turned back to Captain Marshall and opened his mouth to speak, but stopped as Captain Marshall continued.

"Lieutenant Yates, you will be held in confinement pending formal notification of the charges to be filed against you. The evidence presented in this court martial has proven to the panel that you are not worthy of the command of a United States Naval vessel. Commander Mine Squadron Nine has been apprised of these proceedings and has authorized me to inform you that you are hereby relieved of command of the USS *Erne*. You will be escorted by these Marines to the base confinement facility. You will then be escorted on the next available flight to Sasebo, Japan, where Mine Squadron Nine will determine your further disposition. Orders verifying your relief as commanding officer of the *Erne* will be given to you in Sasebo. Your personal effects will be taken from the ship and sent to Sasebo. Lieutenant Yates, do you understand what I have just said to you?"

The Navy had determined that he was unfit for command. There was nothing he could say except, "Yes, sir." He slumped in his chair, a broken man. His elbows were on his knees, and his head was down.

"Captain Harmon. Would you and your men please escort Lieutenant Yates to the detention facility?"

The Marine captain snapped to attention, saluted Captain Marshall, and said, "Aye, aye, Captain."

In a matter of moments, the court room was again quiet. Captain Marshall closed one of the folders that was in front of him on the table and opened another. "Now then. Petty Officer Miller, would you please rise and face the panel."

Buddy did as he was told. The two attorneys did not have to be told. They both rose and faced Captain Marshall.

"Gunner's Mate Third Class J. William Miller, as the presiding official at this court martial, with the concurrence of Mine Squadron Nine, and the Military Advisory Command Vietnam, it is my duty to inform you that all charges filed against you have been dropped. You are free to return to your duty command."

Following those words, one of the legal assistants quietly slipped out of the court room door. A few seconds later a loud cheer was heard from the hallway outside the room. Captain Marshall and the panel were all smiling. LCDR Anderson was hugging Buddy. Tears of joy were rolling freely down Buddy's cheeks.

"Petty Officer Miller, do you have anything you would like to say to the panel?" asked Captain Marshall.

All eyes were on Buddy, but he was frozen. As the tears continued, he managed to blurt out, "Thank you sir."

LCDR Anderson nudged him. Buddy put on his white hat and saluted the Captain.

"Now, Miller, and Commander Anderson, I think we should take a little base taxi ride down to the pier. I need to make a few remarks to the crew of the *Erne*. Commander Boyd, you need to head back to Sasebo. When you get there, tell your boss, Captain Munday that I will be paying him a visit next week. Have you got that?"

"Yes, sir," said Boyd, who continued packing his papers in a valise.

*****

As the two attorneys and Buddy crossed the brow of the *Erne*, Senior Chief Gunther, Fig Newton, and Bob Dawes started raising a ruckus and slapping Buddy on the back. Their noise sounded suspiciously like the noise that was heard outside the court room less than an hour ago.

LTJG Bamino approached Captain Marshall, saluted him, and listened to the Captain. "Lieutenant, would you be so kind as to assemble the *Erne* crew here on the fantail of the ship. I would like to speak to them."

Momentarily an announcement from the 1MC brought all the crew to the fantail.

"Gentlemen," Captain Marshall began. "Because I think there may have been a couple of friendly spies outside the court room, by now most of you know that Petty Officer Miller has been cleared of any wrongdoing for the incident of October 20th. What you may not know is that your commanding officer, Lieutenant Yates, will no longer be your CO."

Heads swiveled as the crew mumbled to each other. Captain Marshall continued, "LTJG Bamino will temporarily assume command until a new skipper can be brought aboard." As he said that, he handed Bamino an official-looking folder, which contained temporary orders for him.

"Please don't ask, because I am not at liberty to give you any details regarding this situation." He turned to LTJG Bamino and said, "Lieutenant, your orders are to sail the *Erne* back to Sasebo to await further instructions, and a new skipper," said Marshall.

"Now, I want to commend the officers and crew of the *Erne*," said Marshall. "You have some very special sailors on this ship, men who would stake their careers on helping each other. You are a good crew.

And now, I think you should all thank LCDR Anderson, Petty Officer Miller's defense counsel. She did a great job to see that justice was done."

Mixed in with the cheering and clapping hands were a couple wolf whistles. After all, they were sailors who appreciated an attractive woman. Captain Marshall, LCDR Anderson, and LTJG Bamino then adjourned to the CO's cabin to go over some other details. The *Erne* would sail the next day for Japan.

That evening, for everyone except the duty section, a party raged at the enlisted men's club on the Da Nang base. There was a true reason for the party. An enlisted man had been cleared of trumped-up charges, which very well could have meant a term in prison. Buddy did not buy a beer all evening, but the table in front of him was covered with full beer bottles.

Try as he might, Buddy could not find the right words to say to Ray Gunther and Bob Dawes. He simply kept saying 'thank you' to both of them; over and over all evening. But it really did not matter to Gunther and Dawes. That's just the way it is with good friends.

Three weeks after the *Erne* reached her home port of Sasebo, there was another court martial. Unfortunately, many of the same witnesses who had testified at Buddy's trial also testified at the trial of Lieutenant Samuel Yates. They all found it to be unpleasant; testifying against their old commanding officer made them uneasy. As a result of the trial, the officer's commission of Lieutenant Samuel Yates was rescinded by the United States Navy. He was sent home to the states as a civilian, with a less-than-honorable discharge. He was fortunate. He would not be spending time in the Federal Penitentiary at Leavenworth, Kansas. For that he was grateful.

In addition, Boatswain's Mate Second Class Mark Schmitt was never again seen on the *Erne*. No one really knew what happened to him. No one, that is, except LTJG Bamino, who had arranged for a set of "quickie orders," PN3 Sorenson in the ship's office who processed the orders, and Senior Chief Ray Gunther, who walked Schmitt to the base Master at Arms facility for further processing.

November 21, 1966
Dear Mom and Dad,

I sure was happy to hear your voices a couple days ago. It was really nice of LTJG Bamino to arrange for that phone call. Things have sort of returned to normal on the Erne. *Rumor has it that we will have a new CO in the next few days. He is sure to be a big improvement over the last one. I never want to see that guy again. Senior Chief Gunther says that now I have even more of a reason to stay in the Navy, but I am pretty fed up with the Navy right now. I'm still having some bad dreams over the whole thing that happened, and I may have to go to the base clinic and see if they can do anything about my headaches. I guess you will get this letter after Thanksgiving. I wish I was there to have a big piece of apple pie.*
Next year, maybe. Say hello to Sarah and Janeen.
Love, Buddy

On December 1, the small wooden ship backed from the pier in Sasebo and pointed its bow once again to the southwest in the East China Sea. The ship and crew later entered the South China Sea and moved toward Vietnam. They had been assigned to Market Time duties again, and after several days, they were in their assigned patrol area. They were all glad the ordeal in Da Nang and Sasebo was over. Hence, no one grumbled about being back to the Navy routine. However, after the respite in

Sasebo, everyone grumbled at being in the hot, sticky weather off the coast of Vietnam again, especially since it would mean that they would be away from their home port on Christmas. There is an old saw in the Navy that says, "A bitching sailor is a happy sailor." It generally means the sailor is busy and working hard. The old saying has some truth to it. But listening to the *Erne* crew moan and groan about the hot sticky weather, one would have thought it might be the happiest crew in the Navy.

From the corner of every eye on the ship, a close monitoring of the actions of Lieutenant William "Will" Spencer was taking place. An academy graduate, with six years of exemplary underway experience, Will Spencer had taken command of the *Erne* in Sasebo only three days before the ship got underway. He would need to be a fast learner and rely on his seasoned crew to help him shoulder his responsibility. In the short observance by the crew, the consensus was that they were now being led by a true leader. This fact, along with daily surveillance of water craft, interception and searching of vessels, and the satisfaction of knowing that they were helping the front line units, served to greatly lift the spirits of the crew. Under the firm and fair guidance of Lieutenant Will Spencer, the *Erne* soon established itself as a leader among the coastal mine-sweepers assigned to Market Time. The ship and crew made several significant seizures of contraband. Captain Spencer was proud of his crew and made sure that his department heads gave credit and awards to their teams.

*****

When he knew that the *Erne* was going to be refueled or replenished by the *Kawishiwi*, Buddy made a special effort to stand by Senior Chief Gunther on the *Erne* fantail so that they could both wave and shout to

Senior Chief John Proctor on the big oiler. Senior Chief Gunther had told Buddy how he had taken the defective rifle to Senior Chief Proctor on the *Kawishiwi* for safe keeping prior to the court martial. Buddy knew that an enlisted man in the Navy did not get to be a chief unless he showed knowledge, skills, and especially, initiative. But the initiative demonstrated by Senior Chief Gunther in helping to thwart the trumped up case against Buddy was truly amazing. Buddy would be forever grateful to the two senior chiefs.

*****

Each time he had visited with the ship's corpsman, he had been given the same advice. But he had not yet heeded that advice. Buddy had been told that he needed to visit a Navy clinic in Sasebo to discuss his condition and receive a true diagnosis after a thorough examination. After scolding Buddy in very pointed fashion and giving his advice, the corpsman would then grudgingly hand over the prescription sleeping pills to Buddy. Without them, Buddy rarely slept more than two hours at a time, only to be interrupted in his sleep by the recurring nightmare. With the sleeping pills, he was able to sleep nearly four hours before the effect of the pills wore off.

Since they shared the same crowded berthing compartment, most of the enlisted men on board the *Erne* knew that Buddy Miller was not sleeping soundly at night. They had heard him talking in his sleep, followed by his waking abruptly after loudly repeating the words, "No, no, no!" Those members of the crew who knew him well could also see that he had lost weight and did not seem to have much interest in food. Bob Dawes and Senior Chief Gunther also noticed that Buddy had developed a habit of rubbing the sides of his head near the temples several times per day. When they asked Buddy about it, he simply replied that he had a headache. In truth, Buddy's headache never stopped. With the constant pain in his head, there were times when he thought that if he was not already insane, he soon would be. In his mind, he was certain that he had developed some sort of horrible illness, and he was afraid to see a doctor for fear of confirming this unfounded fear.

Buddy's medical condition did not seem to affect his work performance. The ship's armory could stand up to any inspection, the department records were flawless, and the maintenance was always up to date. But Bob Dawes could see another change in Buddy. When Buddy became frustrated, over even the most trivial item, his frustration would turn into mild violence. He would slam books to the deck of the armory and throw discarded and useless metal gun parts against the bulkhead, mumbling and groaning as he did these things, as if he was in pain. Dawes was understandably worried about his friend.

Unexpectedly, as the ship had only been patrolling for ten days, in the latter part of December, the *Erne* was relieved on station by another ship and made its long return voyage to its home port of Sasebo. The crew was looking forward to time with their families and leisure time with their friends after work hours.

With the ship in Sasebo, and as time went on, Dawes's concern for his friend heightened. It seemed that each time the men left the ship for liberty, Buddy would find one of the favorite hang-outs and begin drinking heavily. When he drank, he would become loud and demonstrate combative behavior with companions. Contemptuous, profane remarks directed toward anyone within sight would then follow. This was not the Buddy Miller that his friends knew. There was something wrong. Bob Dawes turned again to his best resource and had another long talk with Senior Chief Gunther, telling him of his observations.

Chapter Twenty-Three

Christmas Eve, 1968
USS Erne
In Port, Sasebo, Japan

Christmas Eve
Dear Mom and Dad,

Well, it's going to be another Christmas on the ship. I sure would like to be there with you guys. I have been having some problems with headaches. It seems like I have them all the time, but I can still do my work OK. Our corpsman wants me to go see a doctor, so I guess one of these days I will need to do that. I had been giving more thought to staying in the Navy as a career, but after what happened a couple months ago, I have pretty much made up my mind to get out when my time is up. Maybe I'll go to college when I get home. Hope everything is good there. Say hi to the girls for me.
Love, Buddy

Christmas passed and final preparations for a gala New Year's Eve party were being made by the owner of the *Pony Up Bar,* another favorite watering hole of the sailors in Sasebo. Every ship in port and all of the shore command offices had received flyers of the party. Two different bands would play, there would be free hors d'oeuvres and raffle prizes. Of course, the price of drinks at the bar would be covertly raised to cover these expenses. Shanghai Charlie, the owner of the bar was nobody's fool. He and his staff of bartenders, bar girls, prostitutes, and bouncers were ready to extract every nickel they could from the attendees. But there was little doubt that where there was music, women, and alcohol, sailors would have a good time.

*****

The evening of December 31, 1968 was crisp and clear. Even with the lights of the city, the stars shone brilliantly in the deepening darkness of winter. Buddy stared up at the evening sky and marveled at the beauty of the heavenly lights. It was nearly 2000, and Buddy had only a few minutes left of his quarterdeck watch. He had taken the watch for one of the married crew members who wanted to have dinner at home with his wife and then return to the ship. Buddy would then be free to attend the New Year's Eve party with Dawes and Fig Newton, who were playing cards on the mess deck waiting for Buddy to be relieved on watch and change his clothes.

In a short while, the three young men crossed the brow and left the ship, headed for the *Pony Up Bar*. The festivities had already begun when they arrived. The band which was playing at that moment was made up of a group of American sailors from one of the shore commands. They were cranking out the latest stateside rock and roll tunes while a few couples danced. Three pool tables at the back of the bar were under control of a group of Marines, who, by all appearances, had clearly started their partying earlier. They were easily recognized by their distinctive haircuts, as opposed to the longer hair worn by the sailors. Business was brisk at the bar, and two of Charlie's bullet-headed heavies stood in the shadows casually watching the scene.

The first two beers that Buddy quickly drank assuaged the sharp pain of his headache. The next two calmed the pain considerably, but also lowered his inhibitions and motor skills. Soon, he, Dawes, and Fig were on the dance floor, each with one of the bar girls. To a sober observer, the physical antics of the three men certainly could not be classified as dancing in any known form, but they were certainly having fun. As the evening wore on, Buddy was drinking freely and was clearly inebriated. In this state, he convinced Dawes and Fig that they were the best dancers on the floor, while he tightly squeezed the prostitute with whom he had been dancing. Being paid by the bar to cajole the men to buy as many drinks as possible, the three women accomplices pleaded for money and having gotten it from the three men, quickly left and soon returned with fresh drinks for everyone. Of course, the prostitutes' drinks were simply watered-down tea. The time passed quickly in this manner, but at about eleven-thirty, Buddy, Dawes, and Fig decided that they needed to challenge a table of Marines to a game of pool. Drunken sailors challenging drunken Marines to any sort of game is not a very good idea. It's not even a good idea when no one has been drinking. But the bets were placed on the table, and a small crowd gathered around to watch the inter-service rivalry pool match. Buddy and Dawes were the team playing against the two Marines. As the four men traded shots, Buddy and Dawes seemed to be leading. But the outcome was far from a sure thing in their hampered condition.

No one knew for sure how it started, but suddenly, Buddy seemed to lose focus. For a moment, he stood still and stared into space. The pool cue that he had been holding in his hand clattered to the floor. Suddenly he began yelling with the volume rising as he continued. At first, he held his hands up to the side of his head and yelled, "No, no, no," over and over. His eyes were painfully squinted closed. Then the profanities rolled from his mouth and were directed at anyone in sight, which, of course, included the Marines. Buddy then climbed up on the pool table and began kicking the billiard balls off the table with the toe of his shoe so that they flew around the pool room. One ball struck a Marine squarely on the forehead. The young Marine quickly climbed up on the table and began swinging his pool cue at Buddy. Buddy retaliated with a clenched fist which connected to the jaw of the Marine who then fell off the table to the floor. By this time, the bar's bouncers were hurrying to the pool table, but it was too late. The pool table area had now erupted into a free-for-all with the sailors and Marines going at each other with vengeance. Smaller combatants were simply picked up by larger men and thrown out of the way to land unceremoniously against the nearest wall. Such was the case with scrawny Fig Newton, and he lay next to a wall rubbing a knot on the back of his head. Blood was streaming from many noses and eyebrows as fists and pool cues swung through the air. The melee could not be stopped by a mere duo of bar bouncers. But as is the case in many drunken bar fights, the participants, in their inebriated condition, simply ran out of steam, thereby putting a rather unglorious and anticlimactic end to the disturbance. At midnight, when the band began to play a very sloppy version of Auld Lang Sine, at least three fourths of the combatants lay in drunken stupor heaps on the floor; some still moving and others either knocked out cold or passed out in the melee. Blood flowed from open wounds on numerous drunken combatants. The bouncers began dragging men to the door of the bar and shoving or tossing them outdoors.

Lieutenants Bamino and Spencer had seen enough. They were also in the bar and from their vantage point at the end of the bar, they had seen the beginning through to the end of the fracas and subsequently left the bar to return to the ship.

On the day following the New Year's holiday, eight sailors stood on the fantail of the *Erne*. Periodically, one of the men would be accompanied by Senior Chief Gunther and brought to Captain Spencer's cabin where mast was being held on an assembly-line basis. For seven of the men, the punishment was generally no more than a stern dressing down (ass chewing) by the CO and a mandatory collection of money from those men. The money would be used to make a small reimbursement to Shanghai Charlie for the damage inflicted to the *Pony Up Bar*. The scenario with the eighth man was slightly different. That eighth man was GM3 Buddy Miller.

As he faced the CO, Buddy had to concentrate to understand the words being spoken by Lieutenant Spencer. He was intently concentrating in an attempt to push aside the pounding in his head. The painful headache had nothing to do with the party two days ago. It was caused instead, by the stress of going before the Captain of the ship. The stress only aggravated the ever-present chronic headaches.

He heard the CO saying, "You're damn lucky I don't take that second stripe away from you even before you put it on. What the hell got into you to start messing with a bunch of drunken Marines?"

He heard himself say, "I don't know Captain. I don't know what happened." And in truth, Buddy remembered very few of the details of New Year's Eve.

The conversation went on for a few more minutes, but then Captain Spencer gave his decision.

"Miller, I'm fining you $100 for causing that disturbance, and I am restricting you to the ship for two weeks. I am being lenient with you because I have checked into your past performance and activities. This episode is not indicative of your past. Hell, I don't know what is wrong with you. But I do believe you may have a medical problem; either caused by alcohol, or something even more serious. I have told the corpsman to make you an appointment at the base hospital, and I want you to be thoroughly checked out by the docs over there. Your appointment is tomorrow, and the corpsman will go with you. Miller, I want you to get to the bottom of this, because I think that you still have value to the Navy. Do you have anything else you want to say?"

Buddy answered, "No sir."

Chapter Twenty-Four

January 10, 1969
U.S. Military Medical Hospital
Sasebo, Japan

He had now returned to the clinic for the third time. During the course of the previous two visits, the medical staff had performed a thorough physical examination. Buddy had been poked, prodded, and hooked up to every device available in the clinic.

The same tired-faced physician whom he had met with previously was speaking to him. Buddy listened intently, through the dull pounding in his head. "Petty Officer Miller, I cannot find anything physically wrong with you. In fact, our results show that you are in excellent condition. I am not a specialist in neurology or psychology, but I have a hunch that your condition has something to do with your mental state. Therefore, I am going to refer you to another doctor here in the clinic. He specializes in psychiatry. I am hopeful that he may be able to figure out what is going on with you."

A psychiatrist. The word echoed in Buddy's head. "Are you saying that I might be crazy," he stammered.

"No, I didn't say that at all. What I said was that I can't find anything physically wrong with you, so I want my colleague to take a look at you. I'll make an appointment for you and let your corpsman know when it is. In the meantime, I'm going to prescribe a pain medication for your headaches. I think you should take it when the pain becomes severe." The doctor handed Buddy a slip of paper containing the written prescription.

For the next two weeks, Buddy remained on the medication prescribed by the military physician. The result was that he felt better. The headaches were less painful, and the anxious feelings he had been experiencing also diminished. He slept more soundly, but still had the nightmares which caused him to awaken. He knew he was not cured, but the symptoms were considerably less severe.

It was with a great deal of trepidation, that he had had his first meeting with a psychiatrist. It had seemed so relaxed and casual to talk with the physician that Buddy felt that this session and any future meetings might be a complete waste of time. It was quickly followed by a second session. Those first two sessions with the hospital's resident psychiatrist went well. It now seemed to Buddy that it helped just to have someone with whom to confide, relate his feelings, and unburden himself. He told the physician of the events surrounding the shooting incident and the details of the court martial proceedings. He had not previously discussed these events with anyone else. The sessions did not seem very clinical to Buddy; they were more like just two guys talking to each other, sharing stories. But at the end of each session, Buddy felt better.

At the conclusion of the fourth meeting with the psychiatrist, the young military doctor gave Buddy an opinion. "Petty Officer Miller, I appreciate the time you have given me so that we could talk together. I have been doing some research on your symptoms and their relationship to what has occurred with you in the past few months." The doctor continued, "I have a colleague who was in medical school with me, who is working at Walter Reed in the states. I have talked with him in detail, and he has sent me several new medical articles concerning a condition exhibited by many of the returning veterans from Vietnam. At present, they are calling the condition 'post-Vietnam Syndrome.' I believe your symptoms seem to follow those described in the articles."

Buddy listened intently to the doctor as the young physician continued. "From what I have observed and from what you have described, your symptoms seem to fit into this broad-based condition. Your headaches, your anxiety, the nightmares, sleep disorder, non-specific anger; all these are associated with the diagnosis."

Hanging on every word of the doctor's, Buddy then asked, "Am I ever going to get over this?"

"Unfortunately, I can't answer that," said the psychiatrist. "The data on this condition is very sketchy since no concrete research studies have been done as yet. In the meantime, I want you to come see me once a month when your ship is in port. I am also going to slightly modify your medication in order to further diminish your symptoms. If you develop any new symptoms or changes in your condition due to the medication, please come see me immediately. In addition, you must limit yourself to no more than two alcoholic drinks per day. Can you do that?"

Buddy nodded his head in agreement.

Over the next few days, there was a marked improvement in Buddy's demeanor. He felt better, and the headaches were under control. His physician decided that there was really no need for Buddy to revisit the psychiatrist other than the monthly sessions. The drugs were apparently doing the job for which they were intended. Aside from the dull headaches, Buddy was exhibiting no other signs of the anxiety disorder which was loosely entitled "post-Vietnam syndrome" by the medical community.

After returning to full duty on the ship, he had once again gained the respect of the officers and crew on the *Erne*. The full story of Captain's Yates' conspiracy to lay all the blame for the unfortunate shooting was now known by the crew. What Yates had done was viewed as reprehensible behavior by both the officers and crew.

Buddy's life returned to a familiar routine. He, Bob Dawes, and Fig Newton had become inseparable friends, and he continued to receive guidance from his mentor, Senior Chief Gunther. If Buddy went on liberty with his friends, he would nurse a beer or two the entire evening and often walked back to the ship alone. His life was now disciplined and remained on an even keel.

The *Erne* continued its trips to participate in Market Time. While assigned to Market Time, a small change had been made to the boarding party procedures. In answer to his own request, Buddy would no longer be assigned to a rifle or machine gun. Instead, he stood on the fantail of the ship, next to Senior Chief Gunther. He wore a .45 on his hip. Lieutenant Bamino had seen the wisdom in honoring Buddy's request and had made that change. Buddy was appreciative.

For the next twelve months, the small minesweeper carried out its mission cycle: several weeks off the coast of Vietnam followed by several weeks back in its Sasebo home port. The hot, sweaty, drudgery of intercepting Vietnamese water craft continued with many small weapons and supply seizures made. During the remainder of 1969, and in the first month of 1970, the ship's record was unblemished, and the weapons department's standing under Buddy's guidance was impeccable. Captain Spencer had carefully watched and periodically praised Buddy's work.

At the end of February, Buddy had met the time in grade requirement, and due to his hard work, excellent performance, and innate intelligence, he was promoted to petty officer second class. At an awards ceremony, Captain Spencer personally made the promotion presentation of the new rank insignia to Buddy. It was a proud achievement for the young man at the end of five very trying months.

Buddy's enlistment obligation was approaching its conclusion, and he was still undecided as to whether or not he would stay in the military. Aside from the unfortunate incident in October of 1968, and its subsequent repercussions, his record was exemplary. He was at a crossroads in his life and a decision would need to be made by the young man.

Chapter Twenty-Five

April 20, 1970
Somewhere Over the Pacific

One leg was asleep, tingling with needle-like discomfort. His mouth was dry as cotton, and his tongue felt twice its size. His headache was a dull pounding. He never had been adroit at sleeping on an airplane, but the nap had been a welcome break. Petty Officer Second Class J. William (Buddy) Miller uncoiled his body, rose from the seat, and stood in the aisle. While he shook the afflicted foot to increase its blood circulation, he glanced around the darkened interior of the aircraft. The majority of the passengers on this Trans World Airlines overnight flight from Tokyo to San Francisco were either sleeping or reading below the faint glow of the reading lights above their individual seats in the plane's darkened cabin. A roving stewardess, dutifully walking the aisle of the plane, caught Buddy's eye, and he motioned to her his wish for some water by pantomiming the act of drinking. She smiled and held up a circled thumb and forefinger as she continued her night time circuit.

As the feeling returned to his leg, Buddy reached above his seat, opened the luggage compartment, and dug into his travel bag. He finally retrieved two pills that he would wash down with the water the stewardess was bringing to him. As she reached him with the cup of water, Buddy thanked her.

"Looks like your friend is sleeping well," the stewardess said quietly.

It suddenly occurred to Buddy that this was the first round-eyed girl he had stood this close to for many weeks. He could smell her cologne and was taken by her bright smile to the point that he stammered a bit when he replied.

"Yep, I think he could sleep anywhere," was all he could manage to say.

She smiled again, patted Buddy gently on the arm, and returned to her walk through the aisle.

Buddy placed the two pills on his tongue and swallowed them with the water. A slight snoring sound drew his attention back to the airplane seat next to his own. Bob Dawes' mouth gaped open, and the quiet noises of sleep continued. There was not a worry line on his face. But there were a few wrinkles elsewhere; Dawes' rumpled white uniform looked like he had slept in it for weeks instead of a few hours.

*****

Toward the end of January 1970, three months ago, a message had arrived in the *Erne*'s radio traffic. In essence, it said that the Navy was going to begin drawing down its forces in specific enlisted ratings throughout the Navy, thereby reducing the number of men and women who held those ratings on active duty. Because of the evolving dependency upon more technical ratings, the need for traditional ratings was diminishing. Some of the sailors occupying slots in these old ratings could leave the Navy to make room for more of the technically rated sailors. One of the ratings targeted was that of the traditional gunner's mate. Many gunner's mates in the Navy whose skills were not associated with the Navy's modern electronic weaponry would soon begin receiving orders terminating their service. With the great number of gunner's mates serving in the Navy at that time, the odds of this happening to two gunner's mates on the same small ship were very small. But defying the odds, four weeks after that initial message had arrived on the *Erne*, the names of Gunner's Mates Dawes and Miller showed up on a subsequent radio message, informing them that they were receiving "early out" orders. The Navy also gave each recipient the option of staying in the Navy if they would immediately reenlist. Apparently, the Navy saw logic in this convoluted arrangement. But neither Buddy nor Dawes chose to reenlist, and very soon the *Erne* would be without a gunner's mate.

Bob Dawes didn't have to think twice about whether or not to reenlist. He immediately began sending letters to colleges and universities to gain entrance. He was going to return home and go to school.

The decision was not made as quickly by Buddy Miller. For the past two years, he had been giving serious consideration to staying in the Navy as a career. He had talked at great length with Senior Chief Gunther and other senior enlisted men on the ship. But the factor that tipped the balance was his last visit to the Navy psychiatrist. While there, he had discussed his thoughts about making the Navy a career with the doctor.

"Much as I would like to see you remain in this 'canoe club,' I do not believe you should do that, Petty Officer Miller. It is simply not in your best interest." The doctor advised, "Many of the stressors that caused your anxiety attacks are still around you. You could be thrown into an identical situation in the future if you choose to remain in the Navy. To continue your improvement, and for your own mental health, I am advising you as your treating physician and a friend, that you should think twice about continuing a military career."

To Buddy, the doctor's advice had seemed definitive enough. Therefore, he would exercise his option to leave the military.

Due to the Navy's drawdown in certain ratings, the *Erne* was losing six experienced petty officers. And like all Navy ships operating during the Vietnam War, the ship would be expected to carry out its mission in spite of its shortage in personnel.

*****

As he slowly slid back down into his seat, the seat jostled slightly. Buddy could see a cloud-enshrouded, gray-red glow beginning to show under the window shade that had been drawn down to cover the airplane's window in this row. With their eastern path, full morning light would soon bounce into the cabin of the streaking aircraft. The drugs he had swallowed were slowly taking effect, and Buddy's headache was receding to its normal low throb. He had resigned himself to believe that he would have these nagging headaches the rest of his life.

He glanced over at Dawes. One of Bob's eyelids cracked ever so slightly, and the eyeball behind the lid turned toward Buddy, while his mouth opened and closed a couple of times. Buddy grinned as he watched his friend awakening.

"What the hell are you grinning at?" rasped Dawes. "I ain't funny, and what the hell are you doing awake, anyway?" Dawes was now unkinking his lanky body, rubbing his eyes, and sitting upright. "Damn, I've gotta go to the head."

Buddy again got up from his aisle seat to let Dawes out and watched him slowly walk up the aisle to the toilet. Buddy slowly shook his head. For some strange reason, in the past year, Dawes always made Buddy feel a bit happier. Dawes had proven himself over and over to be a good friend, even though sometimes the immature kid in Dawes showed itself. There was a strong bond between the two young men, forged over time and through pleasant and not so pleasant shared experiences.

Dawes's perverse sense of humor at times bordered on mischief for which there could be unpleasant consequences. One such incident had occurred only a few days before, when the *Erne* was at sea, enroute to her home port of Sasebo. Sometime during the last day at sea, Dawes had

251

scrounged up a large handful of steel ball bearings from one of the ship's machinist mates. He carefully painted his name on two of the steel spheres. That evening, while the ship steamed toward Sasebo and the XO and CO were on the bridge, Dawes had stolen into their cabin. He placed the steel ball bearings in every nook and cranny he could find in the cabin, which the CO shared with the XO. In each of these hiding places, he ensured that the steel balls would be free to roll to and fro in their hiding places. He even opened the locker drawers under the bunks of the two officers and put some of the bearings at the back of the drawers while carefully arranging the officers' clothing to the front of the drawers. Finally, the two balls that had been painted with Dawes' name on them were placed inside one of the uniform dress shoes of both the CO and XO. He knew that once the ship reached port, the two officers would change into these shoes, which were the proper uniform while in port. Dawes knew that both men wore boondocker boots at sea and only wore their dress shoes while in port. Needless to say, that evening, when the CO and XO finally hit their racks, a great deal of time was spent by both men trying to locate every single clattering ball bearing as it rolled about in its hiding place. The CO and XO vowed to get to the bottom of this prank after quarters the following morning.

Just before morning's first light, the *Erne* began approaching Sasebo harbor, and justice would have to wait. But when the CO and XO arose early to take the ship to its mooring and both were dressing and putting on their uniform shoes, they each found the painted ball bearing with "Dawes" painted on it. They couldn't help but laugh, but they decided they would get Dawes. After the ship was secure at the pier, the crew assembled for quarters. In a few minutes, LTJG (recently promoted) Kramer joined his department.

The first words out of Kramer's mouth were, "What the hell have you done now, Dawes? The CO wants to see you on the bridge after quarters." Kramer just looked at Dawes for a minute, then shook his head. "But before you go up on the bridge to see the CO, I suggest you go back on the fantail and see Senior Chief Gunther."

After they were dismissed from quarters, Dawes grabbed Buddy's arm. "C'mon, quick," he said. Buddy looked at LTJG Kramer's back as he walked away. He did not know what to think, so he followed Dawes as he quickly made his way to the fantail.

Senior Chief Gunther, who was uncharacteristically in on this joke, was standing by the brow. "Hurry up, you two." He shoved their respective sea bags into the hands of Buddy and Dawes and told them to hustle to base admin. As soon as the two men began walking across the ship's brow, Gunther trotted up the ladders to the bridge, where he met the CO and XO. The CO was holding a large sock that was tied at the opening. He kept dropping the sock on his free hand and as he did so, the sock made a strange metallic clinking noise. It was nearly half full of ball bearings.

"Where's Dawes, Senior Chief?" asked the XO.

"Well sir, Miller and Dawes are walking down the pier. You see, their orders state that they are to report to the base administration office by 0800 to begin their out-processing. And since it's after eight, I figured they would need to hustle so they wouldn't be counted as AWOL by the base admin office. The CO and XO looked down from the bridge to see the two gunner's mates strolling down the pier past the ship with their sea bags on their shoulders.

"Aw, shit," was the entire exclamation of the CO. But then, he swung the sock with its cargo of ball bearings over his head and threw it toward the pier and the two sailors who were making their escape. WHAM! The sock full of ball bearings landed a mere two feet from where Dawes was walking. On impact the sock burst and ball bearings went in all directions, just as Bob Dawes was taking his next step. His foot landed on six ball bearings, and his foot and leg flew skyward while the rest of his body landed unceremoniously on his rump. The CO, XO, and Senior Chief laughed as they leaned out the open bridge windows. Buddy was bent over laughing. Unflustered, Dawes picked himself up, shouldered his sea bag, stood at attention, and saluted the CO on the bridge. Still laughing, Lieutenant Spencer returned the salute. He then shouted, "Best of luck to you two guys. We will miss you."

Senior Chief Gunther also shouted, "Stay in touch, Miller. I want to know how you are doing."

*****

The two men ravenously ate the airline-provided breakfast as the cabin filled with sunshine and passengers greeted another day. In only a few more hours, the plane would land in San Francisco. Buddy and Dawes, as well as several other military men would then be bussed to Travis Air Force Base near Fairfield, California. There, they would complete the necessary paper work to be mustered out of the Navy in April 1970. And finally, in a day or two, they would be booked on a commercial flight to return to their homes of record. Iowa would regain two of its native sons.

Chapter Twenty-Six

April 25, 1970
Des Moines International Airport
Des Moines, Iowa

Their true feelings were masked in male bravura as they shook hands before parting that early evening at the Des Moines airport. They would miss each other, as they had become best of friends. Promising to keep in touch, Bob Dawes and Buddy Miller walked away from each other and toward their respective families who had come to the airport to pick them up for the final leg of the trip home; Dawes would go to his family home in the city, and Buddy to his family farm in Mahaska County. Irene Miller lovingly clung to the arm of her son as they walked through the airport to the baggage claim area.

Springtime in Iowa should have been well underway, with temperatures above freezing both night and day. But this year, spring had not yet fully "sprung" as Iowans were wont to say as the planting season was approaching. Even in April, when all the winter remnants should have been long gone, the airport parking lot had small pockets of dirty black ice in the sheltered corners of the concrete structure. The sun had dropped on the western horizon, and it was a chilly walk to the car.

Jim Miller put the key into the trunk lock of his new Oldsmobile 88, and stood by the trunk lid smiling. Buddy whistled. "Wow, Dad. Finally got rid of the old Plymouth, I guess."

Irene smiled. "It's about time that old car got traded. It was literally falling apart."

After putting his sea bag in the trunk of the car, Buddy crawled into passenger seat beside his dad. Irene sat in the back seat. "Where are the girls?" asked Buddy. Irene answered, "Oh, they have so much homework they needed to stay home and finish it. They're over at the Nelsons, working on team projects with their girls. They can't wait to see you," she said.

"It sure is good to see you again, son," said Jim Miller as he laid his calloused hand on Buddy's shoulder. "Gosh, it seems like it has been darn near forever since you were home."

The conversation was non-stop as the Oldsmobile comfortably jounced along, eating up the miles toward home. Buddy watched as the greening low hills swept past the car window. But the conversation and hours without sleep were beginning to wear on Buddy. The headache was beginning to build.

"Say Dad, could you please pull into a filling station up here in Indianola? I need to get something out of the trunk," said Buddy.

Jim Miller looked over at his son. "Sure, Buddy. I'll stop up ahead here."

The car pulled off the highway and rolled to a stop. Buddy leaped out and went around back and opened the trunk. He then rummaged into his sea bag and retrieved his shaving kit. He took two of the pills from a vial in the kit and closed up the sea bag. As he did so, he knew his father was standing beside him.

"What are the pills for, son?"

Buddy was hoping he would not have to get into this conversation until sometime later after they had gotten home, but the headache was too intense to ignore. He swallowed the dry pills. "They're for my headaches, Dad. I'll tell you all about it when we get home," said Buddy, and he slammed the trunk lid and got back in the car.

When they reached home, Jim dropped Irene and Buddy off and continued to the Nelson farm to pick up the girls. Buddy went to his room to change out of the soiled uniform. Nothing had been changed in his old room in the nearly four years he had been away. Looking around, it was as if he had never been gone. After getting dressed, but before putting on his shoes, he lay down on his bed and studied the ceiling for a moment while a myriad of thoughts went through his head. He soon fell into a sound sleep. He did not even hear when Sarah and Janeen poked their heads into his room while not so quietly whispering and giggling.

Buddy slept until the following morning. His sisters once again giggled and entered his room, where they wiggled Buddy's feet to wake him. Still in the clothes he had changed into the night before, Buddy slowly opened his eyes. His senses deceived him, and momentarily, he thought he was still on the ship. But then he heard his sisters giggling. He turned his head, smiled at the girls. He could not believe how his sisters had grown. They were now in junior high school, approaching their teen-age years. He really was home.

Sarah said, "Get up sleepyhead. Mom says you are going to miss breakfast."

"OK, OK. Now beat it," replied Buddy. The girls laughed and left his room.

I could stay here forever, Buddy mused. As he stood with the warm shower massaging his back, he thought to himself how great it was to finally be home. He quickly shaved and dressed and headed to the kitchen.

As he sat at the kitchen table drinking his second cup of after-breakfast coffee, Buddy watched his mom begin washing the dishes. Jim Miller sat on the other side of the table sipping his own coffee and watching his son. "I sure am glad to see you, son, and glad to have you home. I've got some work to do here, but before I do that, I need to run into town to the elevator and order our seed corn. If you're up to it, you can ride along with me." Buddy smiled and said, "Sure, Dad."

In the nearly four years that Buddy had been away from home, nothing had changed about his father's favorite mode of transportation. The rusty, old, red International pickup chugged along the gravel road churning up a large flume of white gravel dust which trailed in its wake. As they drove his father asked, "Buddy, how are you getting along? I mean, really, how are you? We have been so worried about you. What were those pills you were taking as we came home from the airport?"

For the next fifteen minutes Buddy related more of the details of the shooting incident in Vietnam, and the resultant medical problems that seemed to be the result of the incident. He told his Dad that he had talked with Navy doctors, including the Navy psychiatrist, and told him of the pills which had been prescribed for his headaches and for keeping the post-Vietnam condition symptoms from flaring up. Jim Miller listened intently while his son spoke of the events and medical treatment. When Buddy was through talking, Jim Miller just nodded his head, but said nothing for a few moments. Love and concern were apparent in his voice as Jim finally said, "Well, maybe being home again will help everything."

The old gray-colored concrete twin silo elevator where Jim Miller bought his seed and sold his corn crop in the fall also had not changed in the years of Buddy's absence. Two other farm pickups were parked outside the office door of the elevator. Enod Hassleberry had managed the cooperative elevator ever since Buddy could remember. In truth, he had been hired at the elevator when he had come home after serving his country in the Korean War and never left. Enod smoked a crusty old briar pipe that had layered the elevator's office walls with an earthy hue and pungent odor over the course of nearly twenty years. That smell, mixed with the smells of grain, dust, straw, and a faint hint of mouse urine hit Buddy's senses, bringing back years of memories of accompanying his father to the elevator in the spring and fall.

"Well for crying out loud," said Enod as the Millers entered the elevator office. "Just look what the cat dragged in," he said. Buddy had heard that same line every time he had come to the elevator. Enod was behind the makeshift counter of the office, leaning on his elbows next to an old brass-colored National cash register. A spill-stained coffee urn was perched on the other end of the counter. A dusty old 1955 calendar with a picture of a scantily clad woman still hung it its place of honor on an adjoining wall. Every year someone would tell Enod that 1955 was long gone and that he should replace the calendar.

Enod would just laugh and talk around his pipe stem. "Yep, and my girlfriend hanging up there looks better every year, don't she?" Then he would laugh some more.

Two other farmers were sitting on folding chairs that were pulled up to a makeshift table made of an old door resting on saw horses. They both had well-stained coffee mugs resting on the table in front of them. A faded checker board and box of checkers sat unused on one corner of the table.

"So our Navy man returns home, eh Jim?" said Enod.

"Yep, we're glad he's back," said Jim.

"Well, how was it over there, Buddy?" asked Enod.

"Not too bad, Enod. But it's sure good to be back home," said Buddy. He knew very well that Enod Hassleberry was an ex-Marine who had seen more than his fair share of action in Korea and had a Purple Heart award to prove it.

While Jim Miller worked on his seed order with Enod, Buddy spoke briefly with the two other farmers whom the Millers knew, and then Buddy left and wandered around the old elevator while he waited for his dad. He stood and watched as one of the elevator's hired men helped a farmer load large bags of Pioneer seed corn into the back of a pickup truck. He waved at the men, and they waved back.

Soon he heard his dad's old pickup horn honk, and he walked back and jumped into the truck.

On the return trip home, Jim Miller was a bit somber. "Every year, we spend a heap of money on seed and fertilizer and pray that the Good Lord will look after us and give us the weather to raise a good crop. All we can do is work hard and hope for good weather. It's pretty much out of our hands," he said. Buddy thought about what his dad said for a minute. He had heard him say it before. He understood that that was just the way it was for farmers. It took a tough, gritty man to be a farmer, and the same man had to be a gambler besides. There were good years, and there were lean years. And even though he loved the home farm, and greatly loved and admired his father, Buddy was not sure he wanted to make farming his life's work.

Chapter Twenty-Seven

May 30, 1970
Mahaska County, Iowa

Buddy had now been home for four weeks. During that time, he worked almost daily alongside his father and was a great help, as he had taken over many of the never-ending chores associated with running a successful family farm. Planting was now in full swing, and he spent many hours on the tractor, plowing and disking the fields. The outdoor, hard work was good for him. He felt good riding on the open tractor in the pleasant spring air. The headaches had diminished, and he was sleeping soundly at night, without nightmares. At the urging of his parents, Buddy had completed all of the required application paper work to enter Iowa State University in the fall and would be taking advantage of the GI Bill to help pay for his education.

At about this same time, the medication that he had brought home with him had run out. In his naivety, Buddy didn't care. He felt so good that he ignored the empty pill bottles that sat on the top of his dresser.

*****

He had looked up some of his old high school friends and spent several evenings in town shooting pool and having a beer or two while he and his friends caught up on the events of the past four years.

He had heard from his friends that she might be here. He eased the car into the diagonal parking space on Main Street in front of the Crown Insurance Agency. He turned the key to shut off the engine of the Oldsmobile. The car wheezed a sigh as it shut down. Buddy stepped from the car and clunked the car door closed. Shirley Moore was sitting behind the reception desk in the insurance office and looked up as Buddy came through the door.

"Buddy," she squealed, as she jumped up from her chair and ran around the end of the desk. She hugged him and then stepped back from him to look him up and down. "Gosh, you look good. The Navy must have fed you all right," she said.

Buddy's heart was thumping as he looked at the girl he left behind nearly four years ago. Shirley was just as cute as the day he last saw her, with a body that had matured further and still stirred the same primal urges in him.

"Now somebody told me you have been home for a good while and you haven't even called me," said Shirley. "That's a fine way to treat a girl," she said, but she had a twinkle in her eye as she said it.

"I know," said Buddy, "and I'm sorry. I should have gotten hold of you sooner, for sure. But I needed some time at home to unwind. I was hoping we might be able to go to a movie tonight, that is if you don't have any plans."

Shirley just looked at him quizzically. Finally she said, "Why Buddy, I thought you knew." As she said this, she held her left hand in front of her body with the diamond ring facing up. "I don't think Kevin would want me going to movies with other guys."

"You mean you're engaged?" said Buddy. He then stammered, "Kevin who?"

"Well, Kevin Ward, you silly. He's finishing up at Grinnell College and already has a job lined up at a bank in Newton when he graduates. He's going to be a loan officer. We're getting married as soon as he graduates from college."

Kevin Ward, thought Buddy; the same Kevin Ward who was halfback on Buddy's high school football team. Most of the time, remembered Buddy, the arrogant bastard thought he was running the football team instead of me, and the same guy who breezed through every hard course in school. Buddy and his circle of friends never much cared for Kevin Ward, and now his old girlfriend was going to marry the guy. Buddy was so irritated at this turn of events that he did not know whether to laugh or cry. He knew one thing though. He no longer cared to stand there looking stupid to Shirley Moore. It was time to leave.

He mumbled something about congratulations, and as he said it, Buddy felt the headache coming on. His chest was tightening. He was mad, even though he had no right to be mad. When Buddy had gone into the Navy, he and Shirley had made no promises to each other, and each had been free to date other people. But to get married? After a few more moments of trivial conversation, Buddy told her that he needed to get back home to help his dad. He took a last longing look at Shirley Moore, turned, and walked out of the insurance agency. His head was pounding.

At the exact moment that Buddy walked out of the door at the insurance agency to return to the car, an old orange colored tractor pulling a grain wagon rolled down the street. Desperately putting his muscle into it, the elderly man driving the tractor could not seem to get the gear changed on the tractor. As the tractor continued to roll, the old man struggled with the throttle and the clutch of the tractor, trying to get the transmission gears to mesh, while firmly grasping the gear lever. The tractor was objecting, and as the engine slowed its revolutions, the tractor immediately responded with two rapid-fire, loud backfires that echoed against the buildings lining the street. Buddy physically jumped at the noise. His jump was followed by a ringing in his ears. His headache was building as he entered the car, slammed the car door, and turned the key in the ignition.

As he left town and the paved roads behind, he drove onto the rural, gravel road, and gray oil smoke rolled from the tailpipe of the Oldsmobile and mixed with the roiling cloud of white road-dust. The accelerator of the car was pressed to the floor by Buddy's foot. The engine strained and roared. With the passing of each telephone pole, the pounding in his head became more painful. The stress disorder was viciously taking over his entire body. A portion of his brain was disengaged from reality. It was as if he was driving in a dimly lit tunnel. His brain had focused only on getting home as fast as the roaring car would go. The soft springs of the car yielded, allowing the car to lean noticeably as it slid and rounded the corners on the gravel road. With the billowing white road-dust cloud rolling into the yard behind him, Buddy slammed on the brakes and stopped the car in the front driveway close to the house. He was breathing heavily as he stumble-stepped out of the car and slammed the car door. He slowly made his way into the house and slumped into a chair at the kitchen table. He held his face in his hands and leaned his elbows on the table. His head felt as if it had been split in two. Sharp needle-like pains were attacking the backs of his eyeballs. He may not have known the exact medical term for it, but he was on the edge of hysteria.

Irene Miller had heard her son come in the house. As she and daughter Janeen came into the kitchen, Janeen was holding several sheets of paper. She proudly held them out toward Buddy and said, "Hey, Buddy. Take a look at this. It's a history project that I have been working on for school."

The small soprano voice of his sister cut through his ears, immediately raising the tempo of the headache. Buddy felt as if his head was going to explode. As if striking out involuntarily against his excruciating pain, Buddy's hand flashed out. The back of the hand struck Janeen's face and jaw as she neared the table, and she danced backwards, falling and striking her head on a corner of the kitchen cabinet as she crumpled to the floor. She did not move while lying there on the floor. Blood was slowly dripping from her nose and from the cut on the back of her head. His mother screamed. A strange psychotic impulse coursed through Buddy's brain, telling him to flee.

Buddy jumped up from the chair, sending it tumbling backwards, and he ran toward the back porch. On his way through the porch, he grabbed his shotgun from its rack, loaded five shells into the gun and charged through the door of the porch. When he reached the farm yard, he began wildly shooting the shotgun. His vision had narrowed to the point that it appeared that he was looking through two long black tunnels. He fired the gun through the tunnels, peppering the trunk and back window of the Oldsmobile which was in his field of vision. He next turned and wildly shot at the back porch. He ran toward the barn and fired another round.

Buddy's next shot echoed and was immediately followed by a piercing scream. The Miller farm pigs were in a muddy yard to the side of the barn. Buddy's shot had hit one of the sows. The terrified screams of the pig added to the monstrous cacophony pounding in Buddy's brain. He fired the gun one more time, but it was empty. He threw the gun wildly into the air and then ran to the car. He got in the car and turned the key. The Rocket V-8 rumbled to life, and Buddy pulled the gear lever down violently into gear. After smashing his foot down on the accelerator, the car immediately tore out of the driveway, fishtailing and careening around the corner at the end of the drive. He kept the accelerator on the floorboard. The car lurched as the transmission shifted into a higher gear with the accelerator still on the floorboard. Dust clouds billowed behind the car as it continued gaining speed. The roar in Buddy's head was the only sound he heard. His painful, narrowed vision certainly did not help, and at the next corner, the racing car slid sideways as Buddy strained against the steering wheel to round the corner. But it was not to be. The left front wheel reached the shoulder of the road where the gravel had been graded into a slightly higher edge, slid through the soft gravel, and continued down the embankment at the side of the road. In an instant, the car plowed down from the road and was quickly at a forty-five degree angle. It held for a split second, but then continued its trajectory, rolling over twice before finally coming to rest on its top at the bottom of the ditch alongside the road. Steam rose in a hissing jet from the broken radiator, and one front wheel slowly continued turning its final few revolutions. The dust clouds on the road slowly settled as the afternoon sun rays pierced the dust. A red-winged blackbird whistled its protest to the disturbance of its normally quiet territory. A rural country silence ensued. There was no movement inside the car.

Chapter Twenty-Eight

Evening
May 30, 1970
Mahaska County Hospital

As a general rule, the small county hospital was a quiet sanctuary. The majority of its patients were elderly with the gamut of medical conditions related to aging, along with the occasional auto or farm accident cases and the minor injuries sustained by the small town's youngsters while participating in childhood games. The hospital's emergency entrance was a popular place for some of the hospital staff to congregate for a smoke break before returning to their duties. Two of the staff members watched curiously as an old, rusty, loudly rattling, bouncing red pickup rolled quickly to the emergency entrance and gave a wheezy cough as its engine was shut off. Four people were wedged into the cab of the truck, and a girl slowly stood up in the bed of the pickup. Jim Miller jumped from the cab of the truck and looked at the two staff members.

"Please help me. My son and daughter are hurt and need help!" he said.

An hour later, Janeen Miller sat in the waiting room with her parents and her sister. She had cotton plugs in her nostrils, which had stopped her nose bleed and her head was wrapped to hold the dressing onto the back of her head. After placing two sutures in the head wound and wrapping the injury, the doctor on duty had pronounced Janeen fit to return home. Sarah sat next to her sister and slowly stroked Janeen's arm. Both girls had been crying.

Another hour passed, and then another as the Millers waited for word from the doctor on Buddy's condition. The only window to the outdoors revealed that the gray dusk was fading into early evening. It would soon be dark.

A white-coated gentleman approached the family. The tall, gray-haired doctor knew the Millers. In this small town, he had treated almost every resident over the course of twenty years of practicing medicine. He lowered his head a bit as he began talking to the family, and then raised it to look in Jim Miller's eyes.

"Jim and Irene, Buddy is in a coma. He has not awakened since he was brought in, and I am worried about his condition. I have to tell you the truth. I have never treated a case like this. He is badly bruised up from the car wreck, but has no broken bones. We've looked him all over, but we don't know the reason for his coma. I don't want to take a chance on his condition getting worse, so I am arranging to have him transferred to the university hospital. An ambulance will be here in a few minutes and rush him to Iowa City. I'm sorry I can't give you any answers. We are just not equipped to treat this kind of case. But don't worry; the university hospital will take good care of him. They've got good people up there who can figure this out."

The Millers were speechless. There was really nothing to say. Their son was in a coma and would soon leave for further treatment in another city.

Chapter Twenty-Nine

June 15, 1970
Interstate 80 in Iowa
Nearing Iowa City

On balding tires and a prayer, Jim and Irene Miller were making the trip again to Iowa City in the old truck. Buddy had been in the hospital now for nearly two weeks. But for the past few days, whenever he and Irene could make the trip, they had seen Buddy sitting in a chair beside his hospital bed in his worn plaid bathrobe, either reading or drawing diagrams. The parents could see nothing wrong with their son. His outward appearance was good, and he acted as if nothing had happened. He discussed current events, sports, and other items of conversation, but made no mention of the episode that had put him in the hospital, which baffled Jim and Irene. Although it appeared there was nothing physically wrong with Buddy, the doctors had not yet granted permission for his release. As they entered Buddy's room, he looked up.

"Hi. How's everybody doing at home?" said Buddy.

"The girls are fine, and they miss you. How are you feeling, son?" said Jim.

"I'm doing okay. I just wish I could get out of here. Have any of the doctors talked to you about when I might be able to go home?"

As if on cue, the Millers watched as two doctors wearing long white coats entered the room. They had seen one of the doctors, Dr. Richard Wells, almost every time they visited Buddy. His companion was new to the Millers.

The couple was then introduced to the other physician, Dr. Walter Boone, a man of late middle age with a shock of white hair, silver framed spectacles, bright blue eyes, an easy smile, and a slight bend in his back.

Both doctors exchanged pleasantries with the Millers. Then the two doctors began getting more technical in their conversation.

"You folks need to meet Dr. Boone. I have known Walt for many years, and he wanted to meet with you today. Dr. Boone is a practitioner with the Veterans Administration hospital here in Iowa City. He and I have agreed that Buddy will be under the care of Dr. Boone when he leaves me; that is, if it's OK with you folks." The Millers were listening, but gave no reply. Dr. Wells continued, "Walt, why don't you brief the Millers on Buddy's treatment plan."

Dr. Boone smiled at Jim and Irene and glanced over at Buddy.

"Mr. and Mrs. Miller, as Richard said, I am on staff at the VA Hospital here in Iowa City, and I have been there many years." Looking over at Buddy, Dr. Boone continued, "With his years of military service, Buddy is eligible for our services, and I will be his treating physician." Dr. Boone glanced again at Buddy and could see that the young man had a pencil in his hand and was intently studying some drawings which he had made.

"Why don't we go out in the hallway for a minute so we don't bother Buddy?"

Jim and Irene Miller followed the physicians into the hall, where Dr. Boone continued his conversation.

"At our VA center for returning veterans, we are seeing a number of young men who are exhibiting many of the same behavioral characteristics as Buddy. I have been studying them, especially the boys who just seemed to be unable to be of further use to the military due to a severe mental condition."

Jim Miller's internal alarm sounded. He looked intently at the middle-aged doctor. "What do you mean by mental condition?"

"Let me explain," said Dr. Boone. "As you will recall, during the First World War, and again in the Second World War, young men were returning with condition that doctors loosely classified as 'shell shock.' The effect rendered the men unable to continue in the war theater. But very little was really known about the cause and the effect on the psyche of the men who exhibited these symptoms. They were simply sent home to live the rest of their lives as best they could. I have had the opportunity to study the young combat veterans coming home from Vietnam. I have learned that the same symptoms resulting from having been in a horrific combat situation can also arise from less violent incidents that are unrelated to wartime experience. That is, we have learned that the symptoms can arise from any extreme stress incident which might occur in a person's life."

"But what does this have to do with our son?" asked Irene.

"Are you implying that Buddy might have some sort of shell shock?" asked Jim.

"Let me answer your questions in just a moment," said Dr. Boone. "At our hospital I have observed and treated many young men who displayed the same kinds of symptoms as those of your son. But unlike the previous wars, the condition was generally downplayed until large numbers of young men who had served in Vietnam were experiencing the symptoms. Because of the sheer number of these cases, the condition was finally given the name 'post-Vietnam syndrome,' which has since been termed 'Post-Traumatic Stress' syndrome, or PTS."

"Are you saying that this is what is wrong with our son?" asked Jim.

Dr. Wells answered, "Yes, Mr. Miller, I believe that is what is causing your son's problems. For the past few weeks we have been monitoring Buddy's condition and his symptoms. I also did an in-depth study of his military medical records, which we were able to obtain. An interesting aspect of his case is that he was diagnosed with a case of malaria at the same time as a very traumatic event occurred in his life. I believe he has told you some of the details of that incident. I am not certain that

Buddy had malaria at that time, but he had some sort of illness which caused a high fever. As you know, a serious fever can cause a person's brain to react differently than it would under normal conditions. So, I am theorizing that the fever associated with the malaria, or other virus, may have caused his brain to react more severely than it might have if he had been healthy at the time of the incident."

Dr. Boone then said, "Buddy has been experiencing the classic symptoms of PTS. He described to us the traumatic event that happened to him on his ship, which involved a life or death situation. This event and the subsequent treatment of the boy by his superior officers have scarred him deeply. His symptoms have been affecting him for months. He has been experiencing excruciating headaches; he does not sleep well, has graphic nightmares about the incident, is startled easily, and is very nearly paranoiac. In addition, he sometimes has outbursts of anger and does not seem to remember these incidents."

In a very low, quiet tone Jim Miller said, "I guess that would explain why he has never mentioned to us the incident which occurred at home just before the accident."

Jim Miller then explained to Doctor Boone what had taken place in the hours before Buddy had been admitted to the Iowa City Medical Center.

"Well, you are correct, Mr. Miller. It is very possible that Buddy does not even remember those incidents. He only knows that something happened, but not the details," said Dr. Boone. "I also understand that before his car accident he was on some meds that the Navy had given him, but he stopped taking the medicine. That could explain why he has had some difficulty recently."

"Excuse me, Doctor, but how does it happen that you know so much about this condition, PTS, or whatever it's called?" asked Jim.

"Mr. Miller, in addition to my hospital observations of returning Vietnam veterans, I have continued my research on the condition by handling cases of some of the boys who have returned here to Iowa from Vietnam. And while I am a doctor, my specialty is psychiatry," said Dr. Boone.

Irene Miller audibly gasped and almost immediately began quietly sobbing.

"Now Irene, what's got into you? What's all this about?" said Jim.

"A psychiatrist," she said. "Our boy needs a psychiatrist," and she quickly blew her nose as she shed a few more tears.

Dr. Boone placed his hand on Irene Miller's arm. "Mrs. Miller, please rest assured that Buddy is going to be just fine. He is on a new regimen of medicine and is getting along beautifully. You will notice very quickly that he is calmer and probably will not experience the full range of the symptoms again. That is, if he keeps his appointments with me, and we continually monitor his medication. He will still experience some of the milder headaches, but it will not be nearly as severe as it has been. Given what he has told me about his supportive family situation, I am confident that he will be able to live a very normal life. In fact, with the concurrence of Doctor Wells, I am going to have him released tomorrow to go home."

Irene dried her eyes and beamed at the doctor. "That's wonderful," she said. "But will he be all right to work at home and to go to the university? He was so counting on that."

Dr. Wells took her hand and led the Millers back into Buddy's room, where they went over to his side. "Let me show you something," he said. "Buddy, show your parents some of your drawings."

Buddy picked up a folder that was on the floor next to the chair and put it on his lap. He chuckled. "I don't think Mom or Dad will have much interest in this stuff," he said.

He opened the folder. In it were rough drawings of various shotguns which had elaborate artistic designs on them. There were also drawings of other equipment related to handguns with which neither of his parents was familiar. "They're just some ideas I have," said Buddy. "It helps me pass the time," he said.

"I think they're pretty neat," said Dr. Boone. "One of these days your parents are going to see these drawings come to life, and I have encouraged Buddy to see if he can patent that gadget he has been telling me about."

Jim and Irene looked at each other. They had no idea what the doctor meant.

"Buddy, I'll see you later," said Dr. Boone. "Mr. and Mrs. Miller, take a little walk with me and get a cup of coffee." Dr. Wells stayed behind to chat a bit longer with Buddy.

They sat in the small hospital lunch room and absently stirred their coffee. The pale green walls of the cafeteria seemed rather sad to Irene, and she thought to herself what some fresh paint and curtains could do for the large room.

"Mr. and Mrs. Miller, I just wanted to tell you what a great kid you have," said Doctor Boone. "Buddy is going to go places. I am amazed at his quiet intellect and those drawings that he is doing tell me that he has real drive and determination to be successful. I want you to get rid of your worries about him. With the proper medication and monitoring, he will surprise you."

The three adults talked a bit longer before Dr. Boone excused himself to go back to his work. Jim and Irene Miller held hands under the table in the pale green-walled hospital cafeteria and pretended to sip their coffees, but very soon both of them had to quietly blow their nose and wipe their eyes.

PART II

Industry
(The Man)

Chapter Thirty

It had taken nearly six full years for Buddy to complete the goal he had set for himself in a hospital room those years ago. With the help of the G.I. Bill and part-time jobs, he now possessed a mechanical engineering degree and bachelor's and master's degrees in electrical engineering. And in his first two years of college at Iowa State University he had taken a number of business courses to augment the engineering grind. His primary area of interest had been in the study of electromagnetic radiation, a relatively new and emerging science, commonly referred to as laser science. The first part of his plan was complete.

School for him had been easy. But it had been an eye-opening experience. During his first year, Buddy had lived in a men's dormitory occupied primarily by eighteen-year-old freshmen. Although he got along well with the younger residents, he continually marveled at their immaturity. He was at least four years older than the majority of other freshmen and had seen a great deal of the world. His perspective was certainly not the same as the others.

Buddy's focus was on his studies. As a result, his social life on campus was a bit limited. He had occasional dates with interesting coeds, but the thought of getting seriously involved with a member of the opposite sex did not even enter his head. And although they liked Buddy, some of his young friends thought he was one of the strangest fellows they had met. After all, they thought, when there was such a wonderful, enticing atmosphere of social interaction with friends and members of the opposite sex, what college freshman would ever want to spend all of his free time at the university library diligently studying. Buddy was certainly different. He was nearly totally immersed in the self-imposed challenge of absorbing all the knowledge that he could while at school. To help with that endeavor, after his freshman year, Buddy moved out of the dormitory and rented a cheap two-room apartment. He reveled in and excelled in his solitary quest for knowledge.

Buddy was up to the challenge of the difficult studies, resulting in an excellent scholastic record. Several business recruiters who held job fairs on the university campus had tried their best to recruit the intelligent, quiet young man with the impressive academic record. None of them were successful. Although he was tempted, at times, to go to various companies for a second interview, Buddy could not help but remember how his boss on the *Erne* had betrayed him. Hence, he was leery of going to work for other people. He had it in his mind that he was going to work for himself. And although he had a plan for how that was going to happen, he was also a realist and fearful of failure.

He had loaded the last of his college apartment belongings into the old Ford sedan he had purchased with the earnings from his part-time jobs. The early sixties-era car showed signs of hard use and the see-through rust holes on the sides of the green sedan gave evidence of the prodigious amounts of salt used on the streets and highways during long Iowa winters. But even so, the old car had faithfully carried Buddy back and forth from home to college each year in the fall and spring and again at holiday times. Buddy affectionately called it 'the tank' due to its dark green faded paint job. He had said his good-byes to friends at school and was ready to head southeast to the farm.

*****

For the next eighteen months he worked for his father on the farm, contributing to a flourishing farm enterprise. But it was not all farm work that occupied Buddy. He had partitioned off a corner of the farm's machine shop for his own use. He spent every free moment in this make-shift laboratory. He spoke for hours on the telephone talking with the engineering and science professors at the university and went through a complete set of tires on the old Ford as he travelled various places to purchase the necessary equipment he needed in the laboratory. Jim Miller didn't say much about the exorbitant telephone bills. It was difficult for Buddy to try to explain to his parents what he was doing, and it was especially hard to ensure that his sisters stayed away from the laboratory.

The experiments he was conducting were dangerous. The optical amplification testing was dangerous to the point of blinding a person or even causing fires or explosions under certain conditions. Therefore, he preferred to work in his laboratory after the rest of the family was in bed. Midway through his experimentation, he had filed for several patents on his ideas and after patiently waiting for the government to act on his requests, two of the most important patents had been approved. At the end of the eighteen months, this part of his business plan was ready. He had perfected his own idea for a specific use of the laser, and he alone held the patents on the concepts.

During the same eighteen months he had been working with his father, Buddy had enjoyed hunting every season with his dad and a periodic surprise visitor. He looked forward to dove season, pheasant and quail season, and deer season. He never missed an opening day with his dad. And for the past two Thanksgiving holidays, a third man had joined their holiday hunting days.

Over the years following his military service, Buddy had kept in touch with four of his old friends from military days. Among them was

Bob Dawes. Goofy as ever, but a true friend, Dawes had graduated from Drake University with a degree in marketing. He was now doing sales work for a trading stamp company. He travelled the state, as well as neighboring states, selling merchants on the idea of carrying trading stamps in their stores. Surprisingly, at least to Buddy, Dawes was very good at his job. Trading stamps were the rage for shoppers at the time. Housewives hoarded their stamps, which they received primarily at their local grocery stores. Shoppers glued the stamps into little books, and when they had enough books, they could trade them in for merchandise. Consumers loved their trading stamps. With his big smile, boyish charm, and calm, honest manner, Bob Dawes had enlisted merchants all over Iowa and its adjacent states to carry the stamps. He was successful and financially secure. But even hard working achievers needed short breaks from their work. Therefore, each year at Thanksgiving time, Bob made the trip to Mahaska County to hunt pheasant and quail with Buddy and Jim Miller.

The first time that Bob Dawes had travelled to rural Mahaska County to hunt with the Millers had been a watershed moment for Buddy. Buddy had heard a car approaching on the gravel road and sat on the front porch to await the arrival of his friend. Very shortly, a chrome-laden highway yacht drove up the driveway to the house. Bob Dawes slowly got out of the two-door Lincoln Coupe with its chromed continental kit on the back bumper, and slammed the door. Buddy only stopped laughing long enough to shake hands with Dawes, and the two men clapped each other on the back.

"What in the hell is that thing you are driving, Dawes?" asked Buddy as he continued laughing and ribbing his friend. "It's a rolling pile of chrome!"

Dawes grinned and said, "That, my boy, is the finest highway cruiser known to man. I know it's hideous, but man it flies. Just like sitting in

279

an airplane. And when you pound the highway as many miles as I do in a year, my poor back side needs something comfortable," said Dawes. He was also grinning from ear to ear. He knew that his glistening Lincoln was a bit over the top.

"That thing covers a half acre. I'm going to have to charge you rent for taking up the whole front yard," laughed Buddy.

In a moment they were joined by Jim Miller, who walked around the mammoth car looking in the car windows and shaking his head. "Ooo-wee. What kind of mileage do you get with this thing," he said.

"I really don't know, Mr. Miller. But I do know that when I fill that baby up, I'm happy I'm on a company expense account instead of my own," replied Dawes.

Another surprise came the next morning when the three men were getting ready to begin their hunt. After breakfast they went to the porch. Jim and Buddy had their well-used Remingtons and were dressed accordingly for the cool, but pleasant, early winter temperatures. As Jim and Buddy watched from the porch, Dawes walked to his car and opened the massive trunk. He then brought out a large hard-sided gun case that he brought over to the porch and quickly opened. He retrieved the shotgun from the case, broke the gun, and placed it in the crook of his elbow while he put the case back in the trunk. He brought out two boxes of shells and closed the trunk of the car. He then walked back up to the porch to join Jim and Buddy while he stuffed the shells in his hunting vest pockets.

Buddy and Jim's eyes locked on Bob Dawes' shotgun. They had never seen anything quite like it. The gun had a beautifully grained walnut stock, a color that was much deeper and richer than the stocks of their own guns. But there was another aspect of the gun that really caught their attention. The body of the gun was etched in intricately carved, floral patterns, while the side-by-side barrels were of a metal color that neither man had seen before. It was certainly not the bluish tint of the metal work on their guns.

"Geez, Bob. What kind of gun is that?" asked Buddy. By now, both Buddy and his dad were examining the shotgun in much closer detail. Neither had ever seen a shotgun that looked like this.

"Well, it's a Purdey," said Dawes. "They are made in England. I was meeting with a customer up in northern Iowa, and we got to talking about hunting. Well, one thing led to another, and he got this gun out of the back room of his store and had me look at it, and I knew I wanted it right then and there. And I didn't know it, but he actually needed some fast cash, so he was willing to sell the gun. I talked him down in price some and made him buy a contract for our stamps, and I bought the gun. I'm kinda embarrassed because I found out later that the gun is worth a whole lot more than I paid him for it. It sure is neat, though, isn't it?"

"Let me hold it for a minute, Bob," said Buddy. He raised the shotgun to his shoulder and held it for a moment, marveling at the gun's balance. Then he brought the gun down and closely examined the works of the gun and the craftsmanship of the beautiful filigreed etching on the gun. He was awestruck with the foreign made shotgun.

Buddy held on to the gun so long that Jim Miller finally said, "Are we going to hunt today or not?"

Buddy handed the Purdey to Bob Dawes, and as he did so, a smile spread across his face. In his head, he remembered the drawings he had made while he was in the hospital and knew that he would soon get started on the second piece of his business plan. The next day, before Bob Dawes had a chance to leave, Buddy walked him out to his car.

"Bob, I've got a favor to ask you," said Buddy.

"Shoot," said Bob.

"I want you to leave your Purdey here for a while."

"Man, Buddy, you don't ask much do you. What do you want it for, anyway?" asked Bob. He knew Buddy didn't want the gun to hunt with, since he could hit anything with the worst of shotguns.

"I'll tell you the next time we get together," said Buddy. He watched as Dawes opened his car trunk and retrieved the gun case.

"Here you go. Just remember where you got it," said Dawes as he handed the case to Buddy.

During the next few days Buddy helped his dad with chores around the farm and then disappeared for hours into the workshop lab. A few days later, as Buddy was working in the lab, Jim Miller entered the machine shed/lab to tell his son to go to bed. It was nearly midnight, and Buddy was still in the workshop. He entered the lab to find Buddy deeply engrossed and bent over one of the work tables. A small kerosene space heater burbled in the corner, taking the night-time chill from the air in the shed. As Jim looked around the room, he saw that every work table was covered with shotgun parts. As he looked more closely, he saw that most of the disassembled guns on the table were his own shotguns. There were a couple more he was not familiar with, along with the Purdey.

"My God, Buddy, what have you done? These are all my shotguns," said Jim.

Buddy had not heard his father come into the lab and was startled. He turned to face his dad. "Don't worry Dad, they'll all get put back together. Look at what I am doing."

Jim Miller listened to his son as Buddy explained that he had taken apart the various guns to compare them all. He had made micrometer measurements of all parts of the guns and had written them into tables showing the comparisons. In addition, he had made detailed drawings of all the parts, labeling the dimensions, the thickness of the metal of each part, and the specific metal used for each part. He had taken apart a

Mossberg, a Winchester, a Remington, and the Purdey shotgun and logged every part of each gun.

Jim Miller was dumbfounded. "Buddy, how do you know how to do all this?" he asked.

Buddy chuckled. "It's what engineers do, Dad," he said. His eyes gleamed. "Along with our laser sights for both pistols and rifles, we are going to build one of the finest shotguns on the market, right here in Iowa."

Jim Miller didn't know what to say to his son's lofty plans. "You need to get some sleep, son. Time to go to bed," he said and turned and trudged back to the house. In a few more moments, Buddy turned off the old heater, put out the lights in the lab, and followed his dad.

*****

From the time he had left the military, Buddy often travelled to Des Moines to visit Dawes. Along with other interests, while Buddy visited Dawes, the two men would attend a very large gun show held twice per year in the Veterans Memorial Auditorium in Des Moines. At each show, while Dawes chatted up the comely female vendors at the show and tried to sell trading stamp contracts to the various larger vendors, Buddy was very seriously looking for specific guns; guns that had been crafted by artisans, instead of assembly line products. When he was lucky enough to find an artisan gun maker, he would spend hours questioning their methods and gaining information on machining, metal carving, metal alloys, various exotic woods, and other subjects. He had not yet told Dawes why he seldom bought very many items at the shows, but he always left the show with a smile and a stack of catalogs which he had obtained at the show. The catalogs listed numerous sources for gun parts and special order components for guns. Of course, Dawes always left the show with a smile too, and a few new business and personal phone numbers in his pocket.

It was on one of those Thanksgiving hunting trips that Bob Dawes had stepped out of Buddy's car just off the county road near town. He and Buddy stood in front of an old, sad-looking, metal-clad building, which showed no sign of any recent human activity either in or around the building. The building had dirty, cracked windows resembling eyes looking forlornly out on the world. Over-achieving wild bushes covered the southern side of the building, as if hiding from any pending winter storm which would beat mercilessly at them from the north. The building had once served as a tractor and implement sales and repair facility. A faded, rusty blue sign attested to the fact that selling Ford tractors had once been the livelihood of one of the previous owners. A weathered, sagging set of broken wooden steps led to the porch and the front door of the building. A local realtor's 'For Sale' sign lay in the dirt where it had blown over many months ago.

"Hey, nice place ya got here, Miller," said Dawes.

Buddy just grinned at his friend. "Let's take a look around," he said.

Dawes looked at his friend quizzically, but Buddy was already walking away and around the corner of the building. They walked down the side of the building, past several more dirty, cracked windows until they reached the back of the building. As he passed each window, Buddy cleaned a bit of the glass with the heel of his hand in order to peer into the old business. Dawes watched him, but said nothing. At the rear of the building was a large metal door that rolled to the side to allow vehicles to enter the rear of service area. Buddy shoved the door, and it moved slightly, allowing the two men to see into what had once been the mechanical repair shop of the business.

"Bob, look at all that equipment in there."

Dawes looked through the door opening. "Yeah, a lot of old dirty machines and tools. So what?"

Buddy still didn't answer Bob, but instead pressed his face up to the door opening and continued surveying the equipment. Although he said nothing, his brain was going a mile a minute. Finally, he turned to Bob and said, "Bob, do you want to sell trading stamps the rest of your life?" Dawes was confused and did not answer.

Dawes looked at Buddy as the two men moved around to the front of the building. They sat on the unpainted, front porch, and for the better part of the next hour, Buddy filled Bob in on his plans. He told Bob that he intended to build his own company, and that he wanted him to come to work with him and be the marketing manager for the company. The company would manufacture laser gun sights for small arms with a sideline of hand-crafted collector quality small arms; specifically shotguns. Buddy told Dawes that the old broken down building would become their office and manufacturing facility.

Bob was aghast. His mouth hung open and he stared at his friend as Buddy rose and walked around the corner of the building. Dawes joined him and the men walked again to the rear of the old business.

"So, in addition to your other quirky problems, it turns out that you are completely delusional, too," said Bob, and he turned his head to again look through the metal door. As he gazed through the opening he repeated himself, "Buddy, you truly must be crazy." After a few seconds, he looked back at Buddy and aimed a rapid fire series of questions at his friend. But to each of the many questions that Bob Dawes asked, Buddy had a plausible, well thought-out answer.

"My God, Buddy. I don't know. What do you and I know about starting and running a company? And where are we going to get the right people to start up the manufacturing. And more importantly, where in the hell would we ever get the money to do all this?" Dawes paused momentarily and rolled a few thoughts around in his head, followed by an alarming thought. "Ah, gee, Buddy. I've got a pretty good thing going with the stamp company."

"Good. That means that if you don't want to join me, then at least you've got some money set aside to invest in our company," said Buddy. To this statement, Dawes whipped his head back to face Buddy. From past experience, Buddy knew that being blunt with Dawes was always the best way to make him understand things.

"Oh, great, now you even want my money. Now that's what I call a true friend," said Dawes. "But since I asked you before and you didn't answer, where do you propose to get all the money you need to even clean all the rats and mice out of this old building, let alone actually starting a company with lots of machines and people and all the rest of the headaches of running a business?"

"And that, my friend is the only hurdle I haven't cleared quite yet," replied Buddy. "But I'll figure out a way."

"So what is going to be your job in this company, anyhow? You're going to have to have somebody who knows how to manage some employees and the production in the company. Did you even think about that?" asked Dawes.

Buddy looked at his watch, cocked his head, and listened; only slightly paying any more attention to Dawes. They walked back to the front of the building.

"Ah, right on time. Get ready for a surprise, oh ye, of little faith," said Buddy. He was listening to the sound of an approaching car.

Dawes kept looking at Buddy. He had no idea what Buddy was talking about. But momentarily, a dark blue sedan rolled up beside Buddy's shabby looking old Ford. A sign on the door of the sedan said, "Jones Real Estate." As the driver exited the car, the passenger door opened, and the passenger emerged.

Once again Bob Dawes looked like he was a study in how best to catch flies as his mouth dropped open, and he stared at the passenger.

"Senior Chief Proctor!" said Dawes. "Holy shit, Buddy, look. It's Proctor."

For the past three weeks, Buddy had been on the telephone with his old Navy supervisor, John Proctor. John had retired from the Navy, was still unmarried, and coincidentally, was finding civilian life to be quite boring in Omaha, Nebraska. He had half-heartedly looked for a new job or career, but nothing seemed challenging to him. When Buddy Miller had called him out of the blue, and they had brought each other up to date on their respective lives, Buddy told John of his plans. The fire was lit in John Proctor. He loved the idea of the challenge of starting a new company; a new adventure. John and Buddy had arranged for this meeting in front of the sad, old, implement building.

Buddy just laughed as he walked toward John Proctor and shook his hand. He was quickly followed by Dawes who laughed and said, "Proctor. Man, oh man, what are you doing here?"

"I might ask you the same question, lame brain, except that Miller and I were both in on this little venture. Why Miller still wants you around is beyond me, but I guess he thinks you can sell ice water to Eskimos," said John Proctor while he laughed good naturedly.

Bill Jones, the real estate salesman then spoke up. "Gentlemen, let's go see if we can get the front door open."

In a few moments, they stood in the middle of the machine shop while John and Buddy sifted through all the old machines and tools. Several old rusty farm implement parts littered the floor along with old rags and newspapers. Looking at several of the old machine tools, Buddy asked, "Can we use any of this stuff, John?"

"Yep, there's a good metal lathe, drill presses, welders, and a bunch of hand tools that are in decent shape, but for what we have in mind, we are going to need a lot of other specialized equipment; equipment that can do all the tight-tolerance, precision work we need for our products. From what you've told me, you have a line on the equipment and have identified sources for all the other machinery. Is that right?" asked John.

"Yes, but I want you to go over everything I have recorded and double check with the vendors when we get to that point. I also have two machinists and two artisan gunsmiths who are just waiting for our call to come to work, and I want you to interview them, too. They can also bring some of their tools and projects to show you," said Buddy.

Just then, another man entered the building. Jim Miller joined the group and stuck out his hand to shake with Bill Jones, whom he had known for many years, and then he came over and was introduced to John Proctor. The men talked for a few moments, after which Jim said, "John, do you think this idea has any chance of success?"

John Proctor laughed. "Yeah, I think it has a chance of success, and I think it has a bigger chance of going belly up. But I think it will be a whole lot of fun trying to make a go of it."

Jim Miller slowly shook his head as he looked around the old building. "Bill, you better just give this place to my son. It sure isn't worth anything to anybody else except the mice and rats that all call it home."

Jones chuckled. "Actually, Jim, I own the property myself. I've already made a tentative agreement with Buddy. For two years he just has to pay the property taxes, utilities, and improvements. After that he can buy the property from me on contract at today's asking price. Can't get much of a better deal than that."

"But in the meantime, Buddy will have to make improvements to the property, which will then enhance its value," said Jim. "Then, if the company doesn't make it, you're going to get a much better building to resell. Ain't that right, Bill?"

"Well, that's about right, Jim. But you being in business for yourself, you know that business is business," said Jones as he winked at Jim.

Jim scowled slightly, shook his head, and turned to look at Buddy and Proctor. "You boys are of legal age. I hope you know what you are doing."

*****

Sure enough, as the men had predicted, financing was the toughest hurdle to starting the small company. The three men pooled their resources, which were somewhat meager. Jim Miller even sold ten acres of rich, black Iowa farm land from his farm to the Nelsons, thereby adding a tidy sum to the venture. In turn, he was promised a share in the eventual earnings or the eventual demise of the company. And while it pained him greatly, Bob finally agreed to put the bulk of his savings into the project. He was now fully committed to helping the company succeed.

After being turned down by all the local banks, it took another two weeks to finally find a bank in Des Moines that would lend the men the money for the unsecured start-up loan. During the two weeks that John and Buddy tramped from bank to bank searching for a loan, John was earning his keep on the farm. He helped Jim Miller make repairs to almost every piece of equipment on the farm. Jim Miller could now see the reason that Buddy needed John in the business. He was convinced that John Proctor could turn junk metal and parts into a productive machine.

A bank was finally located. It just happened that the banker was a golfing buddy of Bob Dawes' father, who carried a great deal of influence on the bank board. Dawes's father had very subtly suggested that his son contact this bank. Bob knew nothing of his father's connection to the bank. On the day that the loan was to be signed, Buddy, John, and

Bob all signed the loan as co-signers. As they were about to leave the bank, Bob noticed his dad in the bank president's office. Bob and his dad waved at each other.

"Hmm. Wonder what the old man's doing here," said Bob. "C'mon you guys, I'll introduce you to him."

Later, as they walked out of the bank, Buddy told Dawes to leave his car in the bank parking lot and to jump into Buddy's car. The old Ford rumbled its way down the avenues of Des Moines.

"Where we going, Miller?" asked John.

"Yeah, what's up, Buddy?" Dawes piped in.

"Sit tight, boys. I've got another surprise for you," said Buddy as he looked at his watch. "We'll just make it."

The old rusted-out Ford rolled into the Des Moines airport, and John and Bob just looked at each other. Buddy killed the engine, and they all remained in the car outside the passenger pick-up area. Ten minutes went past, and as Buddy looked out the window, he started to laugh. Proctor and Dawes followed his gaze and watched the small, slim, bespectacled man with the suitcase approach their car.

Dawes nearly screamed it, "Oh man, it's Fig!" The three men climbed out of the car and immediately surrounded Robert "Fig" Newton. The laughing and talking went on for several minutes, with Fig continually pushing up his glasses each time he was pounded on the back. Finally, Buddy put his arm across Fig's shoulders and said, "Gentlemen, meet our new financial officer, Mr. Robert Newton, BA, CPA, and all-around good man."

Bob couldn't stop laughing. "You're kidding, right?"

Buddy was not kidding, and he quickly explained. After his enlistment was up, Fig Newton returned home to Illinois and was accepted at Northwestern University. He graduated near the top of his class in accounting and passed the CPA exam on the very first try. Following college, he began working as a bank examiner. There was no doubt about it; Fig knew his numbers. Fig was still single, and when Buddy had telephoned him and talked about the company start up, Fig had jumped at it. He was bored with the life of a bank examiner. Of course his conservative parents, after having made a significant financial contribution toward Fig's education, thought he had lost his mind and expected to see him return home sooner or later after giving in to his whims. Little did they know how wrong they would be.

Chapter Thirty-One

Some experts would say that a business will either make it or fail within the first year of its existence; many times, sooner than that if the venture is not properly backed by capital. With Miller Arms it took a bit longer. Everything that was needed to get the company up and running was a mental and physical struggle. The days passed quickly, and at the end of each day the men were exhausted. But they could see incremental progress being made.

Crude prototypes of the laser sights were made, discussed, sometimes rather heatedly; revised, and analyzed again. There were times when these discussions took place outdoors while sitting at a crude wooden table and benches as contractors worked on items inside the building. Throughout the stress and turmoil, the bond between the men grew even stronger.

It was a full two years before the principals of the company felt comfortable enough to take a deep breath of air, knowing that the company had turned the corner. It was not without some severe soul searching on the part of Buddy, Dawes, Fig, and Proctor. Had they made a major mistake in their lives? That question ran through the mind of each of them many times. They all suffered many sleepless nights worrying about their fate. More than once, one or more of them had mentioned pulling the plug on the venture and leaving, but somehow, their camaraderie and genuine respect for each other kept them working on the project. Not only did the four men worry about their futures, but the Miller farm was also stressed.

John Proctor, with his Navy retirement, had rented an apartment in town and stayed there when he was not with his partners. Needless to say, he spent most of his time at the farm or at the business. It had been part of his responsibilities to oversee the renovation of the old implement building, and to supervise the proper placement of the new machines and equipment to be used for the production of the laser sights and shotguns. So, it would be more accurate to say that he lived at the little factory. But when the evening meal time arrived, Irene Miller found herself packing a large picnic basket and driving to the small factory to feed her "field crew." It seemed to her that she rarely stepped away from the kitchen stove. No sooner had she fed her own family and the four men at the new business, but she needed to begin the next round of meals. She was becoming a bit worn.

Outwardly, Irene Miller watched over the four men and was amazed at the progress of the little company. Inside, she worried greatly about the men and whether they would succeed. But most of all, she worried about her son. She knew what the doctors had said about Buddy, and she wondered if the stress of setting up a company was more than Buddy should take on. Irene was the key in making sure that Buddy kept his psychiatric appointments in Iowa City, and with a mother's love, she went with him to the appointments. Many times, she would lovingly ask Buddy, "Have you taken your pills today?"

Fig Newton had left his comfortable bank examiner position to come to Miller Arms and had no income and no place to live. Without saying a word, the Millers welcomed him into the family. He slept in the spare room, worked with his partners all day, and fell asleep nearly right after supper each evening. His job was to oversee and manage the loan funds properly and to ensure that all expenses were completely justified. He quickly earned the respect of his partners when he discovered that one of the contractors was double-billing the company. Fig took it upon himself to fire that contractor and hire another one at considerably less cost, but not before he threatened the old contractor with a civil suit unless he repaid the company. The money was returned.

Fig felt comfortable being around the conservative, but loving, Miller family. The Millers also enjoyed Fig's company and treated him as one of their own. But would the close relationship possibly have consequences? Was it Irene Miller's imagination, or was she seeing a spark of romance between her oldest daughter, Janeen, and the bespectacled young accountant? Irene couldn't help but like Robert Newton, although she didn't care much for the nickname Fig. He was a courteous, sweet man; handsome in his own diminutive-statured way. But it was the boyish manner of Fig that everyone liked. He gamely tried to earn his room and board by helping with chores on the farm whenever he was not involved at the factory. But being a city boy, he was not very good at farm chores.

One weekend when Janeen had been home from college (she was a junior at Truman State University in Missouri), Fig had been following her, carrying two buckets made up of pig feed and supplements. Janeen had entered the hog pen and was waiting for Fig. She held the gate open, and Fig brought the two buckets into the enclosure. Fig should have stepped more lively to the feed trough and emptied the buckets, but instead, he was gabbing with Janeen. Pigs are intelligent animals, and when they saw the two buckets sitting in the mud next to Fig, they raised the appropriate pig noise alarm to signify food, and all of the pigs rose from their mud hole and charged toward Fig. Janeen saw the activity of the pigs, and she gave a short scream of warning and hopped over the low fence to safety. But poor Fig was soon overrun by hungry porcine beasts. The animals shoved the buckets over, right along with Fig. The pigs trampled poor Fig to get to the food, and in his effort to get away, he fell several more times into the wet, sticky mud. As he finally rose and walked to the gate, the pigs eyed him, but went about their gustatory activities. Fig was unrecognizable with all the black, malodorous mud covering him from head to toe. Janeen took Fig to the side of the barn and turned a water hose on him to remove most of the mud. But she couldn't help laughing at the poor city boy. John Proctor had observed the whole sequence from the window of the lab when he had heard Janeen's scream. From then on, when things needed a bit of humor at the factory, John would catch Fig and ask him, "Wrestled any more pigs lately, Fig?"

*****

Bob Dawes had not yet left his job with the trading stamp company. His role in the new venture meant that he would need to travel around the country and begin a sales campaign to sell the new laser gun sights. He could do this and furtively combine it with his present sales job. His first few sales of the laser sights were made to small privately owned gun shops. It was certainly a good start, but what was really needed was an order from a large sporting goods retailer. The day that occurred, Bob Dawes was in Kansas City. He could barely contain his enthusiasm as he called the Miller farm and gave Jim Miller the news to pass on to Buddy, John, and Fig. The "Sports Outdoors" stores had purchased two hundred laser sights for distribution in their four Kansas City area stores. Miller Arms had just received its first substantial order, which enabled Bob to finally sever his ties to the trading stamp company. The following day, Bob Dawes called his boss and gave his resignation notice.

A major windfall came just a few weeks later when Dawes traveled to Hartford, Connecticut. He called on the Colt Firearms Company, where he was relentlessly grilled by a team of four hard-nosed, quality-conscious corporate buyers. Four hours later, and thoroughly mentally drained, Bob Dawes left Colt with a contract order that would ensure not only the survival of Miller Arms, but would begin to make the company highly profitable. The laser sights would be offered in Colt's catalog and made available to police departments in all the major cities of the nation that relied upon Colt firearms for the protection of their police officers.

Bob was also attending every gun show and exhibition he could, as many as his physical stamina would allow. In addition to the laser sights, a keen interest had developed in the hand-made Miller shotguns. Under Bob's relentless salesmanship, they were sold as fast as they could be made, with a backlog of orders. Miller Arms manufactured two models of their shotguns; a break-open over-and-under, and a semi-automatic. They were called the Hawkeye model and the Cyclone model respectively. Both were offered in either 12 gauge or 20 gauge. Demand for the shotguns kept the Miller Arms artisan gun makers busy, with no let-up in sight. The work force in the small company grew in relation to sales.

*****

Miller Arms quadrupled in size in its first five years. The old implement building had increased in size accordingly. Buddy's design and experimental lab had moved from the farm to the factory; much to the relief of Jim and Irene Miller, who, perhaps unfoundedly, harbored a fear that "Buddy's lab" would someday, inexplicably erupt in a huge mushroom cloud explosion, thereby leaving only a smoking crater where the peaceful Miller farm had once been.

The architecture of the old implement building changed drastically, but the four principals agreed that the front door of the building should retain a bit of its original rustic look. So the old façade was painted and spruced up, giving the front of the Miller Arms building a quaint rural charm.

Buddy, John, Bob, and Fig continued to work hard, putting in long hours at the company, even though they were now wealthy men. An upshot of the success of the company was that they had branched into the gun parts and accessories business and manufactured special order, hard-to-find parts for antique guns. They also started a catalog business for all of their products. They had long ago paid off the initial loan for the old building, their start-up manufacturing loan, and purchased the surrounding land and properties.

Bob, John, and Fig had each purchased their own homes. In 1981, Buddy, at thirty-three years of age, still lived at the farm with his parents. Only one of the men had married. Even though there was nearly eight years difference in their ages, Janeen Miller had become Mrs. Robert Newton shortly after she had completed her marketing, management, and accounting courses at Truman State University. Janeen was now over-seeing the company's catalog operation. Their three year old daughter, Jeanie Newton, wandered from the accounting department to the catalog department on most work days to sit on the laps of her parents. John Proctor called her "Little Figette." John was dating a local school teacher, Betty Rhodes, but had no plans to get married. Dawes, as usual, was dating any woman within eyesight.

Thoughts of marriage simply did not enter Buddy's head. Ever since attending Shirley Moore's wedding a decade prior, he had not had a great deal of time or thought for dating. He was married to the company. Even so, he was content with his life, and he was happy. And yet, on those occasions when his friends and family would gather for a special event, he could not help but notice the visible love between his father and mother and between his sister and Fig as they played with his toddler niece. Once in a while when the group was together, Buddy would glance over at his mother and catch her looking intently at him. Her eyes held a slight sorrowful look, but then she would quickly smile at him and look back at her small granddaughter. On those occasions, he experienced a haunting hollowness in his soul, but he knew he was not yet ready for any new commitments in his busy life.

PART III

Redemption
(The Whole Man)

Chapter Thirty-Two

April 1983
University of Iowa Medical Center
Iowa City, Iowa

"Sometimes there is simply no scientific answer to these things, Buddy." Dr. Will Glenn was shining his glasses using a tissue from the box on his desk. Buddy was sitting in an immensely comfortable brown leather recliner in front of the desk, only giving about three-quarters of his attention to Dr. Glenn.

The routine had changed somewhat over the years that Buddy had been receiving medical treatment. The biggest change had taken place in 1979. For nearly nine years, Buddy had faithfully made the monthly trip to Iowa City to visit the gray-haired psychiatrist, Doctor Walter Boone. Doctor and patient had a warm, pleasant relationship. But during the coldest winter that anyone could remember, the kindly physician who had taken a loving and conscientious interest in the veterans with whom he had contact, succumbed to a raging pneumonia virus and died. Buddy had been one of the pallbearers at Doctor Boone's funeral and was deeply saddened by the death of his friend. But out of that tragedy, another doctor had entered his life. Buddy had returned to the University Hospital, where his old friend Doctor Richard Wells had referred his case to a new physician on the University Staff. That doctor was Will Glenn.

Unlike Doctor Boone, Doctor Will Glenn had served in the military during the Vietnam War. He was considered an expert in the field of Post-Traumatic Stress Disorder. And unlike during his time spent with Doctor Boone, Buddy felt at last that he was making some progress with Will Glenn.

Instead of a visit to the psychiatrist every month, he was now making the trip to Iowa City every three months. With the help of a full regimen of medication, Buddy's PTSD had mostly ceased to be a factor in his life. But the drugs did not cure Buddy. He was still nagged by headaches. They were not nearly as severe as in the old days; only a dull pain that he could largely ignore. There was another phenomenon associated with the headaches which bothered him a great deal. Each time that the headache would begin, Buddy's brain would flash what he described to Dr. Glenn as a "snapshot image" just as the headache was beginning. The image was of a frozen moment in time. In that scene, Buddy was standing at the rail of the USS *Erne* holding a rifle. Next to the *Erne* was a Vietnamese fishing boat. In the boat was the Vietnamese fisherman, Ninh Ba Chau. Mr. Chau was holding his head as blood seeped between his fingers, just before he slumped to the deck of the fishing boat. A pan of the horrified faces of the family members in that instant was gut-wrenching, along with the piercing hate-filled eyes of the teen-aged son. The image would then go black, and the headache would intensify. Buddy had described this symptom in great detail to Dr. Glenn; and each time, he had bared his soul to the physician.

"The image stays with me in my subconscious and surfaces periodically. It doesn't seem to happen every day; maybe two or three times per week. But when it does happen, it fatigues me and tears at my conscience, making me feel very sorry for what I did to that family. Even though I know it was not necessarily my fault, the incident will not leave me. I just feel so sorry for those people," said Buddy. And each time he told this story to Dr. Glenn, he could not help but weep.

At each session with Dr. Glenn, Buddy asked the same question. "Will I ever be rid of the headaches and flashbacks?" And just as many times as Buddy had asked the question, Buddy knew the answer that was coming.

301

Dr. Will Glenn kept his head down and finished cleaning his glasses. He knew there was no definitive answer to Buddy's question. Finally, Dr. Glenn lifted his head, put on his glasses, and looked directly at Buddy.

"I wish that I could answer that question, Buddy," said Dr. Glenn. "I am so sorry that your soul is in such torment. You come from a family with good moral fabric. It's understandable that you have such angst. I wish I could give you good news, but I just cannot unequivocally tell you that your symptoms will ever completely leave you. But, having said that, let me tell you that our knowledge of PTSD is growing because of the wealth of data that we have accumulated as we study cases like yours and thousands of others. As you can imagine, Buddy, over the years, I have been recording my findings from the meetings I have had with my patients. In your case, I believe that we have stabilized your condition. But I, too, feel frustrated because I cannot find the key to open that door to let you pass through and resolve your underlying anxiety."

Over time, Buddy had grown to trust Will Glenn and to consider the doctor his friend. Having been in his company for so much time, in some cases he could also foresee what this friend was going to say. In this instance, Buddy felt as though he was going to hear the same old line from his friend and physician; something to the effect that it was all a big web-enwrapped mystery. But instead, Dr. Glenn was telling him some-thing he had not heard before.

"One of the theories that has recently surfaced in our medical journals is now being widely discussed because it seems to have helped some individuals in cases such as yours. It has not been given sanction yet by medical boards, nor has it been officially named. But unofficially, it is being called confrontational interaction treatment," said the physician.

Uh, oh, thought Buddy; another theory. He hated it when Dr. Glenn espoused another buzz word or phrase that was currently being bandied about in his circle of colleagues. It usually meant that they were simply grasping at the latest theory in mental health. And of course, none of their mumbo jumbo had stopped his headaches. But he continued to listen to Dr. Glenn.

"I don't pretend to be any kind of expert in this new theory, but the gist of the theory seems to be this: if a patient is in a position whereby he or she can somehow physically confront the problem, or the underlying trigger factors of the problem, and then somehow interact with those factors so that they no longer are capable of triggering the anxiety disorder, it is possible that the patient will subsequently remain symptom free; at least that's the premise. Believe me, Buddy, I don't know exactly how this theory would work into your particular case. However, I am willing to hazard a guess and plan of action," said Dr. Glenn.

Buddy had begun concentrating on what Dr. Glenn had been saying several minutes ago. He was now giving the doctor his full attention. It was a new topic, one that he and the doctor had never before mentioned.

"OK," said Buddy. "How do you propose that I confront my problem?"

"Remember, Buddy, I don't have answers," said Glenn. "I only have educated guesses."

"Yeah, yeah," said Buddy, who was once again thinking that he was not going to hear anything more of any value. "What's your educated guess?"

Dr. Glenn hesitated, turned and looked out the office window, then turned back again and faced Buddy. He pushed his glasses up on his nose before he spoke.

"I am quite sure I know the answer to this question, but I will ask it anyway. Buddy, since you left the military many years ago, have you ever been back to Vietnam?"

Almost immediately, Buddy thought to himself, what a dumb question. Of course he had not been back to Vietnam. "No, of course not," he answered and looked at Glenn as if the doctor had lost his mind.

Dr. Glenn chuckled. "You're looking at me wondering where that question came from. Well, I'll tell you. Did you know that many Americans are now traveling to Vietnam? Many of these travelers are ex-military men who served their country during the Vietnam War."

Buddy continued to stare at the doctor and said, "I don't believe that I would ever have any interest in taking a trip to Vietnam. As you know, I don't have too many pleasant memories of my military time near that country."

Dr. Glenn nodded his head in understanding. "I want you to focus on something for a minute. Buddy, how many times have you told me in our meetings that you could see the members of that Vietnamese family in the dreams that you have? And how many times have you told me that you felt so sorry for that family?" Dr. Glenn paused to let Buddy think about those words.

Buddy then suddenly grasped the thought process that Dr. Glenn was following, and his eyes held a look of understanding as he looked at Dr. Glenn. "Let me get this straight. I think you are telling me that in light of this new 'confrontational' treatment jargon you just hit me with, that you are thinking that maybe I should go back to Vietnam. Is that right?" asked Buddy.

"I didn't say that," said Dr. Glenn. "You did. But since you are now with me, what would you think about taking that trip? More importantly, what would you think about confronting the very problem that has given you this anxiety for many years? And by that, I can be even more specific. What would you think of going back to meet that family who was in the fishing boat on that fateful day many years ago, to do your best to make amends with them?"

Glenn continued, "There is also an inherent risk in this whole idea. For instance, what if you could not find the family? And even if you did find them, what would be their reaction? They may harbor such hate that they might simply want to kill you." He then quickly said, "Maybe this isn't such a good idea after all."

Dr. Glenn paused and then continued. "I am certainly not saying that such a meeting would cure you. But in my opinion, it might be worth trying." Dr. Glenn looked quizzically at Buddy.

Buddy knew he was supposed to say something, but words failed him. "I'm going down the hall to the restroom," he said, and got up and left the doctor's inner office. A minute later he was standing in the restroom looking in the mirror over the sink as he washed his hands. The man looking back at him from the mirror did not look like a happy person. Buddy did not like what he saw. A tear rolled from the corner of Buddy's eye, which he quickly dabbed with the paper towel in his hand. In fact, thought Buddy, the man in the mirror looked sad and hollow, as if he carried a crushing burden in life. Buddy tried to smile then. The man in the mirror did not smile back.

*****

They say that in life, every man bears burdens. Some are heavier than others; some are physical, and some are mental. Buddy Miller had been carrying a heavy mental burden ever since October 1968. For the past four years Dr. Glenn had been attempting to help Buddy carry and balance that load in his life. But unbeknownst to Buddy, Dr. Will Glenn was carrying a burden in his own life that very well may have been equally as heavy as that carried by his patient, Buddy Miller. He had come to the conclusion years ago that he would someday rectify the set of unfortunate circumstances that had placed that burden on his shoulders.

Chapter Thirty-Three

Dr. Glenn had been a brand new physician who wanted to make a difference in his practice when he graduated from medical school so many years ago. As he watched Walter Cronkite on the evening news each day while completing medical school, he could see that many of America's finest young men and women were putting their lives on the line in Southeast Asia. These young people were being killed or severely wounded at an alarming rate. Young Dr. Glenn knew that as a physician, he would never be called upon to make the same sacrifices as those at-risk soldiers he saw on the nightly evening news. As he watched the world events unfold, for reasons he could not explain, he felt that he somehow must make a contribution to this effort for his country after his graduation from medical school. Following through on his personal commitment, Dr. Glenn decided to offer his services as a physician to the military. In a few weeks, after a cursory Army Officer Indoctrination course, he had found himself with a new set of shiny captain's bars and was headed for Vietnam in 1971. After arrival in-theater, he got exactly what he had wanted; a non-stop learning experience in healing and emergency, state-of-the-art trauma surgery at the Cam Ranh Bay military medical facility. He was now making his own personal effort to help the young men who faced an enemy's fury.

At the same time as he was treating the physically broken, he was learning a great deal about the mentally broken and dispirited warriors that he treated. He had become very interested in the medical condition known at that time simply as "post-Vietnam syndrome." With this experience, he would later turn the focus of his medical practice to psychiatry. In the meantime, he was making a much needed difference in the lives of scores of young men and women through his medical healing. In addition, he gained a great deal of satisfaction from his personal contributions to the war effort.

But Dr. Glenn did not spend his entire time in Vietnam working. There was also time for extracurricular activities. One of those activities resulted in his falling in love with a Vietnamese national who was working for the Americans as a medical clerk on the base. Bich (pronounced "beek") Thi Nguyen was given the nickname "Becky" by the Americans with whom she worked. Although somewhat unusual, the office manager thought calling her Becky would defuse the potential of having other Americans discourteously bandying her Vietnamese given name about in a derogatory manner. In the Vietnamese language, her name meant 'Jade Poem.' Dr. Glenn thought that she was the most beautiful girl he had ever seen. In short order, Dr. Glenn and Becky set up housekeeping in a small off-base apartment. Will subsequently sent a request form through his chain of command for permission to marry Becky. He was somewhat daunted when he was told by his company clerk that he had never seen such a request granted by MACV, and not to expect a quick answer.

Life was wonderful for the two lovers. They rode a small motor scooter to and from the base to work. They were deeply in love and dreamed of the day that they would be together in peace. Their love produced a baby boy in late 1973, whom they named An Dung, (peaceful hero), and whom they would call Andy.

Following a major North Vietnamese advance on allied-held positions in and around Cam Rahn Bay, many of the military medical personnel were hurriedly moved from Cam Ranh Bay to the southern port of Vung Tau. Captain Will Glenn, Becky, and their small son, Andy, rode a military bus through the South Vietnamese-controlled countryside to arrive at the sea-side, resort village of Vung Tau, where they were able to find a small apartment. Life returned to normal for the couple, or as normal as can be expected within a country at war. Becky was again hired to work in the medical records section of the hospital, and Will stayed busy with his warrior patients. His treatments changed drastically though, as there were far fewer war casualties in the southern area of the country, but he was still happy with his life. When the political winds in the United States indicated that the American people had had enough, the American war effort began winding down rapidly. But Dr. Glenn continued on in Vung Tau with the Army. However, his military obligation to the Army would soon be fulfilled, and he would be able to go home.

Will was desperate. He had received no response to the application he had sent through his chain of command, a request to marry Becky and take her and Andy with him to America when he finally left Vietnam. He was told repeatedly that sometimes these applications could take as long as two years to be processed. Even then, many of them were denied. Will knew that with the war effort winding down, there was a possibility that Becky and their son would not be leaving the country with him. The couple was now anxiously waiting for word on their application.

Just when life had calmed a bit for Dr. Glenn and his "unofficial" family, in early 1975, all U.S. forces were given notice of impending evacuation from Vietnam. As frantically as he tried, Will Glenn could not find a government-authorized means to bring Becky and Andy with him to the United States. It seemed that his marriage application had been lost in the never-ending shuffle of government paperwork. The local Army chain of command was powerless. Will reluctantly and tearfully boarded a plane for the United States, leaving a heart-broken Becky and Andy waving at him at the military flight terminal.

Months later, when the entire country had been fully assimilated under the communist regime, the Vietnam populace was placed under much stricter oversight. Travel was generally forbidden within the country and leaving the country by a Vietnamese citizen was impossible. Becky and Andy were forbidden to leave the country by the communist regime. As restrictive as this mandate was, life would get much uglier for Will Glenn's Vietnamese family.

During the war years, the social interaction between the occupying forces and the Vietnamese local population had many foregone consequences. One of them, of course, was the surge in birth rate of children of mixed parent relationships. But because of the fluidity of the military men, most of the American men who fathered the mixed-race children were never aware of the child they helped create. This, of course, meant that many ill-prepared young Vietnamese women were left to care for their mixed-race children.

After the communist regime had fully taken charge of the country, the mixed-race son or daughter of any American military man and a Vietnamese national was henceforth considered impure and an outcast by the Communists. This was the case with nearly all of the children of American military personnel. These children, then, were either voluntarily put up for adoption by their mothers or were forcefully taken from the mothers. An Dung was forcefully taken from Bich Thi and relegated to an austere orphanage, its location not divulged to Bich. In spite of Dr. Glenn's extensive efforts to gain permission to marry Becky, permission had not been granted. Thus, Dr. Will Glenn was forced to leave behind the woman and small son whom he loved deeply, and he was not immediately aware that Andy had been taken from Becky.

In 1978, as a result of co-sponsorship by the Christian Relief Agency, Bich Thi received permission to leave Vietnam, and join Dr. Will Glenn. They were married shortly after she arrived in the United States. But to the best knowledge of both Will and Becky, An Dung, their son, was still in an unknown orphanage in Vietnam. Both parents tried every means they could to locate and bring their son to America. The efforts were fruitless. But in 1981, there had been a breakthrough in the search for the lost boy. The Christian Relief Agency, while working with the Vietnamese agencies that still held children of American heritage, had located an eight year old boy named An Dung, and who had coincidentally told the orphanage workers, as only an eight-year-old could do, that he should be called Andy.

Through exhaustive research and literally door-to-door interviews, the relief agencies were sometimes able to track down many of the mothers of these children. An Dung was lucky. The whereabouts of his mother was discovered and she was subsequently contacted.

Dr. Will Glenn and Becky had only recently learned of Andy's fate, and they were already arranging for their trip to Vietnam. Through the resources of the church agency, a Vietnamese guide and church representative would be waiting for the doctor and his wife when they arrived in Vietnam. Even with that excitement in his life, Dr. Glenn had thought of Buddy Miller. And through their conversations, he had just put the ball into play to have Buddy travel with him to Vietnam to confront his own life's burden. Of course, Buddy Miller did not know the details or motives of the doctor's heart-felt plan.

*****

Buddy dried his hands and walked back to take his place in the chair opposite the doctor's desk. Dr. Glenn was once again cleaning his glasses.

"I'll go," said Buddy, "on one condition. Since you are also a Vietnam veteran, I want you to go with me. And if this experiment works, I want you to do your damnedest to use your observations to help other guys like me."

Dr. Glenn smiled broadly as he agreed with Buddy. His plan had worked. It was at this time that Dr. Glenn revealed to Buddy the nature of his marriage to Bich Thi and the fact that he was going to return to Vietnam on his own accord to reunite with the couple's son who was held in an orphanage. When Buddy had heard all of the facts, he stared at Dr. Glenn.

"You weasel," said Buddy to Dr. Glenn; but he was smiling when he said it.

Later, when Jim and Irene Miller heard about the plan for Buddy to accompany Dr. Glenn to Vietnam, they did not know what to think. On the one hand, Buddy would be going back to an area of the world that had nearly broken him. In the past few years, they had seen their son very nearly healed to become a very successful entrepreneurial business owner. What would happen when he returned to Vietnam? On the other hand, he would be returning to the Far East with his attending physician. Surely Dr. Glenn would look after their son. In reality, it would unfold that several people were looking over his shoulder as Buddy Miller made that fateful trip to the Far East.

Chapter Thirty-Four

August 1983
Miller Arms Co.
Mahaska County, Iowa

"I don't really want to hear any more bullshit argument out of you, Miller." Bob Dawes was pacing Buddy's office at the factory and waving documents above his head. The documents were his passport and an airplane ticket. "Honestly, Buddy, sometimes I think you have a head made of granite. You're my best friend, and if you are going to go back to Vietnam to face your head-case problem, don't you think I might want to go with you?"

Buddy responded, "You know, Dawes, insubordinate employees can be fired. And right now, you're about as insubordinate as they come."

"Employee, my ass. You forget that we are partners," said Dawes.

They were at the end of their thirty minute war of words. Buddy knew that he could never dissuade Bob Dawes. And Bob Dawes knew that Buddy would soon acquiesce. In another minute, both men were laughing at one another. The receptionist outside Buddy's office had seen this same scenario play out dozens of times over a myriad of subjects. The confrontations always ended this way. Even before Buddy came out of his office and asked her to call him, the receptionist had placed a call to John Proctor on the production floor and told him that Buddy needed to see him. When John joined them, the three men began making plans for how the company would function while Buddy and Bob were gone. At the end of the meeting, John looked forlornly at Buddy. "I wish I was going with you guys," he said.

Chapter Thirty-Five

October 3, 1983
40,000 feet
Somewhere Over the Pacific

For the life of him, Buddy could not figure out how anyone could ever get used to twenty-hour airplane flights, the unsavory airline food, confining and uncomfortable seats, and the lack of sleep. He remembered back to what seemed like almost a lifetime ago when he had experienced the same scene. He was now standing in the aisle of the plane, gazing down at his friend, Dawes, lightly snoring in the seat next to his. Even in business class service, where the seats were a bit roomier, he still disliked the restrictive and confining environment of the jet liner. He wondered if he was a bit claustrophobic. He turned his head slightly to see Dr. Will Glenn and Becky as they leaned against each other dozing. The picture of the couple, plainly in love after several years of marriage, touched him, causing him to once again feel the empty spot in his soul.

Dawes roused from his sleep and stretched. "Gotta go," he said and lurched out of the seat and headed to the lavatory. Buddy sat down again in his seat by the aisle and absently looked at the airline magazine. He had already perused the magazine several times as he willed time to pass more quickly. Several minutes later, he began to wonder about Dawes. But as he looked up again and toward the lavatory, he saw Dawes. In the small galley area outside the lavatory he was chatting with the stewardess. He had both of his hands on the shoulders of the beautiful woman, and they were animatedly talking to each other and smiling. She did not seem to be protesting as she talked to Dawes.

In a few more minutes, Dawes returned to his seat. "Miller, you ain't gonna believe this, but one of these days, that little lady could be the one."

"The one what?" chortled Buddy.

"I might lay odds on this, that she could someday have the last name Dawes," said Bob.

"Hmm, think I've heard this somewhere before," said Buddy. "What are the odds on that?"

Dawes grinned. "Three to one. If I marry her within two years, you owe me three hundred smackers. If I don't, I pay you a hundred bucks."

Buddy was still laughing as the two men shook hands. "You'll forget all about this in a couple weeks," said Buddy, "and you never will pay off."

Ladies and gentlemen, please take your seats as our Captain begins the descent for our landing in Ho Chi Minh City.

The rest of the stewardess's spiel went on, but Buddy didn't pay any attention as he quickly made his way to the toilet. In a short time, he returned to his seat and fastened his seat belt. Dawes had turned to the window. Looking out at the looming, mist-covered green mountains he mumbled, "I never thought I would see this place again," he mumbled.

A cold chill went through Buddy. "I know what you mean," he said.

Chapter Thirty-Six

October 4, 1983
Ho Chi Minh City, Vietnam

The United States did not have an official American Consulate in Ho Chi Minh City in 1983. There was only a working liaison office, which lacked consulate status. That very fact made the trip for the four Americans a bit more tenuous. The Communist Party was strict on allowing foreigners into the country. The Glenns were on firmer ground since they had come to arrange for the emigration of their son and were being sponsored by the Christian Relief Agency. Buddy and Dawes were there under the humanitarian umbrella of the Christian Relief Society. Their story was that they were there to gather information about an incident that had occurred during the war in order to write an article for the Christian Relief Agency's magazine. They carried credentials given to them by the Agency. Dawes carried a single-lens-reflex Nikon camera and a bag with two dozen rolls of blank film. The American Liaison Office in Ho Chi Minh City dealt primarily with military related issues unresolved from the war, as well as humanitarian issues, such as those of concern to the various religious agencies working in Vietnam. The long range goal of that office was to establish communication with the communist government to the extent that a future consulate office would be in the best interest of both countries. The liaison office would be the hub of their activities for the Glenns and for Buddy and Dawes while in Vietnam.

*****

Even though they had been previously briefed by the relief agency, as they deplaned and entered the air terminal, the four Americans were surprised and a bit wary as they observed the dark green uniforms of the Vietnamese secret police sprinkled throughout the terminal. Each policeman carried a rifle and a holstered pistol. To Buddy, it did not seem as though the very obvious police presence was in any way "secret," what with the uniforms and weapons.

The lines of passengers crawled ever so slowly through the bureaucratic quagmire of the communist customs inspectors. Buddy developed goose bumps as he neared the unsmiling inspector. When it was their turn, the inspector read and reread the documents and passports of Buddy and Dawes. For several moments nothing happened, but the inspector finally looked up, stared at the two men, and slowly handed back the documents. Even Dawes was subdued at seeing the many militaristic policemen.

Sweat rolled down the middle of Buddy's back under his shirt. He had forgotten the extreme heat and humidity of Vietnam. The four Americans assembled in the baggage claim area waiting for their luggage. They felt, rather than saw, the unrelenting eyes of the police watching their every move. As they waited for their luggage, it was the sharp eyes of Bob Dawes who noticed a man a short distance away, leaning against the wall. He was wearing black pants and an embroidered, short-sleeved, white shirt worn outside his pants. There appeared to be a small hump on the man's hip, hidden under the shirt. He was short with black hair and looked like every other Vietnamese male. But upon further study, an undistinguishable tattoo could be seen on his left forearm. He was cleaning his fingernails with a small knife. Though he looked attentively at his fingers while wielding the knife, he was not missing any details as he furtively watched the Americans. Dawes whispered to Buddy, "Man, that guy's got cop written all over him." Buddy looked at the man briefly and then looked away. Once again, goose bumps covered Buddy's forearms.

The flowing, white, silk, lower portion of the ao dai swayed as she walked, opening the dress's side slits, revealing the white cotton trousers she wore underneath. Margaret Minh Louis walked with confidence, knowing that she was drawing the attention of several of the policemen as she made her way to the baggage claim area. She was taller than the norm for a Vietnamese woman. An observer would need to look more closely to see that while her eyelids had a hint of epicanthic fold, her nose was narrower and her cheeks were sleeker. She carried a small, but fragrant bouquet of flowers and a small hand purse as she made her way to the waiting Americans.

Another more plainly dressed woman walked by her side. She, too, was an attractive woman, but was easily outshined by the woman in white.

Buddy was not as observant as Dawes, and therefore, received an elbow in the ribs, followed by Dawes's nod toward the approaching women. At the sight of the attractive woman in the flowing white dress, Buddy's heart literally skipped a beat. He struggled to not appear to be staring at the striking woman who was drawing near to them.

As the women reached the Americans, they introduced themselves, with the woman in white doing the talking in nearly flawless English. "Welcome to Vietnam. We are pleased that you have come for a visit. My name is Margaret Minh Louis, but everybody just calls me Maggie. I am from the American Liaison Office, and I am here to welcome you and take you to your hotel." She placed her clutch bag under her arm and clasped the hand of her companion. "My companion is Sang Nguyen, a representative from the Christian Relief Agency. Sang's English is improving, but she wanted me to speak for her." As she looked at the four Americans, she spoke again. "And you must be the Glenns," she said as she handed the flowers to Becky. After shaking hands and gently bowing to the Glenns, she turned her attention to Buddy and Dawes.

While she had been introducing herself, Buddy had not heard a word she had said. His heart was beating too loudly. He stumbled through an introduction and cursed to himself at what a buffoon he must appear to Miss Louis. He was absolutely smitten.

After retrieving their luggage, the group made its way out of the terminal, toward a large black sedan idling at the curb. Police were also in evidence outside the terminal and on every street corner. After they had stowed their bags in the trunk of the car, Sang sat up front with the driver, while Maggie and Dawes sat on fold-up jump seats which faced the rear seat of the car where the Glenns and Buddy were comfortably ensconced.

Becky could not contain herself. Vietnamese words flowed from her and were responded to by both Maggie and Sang. In a moment, Becky began quietly crying while the other two women consoled her. In just another moment of girl banter, though, all three women were giggling.

"Now Beck," said Dr. Glenn. You have three English-only guys here. Would you care to share?"

Becky Glenn daubed her eyes. "No. We were talking girl talk. You have no idea how I have missed having someone to speak Vietnamese with," and she laughed again.

When things were quiet again, the soft rumble of the old Chinese-made limousine lulled Buddy's jet-lagged body. He began to relax and realized how tired he was. All he could think of at the moment was falling into a comfortable bed. Suddenly he sat up straight. Where had that thought come from? That of him and Maggie Louis falling into that comfortable bed together! He began to relax again, too tired to continue thinking.

"Let me tell you how our day will go tomorrow," said Maggie. "Sang and I will pick you up at your hotel after breakfast, and we will go to our office. The Glenns will go with Sang to the orphanage, and you two gentlemen will stay with me." Maggie then chuckled as she looked at

Buddy and Dawes. Both men had their heads resting on their chest, very nearly asleep. Becky Glenn was also nodding her head to the drone of the car motor. Maggie looked at Will Glenn. "I guess we can continue this discussion in the morning," she said, smiling.

The next morning, as they sat in the lobby of the hotel waiting for their ride, Dawes observed that the same man who had been cleaning his nails at the airport was seated in a distant lobby chair with his back to the Americans. He appeared to be reading a newspaper. His uplifted arm displayed the same faded blue/green tattoo. There was no time for speculation on this sighting as their driver arrived and beckoned them to the same black car they had ridden in the day before. In broken English, he explained that he would take them to the liaison office. The driver made his way through the myriad of motor scooters and bicycles and sprinkling of small cars on the busy thoroughfare, but soon turned off the main road onto a tree-lined street with considerably less traffic. Many larger, stately, well-maintained homes sat back from and faced the street. The driver pulled up to the curb at an attractive, white stucco building that looked more like an affluent home than a business. Maggie Louis came from the front door of the building and welcomed them.

As they entered the liaison office, the group was met by a young, clean-shaven, short-haired, unsmiling American man dressed in civilian clothing, holding the door. Off to the side in a small, but tastefully decorated room, they saw three more American men sipping coffee with their chairs arranged to face anyone entering the building. They looked very similar to the door man. The thought occurred to Buddy that they certainly looked like U.S. Marines.

Sang Nguyen was waiting for the Glenns and quickly began chatter-ing while she took Becky's hand and led the Glenns down the hall in the center of the building. Buddy and Dawes followed Maggie to a nearby room, which was her personal office, its décor as elegant and gracious as

319

Maggie herself. She took a seat behind the desk and motioned for the two men to be seated. She pushed a small button next to her phone, and in less than a minute, a side door to the office opened and a small, older woman entered with a tray laden with coffee and pastry. She placed the tray on a small side table and quickly left the office.

When they had each filled a coffee mug that was emblazoned with a gold seal of the United States and the words "Liaison Office" written beneath the seal, they resumed their seats. Maggie began, "Apparently the Christian Relief Agency has more clout than I gave them credit for. All I know is that I was told by my boss that I am to be your guide for the next few days. As I understand the situation, you are looking for a specific family. So tell me about it."

For the next thirty minutes, with a brief interlude to refill coffee mugs, Buddy narrated an overview of the events as they had unfolded in 1968, his extreme duress over the years, and his treatment by Dr. Glenn.

"Ah, there's the tie to the Glenns," said Maggie. "If I'm not mistaken, our plain old Dr. Will Glenn also has a father who carries considerable political weight in Washington. I don't know his story, and I don't need to. But I guess that explains how you two were able to ride the Glenn coattails and come to Vietnam." She laughed, put her coffee mug on her desk, and retrieved a pen and yellow legal pad of paper. As he watched her, Buddy was spellbound by the beautiful Maggie Louis. When she laughed, Buddy's ears heard no other sound.

"OK, Mr. Miller, give me as many of the specific details of that day as you can remember. For instance, what is the name of this fisherman and his family?" she asked as she continued writing.

As he told the story of the shooting of Ninh Ba Chau in greater detail, sweat began beading on Buddy's face. He described the Chau family, the number of men and women in the fishing boat, their physical characteristics, the markings and description of the boat, and everything else that came to his mind regarding that fateful day. As he continued, he began to be more animated and agitated. He was reliving the events in his mind, and the low level headache began increasing in intensity. As the details unfolded in his mind, tears began to flow from Buddy's eyes. His speech began to falter, and he gasped for breath.

Bob Dawes watched his friend narrate the story. Buddy's emotions quickly overcame him, and he self-consciously wiped tears from his eyes.

"Perhaps we should take a break for a few minutes," said Maggie, and she stood up and left the office. Alarm clearly showed on her face. In a minute, there was a quiet knock on the office door, and Dr. Glenn entered.

"Bob, let me talk to Buddy for a minute, please," said the doctor.

"Sure, OK," said Dawes as he snuffed his nose and left the office.

"Are you all right, Buddy?" asked Dr. Glenn.

By then, Buddy had recomposed himself and was wiping his face with a handkerchief. "I don't know what happened," he said. "I was just talking away, and suddenly, I fell apart. I think I feel OK now, though."

Dr. Glenn smiled and placed a hand on Buddy's shoulder. "Believe it or not, Buddy, what you are experiencing is a good thing. Remember when you were a little kid and got the winter flu and you were sick to your stomach?"

"Yeah, but what's that got to do with this?" asked Buddy.

"Well, I like to think that the more times you face your problem and talk it out, the process removes some of the barriers to helping you finally get over this anxiety. Kinda like throwing up. When it's over, you always feel better. I have this feeling in my gut, no pun intended," he said as he smiled, "that by coming back to Vietnam you are going to finally whip this problem." He gently squeezed Buddy's shoulder.

Buddy looked up and managed to smile at Will. "I sure hope so," he said.

Will left the room, and Maggie and Dawes returned. "Are you OK, Mr. Miller?" asked Maggie.

Buddy nodded, and said, "Yes, ma'am."

Maggie cocked her head slightly. "Ma'am? Oh, well." She continued, "The two things we have going for us are that the family name Chau is one of the more uncommon names in Vietnam, so there will not be as many families to locate. And secondly, we know that the family fished out of the Cam Ranh Bay area, so it seems logical that they lived somewhere close by."

As she talked, her office door opened again and a stocky, young Vietnamese man entered and closed the door. He was dressed in a white shirt with brown slacks. His arms were well muscled, and his head sat atop strong, broad shoulders and a very short, thick neck. His eyes revealed no emotion and moved very little. A course, small, black mustache desperately clung to the man's upper lip. He had the appearance of a light heavy-weight wrestler; somebody you did not want as an enemy. Buddy shuddered when the stranger met his glance.

"Mr. Miller and Mr. Dawes, I would like you to meet my friend, Bao Nguyen. Bao, this is Mr. Miller and Mr. Dawes."

Bao gave a slight nod of his head to the two Americans, but showed no other emotion and did not offer his hand.

"Think of Bao as a sort of private investigator working for us. He performs a variety of jobs for our office, but we won't go into all of that. Bao is going to begin the search for the Chau family. In the meantime, there is nothing more that can be done but to wait for his results. So, I am going to make a suggestion. Why don't I meet the two of you for dinner tonight? I know a very nice restaurant within walking distance of your hotel where I could introduce you to some Vietnamese cuisine. What do you think?" asked Maggie.

"Sure," said Bob. "What time?"

Maggie smiled and looked at Buddy. "Mr. Miller, could we meet in your hotel lobby at seven?"

Buddy had been staring at Maggie, but finally found his tongue. "Yes, ma'am, seven would be fine."

"Great," said Maggie, and she cocked her head to the side as she looked directly at Buddy. "Our driver will take you back to your hotel. I'll see you gentlemen tonight."

*****

From the corner of his eye, Buddy watched the purposeful walk of Maggie Louis as they made their way to the neighborhood restaurant. Dawes was a bit less discreet and would fall back a step or two to admire the alluring walk of Maggie, and then he would catch back up to the couple. Unseen by the two men, the trailing figure of Bao Nguyen followed from a distance.

After they were seated, a waiter brought a beautiful bottle to their table and poured three small glasses. The bottle had the words "Son Tinh" written on it in gold letters. Maggie explained to Buddy and Dawes that this was sticky-rice liquor, of premium grade, and they should sip it very slowly. She then held a long conversation with the waiter, giving him instructions for their dinner.

"This restaurant was always a favorite of the elite French when they occupied the country. Occupying armies and battles in the country have come and gone, but this little place has survived through the years," said Maggie.

It was a beautifully furnished, small restaurant with the majority of the tables occupied. Striking paintings were displayed on the walls, which, for the most part, depicted serene landscapes of forests, streams, and green mountains. But mixed in with that lot were a few pictures depicting the struggles of the people of Vietnam in overthrowing military armies that had occupied the country through the ages. It seemed odd to Buddy and Dawes to see the mix of the pictures of serenity with the pictures of fighting. Off to the side of the main dining room was a quiet, smoke-filled bar with many of the bar stools also occupied. It appeared that the restaurant/bar was favored by both local residents and travelers. Buddy studied the patrons at the bar for a moment and noticed that Bao Nguyen occupied a bar stool where he could plainly see Maggie and her guests.

The three adults made small talk, and Buddy and Bob answered a fusillade of questions posed by Maggie regarding happenings in the United States. True to his bold nature, Bob soon asked Maggie about herself. Surprisingly, she was very open in her response.

"Now, Mr. Dawes, you know you should not get too nosy about a girl's past," she said. But then she laughed. "Well, as you can see, I am not a complete Vietnamese person. When I was born in 1947, the French were still a major presence in Vietnam. My father was a French military officer, and my mother was his concubine. His last name was Louis, apparently spelled like the first name of some of France's kings. Margaret was his mother's name. My father's family in France were farmers. While in Vietnam, he missed the agrarian life. So he and my mother had a small farm just outside of Saigon where they raised vegetables and had chickens and a milk goat. And that is where my sister and I grew up. Those few years were the best years of my life. I loved that little farm," she said.

"What happened when the French left Vietnam?" asked Buddy.

"When the French left Vietnam in the early fifties, my father left too; never to be seen again," she said. "So you see I have a great deal of empathy for the war orphans, such as the Glenn's son. I was one also."

Buddy and Dawes were fascinated by Maggie's story. "Geez, what happened to you and your mom and sister after that?" asked Dawes.

"When the Communists began making strides to take over the country, my mother was very astute. Before they clamped down on travel, my mother sold the small farm and took me and my sister to the United States. We were sponsored by a church in Houston, Texas. We gained our U.S. citizenship, and my mother and sister still live in Houston. Later, after graduating from Rice University and the University of Texas with a Ph.D. in International Affairs, I went to work for the State Department, so I have travelled around a bit. I guess I really don't call any place home anymore."

Their conversation paused when a very pretty young woman approached their table and removed the small liquor glasses. In their place, she arranged three new glasses and filled them with an almost-clear liquor. Dawes could not keep his eyes off of her, as he watched the woman's delicate hands pour the wine. He then watched her back side as she left the table and returned to the bar area. Maggie explained that the liquor was a very fine rice wine, and that it should also be sipped slowly with dinner.

Their waiter soon reappeared and placed steaming soup bowls in front of each of them, along with an almost translucently-wrapped spring roll. Maggie explained that the soup was called sup mang cua, an asparagus-crab soup. She also said the rolls were called goi cuon, or salad rolls. They were delicious, and Buddy and Dawes ate hungrily. After the soup bowls had been cleared from the table, the main course arrived. Each of them was given a small bowl of sticky rice. A plate was placed in front of each of them, and the waiter began filling their plates from two serving bowls. Maggie explained that one dish was com tam, a grilled pork dish served over broken rice with various vegetables. The other was a small dish of grilled prawns that was placed beside the larger plate in front of each of them. And finally, a very small bowl was also placed in front of each of them, and the waiter poured a reddish-brown liquid into each of their bowls. Quiet ensued at the table, as they began eating. Dawes asked about the small bowl of liquid as he lifted it and smelled it. He immediately placed it back on the table and had a strange expression on his face.

"Nuoc mam," chuckled Maggie as she watched Dawes screw up his nose. "It's a fermented fish sauce. Vietnamese use it for garnish on almost everything they eat. It takes some getting used to," she said. The men watched as Maggie dipped a bit of her grilled pork into the sauce and placed it in her mouth. She smiled, and said with her mouth full, "It's good. Really."

"We'll take your word for it," said Dawes.

Over a dessert of che, a bean and rice pudding, and coffee, the three spoke of their homes, families, and other topics of mutual interest. Maggie continued to ask about the states, while the men asked more about Vietnam and the customs of its people.

It was over the second or third cup of coffee that Dawes noticed it. With a bit of experience under his belt, he could not help but see that there was human electricity flowing across the dinner table between his best friend and Maggie Louis. He watched for a moment as Buddy and Maggie continued to talk, laugh, and pay very close attention to one another. He did not feel the least offended that they had begun leaving him out of the conversation. He just grinned slightly and watched them. Bob had not seen his friend respond to a member of the opposite sex in a very long time. As a result, he found this exchange to be quite fascinating. After a few minutes, he excused himself with the premise that he needed to use the rest room.

They continued to talk, Buddy telling Maggie about his family back in Iowa and the farm where he grew up. At first, as he talked, he did not notice that her hand had been ever so gently placed on the top of his hand. When at last he noticed, he abruptly stopped talking.

Since she first met Buddy Miller and began talking with him in her office that morning, Maggie Louis had been assessing the quiet, handsome man from Iowa. She knew that he was extremely intelligent and successful. A confidential dossier received in her office prior to Buddy Miller's arrival had revealed those and a few other facts. What the file had not revealed was that this man was kind, sensitive, and that he had been hurt badly by an unfortunate set of life's circumstances. As he continued to reveal his inner soul, she felt herself being drawn even more to his quiet, unassuming, kind demeanor.

In the moments prior, when Maggie had told Buddy and Dawes a bit about her past, it was natural, of course that she did not tell them all of her previous experiences. It was readily apparent that Maggie Louis was a very intelligent and beautiful woman. In addition, she guarded her inner self from outsiders. Part of the reason for this was her having been a minority individual living in America, and another part was that she was not stimulated by boorish behavior, a behavior that she had found all too common on the college campus when she was a student. Being pawed and mauled by lusty male fellow students was not necessarily her idea of a good time. Oh, yes, she had several occasional romances, but they all fizzled out. Maggie Louis was not a pushover in affairs of the heart. In fact, she had discovered that she was sometimes referred to as "that cold bitch." If she learned of such comments, she paid them little heed. Instead, she found that immersing herself in study and work was far more satisfying to her than romance, and she believed that she would, more or less, happily continue to work for the rest of her life without a life partner. That is, until she met Mr. J. William Miller. She quickly ascertained that in addition to being a very fascinating man, in Buddy she had met a man who was her intellectual equal, and she greatly enjoyed and found herself fascinated by her conversations with Buddy.

"I'm so sorry, Buddy, that you had such a bad experience," she said. It was the first time that she had called him Buddy. "But Vietnam is not such a large country, and I feel certain that we can find the family you wish to speak with." Buddy looked into Maggie's dark brown eyes, and they were staring intently back at him. Their eyes remained locked on each other for several minutes. They both smiled, and Buddy, ever so gently, turned his hand over to grasp Maggie's hand. "Someday," she said, "I would enjoy seeing your family's farm. I have such fond memories of the time I spent in the countryside."

Buddy lowered his eyes, but then glanced away briefly and began to laugh quietly as he looked back at Maggie.

"What in the world are you laughing at?" asked Maggie.

"Slowly turn around and look at the bar," said Buddy.

She turned and saw Bob Dawes sitting at the bar with his arm on the shoulder of the pretty bar waitress. They were both laughing and enjoying each other's company. She also saw a dour-faced Bao Nguyen watching from his vantage point at the far end of the bar. She turned back and grinned at Buddy. "See," she said, "Vietnam isn't such a bad place, is it?" Buddy returned the grin.

*****

Walking at least a hundred alleys and crowded back streets in the city of Cam Ranh, along with a bit of physical intimidation and small monetary persuasion gifts had finally paid off. Bao Nguyen now had the names and addresses of three families named Chau who lived in the area and made fishing their livelihood.

Dressed in the more shabby attire of a local, Bao had personally walked slowly by each of the three residences. As he had done this, he also watched from the corner of his eye. He now knew that he had picked up a tail. Eluding the tail, and watching from a vantage point, he could see that his tail was a plain-clothes member of the police force. It did not matter that Bao did not know to what force the policeman was attached. To Bao, a policeman was a policeman. Even knowing the multitude of stories about the none-too-gentle treatment of citizens at the hands of the secret police, he did not fear them.

Two of the Chau familys' homes were typical of the local fishermen. Their homes were somewhat squalid with no electrical lines attached to the homes. But the third Chau family home was definitely above the norm for the neighborhood. It was considerably larger than the other houses, and the home was stucco construction instead of being covered by corrugated tin like so many of the other neighborhood homes. There was an electric line attached to the side of the house. A small car and a powerful motorcycle were parked next to the house. These expensive modes of transportation were certainly not typical of hard-working, honest fishermen. There was something very strange about that family. Bao felt certain that there was, somehow, a connection between this house and the policeman tailing him.

Chapter Thirty-Seven

October 8, 1983
Ho Chi Minh City, Vietnam

It was a wonderful clear morning, with no rain in the forecast. The humidity had backed off somewhat with a cool breeze rolling down the mountain sides and coming into the city from the west. Buddy, Dawes, and the Glenns were seated in the hotel restaurant enjoying a breakfast of pastries, fruit, and an endless supply of coffee. Becky Glenn could not keep the smile on her face under control. She was giddy with excitement, and her joy bubbled over to the men at the table. Finally, she could contain herself no longer.

"He is such a handsome boy," she said. The Glenns had now visited the orphanage twice with Sang Nguyen, and Becky was, of course, referring to their long lost son, ten-year-old An Dung (Andy). "He is healthy and seemed to recognize me," she said. "But he is so skinny!"

"Now Beck, I'm not real sure that Andy knew you after all these years," said Will. "But even so, I agree that he sure is a neat kid. Boy, I hope nothing fouls up this adoption procedure. No one at the orphanage has yet confirmed that we will be able to take Andy with us." He wagged his head from side to side and again turned his attention to the small fruit bowl in front of him.

"Well, I'm confident," said Becky. "Sang seems to think everything is going according to plan." Will made no further comment. He certainly did not want to put a damper on his wife's exuberance. But he was also practical enough to know that in a Communist controlled country, the wishes of a western couple were probably a very low priority, indeed. But he would never reveal this thought to his wife. He could only pray that things would turn out all right.

They parted again at the liaison office, with the Glenns going with Sang Nguyen, and Buddy and Dawes taking a seat in Maggie's office.

"Gentlemen, I have some news for you. Bao Nguyen had been making inquiries in Cam Ranh . . ." said Maggie, but she was interrupted by Bob Dawes.

"Excuse me for interrupting, Ms. Louis, but just what is the story on Bao anyway. I seem to see him lurking about every time we are with you. Is he your bodyguard or something?"

Maggie thought for a moment. "Yes, Mr. Dawes. I guess you could call it that. Bao Nguyen works for our office, and I think of him more as a facilitator. When we have projects that need the skill of a local resident who can fit in with the populace, we enlist the help of Bao. He is able to cut through a great deal of local red tape. When we hired him he was truthful with us, telling us that he is loyal to the Communist Party, but that he is also an opportunistic capitalist. Translated, that means that he will stay within the law to carry out our tasking for money. And yes, he does seem to take it upon himself to ensure my safety in the streets. I consider him my friend, and vice versa. Does that answer your question, Mr. Dawes?"

Dawes nodded his head and grinned.

Maggie continued, "As I was saying, Bao has been busy in Cam Ranh city. He has identified three families that we need to visit. We are going to do that tomorrow if that is all right with you gentlemen."

A knot formed in Buddy's stomach. When he first agreed to make this Vietnam trip, he had felt reasonably confident that he would be unable to locate the specific Chau family. He had not counted on the bulldog tenacity and skill of Bao Nguyen. Now he was a bit frightened. If one of these families proved to be the correct one, how would they react to his attempt to make amends with them?

Dawes and Buddy were taken back to the hotel where they each filled an overnight bag. They would be taking a Five Star Express train to Cam Ranh and would be overnight on the train. That afternoon, their driver took them to the train station where they joined Maggie and the ever present Bao, who stood idly to the side and slowly scanned the crowded train platform.

That evening, as the lurching train hugged the green mountains and made its way northeastward, Buddy and Dawes ate meals that they purchased from the food cart that went up and down the aisle of the train cars.

"I'm not sure what it is, but it tastes OK," said Dawes. He washed it down with a beer. They were assigned to a small sleeper compartment that they shared with two flatulent older Vietnamese gentlemen, who, when they were not asleep, were smoking pungent pipes. As a result, Dawes insisted that the compartment window remain partially open. Maggie was in a nearby compartment that she was sharing with three women. Bao's whereabouts was unknown.

Chapter Thirty-Eight

October 9, 1983
Cam Ranh, Vietnam

When they awoke in the morning, it was ironic that both men re-marked that they had dreamed of life on the *Erne* many years ago. The noise and the rocking motion of the train must have triggered the same subconscious thoughts in their heads as they slept.

When they reached Cam Ranh, Maggie and the men waited on the train platform. After nearly thirty minutes, a small sedan pulled to the curb. Bao Nguyen was driving.

"Man, old Bao sure gets around, doesn't he," remarked Dawes.

Blessed cool air came from the air conditioning vents of the small se-dan as they drove from the train station. The roads, while crowded, were not nearly as frenetic as those in Ho Chi Minh City. For thirty minutes, Bao navigated the car through narrow alleys, honking his horn to clear playing children from the path of the car, and finally came to a stop on a quiet, cluttered, and run-down street. He shut off the engine, and the four of them got out of the car. The smell of the ocean and that of fish was suspended in the cool air. Maggie conversed with Bao for a few mo-ments as Bao pointed to one of the houses on the street.

"Let's proceed, gentlemen," said Maggie. Bao stayed by the car as Maggie led the way to the ramshackle house that Bao had pointed out to her. Maggie had briefed Buddy and Bob on how she would proceed. She would knock on the door and ask several specific questions to the home owners. If there was any confirmation that this was the family whom they were seeking, she would summon the two men.

While Buddy and Dawes waited in what could more aptly be called an alley than a street, Maggie knocked on the door of the house. The

knot in Buddy's belly grew tighter, and his hands were clenched unconsciously into tight painful fists. When the door of the house finally
opened, it only took five more minutes, and Maggie began walking back
to the two men.

"It was a very young couple with small children. They are not the
ones," she said.

Again, they got in the car and watched through the windows of the
sedan as Bao threaded the little car through more narrow streets, narrowly
missing several slower bicyclists, each with large baskets precariously
perched on the rear of the bicycle. Fifteen minutes later, Bao again
parked the car, after which Maggie led the two men to another sad-
looking house. The result was another dead end.

"The man there worked in the local fish cannery. The family never
fished and never have owned a boat," she said. She looked at Buddy.
"Sorry," she said. "This might end up being a complete waste of our
time."

If asked, he probably could not have readily described his feelings.
On the one hand, Buddy was relieved that they had not found the family.
Yet on the other, he was also disappointed, thinking that without finding
the family, he was not confronting his source of anxiety. He finally
spoke to Maggie. "We still have another family to visit."

She smiled. "Let's go men," she said, as she began walking briskly
toward the car.

As they approached the car, Dawes stopped to bend over and tie his
shoelace that had become loose. As he stood to follow Buddy and
Maggie, he happened to look around him and was sure that he saw a
small man with black slacks and a white shirt sidle back into the shadow
of a nearby home. What the hell, thought Dawes. It's the same guy, he
said to himself.

As the car negotiated the narrow streets, it began to climb a small rise at the edge of the sea. The houses in this neighborhood were somewhat larger, but were still clad in corrugated tin. Spaghetti-like entanglements of electrical wires crisscrossed above the street. A half block away from the house they were seeking, Bao stopped and shut off the car. He stayed in the car and pointed out another house to Maggie. She and Buddy and Dawes got out of the car and began walking toward the front door. As they approached the house next door to their target, two unsmiling characters dressed in black shirts and slacks stepped into their path and began conversing in Vietnamese. Maggie stepped up to them and began speaking to them very quietly but firmly. The two men looked over Maggie's shoulder, slowly parted, and made room for the group to pass.

As they walked further, Buddy said, "What did you say to those guys? What did they want?"

Maggie answered, "I don't think they wanted us to visit this house, but I told them if they did not let us pass, I would call the policeman who is following us to see if he could persuade them."

"So you knew there was some guy following us?" said Dawes excitedly. "I saw him too."

Maggie did not reply and continued walking. Dawes looked at Buddy and smiled. Buddy just squinted at Dawes. He had no idea what they were talking about, and the knot in his stomach was tightening again as they approached the third house.

*****

As Buddy watched with trepidation, it seemed that Maggie remained at the open door of the house for an eternity. But then, as he looked again, Maggie stepped back one pace and deeply bowed to the woman in the doorway. She straightened, said a few more words, turned, and with her hand pointed down in Vietnamese fashion, she waved her hand and motioned for Buddy and Dawes to join her.

It seemed that Buddy's feet were locked in thick sticky mud. He could not move. Dawes hooked his arm under Buddy's armpit, and literally pulled Buddy forward. The knot in Buddy's stomach made him gasp for a breath of air. Somehow he found himself standing next to Maggie, and she was holding his hand while she spoke to the woman. The woman then bowed, and Maggie returned the bow. The door then opened wider.

Very quietly under her breath, Maggie said, "C'mon Buddy, we have been invited to tea." Dawes followed behind as Maggie and Buddy were led by the woman to a dining table at the rear of the house. The table was a bit unusual, as it was of western style and height with matching chairs. They were seated at the table, and the Vietnamese woman sat at the head of the table, between Buddy and Maggie. The two women then kept up a steady conversation, pausing only long enough for the older woman to turn back and gaze steadily at Buddy before turning her attention again to Maggie.

In the dining room, there was a window that faced an azure expanse of sea. The house had a small back terrace that was ringed by a white, ornate, metal fence. Houses below the back yard were low enough that they could not be seen. Beyond the fence, one could only see the vast expanse of the bay and ocean. It was a magnificent view.

The dining room walls were covered with gaudy, gold foil, leaf-enhanced wallpaper. Two intricately carved wooden cabinets sat next to two of the room's walls. Several wooden-framed pictures hung randomly around the room. A mantel-style wooden clock ticked softly on the top of one of the cabinets.

Their conversation was interrupted when a beautiful, well-dressed, younger woman entered the room carrying a tray with a decanter, cups, and saucers. They watched as she poured the tea and placed the full cups in front of each of them. The older woman again conversed with Maggie, who in turn interpreted their conversation to Buddy and Dawes. Buddy slowly turned the teacup on its saucer, but did not drink the tea.

Maggie turned to Buddy and said, "They were fishermen in 1968. She said that they lived in a small house near the water, and they had a fishing boat at that time. I also asked her if she had ever seen you before, and she said that she thinks you are the sailor who shot her husband."

"Oh, my God," whispered Buddy. "She remembers me?"

Maggie nodded and said, "Apparently."

Buddy began rapidly perspiring. A wave of nausea swept over him. He was afraid he might be sick. He forced his hands to remain in his lap and gently wiped the sweat from his hands to his pants.

Maggie turned back to the woman, and they talked for several more minutes. While the women talked, Buddy thought that he would be ill. He asked Maggie to ask Mrs. Chau for permission to use their restroom. Maggie asked, and then pointed. "Through that door and around the corner to the right," she said.

Buddy followed the directions and passed through a larger living room area. His eyes wandered around the room. It was very clean and neat, but sparsely furnished; unlike the typical American home. There was a television with a skewed set of rabbit ear antennae perched on top of the set. An attractively upholstered couch and side chair faced the television. Buddy then noticed a bookcase filled with books. In addition, two stacks of books rested on the floor next to the bookcase. He then noticed several photographs tacked to the wall near a doorway. He slowed and looked at them, and then stumbled against the wall, holding himself against the door frame. Mrs. Chau, Maggie, and Dawes turned to look at Buddy leaning in the doorway. One of the pictures Buddy was staring at was of the same fishing boat with the family members, including the man he had shot, smiling and waving from the boat. It must have been taken some time prior to the shooting. Buddy quickly went to the restroom and suffered a case of dry heaves. He was clammy and perspiring. He splashed cold water on his face. He felt horrible.

Buddy returned to the table where Maggie and Mrs. Chau were still talking. Buddy sat down, and Dawes looked at him quizzically. "Are you all right, Buddy?" asked Dawes. Buddy nodded affirmatively. Just then, the young woman who had served the tea came to the table and stood deferentially behind Mrs. Chau. She was soon followed by a young man. Mrs. Chau introduced them as her youngest daughter and youngest son. Those siblings had been on the boat the day that their father had been shot, and Mrs. Chau explained to them that the American man sitting at the table was the man who had shot their father during the war. The expressions of the Chau siblings did not show any anger; instead it appeared that they were more curious than angry as they looked more intently at Buddy and Dawes. Buddy forcefully willed himself to look at the two young people.

Maggie said very quietly, "Buddy, this would be a good time to make peace with Mrs. Chau," she said. "Place both your hands on the table in front of Mrs. Chau, palm up. Then look directly in her eyes and tell her exactly how you feel."

Buddy did what he was told. He began talking to Mrs. Chau, while Maggie interpreted.

Tears began to fall from Buddy's face as he said, "Mrs. Chau, my words cannot express to you how sorry I am for the hurt I have caused your family. As much as I have grieved for my mistake, I am sure your family has grieved ten times more. I have been so sad since that day, and my heart breaks every time I think about it. I have come here today to beg for your forgiveness and that of your children. I am so sorry for my mistake."

Buddy continued, but in a moment while he was still quietly talking, Mrs. Chau slid her hands across the table and placed them on top of Buddy's upturned hands. Buddy stopped talking. Mrs. Chau began talking very quietly. Tears also fell from her cheeks. She spoke so quietly that Maggie had to bend closer to hear her words.

"Clasp her hands, Buddy," said Maggie. Buddy curled his hands so that they gently held those of Mrs. Chau. Maggie continued to listen to Mrs. Chau. "She says you have done a very honorable and courageous thing to come and see her and her family. She said it takes a man of great strength for you to bare your soul to a stranger. She can see that you have been sad, and she believes you have also suffered. She forgives you for your actions that day. She says that she wants you to have a happy life."

Buddy turned to Maggie, but still held Mrs. Chau's hands. "She forgives me. How can she so easily forgive me when I killed her husband?" Tears still came from Buddy's eyes.

Maggie looked at him a moment, then turned and repeated what Buddy had just asked.

A puzzled look came over the face of Mrs. Chau, and then a very slow, slight smile showed. She quickly pulled her hands free and clapped them quickly. The youngest Chau daughter bent over and listened intently as her mother quietly spoke to her. Then she ran quickly to another part of the house.

Mrs. Chau spoke again, and Maggie interpreted. "She says we must all drink our tea, for this is a happy day for her family and the Miller family." Maggie obediently picked up her cup and sipped the tea, followed by Buddy and Dawes. But Buddy's mind was awhirl. He had just listened to the wife of the man he had killed say that she forgave him. He thought, how could that be?

The Chau daughter returned to the group, and she giggled to her mother, who smiled. Footfalls of someone wearing soft shoes, probably slippers, were soon heard. Mrs. Chau turned to face the doorway as a man shuffled into the room. His hair was awry, and he looked like he had just awakened. Suddenly Buddy heard Dawes draw a quick breath, followed by Mrs. Chau saying something to Maggie, and Maggie dropping her tea cup. It clattered loudly and spilled tea to the side of the saucer. She turned to Buddy and said, "It's him, Buddy. It's the man you shot. He's alive!"

Nearly simultaneously, Buddy had seen the long, darker-skinned scar on the left side of the man's head. It angled downward from high on the left side hairline, ending just to the back of the ear.

Buddy completely lost his composure. He became a crying, blubbering fool. He was so astonished and happy that he could not stop crying. Having been rudely interrupted from his afternoon nap, Mr. Chau did not know what to make of all this activity at his dining table until his wife rapidly filled him in on the details. He then stared at Buddy, and recognition came over his face. He then began talking so rapidly, answered by his wife, who was talking just as fast, that Maggie gave up interpreting. By now, the son and daughter joined in and the four family members were smiling and laughing.

Mr. Chau then came around the table and grasped Buddy's hand. Buddy stood. Mr. Chau bowed, and Buddy returned the gesture. The men then hugged each other. Buddy's tears were still flowing. Mr. Chau began talking and Maggie interpreted.

"There is no need for sadness," he said. "Many bad things happened during the war. I also learned later that your Navy punished you. There was no need for that, for as you can see, I am very much alive, and my life has been good. If you feel sad over hurting me, please do not be sad anymore. I forgave you and forgot the incident many years ago," he said, and kept shaking Buddy's hand all the while he was talking. A broad smile covered the older man's face.

Ninh Ba Chau had lived after that October day in 1968. According to the family, he had remained in a coma for four days. Everyone, including the doctor who treated him, thought that he might die. But he survived and lived to continue fishing. The family held no ill will toward the American sailor, whom they assumed had pulled the trigger on that day. It had simply been another of the many inexplicable and unfortunate acts that happen in time of conflict between nations. In fact, aside from the ever present visible scar that showed on Ninh's head, the family had forgotten all about the incident through the passing years. Ninh Chau clasped both of Buddy's hands, bowed to him, and again told Buddy that all was forgiven.

Tea cups were refilled. Buddy had finally composed himself and was smiling as he shook hands with all the members of the family over and over again. The conversation and laughter continued. Buddy would forever be unable to describe the joy, elation, and utterly exhausting relief that he felt at this moment.

*****

Such feelings of utter bliss are often short lived. Barely heard over the conversation and laughter was the noise of a door in another part of the house being slammed. The Chau daughter ran out of the room toward the noise. In a moment she came back into the room holding tightly to the arm of another man. She appeared to be trying to restrain him. The man walked to the table and stared at Buddy, then at Dawes, and back to Buddy. Buddy then recognized the man's eyes. He had seen that same look of hate so many times in his nightmares, on the face of the teenage boy who had been on the Chau family boat at the time of the shooting.

This was that same boy who had matured into manhood. In passable, but broken English, the man snarled, "You. You are the son of a bitch that shot my father. I will make you pay for that!" He then made a move to come around the table, but was held back by his brother and sister, who were joined by their father. The man then turned to look at Buddy again and unexpectedly spat toward Buddy. "I will get you," he threatened and shook a fist toward Buddy while his siblings and father moved him away.

Bao Nguyen, who had a knack for being in the right place at the right time, suddenly appeared next to Maggie and whispered in her ear.

Maggie quickly turned toward Mrs. Chau and bowed while saying a few words. She quickly turned and began walking toward the door. Under her breath, she said, "Let's go guys, we're moving out."

Bewildered, Buddy and Dawes quickly followed. They all got in the car, and Bao swiftly drove out of the neighborhood and headed for their hotel. "What was that all about?" asked Buddy.

"It seems that a couple of friends of the quarrelsome Chau son were seen walking toward the house. Bao thought that it might be a good time to leave," said Maggie. "By the way, number one quarrelsome son's name is Huynh," she said. "At least that was what his sister kept saying as she urged him to play nicely."

The altercation with Huynh Chau had upset Maggie, Buddy and Bob. But it was far overshadowed by the pure joy and elation of the scene that had played out with Huynh's parents and Buddy. In fact, Buddy sat motionless in the jouncing car as Bao guided them through the busy streets to return to the hotel. His face held a calm, serene look, and a slight smile. To discover that Ninh Ba Chau was alive, registered as truly a divine miracle in Buddy's mind. It was all so hard to believe, and so astonishing. His head was clear, and he was breathing deeply. A warm feeling of love and contentment overcame him, and he reached his arm around Maggie Louis and kissed her on the cheek. She was startled and said, "My goodness, what was that about?"

Buddy just looked at her and said, "Thank you so much for your help."

"You are very welcome," said Maggie.

*****

"I will pick you up for dinner," she had said, and as Bao drove the car away, she waved from the back window. Buddy and Dawes watched the car for a moment and then turned to enter the hotel. But before they had taken three steps, they were suddenly surrounded by four, armed, green-clad Vietnamese policemen. Not a word was spoken, but the two Americans could not move in any direction. At that moment, a large, glistening black police van stopped at the curb. A side door to the van opened, and Buddy and Dawes were shoved forcefully into the van by the four policemen who followed them into the van. When Dawes tried to protest and stand up, one of the policemen threw a hard uppercut into Bob's stomach, knocking the wind out of him. Dawes quickly sat down, retching slightly as the van pulled away from the curb.

Thirty minutes later, after the two men were separated at police head-quarters, Bob Dawes had been taken to an interrogation room and Buddy Miller sat across the desk from a man he had seen often since his arrival in Vietnam. It was the same short, slightly built man, now wearing black rimmed glasses, dressed in a white shirt and dark slacks that he and Dawes had seen at the airport when they arrived, at the hotel lobby, and another time or two when he had not been quite so sure it was the same man. Now Buddy was sure, as the man sat at the desk with a pocket knife in his hand, once again casually working on his fingernails. The small tattoo was visible on his arm.

In very crisp English, the policeman spoke.

"Welcome, Mr. Miller, to the people's police station. I am Lieutenant Tran. I asked you to come here today because I thought we might have a little chat," said Tran. He did not look up at Buddy, but continued working on his fingernails.

Asked me to come here, thought Buddy. Hardly, I was forced to come here. At this point, Buddy was more curious and mad than worried.

"Didn't I see you in Ho Chi Minh City, Lieutenant Tran?" asked Buddy.

"You may see me many places, Mr. Miller. The People's Police have jurisdiction for the entire country of Vietnam," said Tran.

Buddy was sure now that Tran worked for the secret police, and this sent a shiver up his spine.

"Mr. Miller, you have been very busy while you are in my country," said Tran. "And yet you have not been to visit any of our wonderful tourist attractions. Why is that, Mr. Miller? Please tell me why you have come to Vietnam."

Buddy did not answer right away. He did not know what to say. Should he tell Tran that he was here accompanying the Glenns, or should he really tell the truth? He did not have to answer, as Tran started talking again.

"Mr. Miller, my sources tell me that you are a very wealthy man. Is that correct, are you a wealthy man?"

"I am no wealthier than a great many Americans," said Buddy.

"Indeed, indeed," said Tran. "Mr. Miller, how does it come to be that you are such a wealthy man?"

Buddy thought this was a seemingly innocuous question, but he had no idea what Tran was trying to find out. "I own a small company in the United States," he said.

"Mmm, yes. And what does your small company produce?" asked Tran.

Buddy suddenly went on alert. He hadn't thought of this before. Being in the arms business in a Communist country might not just be the greatest of occupations right now. "My company produces fine hunting shotguns," said Buddy.

Lieutenant Tran nodded his head. "And does your company make any other items?" he asked.

Oh, no, thought Buddy. But then he got it. Tran already knew all the answers to his questions. Buddy was being led on to make sure he answered the questions truthfully. "We also make specialized sight mechanisms for small arms," said Buddy.

Tran was now looking directly at Buddy, but idly playing with a ball-point pen. He suddenly dropped the pen on the desk and slowed down his speech as he asked, "Mr. Miller, how long have you been in the drug trafficking business?"

He couldn't help it. His mouth dropped open. It took him several seconds to answer. "Drug trafficking? Sir, I assure you that I have no idea what you are talking about," said Buddy.

"Mr. Miller, I am not sure you are telling me the truth. I will ask you again. How long have you been trafficking in illegal drugs?" asked Tran.

"With all due respect, Lieutenant Tran, I do not now, nor have I ever been involved with any illegal drugs," answered Buddy.

"Then how does it happen that you are an associate of Mr. Huynh Chau?" asked Tran.

Oh man, thought Buddy. It didn't take him long to put those puzzle pieces together. So that's it. Huynh must be mixed up in illegal drugs. I guess that would explain why the family is living well above the means of their neighborhood.

Buddy decided to come clean with the Lieutenant. For the next forty-five minutes he explained to Lieutenant Tran why he had come to Vietnam. He left out no details. After all, he did not relish the idea of spending time in a Secret Police jail. As Buddy related the entire story and all the details of his life, Tran made no facial expression that might indicate that he believed or disbelieved Buddy. Tran intermittently looked at Buddy and the papers on his desk. It was as if he did not believe a word of Buddy's story.

When Buddy was finished talking, Tran sat still for a moment and then stood up and abruptly walked out of his office, leaving Buddy to contemplate what might subsequently happen. Buddy looked out the window of Tran's office. It was already dark. He looked at his watch; it was nearly eight p.m. For the next two hours, Buddy sat on the hard wooden chair in the darkening office. Lieutenant Tran did not return to the office until ten p.m.

At ten-thirty p.m. Buddy was escorted to the front door of the police building by another armed policeman dressed in green. As they stood in the entryway of the building, Buddy heard a door close and two sets of feet headed in their direction. Another policeman appeared followed closely by Bob Dawes. One of Dawes's eyes was closed with a large, swollen, black and blue bruise holding the eyelids together. There was an angry red swelling of his cheek below the eye. Buddy and Dawes were taken through the door to the street where they were shoved into a small black sedan. Two policemen sat in the front seat. The car sped away, negotiated the slightly less dense traffic at that hour, and subsequently stopped in front of their hotel. Neither policeman said anything. The car continued to idle. The policeman in the front passenger seat finally turned and gestured with his thumb for the two Americans to get out of the car.

"I don't have to be told twice," said Dawes, and he opened the back door and bounded out. Buddy followed, and the police car sped away.

Buddy was soon on his second bourbon while Dawes was on his third scotch in their Cam Rahn hotel bar. It turned out that after some physical coercion, Dawes had finally moved away from the Christian Relief Agency cover story, and had told his interrogators essentially the same story that Buddy had told Lieutenant Tran. It was shortly after that that his interrogator had left the room, followed by his being told that he could leave. Even while nursing the third drink, Dawes was still visibly shaken.

"Jesus, Buddy. I didn't know if we were ever going to get out of that place. That guy that was questioning me really meant business. When he said something about me being mixed up with illegal drugs, I told him he was crazy. He didn't like that very much and hit me a couple of times. God, that hurt! I've heard all kinds of stories of people going in places like that and never seen again. I gotta tell you, I was scared," said Dawes.

"That makes two of us," said Buddy. "I'm sorry I got you into this mess," he said.

"Oh hell, I volunteered," said Dawes. "But we got some good stuff to tell our grandchildren, don't we?" he said as he cracked a smile. But he quickly stopped smiling and gently placed a hand on the hurting eye and moaned quietly.

Buddy returned the smile. After another round of drinks, both men retired to their rooms. A shower never felt so good, thought Buddy. As he brushed his teeth and looked in the mirror, he smiled again. The man in the mirror was returning the smile. It had been a very strange, difficult, and yet wonderful day. A great weight had been lifted from his soul. It was nearly one a.m. when he turned out the light and nearly immediately fell into a dreamless sleep.

Chapter Thirty-Nine

Only one hour later, he was awakened by the telephone ringing next to his bed. It roused him from a deep sleep. Oh no, he thought. Who can that be at this hour? He picked up the phone and groggily answered, "Hello, hello." The line clicked dead. But five minutes later, just as he was nearly asleep again, he heard a quiet rapping on his hotel room door. He debated with himself on whether or not to answer the knock, but he did. Rubbing one eye, he padded softly on bare feet to crack open the door.

She held a black lacquer tray that contained a small pot of tea, two cups, a bowl of fruit, and two scones. As Buddy opened the door further, Maggie entered the room and set the tray on the room desk. "You stood me up for dinner, Miller," she said. "Thought you might need some sustenance." Buddy's heart skipped a beat. She was wearing a tan trench coat and had a pair of colored and bejeweled sandals on her feet. Her black hair was pinned up in the back. She was drop-dead gorgeous, thought Buddy as he quickly became less sleepy. She poured the tea while Buddy slipped on a tee-shirt, and then they sat next to each other on the couch. Maggie asked him what had happened the night before, and Buddy told her of the events with Lieutenant Tran. After they had talked for a while longer and finished off the last of the fruit bowl, Buddy yawned.

"Thanks for the late dinner, Maggie. I appreciate it. But if you don't mind, I really need to get to bed."

"I don't mind," said Maggie, and she walked over and turned off the overhead light. Only the small light next to the bed was still on. "Well, go to bed, silly," she said.

Buddy got into bed, thinking that Maggie would be leaving. But as he laid down and drew up the bed sheet, he looked at Maggie. She was untying the belt of the trench coat. Buddy drew a small gasp. Maggie had dropped the coat on the floor. She was now dressed only in a mid-thigh, sky-blue, beautifully embroidered satin peignoir, which left nearly nothing to Buddy's racing imagination. She slid into bed next to him and turned out the light. It was not long before the peignoir and Buddy's t-shirt and shorts lay on the floor next to the tan trench coat.

The couple embraced, hungrily kissed each other, and began exploring each other's bodies. The thought occurred to Buddy that he was in heaven with a wonderful angel; while the angel soothed and healed his troubled soul. The next hours went by far too quickly.

*****

Filtered by the window drapery, soft morning light edged into the room as the couple lay sleeping in each other's arms. It was a surprising, wonderful, cathartic way to start a new day.

As the room became still lighter, there was another quiet rap on Buddy's hotel room door. Maggie jumped out of bed and headed into the bathroom, after telling Buddy to answer the door. He pulled on his shorts and cracked the door open. Bao Nguyen was standing stoically in the doorway. He looked at Buddy, standing embarrassed in his undershorts, and unceremoniously handed Buddy a garment bag, turned, and walked back toward the elevator. Buddy closed the door and relocked it. The water was running in the shower in the bathroom. Buddy stripped out of the shorts again and crept into the bathroom, cautiously drawing aside the shower curtain. Seeing her in the light, he simply could not believe how beautiful Maggie was. He stepped into the shower with her. Even with both of them sharing the shower "to conserve water," it seemed like it took a long while and a lot of soap and water for each of them to finally be satisfyingly clean.

*****

Dawes was on his third cup of coffee and repeatedly looked at his watch. Buddy was late. As he sat at the table in the hotel restaurant, he gingerly placed his fingers on the skin around his angry, sore eye. Results of the previous evening's events were reflected in the skin surrounding the eye and cheek, which now exhibited bruising in several colorful hues. The swelling had gone down only slightly, but he could see partially through the squint of the eye. What he saw was two very handsome, smiling people heading for his hotel restaurant breakfast table. They were holding hands and smiling as they walked. Dawes broke out a large grin, momentarily ignoring the ache in his eye and cheek. As Buddy and Maggie joined Dawes, he just couldn't hold back; "Guess I don't have to ask where you two were last night, do I?"

Maggie's face showed a slight pink of embarrassment, but she quickly recovered. "It's not nice to be a 'busy body,' Bob." It was then Dawes's turn to turn a slight pink color.

After a light breakfast with plenty of coffee, Maggie turned to Dawes and said, "We're going shopping this morning. Would you like to go along?" She was looking at Dawes, but then followed his gaze to the lobby area where he was watching a very attractive woman come through the front door of the hotel and walk to one of the gift shops. The woman turned and looked at Dawes and gave an ever so slight wave, stepped to her shop, and opened it with a key. Maggie and Buddy both laughed rather loudly.

Dawes broke his reverie, looked at his laughing companions and finally said, "Oh, shopping. Uh, no. I think I'll just stay here and maybe take a walk and take in the scenery." That remark drew another laugh from Buddy and Maggie.

"OK," said Maggie. "But you need to be at my office at one p.m. We are going to go visit with the Chau's again before we go back to Ho Chi Minh City."

"Well, what's that all about?" asked Dawes.

"I want to get Mr. Chau a gift," said Buddy, "and give it to him before we leave the country."

"OK, you two kids have fun," said Dawes with a sly grin.

*****

At approximately two p.m. that same day, Bao Nguyen guided the little sedan to the curb a few houses away from the Chau home. This time, rather than wait with the car, he accompanied Maggie, Buddy, and Dawes to the house, but waited discreetly outside while Mrs. Chau beckoned his companions into the house.

Tea was served to the guests by Mrs. Chau. When everyone had nearly finished their first cup, Buddy placed the package that he had brought with him on the table. With Maggie's help in interpreting, he said, "Mr. and Mrs. Chau, I am deeply honored to have met you, and I will treasure these memories of your family for the rest of my life. Your forgiveness for my carelessness many years ago is the most wonderful thing that has ever happened to me."

It was at this point though, that Maggie placed her hand on top of Buddy's on the table, a gesture that was not missed by the intuitive Mrs. Chau.

"I have brought Mr. Chau a small gift to show my eternal gratitude. I hope he will accept it and remember me when he sees it every day," said Buddy, as he placed the package in front of Mr. Chau. With some urging from his wife, Ninh carefully opened the package. He then slowly retrieved a set of beautifully carved jade bookends. The bookends were pedestals, upon which sat a turtle. By the side of the turtle was a standing crane. An inlaid, carved, gold oriental medallion graced the side of each pedestal base. The turtle, crane, and gold medallion characters all were symbolic of long life and happiness. In addition to the medallion, the intricate lines in the turtles' shells were also inlaid with gold. The bookends were worth a small fortune.

Mr. Chau's fingers traced the lines and indentations on the bookends. He looked at Mrs. Chau and smiled, then turned to Buddy and nodded his head in gratitude while continuing to smile. He rose from the table, came around to Buddy's side of the table and took his hand. He then placed one of the bookends in Buddy's hand, and the other in his own hand, and guided Buddy to the bookcase. Setting the bookend on the floor, Mr. Chau took up several books and placed them on the top shelf of the bookcase and put his bookend at one end of the books. He then motioned for Buddy to place his bookend at the other end of the standing books, which Buddy quickly did. Mr. Chau then took both of Buddy's hands and bowed to Buddy. Buddy was a bit embarrassed, but then he quickly bowed to Mr. Chau. Mrs. Chau then began to laugh and clap her hands.

Apparently, the Chau's daughter had been discreetly overhearing this activity, because at this time she entered the room carrying a small tray holding a decanter and five small glasses. She set the tray on the table in front of her father. Mr. Chau stood and filled the five glasses with rice wine and passed them to each of the adults. Then he remained standing.

"I think he is going to make a toast," said Maggie. "Perhaps we should also stand."

After they stood, Mr. Chau looked directly at Buddy. He then made a very short toast. He said, "I have been honored to have the pleasure of meeting Mr. Miller, Mr. Dawes, and Miss Louis. I would be honored to have you visit our humble family again in your journey through life. I wish you happiness and long life." They all then followed Mr. Chau's lead and emptied their glasses.

Maggie thanked the Chau's and told them that they must depart. As they were walking to the door, Mr. Chau caught up with Buddy and placed an article in Buddy's hand. Buddy studied it for a moment. It appeared to be a military medal. Mr. Chau then talked directly to Maggie, who interpreted.

"He says it belonged to his father. His father was a soldier in the Vietnamese resistance against the French. He said his father was a very honorable man. He always considered his father to be a quiet and humble warrior. He said he believes you are also an honorable, humble warrior, and he wants you to have the medal."

Buddy studied the tarnished, treasured medal with the faded ribbon attached to it and swallowed a very large lump in his throat. He turned slightly to Maggie and asked her to tell Mr. Chau that he would treasure this gift for the rest of his life, and to please thank him profusely. When Maggie was finished, Buddy once again bowed to Mr. Chau, but then abruptly hugged the old man. Buddy's eyes glistened with moisture.

As the Americans moved toward the door, Mrs. Chau grasped the sleeve of Maggie Louis. Mrs. Chau looked at Maggie, spoke to her, and coyly smiled. Maggie's face turned pink, and Mrs. Chau lightly laughed. Curious, Buddy asked her what Mrs. Chau had said.

"She asked me when you and I are going to be married," said Maggie. "Could be she is just a bit impetuous, don't you think?"

Buddy gazed at Maggie with a bit of bewilderment showing on his face. Dawes then spoke up, "I'd put odds of about four to one on that little event," he said and laughed. Buddy shot an elbow into Dawes's ribs. The Americans turned once and waved as they walked back to the waiting Bao, who was standing by the car.

*****

Late afternoon shadows were lengthening. The little car whined a bit as it slowly rolled down the hill from the Chau residence. They were soon passing a street that ran perpendicular to their street and terminated at the edge of the bay. Bao would make a turn onto another street that would take them back to the train station for the return trip to Ho Chi Minh City.

But before Bao could make that turn, a speeding sedan shot out from a side street, nearly collided with their car, and screeched to a halt in front of them, thereby blocking their way. Three armed men jumped out of the car, ran to the American's car and jerked open the car doors. One of those men was Huynh Chau. Bao did not have time to react and found himself with a gun pressed to his head while Bob Dawes and Buddy were dragged from the car by Huynh Chau and one of his cronies. The gun-men told Maggie to remain in the car or she would be shot.

Buddy and Dawes were forced to stumble in front of the two thugs as they were pushed a half block down the street and shoved into a small industrial warehouse-type building where the thugs began to pistol whip and beat the two men. After a few minutes, both Buddy and Dawes lay on the cool cement floor of the building. Both men were battered, bloody, and very nearly unconscious.

It took only a split second. As the third henchman, who was still at the car with Bao and Maggie, turned his head to watch his cohorts enter the building with Buddy and Dawes and close the warehouse door, Bao heaved himself against the car door with all his strength. The force of the opening car door threw the gunman back, and he tripped on a rough spot in the road and fell backwards. Before he could recover, Bao's foot was on the gunmen's wrist. Bao wrested the gun from the fallen man's hand and viciously cold cocked him with the butt of the gun. The thug lay lifelessly on the street. Bao began running toward the building in which Dawes and Buddy were being held, the pistol in his hand.

Bao cautiously opened the door of the building. What he saw was the two thugs laughing as they stood over the fallen bodies of Buddy and Dawes. Suddenly, Huynh's companion raised his sidearm and aimed it at the fallen Bob Dawes. A very loud shot rang out, followed by a short period of quiet before the thug slumped to the floor; very dead. Bao's shot had entered the back of the head of the criminal, where the hollow point slug had splayed and turned the criminal's brain to mush; thereby shutting down every neural pathway in the man's body. He had died instantly.

At the same time as Huynh's accomplice was crumpling to the floor, Huynh spun around, saw Bao, and fired. His shot splintered the wood of the door frame where Bao was standing. Bao returned fire with his pistol, but his shot also missed the mark and clanged as it struck a steel beam behind Huynh. Before Bao could get off a second shot, Huynh had turned and was running quickly through a side door of the building. Bao ran after him, but just as Bao was exiting the side door, he collided with a dark-green uniformed police officer. Both men fell to the ground. Two other companion policemen paused, but then continued their pursuit of the fleeing Huynh. Momentarily, as Bao and the police officer stood, the white-shirted, dark-trousered Lieutenant Tran walked up to the two of them.

Speaking to the dazed, but recovering policeman, Tran said, "I suggest that you follow me in a rapid and dignified manner," he said, and quickly began trotting after his other two officers who were chasing Huynh Chau. Bao was left standing by the warehouse door, watching the running police officers.

Huynh Chau would not be captured. He had a lead on the police that they could not close, and he had a plan. Upon reaching the boat docks, he quickly scanned the docks, looking for a specific boat. He ran down the boat dock and soon found what he was seeking. The small fishing boat that he jumped aboard was configured quite differently from the majority of other true fishing boats. While the boat was used occasionally for legitimate fishing, this particular boat had a pair of ordinary looking outboard motors on it. But those motors were far from ordinary. They had been extensively modified to enable the small boat to outrun nearly any other boat in the area. Each motor also had an elongated lower unit and was built to withstand ocean swells. Not only was the boat fast, it was powerful. Huynh knew the owner of this boat, because the owner had made several trips for Huynh to rendezvous with other boats at sea to transfer illicit drugs into Huynh's possession. The boat's owner, although only a part-time fisherman, was for all practical purposes, on Huynh's under-world payroll, an insignificant cog in the grinding wheel of world-wide drug trafficking.

The boat owner was on board the boat diligently doing some of the never-ending maintenance work required to keep the boat sea-worthy. The boat's deck was covered with rope in disarray, while the owner spliced frayed rope and made net repairs. Brandishing his pistol, Huynh smashed the boatman across the cheek with the pistol and told the man to untie all the lines on the pier. The criminal underling did so, and then

Huynh forced the man to start the engines. With the fisherman at the controls, the transmission levers were thrown forward, followed by the throttles being shoved forward. The boat quickly gathered speed and headed to sea. A shot from one of the pursuing policemen thudded into the teak wood next to the boat driver. Huynh answered, firing two shots back at the police. As he watched, the group of uniformed policemen and the man in civilian attire ran to a nearby pier and jumped aboard a police boat. The police boat soon left its pier, and with lights and a siren screaming, began its pursuit of Huynh's speeding craft.

Huynh was not worried. He knew the capabilities of both boats. With the large fuel tanks onboard the fishing boat, he could far surpass the fuel range of the small police launch. Huynh set a course that was east, northeast and jammed the throttles forward to their maximum.

But Huynh was careless. With the disarray left on the deck of the fishing boat while the owner was doing repairs, there was a grappling hook that was teetering atop the aft rail of the boat where it had been temporarily placed by the fisherman. The grappling hook would ordinarily be used by the fisherman to retrieve lobster and crab pots along with pre-baited fishing lines. With Huynh now at the wheel of the boat, the grappling hook, fastened to over one hundred feet of rope and tied off on a deck cleat, would be used for something far more deadly. As the speeding boat reached deeper water and the first large sea swell, the grappling hook fell off of the aft rail and began playing out its long length of rope. The rope reached its end and grew taught against the deck cleat. With the forward motion of the boat, the grappling hook flew underwater just above the ocean floor.

While the surface of the beautiful blue sea appears level to the casual observer, the sea bed beneath that surface is anything but level. The sea floor can range from fairly flat, to mountainous. The sea bed that Huynh's boat was passing above was rolling and contained vast beds of coral, but the water was deep enough that the grappling hook was easily clearing the bottom. However, the course that Huynh had charted would take him far out to sea. He was certain that the police launch would run low on fuel and turn back. Huynh's intent was to make a large arc through the night and quietly land in Qui Nhon the next morning, where he had criminal associates who could hide him until this whole business cooled down.

In the police boat, Lieutenant Tran and the uniformed police officers gamely pursued the swifter fishing craft. They knew they were out-classed in power and speed, and there was nothing they could do but keep the criminal boat in sight by binoculars and doggedly follow at an ever-growing distance.

*****

After leaving Tran moments ago, Bao ran back to the car to check on Maggie. He told her where Buddy and Dawes were, and then continued running to a distant street corner where there was a forlorn looking phone booth. He entered the phone booth and disgustedly felt his shoe slide on the built-up combination of tobacco juice and mucus on the floor of the phone booth. He quickly dialed some numbers and spoke feverishly, all the while gesturing with his free hand. He was soon confident that the ambulance would find them. He then made one more call to the U.S. Liaison Office. This time he spoke for only a short time and did not use his free hand. He grimaced while listening to the other side of the conversation, finally pulled the phone receiver away from his ear, and slowly replaced it on the top of the phone. He walked quickly back to the building where Buddy and Dawes were being ministered to by Maggie Louis. There was little that Maggie could do for the two men. Neither man was in mortal danger, but they both had ugly, freely-bleeding wounds on their faces and heads. Maggie wept quietly while attempting to comfort Buddy and Dawes. The wail of sirens from an approaching ambulance and police sedan were soon heard.

*****

A grin spread across Huynh Chau's face. He was certain now that he had made good his escape. The police launch was only a speck in the distance, and dusk was rapidly approaching. It would be dark in only one or two more hours, and he felt certain the police would soon give up the chase. Huynh turned to feel what he thought to be the wind of freedom blowing against his face. With the wind in his face and the boat speeding across the surface of the sea, he was now confident that he would live to once again lead his local crime syndicate. His only regret was that he had not quickly killed the two meddling Americans. He still seethed with hate toward the American who had shot his father those many years ago.

Life is funny in many ways. Gloating is a human frailty that so often turns upon itself to bite the unsuspecting arrogant gloater. And in the unsavory, swirling world of crime, the best laid plans so often go awry.

If Huynh Chau had been able to see clearly through nearly a hundred feet of ocean beneath and to the rear of the boat's path, he would have seen that undersea, the rolling sea bed floor began to contain hundreds of perfectly shaped metal cylinders. Unbeknownst to Huynh, the boat was crossing what the allies had called 'Point Delta' during the Vietnam War. Literally thousands of unexploded bombs and ordinance were dropped in the area by allied planes after they completed their bombing missions in both North and South Vietnam. Among those thousands of bombs were a number that contained the same faulty fuse that had exploded many bombs prematurely, thereby killing a score of the American pilots whose planes had carried such bombs. Some of these deadly bombs with their faulty fuses lay on the sea bed while the sea above carried the drone of the powerful outboard motors on Huynh Chau's boat.

The boat was soon passing over a high, relatively flat-topped ridge which was beautifully encrusted with coral and other sea life. It rose naturally from the ocean floor. That ridge was less than fifty feet beneath the surface of the sea. Lying benignly amongst the coral on that ridge were many of those unexploded allied bombs. And within that group were two bombs with the faulty fuses. With such an extreme set of odds, even the most gullible fool would not bet on such a scenario. But with an echoing clang, the grappling hook beneath the escaping boat made contact with the fuse end of the rusty, deteriorating, five hundred pound bomb, thereby causing the powerful explosion of the bomb. Enormous shock waves were quickly carried through the salty water. The force of the explosion of the first bomb almost immediately caused the explosion of the other five hundred pound bomb with an identical faulty fuse. The force of those thousand pounds of explosives detonating under relatively shallow water sent a powerful shock wave to the surface of the sea, opening a round crater momentarily void of water. The force of the explosion violently pushed the stern of Huynh's boat skyward and broke the keel of the boat. With no water resistance, the outboards screamed a frenetic pitch as the propellers met only the resistance of air. Pulled quickly by sheer gravity, the boat then shot downward, bow first and plunged beneath the resultant rush of water to refill the void caused by the explosion. The ruptured boat rapidly filled with roiling sea water and did not rise to the surface. The beautiful blue sea water replaced the gases in Huynh's lungs as he struggled beneath debris to find a way out of the wreckage pressing down on him from above. A final desperate gasp completed the displacement of air in his lungs with seawater. Fate had terminated the life of the arrogant criminal thug. Huynh's life of crime and the shame that he had brought to his family had ended.

Lieutenant Tran had been shocked to see the geyser of water arise on the distant ocean surface and to watch the fishing boat that they had been pursuing, lift out of the water and literally break in half. As the police boat continued onward, he held his binoculars to his eyes and narrated what he observed to his fellow police officers. In a few more minutes, the police launch reached the scene of the explosion. The police recovered the bodies of Huynh and his cohort from the floating debris of the destroyed drug smuggler's boat and soon headed back to port.

Chapter Forty

2000, October 12, 1983
Hospital
Cam Ranh, Vietnam

Maggie had told the hospital staff that the two men should share a double room, and fortunately, such a room was available. In the waning hours of the second night in the hospital, the room was already dark, and both Buddy and Dawes were sleeping peacefully as she entered their darkened room. They had both slept off-and-on since being admitted to the hospital.

She couldn't help herself. Maggie had to smile each time she saw Bob Dawes. The poor fellow looked like the comic character Popeye, with one eye completely closed and the other one just a slit, and his face was all puffed up and black and blue. His nose had been broken, and a web of tape was draped across the bridge of his nose. She felt so sorry for him. She took a seat on the small uncomfortable wooden chair that was between the hospital beds. She laid her hand on top of Buddy's and watched as both men slept.

*****

Two days ago, when the ambulance had arrived at the dingy warehouse building to administer to Buddy and Dawes, she had been at Buddy's side when he regained consciousness. He had stared at her for a moment and then smiled, and said, "When are we going to get married?" He continued smiling and closed his eyes. She quietly whispered, "Soon, my love, soon."

Both men had been beaten rather badly, and the medical crew was careful as the men were placed on gurneys and slid into the backs of two waiting ambulances. Maggie had held onto Bao's arm and cried quietly as they left the worn-out building to walk back to the car.

For the next four hours, she sat across from Lieutenant Tran at the old, scarred, wooden desk. Maggie told him everything she knew, and after repeating the same story four times, Tran finally relented and released her.

*****

She was still on the small wooden hospital chair. Periodically, she would stand and walk about the room. The chair was especially uncomfortable, and her bottom and back frankly needed a break. Dawn was pushing its fingers into the room, slowly blotting out the blackness. As if on cue, a nurse came into the room and turned on the overhead light. "Wakee, wakee, lazy 'Merican boys." She was funny, and very cute, with a larger than average chest size and an astonishing set of deep green eyes. Her laugh and smile covered a third of her face. It appeared somewhat obvious that in addition to Vietnamese, Hoa might have also had some other nationalities in her background. She moved the chair from between the beds and then moved to the window and opened the slatted blinds.

"Hoa, Hoa, (pronounced hway) go away," mumbled Dawes from his bed.

"Now, now, Mr. Dawes. It's time for breakfast. No tell me to go away or I not bring your breakfast," said Hoa.

"Soup and a boiled egg again," moaned Dawes. "I guess they don't have any potatoes to make some good, greasy hash browns." Dawes looked over at Buddy. By this time, Buddy was also awake. "Geez, Miller, you look like hell."

Buddy slowly turned his head and looked at Dawes and then laughed. "You should talk. Have you looked in a mirror?"

"Well," said Dawes, "at least you didn't get the chance to break my nose this time. Somebody else beat you to it."

Sometime after breakfast, Hoa came in the room again. She was carrying a large bottle and two small towels. "OK boys, over on tummies. Time for rub down," she said. Dutifully, Buddy and Dawes rolled over onto their stomachs. Hoa pulled down the sheets and exposed Dawes's back side and bottom through the unclosed hospital gown. "Miss Louis, you watch me, and you can do Mr. Miller," said Hoa as she winked at Maggie.

Hoa spread the alcohol gel on Dawes's back and rubbed it in. Maggie watched and followed suit on Buddy. Hoa worked quickly and was soon at the base of Dawes's back and rubbing his hips and bottom. Maggie did the same. But with a free hand hanging over the side of the bed, Dawes found a shapely leg and was crawling the hand up her leg under Hoa's dress. Hoa quickly jumped back, and with a resounding smack, she whacked Dawes on the bottom.

"Ouch," said Dawes.

"You a naughty boy, Mr. Dawes." Hoa then dried the alcohol from Dawes's back. Maggie suddenly felt a hand creeping up her leg too, but she was out of view of Dawes and Hoa. Instead of moving away, she leaned over and kissed Buddy on the cheek. "Not until you're well, big boy," she teased and stepped back.

Chapter Forty-One

October 15, 1983
Police Station
Cam Ranh, Vietnam

There was a follow-up meeting with the police after the two men were released from the hospital. None of their injuries had been life-threatening, and time would heal the scrapes, cuts, and bruises along with Dawes's broken nose. Dawes and Buddy were once again sitting in Lieutenant Tran's bleak Cam Ranh office. But the coffee was strong, and Tran seemed nonthreatening as he talked with them. He was smoking a rather vile-smelling brown cigarette.

"I should have locked you two up when you came into the country. I knew you were up to no good. And I still don't have anything to hold you on, so fortunately for you, I have to let you go. But I wanted to at least let you know some of the details of that character Huynh. We have been trying to nab him for two years. We knew he was in the smuggling game, and we were sure it was drugs. How else do you think his family could live in a nice house like that when all the neighbors are living in shacks?" Tran took another deep drag on the cigarette. "And then the father quit fishing, so we knew the money must be coming from the son. It is traditional in our country that the oldest son takes care of the family. Normally that is the honorable Vietnamese way, except that this son was managing to look after his family with a life of crime."

"Lieutenant Tran, do you think that his mother and father knew of his illegal activities?" asked Buddy.

"No," answered Tran. "When we questioned them, they honestly thought that he was managing a fish cannery. They were proud that he

was able to take care of his family. By the way, did you get your business taken care of with Mr. and Mrs. Chau?"

"Yes, we did," answered Buddy. "They are really very nice people. I
hope they can get over this bad business with their son."

"Time will heal some of that," said Tran. "But the personal disgrace
that they feel from the family's oldest son being involved in crime will
never go away."

"Well, I'm very grateful that you showed up when you did. Otherwise we might not be here having this chat," said Dawes.

"I think you also owe a great deal to that liaison office fellow, Bao.
He's probably the one who saved your lives," said Tran. He blew
another cloud of cigarette smoke. "Now, if you will excuse me I have
other work to do. By the way, when are you planning to leave my
country?"

"We will be leaving in two or three days," said Buddy.

"Have a pleasant trip," said Tran. And without so much as a hand-
shake, he stood, walked over, and opened his office door. It was a not-
too-subtle sign for Buddy and Dawes to leave.

*****

That evening, their clothing lay strewn on the floor of the bedroom,
leaving them each in the suit in which they had been born. The breeze
from the overhead fan felt cool on their moist bodies as they sat in the
bed and sipped the rice wine. Maggie set her wine glass on the night
stand and rolled over toward Buddy. She gently drew circles on his
stomach as she talked.

"I don't know whether or not you should get too wrapped up with me
or not, Buddy Miller."

Her finger was tickling him, and he grinned as he grabbed her hand. "And just why not, Miss Maggie Louis?" he asked.

"Well, today, my boss fired me."

"What! What happened?" asked Buddy.

"Well, I didn't get fired exactly. I was told that my activities of the last few days have not been in the best interest of the nation's goal of eventually establishing a trusting relationship with Vietnam, which would lead to reestablishing a consulate in Ho Chi Minh City. So the Office Chief has called Washington, and I am being reassigned to, of all places, Oslo, Norway. Norway! Nothing happens in Norway except snow. The whole place is frozen all year."

Buddy was silent for a few seconds and then asked, "So what are you going to do?"

"I told the Office Chief that I would have to think about it," said Maggie.

"I'm sorry you lost your job, Maggie. But, I told you there is an alternative. You can come to Iowa and be Mrs. J. William Miller," said Buddy. "I think you would like it there. 'Course, it's pretty chilly in Iowa in the winter, but at least it's not Norway."

"I know. That's the third time you have mentioned that. And once again I'm telling you; I'm thinking about it. But not right now." She rolled over, turned out the light, and started tickling Buddy's stomach again while she kissed him. It seemed to Buddy that he wouldn't be going to sleep quite yet. While next to him in the bed, Maggie was thinking that maybe there was a pleasant way to keep warm in an Iowa winter.

Chapter Forty-Two

October 17, 1983
Ho Chi Minh City, Vietnam

Maggie had made her decision while riding the train as it returned to Ho Chi Minh City, and she had informed her boss. Later, they had been to lunch with two of Maggie's co-workers, her immediate supervisor, and another analyst who worked in the office. Sang Nguyen, the Glenns, and their son Andy had also been there. Conspicuous by his absence was the Liaison Office Chief, who had begged off with the excuse that he was just too busy. The lunch had served as a sort of going away party for the Glenns, who were taking Andy back to Iowa with them, and for Maggie, who had given her notice of termination. In two days, they would all be catching a flight for the United States.

The Office Chief had asked that Maggie and Buddy come to see him before they departed; again claiming that he was much too busy to attend the going away luncheon. As Buddy sat across the desk from John Mitchell, the U.S. Liaison Office Chief, he was not favorably impressed by Mr. Mitchell. Mitchell's demeanor suggested a career bureaucrat, who had kissed a great many glutei maximi to achieve his promotions, and who seriously believed that the world revolved around him. Buddy thought that he was an arrogant, pompous, effeminate twit.

"We will certainly miss you, Miss Louis," said Mitchell, as he looked down at his shiny manicured fingernails.

Buddy saw right through that façade. Give us a break, Mitchell, thought Buddy. You can't even look Maggie in the eye when you are talking to her. What you really mean is that you are happy to see the last of Maggie Louis.

Mitchell continued, "We wish you good luck in your future endeavors." The smarmy smile never left Mitchell's face. Turning to look at Buddy, he said, "Now is this the little man that is taking you away from our happy family?"

Little man? Family? It was all Buddy could do to remain seated. He would have preferred to knock Mitchell on his contemptible butt and smack the grin off of his face. But he restrained himself as Maggie chatted away with Mitchell. He listened as she told Mitchell all she knew about Miller Arms, the laser sights, the hand-built shotguns, and the success of the small Iowa company.

"Splendid," said Mitchell. "I have gone hunting with relatives in the past, although I am not very good at it. Perhaps I should buy one of your fancy little shotguns. What do you think?"

Buddy had had enough. He stood and took Maggie's hand so she was also standing. "On a government salary, Mr. Mitchell, you could not afford one of our precision field guns."

Mitchell's jaw dropped and a look of confusion came over his face.

"It was a pleasure meeting you, Mr. Mitchell," said Buddy. Making it a point not to shake hands with Mitchell, he escorted Maggie from Mitchell's office. Maggie again said her good-byes to some of her co-workers and left the building, arm in arm with Buddy.

"My God, Maggie, how did you ever get along with that jackass," said Buddy. He turned and looked at his sweetheart. Maggie was having a hard time trying to hold back the laughter and the tears. It was a turning point in her life, and even though she loved Buddy dearly, the clouds of doubt gave her reason to pray that she had made the right decision.

Chapter Forty-Three

October 19, 1983
40,000 feet over the Pacific Ocean

It was well into the flight, with the cabin darkened for sleeping. In business class, Buddy was waking next to Maggie. He needed to use the restroom. Before he stood up, he looked at Maggie sleeping next to him. Her long, dark hair partially covered her face, and Buddy again marveled at her beauty. He was convinced that an angel had been sent to him to share his somewhat lonely life. He was tempted to kiss her before walking to the restroom, but he decided that she needed the sleep. Buddy stood and looked across the aisle at an empty seat, which should have been occupied by Bob Dawes. He briefly wondered where Dawes had gone. Then he turned his head to look two rows back and momentarily watched the Glenns sleeping; Will and Becky flanking Andy, who had his head leaning on Becky. He suddenly felt very happy to see this small family, who were also wonderful friends. He thought to himself that Will Glenn was a very fortunate man. Buddy then walked ahead to the restroom.

He reached the darkened restroom area and noticed that the small sign on the door said that it was occupied. Buddy decided to wait, since he needed to stretch his arms and legs anyway. He heard some sound behind the closed door of the restroom, and thought to himself that it sounded like someone talking. After waiting a few more minutes, the small 'Occupied' sign shifted to 'Vacant.' The door slowly opened, but did not open fully. Slipping through the opening was the flight attendant, who glanced briefly at Buddy as she rearranged her clothing, smoothing down her dress. She then rather hurriedly and purposefully marched down the aisle to the back of the plane. Buddy thought this was very odd, but as he turned his attention back to the restroom door, it opened fully and out stepped Bob Dawes. If he had been able to see in the dim light, Buddy would have seen Dawes's face flush a dark pink. Dawes just smiled and stepped aside to allow Buddy into the restroom.

After a few minutes, Buddy stepped out of the restroom to find Dawes waiting for him. "Dawes, if I didn't know better, I would think you were really disgusting," said Buddy.

"Don't you recognize her, Buddy? She's the love of my life, the same stewardess who was on the plane when we went over to 'Nam. I told you then I was going to marry her. Don't you remember our bet?" Dawes asked.

"Yeah, yeah, you're going to marry her. I'm just waiting for my hundred bucks," said Buddy.

"Well, old pal, you just keep waiting, 'cause you're going to end up paying," said Dawes. "By the way, her name is Nancy, Nancy Green, and we love each other. She's stationed in New York."

The plane's eastward progress soon encountered a rapidly rising sun, which filled the plane's cabin with ever increasing light. Passengers stirred as the smell of brewing coffee from the plane's galley filled the air. Maggie stirred next to Buddy and smiled at him.

"Did you sleep OK, sweetie?" asked Buddy.

"Yep," said Maggie. She stretched and absently pushed her hair out of her face. "By the way, what does your family's farm look like? I had a dream about you riding around on a horse on a farm, looking like a pompous land baron."

Buddy chuckled. "Sorry, we don't have any horses. But just let me know, and I will buy a couple of nags so I can make your dream come true."

"Miller, you're such a smooth talker. You just sweep a girl off her feet, don't you?" The mild sarcasm was not lost on Buddy. He just chuckled and grinned. Maggie reached over and kissed him. Buddy reached out, hugged her, and kissed Maggie, holding the embrace for several seconds.

"I love you Maggie Louis," said Buddy.

"I love you too, J. William Miller," she answered.

Holding hands, they leaned back into the soft leather seats and waited for breakfast to be served. Buddy blissfully closed his eyes. He was looking forward to going home with Maggie. For the first time in many years, he truly felt good. His inner being was finally at peace. He had no headache. The evil demons of darkness associated with PTSD had quietly, but powerfully, been replaced by the beautiful, selfless emotions of love.

Epilogue

The dawn had broken two hours earlier, with the first light reflected in the glistening hoarfrost covering the field. The only sound was that of four pairs of leather boots crunching on the dry corn stubble and debris. Jim Miller, his son Buddy, Bob Dawes, and John Proctor were spread across the field, their eyes looking ahead intently at the roving, four year old German Shorthair; their shotguns held at the ready in two hands by each of the men. Suddenly, two quail flushed on the right side of their line, the side on which John Proctor was walking. John raised his Miller Arms Hawkeye, and the 12 gauge barked twice. The frantic, bobbing flight of the two quail continued as they fled to the cover of the nearby woods. Sheepishly, John looked over and saw Buddy and Dawes grinning at him.

"Yeah, yeah, wise guys. I missed. So what?" said John. Buddy and Dawes cracked up laughing.

They came to the end of the corn field. "I've had enough, boys," said Jim Miller, and he whistled to the pointer. The dog came bounding to him. Jim snapped a lead on the dog's collar. "Besides, Irene wants us back in plenty of time for dinner."

They all began walking to the fence row to cross to the road for the walk back to the truck. All guns were unloaded; the men crossed the fence and began their walk down the dusty road to reach the truck.

The old, rusty, red, International pickup had finally reached its limit a year ago, and a slightly newer, rusty, red GMC had taken its place. It was a great improvement over the older truck, but still would win no vehicle fashion awards. It was well used when Jim bought it from a friend. Even though he was a wealthy man, Jim Miller lived the same way he had lived prior to achieving his wealth. "This truck suits me just fine," had been Jim's words when he brought the newer truck home.

Four hours later, the younger fathers were attempting to round up their respective rambunctious children who would be relegated to their own "kids' table" in the kitchen. The adults would eat in the dining room. Well, that was the plan, anyway.

The Thanksgiving spread on the dining table and the sideboard could have fed a small army. In a prominent place, on the wall next to the sideboard, in a tasteful, plain, wooden frame was the Vietnamese war medal that had been presented to Buddy in Vietnam by Mr. Ninh Ba Chau. The cherished medal had been given with love to Jim Miller by Buddy and would remain on that wall until Jim Miller was no longer on earth to enjoy its presence. Buddy would then place it in his own home, to perhaps give to his own son someday.

At the urging of Jim and Irene, the entire assemblage gathered around the dining table. Parents held small hands and shushed the squirming children while Jim Miller said grace. As Jim continued, Buddy glanced furtively around the table. His sister Sarah was there with her boyfriend. Eight year old Jeanie and six year old Joanie Newton stood by Janeen. Fig held three year old Janet, and Janeen held three month old Johnnie Newton. John Proctor held four year old Sammy, and Betty Proctor held two year old Sylvia. Betty Proctor continued her teaching career, and with John's help, managed just fine.

Just three years ago, Buddy had served as best man and paid Bob Dawes three hundred dollars when he married flight attendant Nancy Green. With her seniority, Nancy Dawes no longer flew international flights, but instead had taken a domestic run two days per week out of Des Moines. She called it the "milk run," but it allowed her to continue to fly and still be home to take care of her family. Nancy held a fidgeting Danny Dawes in her arms. Little Danny was playing with his mother's earrings and was straddling his mother's very pronounced tummy. Nancy Dawes would soon be grounded again for maternity leave.

Buddy squeezed Maggie's hand tightly, silently telling her that he adored her. She squeezed back. Maggie had joined the faculty of Grinnell College and was teaching international affairs. This meant that she commuted thirty miles each way, three times per week, but Maggie loved it. Maggie's other arm was occupied by two year old Michael Miller, affectionately nicknamed Mikey the Mouse, as he was seemingly always scurrying across the floor just out of reach of his parents.

". . . in His name we pray," concluded Jim Miller. It had only just begun, but it was already a great Thanksgiving.

Author's Notes

I hope you enjoyed reading *Market Time Conspiracy* as much as I enjoyed writing it. The idea for the book came to me some years ago when I expressed an idea to my wife that I would like to someday visit today's modern Vietnam. I did not serve in-country during the Vietnam War, but rather in and out of some of its ports on a Navy vessel, much like Buddy Miller. I have attempted to transpose this idea to a fictitious young man who had served in the Navy during the Vietnam War.

There was, indeed, a naval war strategy entitled Market Time utilized by the U.S. Navy during the Vietnam War, and many Allied navy ships were involved in the process of intercepting Vietnamese vessels off the coast of Vietnam during the war years.

The USS *Erne* is fictitious. The USS *Kawishiwi* was, in fact, a real Navy oiler in the service ship squadron of which I was part. All of the characters in the book are fictitious, as is the court martial segment. I am unaware of any similar court martial proceedings being conducted during Market Time.

The conspiracy of the USS *Erne*'s commanding officer is in no way meant to reflect derogatorily on the reputation of the Navy's exemplary force of commissioned officers. After all, I also proudly wore the uniform of a Naval Officer during the Vietnam years and served with many others.

During the war, there actually was an area off the coast of Vietnam where the military pilots jettisoned their unused bombs. To this day, the area would very likely have thousands of unexploded bombs lying silently on the sea bed.

The reference to the faulty bomb fuses is also true. Twenty-plus Air Force pilots were lost in combat by the bombs detonating prematurely when they were released from the plane.

The subject of PTSD is not a topic to be taken lightly. The condition that modern medicine now calls "Post Traumatic Stress Disorder" has been in evidence for centuries, has had several names, and has disrupted the lives of countless individuals. But the psychological damage inflicted by the Vietnam War, at last, put the condition on the front burner for the medical community and the Department of Defense. I salute the gallant warriors who have suffered from the nightmares of PTSD, and I hope that in my writing I have treated this condition with the proper respect and awareness that it deserves.

Acknowledgments

Although I served on two ocean-going minesweepers during my active duty days in the Navy, (see *Heroes in Obscurity*, my book about my active duty days) those particular ships are considerably larger than the coastal minesweepers, such as the fictitious USS *Erne*. My brother, retired Navy Captain Stephen Duermeyer, who served on a coastal minesweeper, the USS *Albatross*, during Market Time, was an invaluable resource for many of my questions regarding life on those small ships, and the procedures used during the interception of Vietnamese water craft. Thank you, Steve.

My thanks also go to retired Air Force Lt. Col. Jack Drain, a retired F4 pilot who flew during the Vietnam War, and has authored *Life on a Short Fuse,* for his information on the malfunctioning bomb fuses that took the lives of many Air Force pilots, and for information on the dump site used by pilots during the war to rid their planes of unused munitions. Thank you, Jack.

But my greatest thanks go to Janet, my partner and wife of fifty-one years. She is the best partner and editor I could ever hope to have.

On Sale Now!

Sign up for free and bargain books

Join the Speaking Volumes mailing list

Text

ILOVEBOOKS

to 22828 to get started.

Message and data rates may apply

www.ingramcontent.com/pod-product-compliance
Lightning Source LLC
Chambersburg PA
CBHW030807260626
47169CB00001B/225